"IS GUILTY OF MASTER STORYTELLING IN THE FIRST DEGREE."
Carl Hiaasen, author of *Strip Tease*

"A CRIME NOVELIST WHO ISN'T JUST PROMISING—HE'S PRODUCING."
Sacramento Bee

JAKE LASSITER

"IS GREAT FUN."
The New York Times Book Review

FOOL ME TWICE

"SHEER ENTERTAINMENT"
Booklist

"KEEPS THE READER HOOKED."
Denver Post

"FIRST-CLASS . . . FINELY ETCHED CHARACTERS, SPIFFY PLOTTING, SNAPPY DIALOGUE AND ENOUGH ACTION TO KEEP PULSES RACING . . . A REAL BARN-BURNER. JAKE LASSITER MAY NOT BE TRAVIS McGEE, BUT THE KNOCK-ABOUT LAWYER WITH THE KNOCKDOWN PUNCH COMES ABOUT AS CLOSE AS COULD BE HOPED FOR. CASE CLOSED."
Tampa Tribune

Other Jake Lassiter Novels by
Paul Levine
from Avon Books

MORTAL SIN
SLASHBACK

FOOL ME TWICE

A JAKE LASSITER MYSTERY

PAUL LEVINE

AVON BOOKS ◆ NEW YORK

VISIT OUR WEBSITE AT
http://AvonBooks.com

AVON BOOKS
A division of
The Hearst Corporation
1350 Avenue of the Americas
New York, New York 10019

Published in hardcover by William Morrow and Company, Inc.; for information address Permissions Department, William Morrow and Company, Inc., 1350 Avenue of the Americas, New York, New York 10019.

First Avon Books Printing: December 1996

To the memory of my father, Stanley Levine,
who paved the way, then left too soon.
There's an empty chair at the table.

ACKNOWLEDGMENTS

I gratefully acknowledge the assistance of Dade County Medical Examiner Dr. Joseph Davis, Associate Medical Examiners Dr. Emma Lew and Dr. Bruce Hyma, Aspen attorney/skier Gary Wright, and Miami attorneys Roy Black and Edward Shohat. Special thanks to Colorado historian and miner Stephan Albouy, who loved the land and kept the faith, even in death.

As always, I am indebted to my agent, Kris Dahl, and my editors, Paul Bresnick and Tom Colgan, for their guidance and support.

Have you a criminal lawyer in this burg?
We think so but we haven't been able to prove
it on him yet.
—Carl Sandburg, "The People, Yes"

I could win most of my cases if it weren't for the
clients.
—John Mortimer
"Rumpole and the Confession of Guilt"

1

In the Shadow of a Corkscrew

Louis "Blinky" Baroso squirmed in his chair, tugged at my sleeve, and silently implored me to do something. Anything.

Clients are like that. Every time the prosecutor scores a point, they expect you to bounce up with a stinging rejoinder or a brilliant objection. This requires considerable physical and mental agility, something like prancing through the tires on the practice field while reciting Hamlet.

First, you've got to slide your chair back and stand up without knocking your files onto the floor, and preferably, without leaving your fly unzipped. Next, your expression must combine practiced sincerity with virtuous outrage. Finally, you have to say something reasonably intelligent, but not so perspicacious as to sail over the head of a politically appointed judge with a two-digit IQ. For me, the toughest part is simultaneously leaping to my feet and yelling "objection" while buttoning my suit coat. Sometimes, I slip the top button into the second hole, giving me a cockeyed look, and probably distracting the jurors.

Blinky's eyes pleaded with me. *Do something.*

What could I do?

I patted Blinky's forearm and tried to calm him, smiling

placidly. The captain of the *Hindenburg* probably displayed the same serene demeanor just before touching down.

"Chill out and stop fidgeting," I whispered, still smiling, this time in the direction of the jurors. "I'll get my turn."

Blinky puffed out his fleshy cheeks until he looked like a blowfish, sighed and sank into his chair. He turned toward Abe Socolow, who was strutting in front of the jury box, weaving a tale of deceit, corruption, greed, and fraud. In short, Honest Abe was telling the life story of Blinky Baroso.

"This man," Socolow said, using his index finger as a rapier aimed directly at Blinky's nose, "this man abused the trust placed in him by innocent people. He took money under false pretenses, never intending to perform what he promised. He preyed on those whose only failing was to trust his perfidiously clever misrepresentations."

Socolow paused a moment, either for effect, or to round up his adjectives. "What has the state proved this man has done?" Again, the finger pointed at my presumedly innocent client, and the cuff of Socolow's white shirt shot out of the sleeve of his suit coat, revealing silver cuff links shaped like miniature handcuffs. In prosecutorial circles, this is considered haute couture.

"The state has proved that Louie Baroso is a master of deceit and deception," Socolow announced, answering his own question as lawyers are inclined to do. "Louie Baroso is a disreputable, manipulative, conscienceless sociopath who gets his kicks out of conning people."

I thought I heard Blinky whimper. Okay, now Socolow was getting close to the line. Still, I'd rather let it pass. An objection would show the jury he was drawing blood. But then, my silence would encourage him to keep it up.

"This defendant is so thoroughly corrupt and completely crooked that he could stand in the shadow of a corkscrew," Socolow said with a malicious grin.

"Objection!" Now I was on my feet, trying to button

my suit coat and check my fly at the same time. "Name-calling is not fair comment on the evidence."

"Sustained," said the judge, waving his hand in a gesture that told Socolow to move it along.

Unrepentant, Socolow shot his sleeve again, fiddled with one of the tiny handcuffs, and lowered his voice as if conveying secrets of momentous portent. "A thief, a con man, and a swindler, that's what the evidence shows. Both Mr. Baroso and his co-defendant, Mr. Hornback, are guilty of each and every one of the counts, which I will now review with you."

And so he did.

My attention span is about twelve minutes, a little more than most jurors, a lot less than most Nobel prizewinners. I knew what Abe was doing. In his methodical, plodding way, he would summarize the evidence, all the time building to a crescendo of righteous indignation. While I was half listening, scrupulously *not* watching Socolow so that the jurors would think I was unconcerned with what he said, I scribbled notes on a yellow pad, preparing my own summation.

I am not invited by Ivy League institutions to lecture on the rules of evidence or the fine art of oral advocacy. Downtown lawyers do not flock to the courthouse to see my closing arguments. I am apparently one of the few lawyers in the country not solicited by the television networks to comment on the O. J. Simpson case, even though I am probably the only one to have missed tackling him—resulting in a touchdown—on a snowy day in Buffalo about a million years ago. I don't know the secrets of winning cases, other than playing golf with the judges and contributing cash to their re-election campaigns. I don't know what goes through jurors' minds, even when I sidle up to their locked door and listen to the babble through the keyhole. In short, I am not the world's greatest trial lawyer. Or even the best in the high-rise office building that overlooks Biscayne Bay where I hang out my shingle, or would, if I knew what a shingle was. My night law school diploma is fastened by duct tape to the bathroom wall at home. It covers a crack in the plaster and forces me to contemplate the sorry state of the justice system a few times each day, more if I'm staring at the world through a haze induced by excessive consumption of malt and hops.

I am broad-shouldered, sandy-haired, and blue-eyed, and my neck is always threatening to pop the top button on my shirts. I look more like a longshoreman than a lawyer.

A dozen years ago, I scored straight C's in torts and contracts after an undistinguished career as a second-string linebacker earning slightly more than league minimum with the Miami Dolphins. In my first career, including my days as a semi-scholar-athlete in college, I had two knee operations, three shoulder separations, a broken nose, wrist, and ankle, and turf toe so bad my foot was the size and color of an eggplant.

In my second career, I've been ridiculed by deep-carpet, Armani-suited, Gucci-briefcased lawyers, jailed for contempt by ornery judges, and occasionally paid for services rendered.

I never intended to be a hero, and I succeeded.

On this humid June morning, I was slumped into the heavy oak chair at the defense table, gathering my thoughts, then disposing of most of them, while my client kept twisting around, whispering snippets of unsolicited and irrelevant advice. Each time, he leaned close enough to remind me of the black bean soup with onions he had slurped down at lunch. Nodding sagely, I silently thanked him for his assistance, all the time staring at the sign above the judge's bench: WE WHO LABOR HERE SEEK ONLY THE TRUTH.

Sure, sure, and the check's in the mail.

Philosophers and poets may be truth seekers. Lawyers only want to *win*. I have my own personal code, and you won't find it in any books. I won't lie to the judge, bribe a cop, or steal from a client. Other than that, it's pretty much anything goes. Still, I draw the line on whose colors I'll wear. I won't represent child molesters or drug dealers. Yeah, I know, everybody's entitled to a defense, and the lawyer isn't there to assert the client's innocence, just to force the state to meet its burden of proof. Cross-examine, put on your case, if you have any, and let the chips fall where they may.

Bull! When I defend someone, I walk in that person's moccasins, or tasseled loafers, as the case may be. I am not just a hired gun. I lose a piece of myself and take on a piece of the client. That doesn't mean I represent only *innocent* defendants. If I did, I would starve. My first job after law school was in the Public Defender's office, and my first customers, as I liked to call them, were the folks too poor to hire lawyers with a little gray in their hair. I quickly learned that my clients' poverty didn't make them noble, just mean. I also got an education from my repeat customers, most of whom knew more criminal law than I did. Nearly all were guilty of something, though the state couldn't necessarily prove it.

These days, I represent a higher grade of dirtbag. My clients are too smart to pistol-whip a liquor store clerk for a hundred bucks in the till. But they might sell paintings by a coked-out South Beach artist as undiscovered works by Salvador Dalí, or ship vials of yogurt as prize bull semen, or hawk land on Machu Picchu as the treasure trove of the Incas. All of which Blinky Baroso did, at one time or another. Sometimes twice.

But back to ethics. I'm not interested in the rules made up by bar association bigwigs in three-piece suits who gather in ritzy hotels to celebrate their own self-importance. Their rules are intended to protect clients and industries with the most money. It's just like my old game, which they sissified to protect the lah-de-dah quarterbacks. To me, a late hit is just a reminder that football is a contact sport.

Anyway, as far as I could tell, no one in courtroom

4-2 of the Justice Building was zealously engaged in truth seeking at the moment. My client had a more elementary quest. Blinky Baroso merely sought a not-guilty verdict ("Gimme a big N.G., Jake") so he could resume his career of shams, swindles, and sleight-of-hand business deals.

Judge Herman Gold, peering at us over his rimless spectacles, just wanted a verdict—any verdict—in time to play a couple of quinielas at the jai alai fronton.

Chief Prosecutor Abe Socolow, looking appropriately funereal in his black suit, wanted another slam-dunk guilty verdict to add to his ninety-six percent conviction rate.

The jurors gave no indication of wanting anything at all, although number five, a female bus driver, looked like she had to pee. It was a fairly typical jury by Miami standards. Besides the bus driver, we had a body piercer (noses, nipples, and ears), a shark hunter, a lobster poacher, a county kosher meat inspector, and a self-proclaimed show girl, who was telling half the truth, since *she* was a *he* who performed at a cross-dresser's club on South Beach.

The jurors sat, poker-faced (except for the squirming bus driver), occasionally shivering in the air-conditioning, usually staring into space, once in a while smiling at an inadvertent witticism. Trials are usually so stultifyingly boring that the slightest glimmer of humor is nearly as welcome as the mid-afternoon recess. When I was a newly minted lawyer, having just passed the bar in what was most likely a computer glitch, a judge asked my first client, a repeat offender car thief, if he wanted a bench trial or a jury trial.

"Jury trial," my client responded, somewhat hesitantly.

"Do you know the difference?" the judge asked.

"Sure, Judge. A jury trial is six ignorant people instead of one."

Ah, from the mouths of babes and felons.

Abe Socolow was still droning on about the evil deeds of Blinky Baroso, whose eyes fluttered three times whenever he was nervous, or whenever he told a fib. His eyes had been flapping like Venetian blinds the last four days.

"You have heard the testimony," Socolow said, his long, lean frame hunched over the podium. "Louie Baroso and Kyle Hornback are con men, pure and simple."

Blinky leaned close and gave me another whiff of his partially digested *sopa de frijoles negros*. "Nobody calls me Louie," he protested, as if we could use that point on appeal.

"These unscrupulous men used what is known as affinity fraud," Socolow continued. "By pretending to be born-again Christians, they ingratiated themselves into the lives of decent, God-fearing citizens at the West Kendall Baptist Church. They conned hundreds of thousands of dollars from their victims, who were taken in by promises of huge returns on their investments. These criminals wove a clever web of deception, promising both profits and holy redemption. The parishioners, honest citizens all, were induced to spend their retirement funds on diamond investment scams only to learn that Mr. Baroso and Mr. Hornback never bought the diamonds. Where did the money go? Into the pockets of Louie Baroso and his underling, Kyle Hornback."

Blinky whispered something in my ear that sounded like *caveat emptor*.

"Next, you heard proof of the real estate scam. *Su casa, mi casa*. Your house, my house. You heard how Mr. Baroso was a regular visitor in the real estate deed room of the courthouse . . ."

"Is that a crime?" Baroso grumbled.

". . . where he researched titles on various expensive homes. Then Mr. Hornback, armed with a fake driver's license and the legal description of the property, persuaded banks that he was the owner, and secured loans on other people's property. Again, honest citizens were shocked to learn that second and third mortgages were recorded on their properties."

"So what, the title insurance company paid," Blinky whined. "The owners didn't get hurt."

At the far end of the defense table, Kyle Hornback, a handsome young man whose clean, chiseled features disguised a reservoir of guile, was scratching furiously on a legal pad. If the jurors looked at his lawyer, H. T. Patterson, they would see a smile so confident, it stopped just short of smugness. H.T. had been around long enough to know the first rule of the trial lawyer: Never let them see your fear.

"Now, when I sit down," Socolow continued, removing his eyeglasses and pinching the top of his nose, "Mr. Lassiter is going to tell you that there is no direct evidence against his client, Louie Baroso. He is going to tell you that all the victims dealt with the salesman, Kyle Hornback."

I just love it when the opposition makes my closing argument for me.

"But you are entitled to use your common sense. Who was the boss? Whose name appeared on all the fraudulent paperwork? Who gave Kyle Hornback his marching orders? You all know who."

Or was it *whom*? I never know the difference.

"Louie Baroso, that's who," Socolow announced, cranking up the volume.

Just then, the ornate wooden door to the courtroom opened with its usual squeak. Three of the jurors looked that way, and three didn't. One of the alternates sneaked a peek, and the other didn't. Okay, so half were paying close attention. About average.

I swung around, too. A tall young woman walked through the door and down the aisle that split the nearly empty gallery. She sat down at the end of one of the church pews in the first row.

Josefina Jovita Baroso. I used to call her Jo Jo, although I suppose the correct pronunciation would be Ho Ho. And we did have some laughs, as well as tears.

"Why's your sister here?" I whispered.

Blinky shrugged. "To wish me bad luck. Maybe you, too. Too much history."

*   *   *

History.

Blinky was right. How many years since we had met? I was still playing ball, Blinky was a small-time bookie who hadn't yet Americanized his name by adding an "o" to Luis, and Jo Jo was a poli sci major at Florida State. Blinky asked me to Christmas dinner at his mother's home on Fonseca, just a block off Ponce de Leon in Little Havana. Why not? I'd blown five grand with him during the last season alone, without once betting on a Dolphins game. I've got ethics, you know.

Señora Baroso was cooking a whole pig, *lechón asado,* in the backyard when Josefina Jovita walked through the wrought-iron gate past the lawn statue of the Virgin Mary. Jo Jo was toting her books and laundry in an army-green duffel bag, and she looked at me with bright, dark, fearless eyes. We sat outside at a redwood picnic table, telling our life stories while sharing the *yuca con mojo,* and over espresso and flan, I asked whether she'd like to be my guest at the Jets game Sunday, maybe come over to the house afterward. She didn't say no.

History.

We became friends, then lovers. Looking back, I cared more for her than she did for me. To her, I was a project. Mature beyond her years, Jo Jo encouraged me to apply to law school when my demi-career was fading. My other choices were tending bar or becoming the assistant to the regional vice president of a beer distributor. I went to law school, and so did she. But we headed down different paths. I always rooted for the underdog, so the P.D.'s office was a natural. She was less forgiving of human failings, so the prosecutor's office was a second home.

Josefina Jovita Baroso was attractive and bright and combative, and seemed to enjoy all three. We debated politics, religion, sports, and her brother. We didn't agree on anything except the virtues of hard pretzels and cold beer. She voted straight Republican, and like most Cuban Americans, viewed Ronald Reagan as a combination of Jose

Martí and Teddy Roosevelt. I always thought of him as a Notre Dame running back, and I never liked Notre Dame.

Eventually, we broke up. Okay, so I broke up with her, but there were no major explosions, just a disengagement of lives going different directions. Blinky kept me informed of major events in her life. On a ski trip out west, Jo Jo met a man and had a whirlwind romance. She took a leave of absence from the state attorney's office, spent six months with the guy on his Colorado ranch, but came back alone. On the few occasions we would run into each other, she never referred to the relationship. To this day, I don't know what happened, though Blinky says it's simple. "She busted his chops, like she did to you, to me, to everybody. Nobody measures up to Josie."

I caught another glimpse of her over my shoulder. She wore a beige cotton dress that stopped just above the knee. Her dark hair was pulled back in a ponytail, emphasizing the strong bone structure of her face. It wasn't her trial uniform, and because of the conflict of interest, she couldn't be assisting Socolow with the case.

I must have been staring at her.

"Hard to believe she's my sister, isn't it?" Blinky whispered, reading my thoughts.

I glanced at Josefina Baroso and then at Blinky Baroso. My client resembled a sausage stuffed into an Italian silk suit. A *green* Italian silk suit that shimmered under the fluorescent glare of the courtroom lights. Jo Jo was tall and slim and in an earlier age would have been called elegant.

I turned my attention back to Abe Socolow, who was prattling on about the utter depravity of preying on the virtuous. He reminded the jury of the witnesses he had brought before them, a retired airline mechanic, an Amway distributor, a widowed schoolteacher. Abe believed in swamping jurors with testimony. As Charlie Riggs, the retired coroner, likes to say, *"Testis unus, testis nullus."* One witness, no witness.

When the victims are likable, the prosecutor's job is easy. Put 'em up there, extract a tear or two, and get a guilty verdict in time for everyone to get home to watch *Roseanne*.

Socolow seemed to be winding down now. "You folks are contributing to a sacred function of government." Abe was not a naturally down-home guy, but he was getting into his flag-waving, Fourth of July, you-folks shtick, and it sounded pretty good. "As envisioned by our Founding Fathers, you folks from the community, not some wigged and robed judges, are to determine what is true and what is false, who is innocent and who is guilty. And when you look at this man . . ." He pointed at poor Blinky again. "What do you see?"

I couldn't help myself. My eyes darted to my client, just as did the jurors'. I didn't know what they saw, but to me, he looked like a big, fat crook.

"You see a thief, a con man, a deceiver," Socolow said, lest there be any mistake. He was dying to mention Baroso's criminal record but he couldn't get it into evidence because I had kept Blinky off the stand. A prior conviction can only be used for impeachment, and that was enough reason to keep Blinky at the defense table during the trial. So was the nervous twitch that made Blinky look like a pathological liar when he was giving his name and address.

"So on behalf of the people of the state of Florida . . ."

All of them, I wondered?

". . . I ask that you convict both defendants on each and every count of grand theft, fraud, racketeering, and conspiracy. Thank you and God bless you."

Socolow gathered his notes from the podium, took down his Technicolor charts that detailed various feats of grand larceny, and lowered himself majestically into his seat at the prosecution table. I stood up, cleared my throat, and thanked the jurors for their rapt attention to the case, but I left God out of the equation. Then I pointed to the U.S. flag behind Judge Gold and started talking about the Constitution, Mom, and apple pie. I wasn't about to let Abe out-folks me.

"Our great democracy depends on citizens like you, leaving your homes, your jobs, your loved ones and serving as the last bastion of protection for your fellow citizens . . ."

I always try to make jury service sound like joining the Marines.

"We have the greatest legal system in the world . . ."

Excluding trial by combat, of course.

"Now Mr. Socolow and I have other cases to try, other fish to fry . . ."

Other fish to fry? Did I say that? Sometimes the mouth moves faster than the brain.

"But Louis Baroso has only one case . . ."

Pending, that is.

"It is here and it is now. This is Louis Baroso's case. This is his life, his fate, and it's in your hands."

I shot a look at my client. He blinked at me. Thrice.

"Our Constitution provides certain rules that protect men and women accused of crimes. Anyone accused is innocent until proven guilty, innocent until you say otherwise, innocent until and unless you conclude after considering all of the evidence, after searching your conscience, after using all your powers of common sense and intelligence and fairness, that the state has proven guilt beyond and to the exclusion of every reasonable doubt. A jury's job is not to presume evidence where there is none. It is not to assume evidence, to fill in evidence, to believe there must be evidence just because the prosecutor says so. We don't guess people into jail. We don't assume people into jail. No, the jury's job is to look critically at the evidence and ask, 'Did the state prove its case beyond a reasonable doubt?' "

I blathered on for a while about reasonable doubt. That's what you do when you don't have much of a defense. When I have favorable evidence, I use it. Hell, I hoist it up the flagpole and salute it. Lacking a defense, I tap-dance around the state's evidence and say it just isn't enough.

"Now, Mr. Socolow told you the evidence *indicates* that Mr. Baroso conspired with Mr. Hornback. The evidence *implies* that Mr. Baroso profited from Mr. Hornback's endeavors. The evidence *suggests* that Mr. Baroso knew what was going on. Well, there's a phrase for that kind of evidence, and you've all heard it. It's called circumstantial evidence . . ."

The jurors nodded en masse. Good, they'd heard the phrase on Larry King.

". . . And I'm going to tell you a story about circumstantial evidence. A mother bakes a blueberry pie and puts it on a shelf to cool. She tells her little boy not to touch that pie, but he climbs up on the shelf and digs in anyway. Now he hears his mom coming into the kitchen, so he grabs his pet cat and rubs the cat's face in the pie. The mother walks in and yells for the boy's father. The father takes the cat out to the barn, and then, boom! There's a shotgun blast. The boy is still there in the kitchen licking off his fingers, and he says, 'Poor Kitty. Just another victim of circumstantial evidence.' "

I paused just long enough to let the jurors chuckle. Then, becoming serious, I lowered my voice and said, "I'm pleading with you not to let Louis Baroso be another victim of circumstantial evidence."

This time, only two jurors nodded, and one of them might have been asleep. I wrapped it up with an appeal to the basic decency of the American people, then sat down. Blinky gave my arm a good squeeze and patted me on the back.

I looked into the gallery again at Jo Jo Baroso, who avoided my gaze.

"We were never close," Blinky said, watching me. "I was hot-wiring cars when Josie was still making mud pies. She always thought she was better than me."

Which didn't exactly put her in an exclusive club. "So

what's she doing here?'' I asked for the second time.

"She hates me," Blinky answered, as if that said everything.

Looking back now, I know that wasn't it at all.

2

The Shyster, the Grifter, and the Lanky Brunette

We all have our little rituals. On the morning of the last day of trial, I always slice a mango and a papaya for breakfast, then toss two paperback books into my briefcase. You never know how long the jury will be out, and reading keeps me from replaying the case in my mind, second-guessing myself and cursing the decision to go to law school instead of doing something productive like bulking up on steroids and joining the World Wrestling Federation.

An hour after the jury disappeared into its tomblike room, Blinky Baroso and I headed down the street to the Gaslight Lounge, where many a lawyer has washed away the memories of judges and juries in rivers of icy gin. The lounge was dark and windowless with red Naugahyde barstools. Even half empty, the place reverberated with the pleasant clink of ice against glass.

I don't chitchat when the jury is out, so I sat there, sipping a Samuel Adams draft, reading Nelson DeMille's *The Gold Coast,* a tale of an honest lawyer who is compromised by a charming Mafioso, when Blinky Baroso started his chatterbox routine.

Some clients clam up when waiting for a verdict. They become pale, withdrawn. Maybe they're apologizing to their Maker, making silent promises to go straight if only they're given a second (or fifth or sixth) chance. Other clients become nonstop motormouths.

Nerves.

Blinky Baroso, his face flushed, his pudgy hands gesticulating, was keeping his mind occupied and mine distracted with a loud soliloquy retracing the many stages of his misspent life. Plopped onto his barstool, he used a nail file to amputate the filters of an endless chain of Marlboros, which he occasionally smoked, the ashes dropping into his lap as he told his tales. He interrupted himself every few minutes to ask, "That right, Jake?" which was probably intended to determine whether I was listening.

"Maybe I should go to Russia," Blinky said, exhaling a cloud of smoke. "There's no more free-enterprise system in this country. Too many controls. Too many regulations. I remember when I started selling waterfront homesites. We made a killing for what, eighteen months. Then those rubes from Tallahassee came down here in their Sears sports coats and short-sleeve shirts. Restraining orders, permanent injunctions, cease and desist orders. Jeez, all the profits went to the attorneys. That right, Jake?"

I drained my beer and put down the book. "The homesites weren't waterfront, Blinky. They were *under water*. You were selling swampland in the Everglades." I *had* been listening. He brushed me off with a wave of his hand, his diamond pinky ring sparkling, even in the muted light. I must be slipping. Rule number one for trial: no gold chains, no flashy rings, no dark glasses. The trick is make a hoodlum look like a choirboy.

I ordered my second beer and Blinky went into a loud lament about the demise of his precious metals business. "Who would think you could sell gold bullion on the phone? Who the hell thought that farmers in Iowa would give their credit card numbers on the basis of cold calls? Jake, it was a thing of beauty. The world headquarters of

Million-Dollar Minerals Inc. was just up the road in Lau-
der-damn-dale. You should have seen it Jake, thirty sales-
men, twenty-five hundred calls a day.''

Actually, I saw it the day the state padlocked the doors.
Blinky's world headquarters was a boiler room operation
where they sold pieces of paper attesting to the ownership
of precious minerals. Blinky swears he would have delivered the gold, too, if he hadn't presold the stuff at twenty
dollars an ounce less than it would have cost to buy. Like
smoking, breaching contracts was a nasty habit for Blinky.

''The market was moving. If the damn bureaucrats had
given me time, I could have come back. That right, Jake?''

Before I had a chance not to answer, I became aware of
a presence just behind me at the bar. My first thought was
that Ernie Cartwright, the ninety-year-old asthmatic bailiff,
was there to inform me that the verdict was in, but we still
had time for a round together if I was paying. My second
thought was that Ernie Cartwright doesn't wear Panther
perfume.

''Well, well,'' our visitor said, malice in her voice, ''the
shyster and the grifter.''

''Gimme a break, Josie,'' Blinky responded, blowing a
cloud of smoke toward his sister.

She stood there a foot from me, her head cocked, her
hip shot, her look challenging look. I had seen it plenty of
times before, but it had been years since I stared into those
dark eyes from this distance. She was standing, and I was
sitting, and she looked down at me from a position of
geographical and moral superiority. I looked back with my
crooked grin that had been good enough for several bus-
loads of cheerleaders, flight attendants, and dental hygien-
ists.

She shook her head, seeming to dismiss me. Looking at
her brother, she said, ''Thanks to your smooth-talking
friend here, you've had more breaks than you deserve.''

''C'mon, Jo Jo,'' I said. ''Why not call me 'Jake'?
Smooth-talking friend sounds so impersonal.''

Her eyes glinted at me and her dark complexion seemed

to glow. Josefina Jovita Baroso was a self-confident woman with what my granny would call gumption. She reminded me of Dashiell Hammett's "lanky brunette with a wicked jaw."

"You're looking good, Jo Jo," I told her.

"Don't change the subject," she said.

"I didn't know there was one, except that old standard, my many personal failings."

Blinky nudged me. "Join the club. Nobody's as perfect as Josie."

She narrowed her eyes at me, or maybe it was the noxious cigarette smoke blinding her. "Just like old times, isn't it? Luis is in trouble, and Jake is here to help."

"I know it doesn't rank with feeding starving children or even prosecuting shoplifters, but it's my job. And for what it's worth, your brother is my friend."

Without an invitation, she swiveled a hip onto the barstool next to mine and gave me a little smile. A very little smile. "My brother," she said, rolling the words on her tongue to see how they tasted, "is a major embarrassment. My brother is a lazy, cowardly criminal, and you are his mouthpiece."

"Blinky's not lazy," I said, in my client's partial defense.

"I don't have to listen to this garbage." Blinky slid off his barstool. "I'm gonna take a leak."

I turned my attention to Josefina. Her mouth was wide, the lips full, the face oval with prominent cheekbones.

"Look, Jo Jo, I could give you the standard spiel about how every client deserves the best representation possible, but I won't. I won't apologize for defending your brother because I like him. I'd like him even more if he went straight, and maybe he will. I once got him a job selling time-share condos in Sarasota."

"I know all about it. When sales were slow, he stripped the units. Everything from the microwave and VCR right down to the copper wiring."

"That was never proved," I said, sounding like a shyster, even to myself. "Blinky wasn't even charged."

"Thanks to you," she said with some bitterness. "Look, Jake, you may not believe me, but this isn't personal."

"Really, do you chase down every defense lawyer to criticize his character, or just the ones you've slept with?"

Unlike her brother, she didn't blink. "That was beneath you, Jake. You weren't always like that, but I suppose that's what comes from hanging around the Justice Building, spending every day with sociopaths."

"Some of the judges are okay."

"You're not funny, Jake. Not to me, anyway. You're just an aging jock who's never grown up."

"Is this the part I'm not supposed to take personally?"

She sighed. "Okay, you're right. I'm disappointed in you. You had such potential, but you never explored it. You never reached higher. You were a second-rate football player, but maybe you couldn't help that. You went to a second-rate law school, and maybe that's the best you could have done, too. Now you have a second-rate practice, and you seem happy with it, and that's what disappoints me so much. You don't strive anymore. You take pride in negatives, like that stupid line you always say, you've never been this, you've never been that . . ."

"It's true. I've never been disbarred, committed, or convicted of moral turpitude, and the only time I was arrested, it was a case of mistaken identity. I didn't know the guy I hit was a cop."

She didn't laugh or even crack a smile. "I don't blame you for the way you are, Jake. You were raised without a family, and it made you a loner. You're really dysfunctional when it comes to relationships."

"I hate words like 'dysfunctional.' It's right up there with 'prioritize' in bullshit quotient. Besides, I had a family. I had my granny."

"That's what I mean. You were raised on moonshine whiskey by an old woman who's half *loco*. You had no parents, no siblings, and it shows. Where do you hang out? The morgue! *Dios mio!* Who's your best friend? A retired coroner who still does autopsies for fun! When you picked me up on Saturday nights, you smelled of formaldehyde.''

She was shaking her head. I seem to have depressed her. Then she reached over and took a sip of my beer, leaving a faint impression of lipstick on the glass. It was the most intimate gesture she'd shared with me in years.

"You know what Abe Socolow says about you?" she asked, sliding the beer in front of me.

I wasn't sure I wanted to know.

"That you're not as bad as most defense lawyers. Is that how you want to be known?"

"Abe's a good man. A bit rigid, haughty, and self-righteous, but what prosecutor isn't?" I smiled and hoisted my diminishing beer in her direction.

"You mean me, don't you? You think I'm rigid and haughty.''

"And self-righteous," I added, in case she had forgotten.

She seemed to think about it, little vertical lines creasing her forehead. If she didn't dislike me so much, and if I wasn't such an enlightened man of the nineties, I would have mentioned just how fetching she looked just now. Okay, if she didn't dislike me so much, I would have mentioned it.

"Maybe I am," she admitted, "and maybe those aren't such bad traits.''

"I agree. They're just what I'd look for in an executioner.''

"And what about you? What are your character traits, Jake?''

Her voice was growing softer. Was there a touch of wistfulness there or was I imagining it?

"Me? I'm humble, honest, and congenial, not to mention sexy.''

She let the bait drift across the water. After a moment, she said, "We could have had something, Jake. We really could have.''

"If only I'd been different, right?''

"That's your way of attacking me, isn't it, Jake. You're saying it was wrong of me to try and make something out of you."

"No one can make anyone else anything," I said. "I can't make your brother into Albert Schweitzer, and you can't make me . . . whatever it is you wanted me to be. I can't live up to your schoolgirl image of me."

"Is that what you think it was?"

"Yeah. I think if we'd met when you were older, maybe you would've been more realistic, a little less idealistic."

"You never knew how much I cared for you," she said, her voice a whisper.

"I thought I did. I thought I knew precisely how much."

"You're being sarcastic, aren't you? Well, you're wrong. I loved you once."

Why did *once* sound so achingly long ago?

There were a lot of things I wanted to say, and if I had twenty minutes or so, I could have come up with something meaningful and sensitive. Instead, I stood up, steady as a newborn calf on spindly legs. But I had nowhere to go, so I sat back down again, feeling foolish. I didn't say a word, and in a moment, Mickey Cumello, the bartender, asked Ms. Josefina Jovita Baroso, prosecutor, judge, jury, and woman, if she'd care for a drink of her own.

"Absolut Citron on the rocks, just a splash of soda," she said.

"Don't have the Citron," Mickey replied, politely, a clean white towel draped across a shoulder. He was a bartender of the old school, white shirt, black bow tie, hair combed straight back. "We have Absolut, and I could drop a twist into it."

Jo Jo wrinkled her mouth into a frown. "How about a San Pellegrino, no ice?"

"Club soda okay?" Mickey asked, his eyes shifting to me. We both knew he had San Pellegrino, but he's entitled to some fun, too.

She shook her head. "Sodium. No can do."

Life can be so difficult.

She started to ask about chardonnay by the glass, and I was still thinking about my possible reply to her belated professions of ardor, but just then the front door opened, letting in a blast of sunlight. Ernie Cartwright, the ninety-year-old bailiff, stood just inside the door, squinting in the darkness, calling my name.

3

Honor Among Thieves

Waiting for a verdict, I try to think of anything but what is going on inside the jury room. I try to be philosophical. No use worrying. I've done everything I can do to win; now it's up to six strangers to tell me whether I'm worth a damn.

It works, too, until the knock on the door awakens the bailiff, who summons the judge, who sits forlornly in his chambers missing half the evening card at the jai alai fronton. The judge is either reading court files, or more likely, haggling on the phone with his bookie, mistress, or his cousin, the bail bondsman who kicks back a percentage of bond premiums.

The judge orders the bailiff to retrieve the lawyers from the Gaslight Lounge where they are getting shitfaced, something the judge is precluded from doing either by the Canons of Judicial Ethics or his duodenal ulcer.

When the bailiff comes calling, I tighten up. Helpless. In the game I used to play, you chased the butterflies by hitting someone. I did double duty on kickoff and receiving teams, so I was assured of physical contact and a grass stain within the first seven seconds or so.

Now, there was no one to hit. I once let a witness slug me in court, just to prove his dangerous propensity and

23

help my client, a doctor accused of killing his patient with a deadly drug. The best I could do now was to whack Blinky across the back and tell him to look innocent when the jury filed in.

Riding up to the fourth floor, Blinky Baroso was silent and seemed a shade paler than an hour earlier. We were joined in the elevator by Blinky's one-woman fan club. Nobody invited her along; she was just there.

H. T. Patterson was already in the courtroom, pacing in front of the bench, hands clasped behind his back. He stood all of five six, and that's including three-inch heels on his ostrich skin cowboy boots. I admired Patterson's style, white linen suit and all, but I've always thought the dress code for lawyers should require sharkskin suits and rattlesnake boots.

"Good luck, Jacob, and may Providence smile on you and all who are dear to you," Patterson intoned. Before attending law school, Patterson had been a preacher at the Liberty City Baptist Church, and the singsong of his holy-rolling sermons stayed with him.

"I'm not sure about Providence," I replied, "but I'll take a smile from number five."

"Ah, the lady bus driver. You seated her because she's African American, and you still adhere to the old saw about minorities distrusting authority."

"Right."

"You left her on, despite the fact that she seemed to have an attitude."

"Right again. What are you trying to tell me?"

"Only this, Jake. Throw out the book. Go with your instincts. She's a woman who's driven a million miles for Metro, and her hemorrhoids are flaring up."

"Hemorrhoids?"

"Did you not notice the pillow she carries with her each day?"

I hadn't.

"She works overtime to support her children. She has to deal on a daily basis with rude, tired, angry people who have lost their cars and maybe their homes. So we come into court with a pretty white boy who's never done an honest day's work and a fat con man who'd steal cookies from the Girl Scouts, and you expect her to be sympathetic. Black jurors will cut you a break if they think the cops did wrong, which is always the presumption in the 'hood, but you got to remember this. Your black juror isn't from the streets. She's a registered voter or she wouldn't have been called, and when you bring in some slippery white boys, you got trouble.''

"So why'd you leave her on?" I asked.

" 'Cause, Jake, my boy, in case you haven't noticed, while I may be as bald as a cue ball, I'm as black as the eight ball. I was hoping for some home cookin' from number five.''

"And . . .''

"And she scowled at me worse than at you. We both botched it with Mrs. Cherelle Washington. We bobbled, blundered, and bungled. We fumbled, faltered, and floundered. We looked deep inside ourselves and failed to see the light.''

"Maybe we'll get lucky. You do believe in luck, don't you Henry Thackery?''

"Of course. How else can one explain his enemy's successes?''

I thought I'd heard that somewhere before and probably had. Lawyers are noted plagiarists.

Our respective clients sat at opposite ends of the defense table, and I joined H. T. Patterson pacing in front of the bench. The clients watched us, probably wondering why H.T. and I acted as if we were on trial. I'm not sure why, but that's the way it is.

"Good luck, Kyle," Blinky said, caught up in the spirit of the moment. Foxhole buddies, at least for now.

Josefina Baroso sat in the front row of the otherwise deserted gallery. Her legs were crossed, her fine chin tilted upward, an enigmatic smile playing at her lips. I resented her regal presence. If this were ancient Rome, and we were gladiators, she would be casting thumbs down as a spear pressed against her brother's throat.

Abe Socolow walked calmly down the aisle, whispered something to Queen Josefina, and took his place at the prosecution table. He was one of these guys who never sweated. His shirt always stayed tucked into his pants, and his shoes never lost their shine. I was dying to get him in a headlock and give him a noogie.

The back door banged open, and Judge Gold trundled in, his black robes flapping behind him. The clerk was in her place, and the stenographer sat hunched over her keyboard, stretching her neck. "Bring in the jury," the judge ordered the bailiff.

You try to read their faces. If they won't look you in the eye, they've gone against you. That's what old lawyers will tell you over a dry martini at the Gaslight. As with most courtroom wisdom about verdicts, they're right fifty percent of the time.

These jurors were all over the place. A couple studied their shoes. A couple were clutching their thin sweaters, protection against the spastic air-conditioning that could drip warm water one moment and freeze sides of beef the next. Mrs. Cherelle Washington shot a look at Socolow, then me, then stopped her gaze on H. T. Patterson. She seemed angry with all of us.

"Who do you think's the foreman?" Blinky asked.

"The shark hunter," I guessed, straining unsuccessfully to see who was holding the two sheets of paper on which was written the fate of Messrs. Baroso and Hornback.

"Has the jury reached its verdicts?" Judge Gold asked, in properly senatorial tones.

Mrs. Washington stood up.

Oh shit.

"We have, Your Honor," she said, holding out the verdict forms to the wheezing bailiff, who carried them to Rosa Suarez, the clerk.

"Thank you, Madam Foreperson," the judge said. He

studied the forms and seemed to grimace, but it could have been stomach gas. "The clerk will publish the verdicts," he announced, handing the forms to Rosa Suarez, who stood with an air of self-importance.

Rosa Suarez's uncle was a county commissioner, and her entire family—mother, father, three brothers, and a sister—held county jobs. If you needed a gator removed from a backyard canal or a new water meter on your house, chances are a Suarez would sign the paperwork. Rosa Suarez touched a hand to a silver barrette pinning back her dark hair and began reading in a bored voice: "In the Eleventh Judicial Circuit, in and for Dade County, Florida, Criminal Division, Case Number Ninety-four, Thirteen, Twenty-one, State of Florida versus Louis Xavier Baroso, we, the jury, find the defendant, Louis Xavier Baroso, not guilty on all counts. So say we all."

All right! That jolt of exhilaration, the momentary joy of victory. It always fades so quickly, I wanted to savor it.

Next to me, Blinky sighed and grabbed my hand with a sweaty, hearty shake. Rosa Suarez cleared her throat: "In the Eleventh Judicial Circuit, in and for Dade County, Florida, Criminal Division, Case Number Ninety-four, Thirteen, Twenty-two, State of Florida versus Kyle Lynn Hornback, we, the jury, find the defendant Kyle Lynn Hornback not guilty on counts one, three, and four . . ."

Uh-oh.

". . . and guilty on count two, fraud, in violation of Section 817.29 of the Florida statutes. So say we all."

Hornback's hand slammed the defense table. "What the fuck!"

Socolow shook his head. He wanted Baroso; Hornback was just along for the ride.

I thumbed through the indictment, trying to figure it out. Not guilty of grand larceny, not guilty of racketeering, not guilty of a scheme to defraud, but guilty of common law gross fraud. It's an 1868 law that prohibits "cheating" and sits in the musty tomes next to the statute that forbids cutting off the head of sheep before they're dressed. Just goes to show why prosecutors charge everything in the book. Throw enough mud on the wall, some will stick.

H. T. Patterson didn't flinch. "Your Honor, we ask that the jury be polled."

"Very well," Judge Gold said, nodding judiciously, and turning toward the jury box. "The clerk has just read your verdict in which you have found Mr. Hornback guilty of gross fraud as alleged in count two of the indictment. Is that your verdict, so say you all?"

"You all," chimed the tattoo artist and the body piercer in perfect harmony.

The judge rolled his eyes to the heavens. "Maybe we better do this individually."

It took another couple of minutes, but each juror affirmed the verdict. The judge finished by thanking the jurors for their patience and wisdom, then handed out certificates attesting to the splendid performance of their civic duties. He told Blinky he was a free man and postponed sentencing for Hornback, pending a presentence investigation of his background. Over Socolow's objections, he allowed Hornback to remain free on bond until the sentencing date. The jurors filed out of the courtroom, and the judge ducked out the back door. The stenographer folded up her machine, cracked her knuckles, and left. The clerk gathered up loose papers, stuffed them in a file, and followed.

Abe Socolow packed his briefcase, stopped by the defense table, gave me a friendly pop on the shoulder, and said, "Go figure, huh, Jake?" That was as close to a compliment as I would get.

"I figure it was a compromise," I told him. "Some wanted to acquit them both, some wanted to convict them both. You made Hornback look bad on cross, and they remembered that. Blinky never testified, so the lingering image was Hornback fidgeting on the stand. Just reinforces my long-standing rule against letting defendants testify."

Socolow smiled grimly. "You mean letting *guilty* defendants testify."

"Let's just say I don't want a client to testify if he's subject to impeachment on cross."

"You got a way with words," Socolow said, hoisting his briefcase toward the door.

The rest of us sat there, the four horsemen of the defense, H. T. Patterson and his unhappy client, Blinky Baroso and little old me.

"I don't believe this shit." It was Hornback, his handsome face flushed. He got to his feet and was leaning over Blinky. "You owe me, man. You coulda gotten me off if you'd pleaded out."

"Kyle, Kyle baby," Blinky said, in the same soothing voice I imagined he used when selling swampland to rubes from the Midwest. "You know I couldn't do that. I'm on probation. I woulda done time."

It was true. Two years ago, Blinky was convicted in the Dumpster Diver scam. Police found him up to his elbows in trash behind a rental car agency near the airport. One good dive, and he could come up with a dozen discarded rental contracts complete with credit card numbers. Then he'd order stereos, televisions, and battery-powered dildos from home shopping networks.

Hornback raised his voice. "Yeah, well maybe you'll still do time if *I* cut a deal." He swung to face his lawyer. "How 'bout it, Mr. Patterson? You think the prosecutor still wants to talk?"

H.T. placed a calming hand on his client's arm. "I, too, am confounded and confused. However, now is not the time to discuss such weighty matters. After a good night's sleep, we'll pursue every avenue, explore every venue . . ."

"Climb every mountain," I added, helpfully.

"It'll be okay, Kyle," Blinky said. "I'll take responsibility."

Hornback snorted a mirthless laugh. "Yeah, will you do my time?"

"Kyle, we stand together. That was the plan."

"Me getting convicted was not the plan. You said we'd both be acquitted or only you would be convicted. You never said nothing about this."

Blinky shrugged. "I didn't think it would turn out this way. Did you, Counselor?"

I shook my head. "You can never tell with a jury."

"Well, I can tell you one thing," Kyle Hornback said, his face hardening. "I get time, I've got some things to say to the state attorney. I got stories to tell. I got—"

"Kyle, that's enough!" Blinky tried to look tough. It didn't work.

"I'll tell them about the tunnels in the mountains and what's in them, and what's not," Hornback said, his voice rising. "You sold stock across state lines, so it's federal. They'll send you to Marion where some hard cases will pass you around like a volleyball."

"It's a perfectly legitimate venture, and you don't know anything about it," Blinky announced with such conviction and a flapping of eyelashes I was sure he told two lies in one sentence.

"I see there's no honor among thieves," Josefina Jovita Baroso said, sneaking up behind us, the same way she did in the Gaslight. She turned to me. "I suppose I should congratulate you, Jake. You hoodwinked the jury, so they convicted the lesser of two evils. That is the hallmark of the defense lawyer, is it not, to obfuscate the facts until the jury can only guess?"

"Funny, I thought my job was to force the state to prove its case. Abe didn't do it, so your brother goes free. That's the way the game is played."

"That's what it is to you, isn't it, a game?"

"Sure, it's got rules, like any other game. You can't bang into the receiver when the ball's in the air. You can't admit hearsay, even if it's the truth."

"The rules are intended to do justice, not thwart it."

"Yeah, well justice doesn't enjoy an intimate relationship with the law, and you damn well know it."

Her eyes narrowed, and she lowered her voice. "I didn't realize it before, but you're just like all the rest of them."

"Them?"

"Silver-tongued shysters who can rationalize their every act. It must come with the territory, with the briefcase full of tricks and the amusing stories about bamboozling judges and juries."

"Give me a break, Josie. Some of us just plod along, doing our jobs. We all can't be as saintly as you."

Josefina Jovita Baroso turned on her heel and stormed out. I started to say something, but Blinky was stirring next to me. "Let her go. You can't win an argument with her."

I sat there a moment while Patterson and his client headed out of the courtroom. As he got to the door, Kyle Hornback shot us a look over his shoulder. "I'm warning you, Baroso. You've got to make good to me."

Patterson took his client by the arm and hustled him into the corridor, leaving just Blinky and me, unless you count the portraits of long-deceased judges with fine crops of chin whiskers.

"He's full of shit," Blinky said. "Don't worry about anything, Jake."

"Me? Why should I worry? *You're* the one he's threatening."

"He's a con man. I ought to know. I taught him the trade."

I packed my trial bag, and Blinky started down the aisle without waiting for me. "Well, I guess that's it, Jake," he called back to me. "Thanks for a great job."

"There's one more thing," I said.

Blinky stopped by the door, poking his head back at me, resembling a rabbit sniffing the air for danger. "What's that, Jake?"

"There's the matter of the fee."

4

Sweets and Poisons

We were fishing in the saltwater flats off Key Largo, baking in the heat of a cloudless, still June morning. More accurately, Granny Lassiter was fishing, Doc Charlie Riggs was reminiscing, a skinny, towheaded kid whose name I didn't catch was pouting, and I was poling the skiff through the shallow water, simultaneously working up a sweat, a headache, and a sunburn.

"Jake, you look a tad green around the gills," Granny said. "You're not coming down with the grippe, are you?"

I grunted a negative response, and Granny announced, "Boy always took ill at the worst times. Made me miss a billfish tournament once when he caught the flu."

"I was only eight, Granny. I didn't do it on purpose."

Charlie Riggs cleared his throat. "Have I told you two about the case of the poisoned nasal spray?"

"Not recently," I said.

"Oh hush up, Jake," Granny admonished me. "I'd rather listen to Doc's yarns than hear about criminals you've helped keep on the streets."

Ouch. Why's everyone on my case these days? Now there were two of us pouting.

Charlie gnawed on a cold meerschaum pipe, waiting for a break in the Lassiter family banter. He had been county

32

coroner for twenty-five years, and in retirement, his interests had expanded from corpses to virtually every bit of knowledge worth knowing and a lot that wasn't. Doc Riggs was a short, bandy-legged, bushy-bearded cherub with bright brown eyes behind eyeglasses that were slightly cockeyed, probably because one of the hinges was held together with a bent fishhook where a screw had long since dropped out. Charlie was wearing green work pants cut off at the knees, an army camouflage T-shirt, and a Florida Marlins cap. His nose was smeared with gooey, white sunblock.

"C'mon, Charlie, I was only kidding. What's your story about?"

Charlie shot me a look over his shoulder. "The moral might have been summed up by Horace when he wrote '*Ira furor brevis est.*' "

"Horace had such a way with words," I agreed.

" 'Anger is brief madness,' " Charlie translated. "Two biologists at a research laboratory were bitter rivals, and when one received a government grant and the other did not, professional jealousy erupted into—"

"Poisoned nasal spray?" I asked, digging the pole into the shallow water, and pushing us silently across the flats.

"Precisely. One biologist injected beta-propiolactone into the spray the other used for his sinusitis. The drug is quite useful in sterilizing body parts prior to transplant, but I wouldn't recommend ingesting it. We ran a day's worth of tests on the stuff before we could even identify it over at the old morgue. You remember that place, Jake?"

"Sure. That's before the county built you the Taj Mahal on Bob Hope Road." It was true. Those unfortunate victims of shoot-outs and knife fights—most of whom had lived in squalor—spent a few posthumous days in a splendid brick building with the ambience of a decent hotel. "The nasal spray, Charlie. Did it kill the rival?"

"*Dei gratia,* by the grace of God, no. The chemical in the nasal spray changed the properties of the beta-propiolactone. Stung like the devil but didn't cause permanent damage. The assailant, it turns out, had suffered a mental breakdown, and was given a suspended sentence with intensive psychiatric therapy.''

"I like that story, Doc," Granny said. "For once, nobody got killed, and justice was done."

"He must have made it up," I suggested.

Doc Riggs harrumphed at me, baited a hook for himself, and launched into a lengthy and graphic description of determining time of death by the extent of larvae growth in the corpse. The story seemed to make Granny hungry, because she grabbed a strand of Jamaican jerk chicken from a waterproof bag.

I didn't spend as much time with Granny as I used to, and now I studied her a moment. She was a tough old bird in khaki shorts, an "Eat 'em Raw" T-shirt from a Key West oyster bar, and a canvas hat. Her legs and bare feet were tanned the color of mahogany bark and were just as soft. As she listened to Doc Riggs spin his tales, Granny watched the water, squinting into the morning sun, occasionally giving me directions by pointing her fishing rod in a direction her instincts or her failing eyesight dictated. She let fly a cast, grimaced, and allowed the line to drift in the placid water. "You gotta lay the hay down where the goats can git it. Jake, you see the tails of any bonefish a-wiggling?"

"Only thing I see are snails dancing across my eyelids," I said.

"Too much of Granny's moonshine last night," Doc Riggs told me, as if I didn't know. "We're all liable to be blind by tonight."

Granny Lassiter wasn't even my grandmother, but there was some relationship on my father's side. Great-aunt or distant cousin or something. She raised me after my father, a Key West shrimper, was killed in a barroom brawl, and my mother ran off to Oklahoma with a roughneck. I called her Granny, and so did everybody else. Well, nearly everybody else. There was the sailor in the bar who called her Skunky, a reference to the white streak that creases her

jet-black hair. He only called her that once, a whack across
the ankle from a four-foot tarpon gaff ending the nickname
then and there.

Charlie was going on about how posthumous stench attracts blowflies. It's just like an engraved invitation to col-
onize a cadaver, I think he said. Granny was still chewing
the jerk chicken, washing it down with beer from the
cooler. I kept poling, watching for fish, occasionally looking at the towheaded kid Granny had brought along. She
was always feeding stray cats and little boys.

"How about you, son," I asked. "You try any of Granny's white lightning last night?"

"I'm not your son," the kid said, matter-of-factly and
accurately.

"And we're both thankful for that," I responded. I am
generally able to hold my own in repartee with eleven-
year-olds, though I don't have much practice.

"Kip drank his weight in Granny's mango milk
shakes," Charlie said. "Gave him an orange mustache."

Kip. That's right. I'd heard Granny call out "Kippers"
a couple of times, but I thought she was looking for some
salted herring.

"*Mangifera indica,* such a delectable fruit," Charlie
was saying. "Though it tastes like a cross between a peach
and a pineapple, the mango actually is related to the
cashew nut, and heaven help me, poison ivy. Isn't that
strange, the relationship between a sweet and a poison?"

"Reminds me of the women Jake's been sniffing around
all these years," Granny said. "Except for that one who
became the lawyer, they were a bunch of Jezebels in miniskirts."

"*Non semper ea sunt quae videntur,*" Charlie said.
"Things are not always what they seem."

Charlie went on like that for a while, waxing philosophical about plants, animals, and the human condition.
I watched the kid, who was still pouting.

"Kip," I called out in my let's-be-pals voice, "how

'bout some fishing? Want to chase the wily bonefish with a fly rod?''

"I hate fishing," the kid said.

"Fair enough," I responded. "How 'bout a swim? I could toss you overboard and chum for sharks."

"Jake!" Granny warned me.

"Just like *Lifeboat*," Kip said, nonchalantly.

I stopped poling. "Huh?"

Kip looked at me with the air of superiority kids use when dealing with an adult who's never learned their games. "The movie. After a shipwreck, there isn't room for everyone. Some are thrown overboard so others can live."

"Sounds like plea bargaining in a case with multiple defendants," I said.

"It was filmed during World War Two," Kip continued, "a parable for what was going on in Europe."

"A parable," I repeated, impressed.

"Yes, that means you can take it literally or—"

"I know what it means, kid."

"Jake, don't stifle Kippers," Granny ordered, keeping her eyes on the water. "Movies are very important to him."

I turned back to the precocious pouter. "I'll bet you even know who directed this *Lifeboat*."

The towheaded kid gave me another look of youthful disdain. "*Everybody* knows Hitchcock was the director."

Granny dropped a cast near some green floating gunk. " 'Bout all Kippers does is sit home watching movies on the cable. Makes me want to take the twelve-gauge and blast a hole in that damn satellite dish." She turned and peered at me from under the canvas hat. "I was hoping maybe you could get the lad more interested in the outdoors."

"I could use him to pull weeds in my backyard," I offered, generously.

Granny reeled in a stringy mess of seaweed and cleaned off her line. "That's not what I had in mind. Maybe you could toss the football with him. I told Kippers you used to play for the Dolphins.''

"I looked you up in my card book,'' the kid said.

I grunted an acknowledgment. Little boys are always impressed by athletes, even second-stringers.

"Your rookie card is only worth twenty-five cents.''

"You don't say.''

"That's the minimum,'' he reminded me.

"Sounds like a good investment,'' Charlie chimed in, though nobody asked him to. Then Charlie launched into a soliloquy on the depressed international art market, mainly due to economic woes in Japan, when the kid interrupted him: "Most football movies are yucky.''

"Yucky?'' I asked him.

"*The Longest Yard* was okay. I mean, Burt Reynolds was pretty good. He played at Florida State, you know . . .''

I knew.

"Then he did *Semi-Tough* where he played a running back. Boy, what a stinker. In *Everybody's All-American,* I thought Dennis Quaid's legs were too skinny to be a real football player.''

So did I.

"Now, *North Dallas Forty* was pretty decent, though a little dark,'' Kip said. He gave the appearance of furrowing his brow in serious contemplation, but with his long blond bangs, it was hard to tell. "I give it three stars.'' The kid studied me a moment, shading his eyes from the sun. "You know, you look a little like Nick Nolte.''

"Thanks.''

"But he's more handsome.''

My head was throbbing again. "Hey, Granny,'' I called out. "Did you pack a real lunch, or do we have to start eating the passengers?''

"Just like *Soylent Green,*'' Kip said, showing off some more.

"Granny, how do you turn off Siskel and Ebert here?''

"Edward G. Robinson's last movie," the kid concluded, finally cracking a smile.

We were back at Granny's place on the Gulf of Mexico side of Islamorada. I had lived there, too, in the old Cracker house of cedar planks and tin roof, eaves spouts that collected rainwater in barrels and a sturdy wooden porch with a swing, awning, and rocking chair. Charlie was snoozing in the rocker, the kid was watching TV in the Florida room, and I was keeping Granny company in the kitchen. She was squeezing lime juice over a mess of mullet we had caught when the bonefish proved too elusive.

"So what's bothering you, Jake? You've had a burr under your saddle ever since you got down here."

"Nothin'."

"Uh-huh."

Outside, plump gray clouds were building over the Gulf. The temperature was dropping, and the air smelled of rain.

"Granny, do you think I'm a silver-tongued shyster?"

"You're not silver-tongued," she answered, proving that sarcasm runs in the family. Granny dipped the mullet fillets in flour and poured some oil into a frying pan. She was from the old school, and broiled fish just didn't have enough taste for her. "You got that burned-out feeling again?" she asked.

"Not exactly." I picked up a Key lime and sucked on it, bringing tears to my eyes. "You remember Blinky Baroso?"

"Fat fellow who sells stuff he don't own."

"That's him."

"Now, *he's* silver-tongued."

"Yeah, well anyway, I just walked him in a fraud case, and now, it's one of those times of self-examination."

The wind had picked up, and fronds from a coconut palm were slapping against the side of the house. Heavy raindrops began *pinging* off the roof. I used to fall asleep to that noise, just down the hall and to the right.

"You didn't cheat, did you?" Granny asked.

I shook my head. "I just did my job."

"Then, what's the problem? You're a lawyer, a hired gun. You can't be judge and jury, too."

"I know. I keep telling myself that, but it sounds like a rationalization for what I'm doing, which, let's face it, has no social utility."

She dropped a chubby white fillet into the sizzling oil. "Social utility? Are you the same Jacob Lassiter who used to cut school to go frogging in the 'Glades? Are you the same boy who'd rather hit a blocking sled than study for finals?"

"C'mon, Granny, I've grown up."

She regarded me skeptically. "Is there a woman behind this?"

"Whadaya mean?" Even the dimmest witness knows how to avoid a question by asking one of his own.

"Men generally don't do any self-examining unless they get criticized by someone else first. As far as I know, the only people whose opinions matter to you are Charlie and me, and we both love you no matter what you do. So I figure there's gotta be a woman."

"Now you're playing psychologist." Another delaying tactic, shifting the focus to the questioner.

"Okay, if you don't want to talk about it . . ." She let it hang and returned to her cooking. When the fillets were golden brown, she removed them from the pan, strained the oil, added some flour, lime juice, tomato sauce, garlic, pepper, thyme, and a pinch of pepper and salt for the sauce. Outside the window, lightning flashed across the Gulf, and the rain slanted in silver sheets along the beach. "Well, at least, I hope that sleazebag paid you a bundle."

"You know my rule, Granny. Get paid up front."

"Did you?"

I ignored the question and kept going. "Because if you don't and you lose, you never see the money. The client says, 'What good did you do? I could have been convicted *without* a lawyer.' And if you win, he says, 'What'd I need you for? I was innocent.' "

"So did you get paid up front?"

"Not exactly," I admitted.

"Afterward?"

"Sort of."

"I hope you didn't take a check from that bum. He writes checks on banks that closed in twenty-nine."

"Not a check, either."

"Cash? Did you check to see if all the serial numbers were the same?"

"Not cash, either."

"What then?"

"Stock."

"Huh?"

"Blinky gave me a hundred shares in Rocky Mountain Treasures, Inc. It's incorporated in Colorado, licensed to do business in Florida."

Granny was looking at me as if she'd raised a fool. "What makes me think this so-called corporation is not one of the Fortune 500?" she asked.

"Probably because Blinky is the incorporator, the president, and the sole director."

"And he gave you the stock instead of a fee."

"He's tapped out. Look, Granny, I know what you're thinking, but there's one person in the world Blinky wouldn't stiff, and that's me. Now, it may turn out that company doesn't make any money and the stock could be worthless. I know that. But, for once, it's a legitimate enterprise."

"What's this Rocky Mountain corporation do?"

"Sort of geological research," I mumbled.

"What's that, mining?"

"Not exactly."

"C'mon, Jake."

"They look for things."

"What sort of things?"

"Buried treasure," I said, staring out the window at the rippling Gulf, slate gray in the storm.

"Oh Lordy, Jake. Get me a mason jar. I need a drink."

"Look, lots of lawyers take stock in lieu of fees: Imagine if I'd represented Microsoft ten years ago."

"Microsoft didn't try to sell chunks of a condemned condo as pieces of the Berlin Wall, did it?"

I had forgotten about that scheme. Just then, somebody behind me said, "Gregory Peck would have taken vegetables, instead of worthless pieces of paper."

I turned around. Kip was barefoot and wore torn jeans and a faded T-shirt.

"Vegetables?" I asked him.

"In *To Kill a Mockingbird,* he takes collard greens as his attorney's fee when a client can't pay. At least you can eat them."

"Thanks for the advice, kid. Why don't you see if *Judgment at Nuremberg* is on? It'll keep you busy for three and a half hours."

The kid pouted and backed out of the kitchen. In a moment, I heard him clicking through the channels in the other room. Now Granny was scowling at me. "Jake, I want you to be nice to Kippers."

"Okay, okay."

"And I want you to represent him."

"He needs a lawyer? What happened, did they fail to deliver his *TV Guide*?"

"It's a little problem in Juvenile Court. I'd rather let Kippers tell you about it."

"Let him hire Gregory Peck. He works cheap."

"Jake!"

I stuck an index finger into the sizzling lime-tomato concoction and burned myself. "Holy blazes," I said, repeating a phrase I'd learned from Granny in my youth. I sucked on my finger and turned the heat down on the burner. After a moment, I said, "Okay, I'll get the little brat off, even if he poisoned the nasal spray of the entire PTA."

Granny gave me a smile. She still had all her own teeth, despite fifty years of opening beer bottles without an opener. Then she took a wooden spoon that was older than me and started stirring the sauce. "Good. You've got to promise me you'll treat him like family."

"Like family? Why?"

"Because he's your nephew," Granny Lassiter said, never looking up from the simmering sauce.

5

One of Us Was Dead

I thought I heard a faint knock in the engine of my canary yellow Olds 442. Like its owner, the convertible is beginning to show its age, which is only natural, since it is vintage 1968. The Olds doesn't have a tape deck, a CD player, a cellular phone, or a fax machine. It does have a radio, but no FM band. Three hundred fifty cubic inches under the hood, a four-barrel carburetor, a black canvas top, and a five-speed stick, it is—again, like its owner—a throwback.

On this warm, humid Monday morning, my ancient but amiable chariot, its top down, was growling north on Useless 1, the old highway that runs from Maine to Key West. The radio was tuned to a sports talk show at the low end of the dial, but every time a cloud passed over, the speaker crackled with static, and Fidel Castro or one of his cousins came on the air yelling about the *imperialistas*. It made me miss the latest report on which Dolphin free agents signed multiyear, megabucks contracts, and which University of Miami players had failed their drug tests.

In the black leather bucket seat next to me was this lemon-haired, string bean of a kid who Granny had informed me was my kin, to use her word. I studied him. He had blue eyes with long, pale lashes, fair skin with a faint blue vein showing just over the left temple. His straight, lank hair fell into his eyes. He would be considered cute, and when he filled out and reached his midteens, the girls would probably consider him a stud or a fox, or whatever the word of the day might be.

Granny said he was my half sister's son.

Which was double news to me. I didn't know I had a sister, whole or fractioned, and obviously, I didn't know about a son. It all had to do with my no-account mother—Granny's phrase again—who ran off to Oklahoma with a man she didn't marry, a man who left after fathering a daughter, Janet by name.

My mother had spent her last half-dozen years in an alcoholic fog, living alone in a third-floor walk-up apartment in Tulsa. Although the roughneck was long since gone, dear old Mom never came back to Florida, which is a euphemistic way of saying, she never saw me after dropping me off at Granny's on her way out of state and out of mind. Still, she always sent a card at Christmas and on my birthday, sometimes with a few dollars or a shirt that was hopelessly small.

I know a psychologist would say I'm into heavy denial, but I don't remember missing her, and when she died in my junior year in high school, it didn't mean that much. I still had Granny, and now apparently, so did Kip, son of unknown, unmarried, half sister Janet, who was in drug rehab in Houston or Phoenix or Albuquerque, those cities tending to merge in Granny's mind.

"How come you're not in school?" I asked Kip, as we roared north, passing a Winnebago with mushy tires on the two-lane road lined with conch shell stands and ticky-tack motels.

"It's summer vacation," he answered, giving me a pitying look.

"Right. I knew that."

We both studied the double white line a moment, and he said, "You ever see *Fast Times at Ridgemont High*?"

"Must have missed it."

"It was so co-ol. Sean Penn is this dweeb named Spicoli, who orders pizza delivered to his homeroom."

"Co-ol," I agreed.

I stayed quiet a while, sneaking peeks at the kid's profile as the wind blasted his hair back off his face. Okay, maybe there was some resemblance. He would be more finely chiseled than his roughly hewn uncle, and just now he seemed so fragile that something within me, something buried in the genetic material we shared, made me want to protect him. Trouble was, I had precious little experience with children, and I didn't know where to begin.

"I did see *Blackboard Jungle*," I said, "but that was before your time."

"Yeah, it's been on the classics channel. Sidney Poitier and Vic Morrow were totally awesome, and the music over the credits was way cool."

"Way cool," I agreed again.

I gunned the convertible around a rental Ford Taurus whose occupants had slowed to stare at an osprey nest lodged on top of a telephone pole. "The song you liked was 'Rock Around the Clock' by Bill Haley and His Comets."

Granny had asked me to teach the kid some things. I wasn't sure what I could do, unless he wanted to know some of the history of rock and roll, or maybe how to get by an offensive tackle with the swim move. In the meantime, there was work to do.

"Kip, I have to ask you some questions to get ready for the hearing tomorrow."

"Yeah."

"Why'd you do it?"

"Who said I did? There's a presumption of innocence, and if the state can't prove its case, the judge has to dismiss it, just like Paul Winfield did when Harrison Ford was charged with murder in *Presumed Innocent*."

Most clients who try to teach me the law are jailhouse lawyers. Now I had a kid with a J.D. from HBO. "Listen up, Kip. I'm your lawyer, so you tell me the truth without being a smartass. Got it?''

"Are you a good lawyer or a goofball like Joe Pesci in *My Cousin Vinnie*?"

To our left, the sun was setting over a swampy field of saw grass. Three web-footed terns dipped and cawed, scanning the shallow water for dinner. I gunned the Olds to pass a Jeep hauling a Boston Whaler on a shimmying trailer and said, "Granny gave me the A-form, so I know what the cops say you did. I'm assuming you spray-painted the wall since you were caught with blue paint on your pants, and there's a witness who saw you chuck the can through a display window. If that's not enough, you admitted everything to the cop who came to the scene."

"He didn't read me my rights. Not even like Mel Gibson in *Lethal Weapon 3*, when he knocks the bad guy unconscious, then says, 'You have the right to remain silent.' "

"But they'll testify they did. They always do. Besides, the physical evidence and the eyewitness are enough to convict, even without the confession. So, bottom line, little guy, tell me what was going through that mind of yours."

"What's the big deal? Timothy Hutton did the same thing in *Turk 182* as a protest. That's where I got the idea."

I hit the brakes and the old car groaned and whinnied as we stopped on the edge of a ditch filled with water, weeds, and probably alligators. We were just south of the Card Sound Bridge, and the traffic was slowing down to watch a flock, or is it a gaggle, of herons heading for the water.

Turning to the kid who allegedly shared my blood, I said, "I don't care about movies, okay, and I want you to stop showing off. I know you're bright. I know you wrap yourself in the movies because you don't have a real family, and you've been bounced around so much, you don't have any real friends, either. But I'm here for you. Do you understand what I'm saying?"

"You're my lawyer."

"I'm your *friend* and . . ." I took a deep breath as an eighteen-wheeler roared by, kicking up dust. "I'm family, too."

He looked at me skeptically.

"Look, Kip, neither one of us knows exactly what to do. You don't know how to be a nephew, and I don't know how to be an uncle. So, we'll learn together. When the hearing's over, I'll take you back to Granny's if they don't send you off to Raiford."

He gave me a funny look, like I'd hurt his feelings, but he wasn't going to let it show.

"I'll come down and visit you," I added quickly, "and you can come to Miami and visit me. I'll try to do the uncle things like buying you ice cream, taking you fishing—"

"Or to the movies."

"Right. And you'll do the nephew things like . . ." What the hell were nephew things? "Like cutting the grass, changing the oil in the Olds, and waxing down the sailboards."

"You'll have to show me how," he said happily, seeming to welcome the opportunity to work up a sweat.

"It's a deal," I responded, and we exchanged high fives.

"Can we go to the movies tonight?" he asked.

"No. I have to meet a client."

"A murderer, like Jeff Bridges in *Jagged Edge*?"

"Nobody ever mistook Blinky Baroso for Jeff Bridges," I said. "Danny DeVito, maybe."

I pushed the clutch to the floor, grabbed the chrome ball on the stick shift, eased out the clutch while giving it some gas—leaded, high-octane—and tore up gravel, then burned rubber getting back onto the road. I figured the first lesson in nephew training was safe driving, which I sum up as follows: If you've got three hundred fifty cubic inches, use them all.

*   *   *

I live in a coral rock house between Poinciana and Kumquat in Coconut Grove. The house is a two-story pillbox that has withstood sixty years of hurricanes, a number of Super Bowl parties, and many years of benign neglect. Just after nine P.M., I pulled the Olds under a chinaberry tree that serves as a carport and showed Kip how to put up the canvas top. He seemed to like helping. Then I grabbed the duffel bag with all his worldly belongings and led him to the front door, which I opened by banging my good shoulder into the humidity-swollen wood. The door yielded with a groan, or was that me?

Inside was dark and stuffy. I turned on the ceiling fan to stir the soggy air and opened the blinds to let in the green phosphorescent glare of the neighborhood's sodium vapor anti-crime lights. I cleared some beer bottles from the sailboard that is propped between two concrete blocks and serves as a cocktail table. Then I sat down, put my feet up, and tried to figure out what to do next.

My house is furnished in Early Locker Room. There's a tasteful lamp made of a Dolphins helmet with an orange and aqua shade. There's a rusted scuba tank leaning against a planter filled with parched dirt and the fossilized remains of a rubber plant. There are newspapers and magazines and assorted volumes of *Florida Statutes Annotated* and a few paperbacks by John D. MacDonald.

Kip looked around, surveying my palace. "Wh-at a dump!" he proclaimed, and before he could tell me, I said it was a pretty fair Bette Davis. The kid looked sleepy. It hadn't occurred to me earlier, but now I was getting some vague idea about children's bedtimes. I had been planning to haul him with me to meet Blinky Baroso on South Beach. Now, I saw the kid couldn't make it.

I told Kip the bathroom was on the second floor to the left and he scampered up the stairs. I followed him up and put some fresh sheets on the bed in the spare room, a place former teammates crash when they hit town to check into Mount Sinai for a knee replacement or drug rehab.

I tried calling Blinky Baroso to tell him to come over

to the house, instead of meeting me at our usual spot on South Beach, but all I got was a recording. Damn, he must have left already. I didn't even know why he wanted to meet. He hadn't said much on the phone when he set up the meeting. People were watching him, or me, or both, and we needed to talk. He probably wanted to tell me about his latest scheme to turn horseshit into gold, and I was growing irritated that he was dragging me out of the house and away from my kid.

Whoa, my kid?

Is this what fatherhood—or uncledom—does to a man? Was I finally getting domesticated?

I changed into my client conference attire, a clean tank top to match my cutoffs, deck shoes without socks, then came back downstairs. Maybe I could tuck Kip in bed and ask one of the neighbors to stop by. But it was Sunday night, and Phoebe, a thrice-divorced redhead across the street, was hosting one of her swingers' parties, complete with bobbing for apples (and what not) in the Jacuzzi. I could do without a herd of her sopping wet friends traipsing through my house, corrupting my nephew.

My neighbors are a fine lot, though not necessarily baby-sitter material in a Newt Gingrich world of family values. Besides Phoebe, there's Geoffrey, who works nights cruising the expressways looking for fiery car crashes to videotape, and Mako, who lives in a wooden treehouse on the other side of the limeberry shrubs. To visit, you have to climb a rope ladder, something that discourages process servers. Mako trades his custom-made hammocks for crawfish with Homer Thigpen, a lobster pot poacher who lives in the first house on Poinciana. I helped Homer beat a federal charge that could have cost him his boat under the forfeiture laws, and ever since, I've been knee-deep in Florida lobster, some of them even corralled in season. I haven't felt so warm and fuzzy about the majesty of the legal system since I walked a parking meter thief who paid my fee in quarters and dimes.

I heard the water running upstairs and yelled at Kip to

make sure he brushed his teeth. "Up and down strokes," I ordered.

I was feeling uneasy about leaving him alone in a strange house. He was a good kid. Okay, so he smashed a window and spray-painted the South Miami Cineplex with a pretty fair drawing of Arnold Schwarzenegger holding a shotgun. "*Hasta la vista,* baby," Arnold was saying in a cartoon bubble of iridescent blue paint.

It was an understandable protest by a kid who had ridden the bus from Islamorada to see *Casablanca* on the big screen only to discover that the theater had, without notice, substituted *Revenge of the Nerds III*. I thought the theater manager overreacted in reporting the incident as a terrorist act, and when Kip asked, I assured him he wouldn't get the chair like Jimmy Cagney in *Angels with Dirty Faces*.

I was thinking about the juvenile court hearing when Kip came back down the stairs. He had changed into his pajamas, I thought at first, but then I saw he was wearing an old Dolphins jersey that hung down past his knees. "I found this in the closet," he said. "Okay if I wear it to sleep?"

He turned around, modeling it. Across his back, the lettering said LASSITER. Below was the number, fifty-eight. "Looks great on you," I said. "It's yours."

He smiled, stifled a yawn with a dainty fist, and came up to me. I didn't know what he wanted, but I figured it out after a second. I gave him a good-night hug, then on impulse, scooped him into my arms. We went up the stairs that way, his legs curled around me, and I dropped him into bed and pulled up the sheet to his chin.

"Good night, Kip."

"Good night, Uncle Jake," he said, his eyes half closed, his face a tranquil reflection of childlike innocence.

I took Douglas Road up to Grand Avenue, hung a right and headed into downtown Coconut Grove. To avoid the teenyboppers cruising Cocowalk on a Sunday night, I swung onto Oak and then by Tigertail going north. I turned left on Seventeenth Avenue, picked up I-95 to hook up with the MacArthur Causeway and drove east across the bay to Miami Beach. I found a parking spot next to a Dumpster behind a sushi bar and walked to the coral rock wall that runs along the east side of Ocean Drive.

A three-quarter moon was hanging above the ocean, spreading a creamy glow across the black water. A warm breeze from the southeast swirled sand across the sidewalk and into the street. Lovers of every persuasion strolled by the sidewalk cafés across the street, and the usual collection of models, photographers, would-be actors, wannabe trendies, and assorted semi-hipsters crowded the sidewalk, pausing long enough to be ogled by patrons sipping decaf cappuccino under Campari umbrellas. This season's color seemed to be black. Billowing black silk pants, square-cut black jackets with shoulder pads over white T-shirts. And those were the men. The women wore black minis and black fishnet stockings.

As is my custom, I was on time. It is a harmless obsession. I don't like to be kept waiting, and it's only fair to return the favor. So I sat on the low wall, watching the parade of characters go by on foot, in limos, on choppers, and occasionally on Rollerblades. I thought about Jo Jo and Blinky, the beauty and the bullshit artist. In my life, there had been women before Jo Jo, and women after her, but she was unique. Always pushing me. Reach high, be the best. She reminded me of a recruiting pitch for the Army.

I had cared for her, but I went on without looking back. I'm not proud of that, but it's the way I am. Introspection is not my strong suit. I am an ox, head down, plowing ahead to newer, if not greener, pastures. So when I am forced to revisit my past, I am confused. I do not see the present clearly because the past is still misty. I have not resolved old issues. Hell, I didn't even know they were issues at the time.

Now I waited for Blinky. If I smoked, which I don't, I would have struck a match. If I drank, which I do, I would have strolled across the street and sat at the News Café, watching for Blinky at the wall. So I did, at an outdoor table, ordering a Grolsch, the fine Dutch beer, in the sixteen-ounce bottle with the porcelain top.

As it turned out, I had a three-Grolsch wait, and still no Blinky. I found a pay phone and called his apartment. "Hello, this is Baroso Enterprises, Inc. Please leave a message at the tone, and I . . ."

It was nearly eleven, so I said to hell with it and walked back to my car, which still had its aerial, hubcaps, and AM radio intact. It occurred to me that Blinky might have gotten mixed up. Ever since the trial, he had been in a daze. He might be at my house, probably waiting on the front porch, cursing me. Hitting seventy on the brief stretch of the interstate, I was back on Kumquat Street in the Grove in fourteen minutes.

I parked under the chinaberry tree, same as always. The moon was higher in the sky now, the night warm and muggy, no trace of an oceanfront breeze here. I listened for the warbling of my mockingbird. He is *my* bird the way the raccoon who knocks over my garbage cans is my raccoon. But the mocker usually is perched in *my* marlberry bush, singing nighttime songs. *Mimus polyglottos,* Doc Riggs calls him, mimic of many tongues. He's not much to look at, sort of a battleship gray with white wing patches, but like the bobwhite, nighthawk, and whippoorwill, he's got a voice.

As I approached the front porch, I heard a sound from the hibiscus hedge, or maybe I sensed movement there. It could have been a variety of nighttime animals, including *Perfidus nocturnus,* who might be waiting to mug an honest citizen such as myself. I'm as brave as the next guy, and I don't mind a fair fight, but a punk kid with a semi-automatic could tattoo a ring around my heart before I got off a punch, so I hurried to the front door.

The sound was barely more than a squeak. "Uncle Jake."

I turned and ran back to the hedge. Huddled in the dirt,

hidden by leaves and floppy red flowers was the boy in the Dolphins jersey. I reached down to him, and he crawled into my arms. "Uncle Jake, you're home."

He was crying, his tears tracking down grimy cheeks.

I was stunned. "What the hell's going on?"

He pointed toward the house, his hand shaking. "I woke up and heard voices downstairs. Then, somebody came up the steps. Slow, like he was listening for something. I got so scared, I crawled under the bed. Somebody opened my door, looked in, and closed it. Then he went into your bedroom. I heard sounds in there, but I just stayed under the bed. He went downstairs again, and I heard voices, real soft, then a noise like furniture being moved. Uncle Jake, I was so scared . . ."

I squeezed him in my arms. "Kip, I'm sorry. I shouldn't have left you. I'll never do it again, but you were dreaming, that's all. No one was in the house. You've seen too many of those movies where maniacs with razors go after the kids."

He was shaking his head. "Honest, Uncle Jake. You gotta believe me. After a while, I heard the front door close, so I sneaked to the stairs. Then I saw it. Even though it was dark, I knew what it was."

"What?"

Again, he pointed at the house with a shaky hand. "I didn't want to go out through the front. I just couldn't go into the room, so I ran back to my bedroom, climbed out the window, and crossed the roof to the tree in back."

"You came down the tree? Why?"

He started crying again.

"Hey, Kip. Everything's okay. Here's what we'll do. We'll go in the house together."

He shook his head and squeezed me tighter.

"Okay, Kippers, I'll go in. Will you wait for me?"

He nodded and wiped his nose on the sleeve of my old jersey. I carried him to the car and put him in the front seat. He sat there, rocking back and forth, hugging his knees. I went back to the porch, hit the front door with a solid shoulder and barged in. Moonlight slanted through the windows and lit the room in ashen grays. It was silent, except for the *whompeta-whompeta* of the ceiling fan. Which seemed to *whomp* slower than usual.

I saw it then, or sensed it.

A shadow, a shape, a movement.

I looked up. A dark silhouette flew just over my head.

A whirling, twirling, unidentifiable mass.

My first impression was that someone had leapt off the landing of the stairs at me, like a cowboy in a Western. I ducked and head-rolled on the old pine floor, coming up in a crouch, adrenaline pumping, knees bent, legs spread, fists clenched.

My second impression was different. There were two of us in the room, all right, but one of us was dead.

He was suspended from the ceiling fan and looked like one of those circus performers on the high rings, spinning dizzying circles. The body swung at a forty-five-degree angle from the ceiling, circling above me in endless, hypnotic motion. The legs were straight out, the arms flung back from the centrifugal force. In the moonlight, the shadow danced crazily across the floor and up the wall.

A jumble of emotions. On South Beach, I had the strange sensation that something was wrong. Blinky was usually late, but he always shows. Tonight he had been afraid of something, someone. What, who?

I felt my heart beating and beating hard. I tried to calm myself down and think. What to do first? Cut him down, call the police, take care of Kip? They don't train you for this stuff, not in three-a-day practices in August, and not in night law school in September.

Now my mind was tearing along at a speed I couldn't control. Flashes of overlapping thoughts and unanswered questions kept jolting me with each spin of the body. Who killed Blinky Baroso and why, and had the killer been looking for me? I said a silent prayer of thanks that Kip was unhurt.

I duck-walked out from under the body and got to the wall, reaching for the light switch. Overhead, three spots flashed on. I squinted through the glare and saw how he was fastened to the motor housing of the fan. What looked like a bolt of colorful silk cloth was digging into his neck and tied to something, a wire coat hanger maybe, that was attached to the fan.

In the brightness, I could see his eyes were bulging open, and his tongue, black and swollen, stuck out the side of his mouth. And I could see something else, too.

It wasn't Blinky Baroso.

6

My Alibi

I called Charlie Riggs first, getting a recording that informed me he had gone fishing, telling all his friends, *"Vive valeque."* I should have figured he was still in the Keys. Granny never complained when I headed north early, leaving Charlie behind to keep her company. I think it was Father Andrew Greeley, with the aid of the Gallup Poll, who determined that couples in their sixties have the best sex. Something to look forward to.

Granny answered on the second ring, and I pictured her rolling over in bed and handing the phone to my old friend. Charlie said he'd get here in an hour-fifteen if his old Chevy pickup didn't throw a rod.

Next, I called Miami Homicide where I am known, but not necessarily liked. A woman with a faint Cuban accent took down the information, calmly checking the address three times, and politely asking me not to leave the premises. From her tone, she might have been taking an order for a pizza with anchovies, but that's the way cops act, particularly in a city where homicides are as plentiful as mosquitoes. Next I called Abe Socolow at home, figuring if I hadn't, the cops would have, and Abe's the kind of guy who remembers the small stuff.

At first, I tried not to touch anything, having been ed-

ucated by television that I might foul up the crime scene
with my fingerprints. Once every hundred years or so, a
crime will be solved by finding an unknown assailant's
fingerprints at the scene. Usually, fingerprints merely corroborate what everyone already knows: Three witnesses in
the liquor store identify the gunman, and a fingerprint spe-
cialist confirms his prints are on the gun dropped at the
scene.

Then, I remembered Kip was still in the car. I didn't
want him to see the body a second time, so I hit the switch
for the fan, went into the kitchen, hauled out a high stool,
and climbed up until I was looking straight into the face
of a dead man. A thin copper wire circled his neck and
was looped through the motor housing of the fan. But
that's not what killed him. The bright splash of cloth was
an imported silk tie knotted by someone unfamiliar with
the double Windsor. The knot dug deeply into the neck,
just below the Adam's apple.

The tie was a palette of blues and reds and would have
looked swell with a dark suit and a white oxford cloth
shirt. In fact, it always looked swell just that way.

I should know. It was my tie.

I climbed down and went into the kitchen where I found
a knife I use for cleaning fish. Up again, and this time, I
hoisted the body with one hand placed under his chin and
sawed through the copper wire. He dropped like a tree,
banging the floor. I got down, covered the body with an
old beach towel, and went out to the car.

I hustled Kip inside, told him he had been right, apologized for doubting him, and said everything would be
okay, the cops would be here soon. I turned on the TV to
distract him from the lump in the corner of the room, but
in what must have been a first, he wasn't interested. It took
about ninety seconds, but he wasn't scared anymore. He
began babbling excitedly, asking questions, wanting to
help, telling me how totally awesome and off-the-Richter
it was to have a murder in the house, and did it happen
often, and was somebody trying to set me up, like Gene

Hackman did to Kevin Costner in *No Way Out,* which was a remake of *The Big Clock* with Charles Laughton and Ray Milland, in case I didn't know, which I didn't. He asked if we could keep the body a while, like the boys did in *Weekend at Bernie's.* I told him to calm down, but he kept chattering away, and I finally figured that it wasn't quite real to him. Just another movie.

I was trying to concentrate, to figure it out, but Kip was carrying on about murder plots, so I led him to the kitchen, opened the refrigerator and popped the porcelain top on a sixteen-ounce Grolsch. I found two glasses that didn't appear to carry contagious diseases and poured half into one and half into the other.

"How 'bout a beer, Kip?" I asked, handing him a glass.

"Wow, that's completely broly of you, Uncle Jake," Kip said, which I took as well-deserved praise of my child-rearing skills.

I drained my beer while Kip sipped at his, making a face. Then I had another, sitting on a stool at the kitchen counter, feeling my pulse rate subside. I needed to think, to consider what I knew and what I didn't. There were a hundred questions, but they all boiled down to two.

What was Kyle Hornback doing in my house, and who killed him?

To answer those two, I needed to consider what Charlie Riggs called the threshold question in any unsolved crime. *Cui bono?* Who stands to gain? If I couldn't figure that one out, Abe Socolow would be the first to tell me. First, though, he'd probably ask me something I'd been wondering ever since I cut down the body.

Where the hell was Blinky Baroso?

Two detectives showed up first, an Anglo major near retirement age and a young Hispanic who didn't give his rank. The older cop had tired eyes and wore a lightweight brown suit with shiny black shoes. The younger one wore a short-sleeved white shirt and a blood-red tie. He had the sloping shoulders and bulging arms of a weight lifter. I had known the major from my days as an assistant public defender, but we'd never had a case together. The young one was a stranger to me.

Abe Socolow walked in five minutes later. After they convinced themselves that there was indeed a death not from natural causes, they called the assistant medical examiner lucky enough to be on weekend duty. Socolow spent the next ten minutes chewing me out for contaminating the scene, as he put it. Then the younger detective flexed his triceps and called the station, asking for what used to be called the crime scene boys, who turned out to be an African-American woman and an Asian-American woman. They arrived, toting their cameras, tape measures, fingerprint kits, and assorted technological doodads. Kip followed them around for a while, eyes wide, mouth closed, except when he asked the difference between the Glock nine-millimeters city cops carried and the Beretta used by Mel Gibson in the *Lethal Weapon* movies.

I was sitting on the battered sofa with the two detectives in mismatched chairs at slight angles to me. Abe Socolow paced in front of me. He wore his trademark black suit, white shirt, and black tie, but it being a Sunday night, the tie was loosened at the neck.

The major asked all the right questions, and I had none of the answers. No, I didn't expect Kyle Hornback here. That's right, I leave the front door unlocked, preferring burglars to walk in, rather than busting up the place. Besides, unless you know to batter the door, it's stuck shut by the humidity.

Where was I earlier in the evening? On South Beach. That's right, I left the youngster here alone.

The crime scene investigators had shooed Kip away while they photographed the body, and now the lad joined me, moving close on the sofa, where I put my arm around him. Even under the paddle fans, it was about eighty degrees in the house, so the goose bumps on Kip's arms couldn't have been from the temperature. Maybe it was starting to sink in. Maybe it was becoming real.

The major asked Kip what he saw, and he ran through the story. Footsteps, his door opening and closing, someone in my bedroom . . .

"That's when they must have taken my tie," I chimed in.

"Shut up, Jake," Socolow said, still pacing.

Voices downstairs, Kip continued, furniture moving, the front door closing again. He sneaked down the landing, saw the body spinning, tossing shadows across the moonlit room, ran back upstairs and climbed out his window. Same story he told me with no embellishments.

"Good try, Abe," I said, "but I don't think the kid killed him, even though he doesn't have an alibi."

"What about you, Jake? What's your alibi?"

"What's that supposed to mean?"

"Hey, Jakie, let's get something straight here. This is a murder investigation, so I ask—"

"The questions," Kip interrupted. "Or if you want, we can finish this downtown."

I hushed the kid with what passes for a stern look. "Go ahead, Abe. Fire away."

"Where's your client?" Abe Socolow asked.

"Which one? I've got two or three, you know."

"Jake, don't jerk me around. Where's Louie Baroso?"

"I don't know," I answered, truthfully.

"When's the last time you saw him?"

"Three days ago."

I could have added, "in my office," but the question was *when,* not *where,* and I preach to my clients just to answer the question, no more, no less.

"Where?" Socolow asked.

"In my office."

"What was he doing there?"

"The usual, dropping ashes on the carpet, flirting with my secretary."

Socolow gave me a pained look. "Did he mention Kyle Hornback?"

"Yeah, he asked if he could use my house to kill Kyle,

maybe add him to the living room furnishings along with the beanbag chair and lava lamp.''

The muscular young detective looked up. "He said that?"

The major rubbed his forehead as if he had a migraine, and Abe stopped pacing and squarely faced me. "Jake, don't fuck with me, okay?"

"Yeah," Kip said in his tough-guy voice, or at least as tough as his eleven-year-old tenor could make it. "We can do this the easy way or the hard way, it's up to you, pal."

"What is it with you two?" Socolow demanded, scowling.

Just then, Kip leaned over and whispered something to me. I patted him on his goose-bumped arm, held his hand, and whispered something back. Abe Socolow's dark eyes shot me a question, so I answered. "He said you remind him of Frank Sinatra in *The First Deadly Sin*."

"Yeah?"

"And I told him Sinatra wore a better toupee."

"I don't wear a toupee."

"Really? No one can tell."

The major cleared his throat and said, "Mr. Lassiter, were you expecting any visitors here tonight?"

"No," I said, softly.

"Why did you leave the house?"

"Like I said before, I had to meet someone." When possible, I like telling cops the truth.

"Someone?"

"Call it a date if you like." Okay, okay, so it wasn't the whole truth and nothing but the truth.

"What was the lady's name?"

"I didn't say she was a lady." True enough. I also didn't say she was a she.

Socolow couldn't stand it. "Jake, what's her name, for chrissakes. We gotta establish your whereabouts, you know that."

"That could be embarrassing," I said. Still true. I should get a Boy Scout badge for this.

"Why? She married?"

I gave my best bashful grin. "You said it, Abe, not me."

I felt Kip's hand squeeze mine, but he didn't flinch, didn't say a word. What a trooper the kid was, and what a role model his old uncle Jake. In just a few hours, the kid learned how to drive recklessly, witnessed a grisly murder scene, drank his first beer, and watched his blood kin mislead the cops. And poor Granny was worried about a little spray-paint graffiti. If the kid hung out with me much longer, he'd be knocking off Wells Fargo trucks before he hit puberty.

Abe Socolow was prowling again. "When Baroso was in your office on Thursday . . ."

Socolow let it hang there, but if he thought I'd start a narrative like some motormouth witness, he had a long wait. After a moment, he continued, ". . . what did you talk about?"

"C'mon, Abe. That's privileged, and you know it."

"Not if Baroso disclosed a plan to kill Kyle Hornback, it isn't."

"Hey, Abe. We've known each other a long time. If that had happened, don't you know I would have stopped him one way or another?"

"Yeah, I like to think so."

"Besides, Blinky Baroso isn't a killer. Even if he wanted to, he wouldn't have the physical ability to . . ." I gestured to a corner of the room, where the crime lab cops were taking the body temperature of the corpse. "Hornback must go about one eighty, one eighty-five," I continued. "Blinky couldn't bench-press a breadstick, much less strangle the guy and hoist him to the ceiling. You're looking for someone bigger and stronger, someone who's good with his hands."

"You're right," Socolow said, softly, "someone like you."

*　　*　　*

I made coffee for my guests while they waited for the assistant medical examiner, who either was lost or had other customers. Take a number, there were three other homicide scenes ahead of ours, according to the younger detective.

While we waited, the female crime scene cops were smoking cigarettes, talking to each other about overtime and the supervisor who calls them babes. The detectives were scribbling in their little notebooks and whispering. Abe Socolow's face was set into its usual frown with an occasional glare thrown in for variety. "I suppose you know Hornback wanted to cut a deal before sentencing," he said.

"I figured."

"He was supposed to come in tomorrow with his lawyer. He had something to trade about your client, something that could make a bigger case, maybe involve the feds."

"Uh-huh."

"What do you know about it, Jake?"

"Nothing," I answered, which for once was entirely accurate. "I heard Hornback and Baroso exchange words in the courtroom at the end of the trial, and that's all I know. Blinky has another deal going out west, but I don't know the details, and I wouldn't tell you if I did. Besides, he assured me it's legitimate."

"And you believed him?"

"I've been trying to get him into something straight for years."

"I know that, Jake. You see the glimmer of good that's in all these jerkoffs. It's your flaw, your weakness. Can't you get it through your head that you can't make a citizen out of a wise guy? You can't change a lifetime of habits. Jeez, you'd think your days as a public defender would have taught you some cynicism."

"They did. They made me cynical about cops, judges, prosecutors, defense lawyers, and defendants. They made me distrust the system and everyone in it. But I'm a cynic with hope.''

''Me, too,'' he said, after a moment. ''My hope is bigger prisons, longer sentences, fewer paroles.''

I was willing to spar a couple more rounds with Abe, but my attention was distracted. Someone was pounding at the front door. It groaned, shuddered, and opened with a thud. The cops looked up excitedly, as if their suspect would walk into the room and surrender.

''*Deus miseratur!*'' Charlie Riggs proclaimed. ''Now where's the *corpus delicti*?''

7

The Bates Motel

"State of Florida versus Sylvester Houston Conklin," the bailiff announced. "Adjudicatory hearing."

"C'mon," Kip said, nudging me. "That's us."

I gave him a look.

"My mom loves Sly Stallone," he explained. "I was born in Houston, and best she knows, my dad's name was Conklin."

The bailiff called out the case again, louder this time, and we hustled from the small gallery toward the bench. Earlier that morning, I had told Kip, or Sylvester Houston, to put on his Sunday best, which he interpreted to mean his Reebok high-tops without socks, jeans with holes in the knees, and a T-shirt that celebrated "The Fish That Saved Pittsburgh." I wore a seersucker suit in a half-successful effort to look like a Southern gentleman.

We were in the courtroom of the Honorable T. Bone Coleridge, longtime Dade County Juvenile Court judge and Bull Gator in the University of Florida Alumni Society. He was, as far as I knew, the only judge in the state to wear orange and blue robes. His chambers were festooned with autographed footballs, photos of His Honor with various coaches and athletes, and memorabilia ranging from shoulder pads and helmets to the jockstrap Steve

Spurrier wore the day he clinched the Heisman Trophy.

The Juvenile Courthouse, a concrete block affair with open walkways surrounding a cheerless concrete court-yard, sits on northwest Twenty-seventh Avenue in what police maps used to call the Central Negro District. It is a neighborhood of pawnshops and used car lots, lumber-yards, and hubcap bazaars. About a block away is a gun shop with a pass-through window, like a hoagie stand in South Philadelphia. I had parked in a public lot surrounded by a razor-wire-topped fence. I took Kip by the hand, which felt small and moist, and led him through the maze of administrative buildings into the courthouse.

"Afternoon, numbah fifty-eight," the judge greeted me, in homage to my short but unspectacular career on the football field. "Don't see you much in kiddie court."

"Good afternoon, Your Honor," I acknowledged, bow-ing my head slightly. Like most lawyers, I would curtsy or kiss the hem of a judge's robe to help win a case.

"Say, Jake, what do you think of my dog-ass Gators this fall?"

"I think they'll play eleven games, twelve if they go to a bowl."

"Ah believe those boys will go all the way," the judge opined, as he did each summer. "Sugar Bowl and a num-bah one ranking." It galled him that the University of Mi-ami had won four national championships while his alma mater had failed to notch even one. "Now, let's see what roguery brings you here today."

The judge hunched over the bench and riffled through a court file. He had a bulbous nose lined with purple veins, a large bald head that reflected the overhead lighting, and he carried close to three hundred pounds on a five-eight frame. He liked to let people think he played football in college, but according to an ancient yearbook some lawyer friends passed around, the closest he got to the end zone was as a cheerleader. The judge, still peering into the file, made a *tsk-tsk-tsking* sound. Part of the role, as played by T. Bone, was to scare kids straight. "Malicious mischief!"

he thundered, lifting his large head and glaring at Kip. "Trespassing and willful destruction of property. Serious charges, one and all. Son, how do you plead?"

I was ready to say "not guilty," but my half-pint client was too quick for me.

"Hey, Judge," he called out, "when you go through the metal detector downstairs, what goes off first, the lead in your ass or the shit in your brains?"

The judge turned red.

I was speechless.

Kip smiled a sinister grin I hadn't seen before. It didn't even look like him. Which made me think it wasn't him at all. I was tossing around that idea, but the judge's booming voice interrupted my train of thought.

"Young man, you're in direct contempt of court! Ah'm looking at your face, and it's got Youth Hall written all over it. Jake, you got yourself a real in-cor-rigible here."

"Your Honor," I responded, "that wasn't him talking."

"What are you saying, that Ah cain't believe my ears?"

"No, just that he didn't have control over what he said."

"Why not? Is he on ecstasy or crack? Is he one of those dopeheads who puke on my Dodge in the parking lot?"

"Your Honor, I believe what the boy said was from a movie." I turned to Kip, my eyes pleading. "Isn't that it, Sylvester?"

"Bruce Willis in *Die Hard 2*," Kip declared, proudly. "It just sort of popped into my head."

"That's part of our defense, Your Honor," I volunteered, making it up as I went along.

"Jake, that dog won't hunt. You know me, Ah'm just a simple country lawyer who's now a simple country judge . . ."

Four million people from Miami to Palm Beach, and we still have judges chewing straw and handing out that aw-shucks routine.

". . . and while I may not read everything in the law books," he continued, gesturing to a shelf of pristine copies of the *Southern Reporter,* "Ah believe there are only three possible pleas—guilty, not guilty, and *nolo con-ten-dere . . .*"

He made the last plea sound like the title of a Tony Bennett song.

". . . unless you're claiming the boy's incompetent. You'all looking for a competency hearing, Jake?"

"Respectfully, Your Honor," I said, employing a term lawyers use to mean just the opposite, "we plead not guilty and seek an immediate adjudicatory hearing, and while the facts of the incident may not be in dispute, there are certain mitigating factors, including the defendant's age, lack of prior record, and psychological considerations we'll be asking the court to consider."

Judge T. Bone Coleridge exhaled a guttural snort. "Ten-minute recess. Then strap on your helmets 'cause we're gonna try this case."

I adhered to the first rule of courtroom recesses: I took a pee, because you don't know when you'll have a chance for the next one. Then I used a pay phone to call Doc Riggs and find out if the autopsy report on Kyle Hornback was finished.

"Obviously, this was neither a natural death nor an accident," he lectured. "I believe we can rule out suicide, though that's often an issue in hangings. So, we're dealing with homicide."

"No kidding, Charlie. C'mon, I'm in court. Cut to the chase." I am not usually testy with Charlie or Granny, but my nerves were on edge. I was worried about Sylvester aka Kip; I was worried about Blinky; and I was worried about me.

Charlie harrumphed and continued: "Well then, you might be interested to know what the toxicology report showed. I happened to be there when the chemist—"

"Charlie, please!"

"All right, all right. *Vincit qui patitur.* He who is patient prevails. Hornback's blood was loaded with barbiturates. Probably pentobarbital, pretty fast-acting, and he was unconscious when throttled by person or persons unknown. If he'd been conscious, there would have been a struggle, and pressure on the neck would have been intermittent. There'd probably be some petechial hemorrhaging, burst blood vessels and the like. With slow, steady pressure, there's less evidence of trauma, and that's the case here. Just a trace of blood in the larynx, some engorged blood vessels in the brain, that's about it. Cause of death was asphyxia. Your tie, and quite a handsome one at that, was the ligature, used much like a garrote. There was a contusion in the middle of his chest. Hornback was probably faceup on the floor when the tie was slipped around his neck. The assailant likely placed a knee on his chest for leverage, then tightened the tie, squeezing off the air supply, and finally tying the knot.''

"That it?''

"Just about. Before the M.E. sliced him open, they tried to pull latents off the body. As usual, they couldn't do it. But one of the technicians wanted me to help with a methyl methacrylate test.''

"Did you?''

"Of course. We used Super Glue, which converts to fumes quite easily, tented the body, and came up with some nice latents on the neck and chin. Checking them out now.''

"Great. I hope there are some besides mine.''

"Yes, well next time, don't fool around with murder scenes.''

Next time? "Okay, Charlie, thanks.''

"Thank *you*, Jake. You know, I'm never as alive as when I'm poking around in a dead body. Strangulation is quite tricky. Not like the old days of execution by hanging when they'd just tie the knot under the left side of the jaw to throw the head back and snap the odontoid process of the second cervical vertebra. No, that was too easy. As Pierrepoint, the former hangman of London once testified—''

"Charlie, hold that thought. I've got a case to try.''

*   *   *

An earnest young woman wearing a blue suit and white silk blouse introduced herself as the assistant state attorney. Her mouth was fixed in a grim expression, and the notes on her yellow pad were printed in precise block lettering. I don't know why, but prosecutors tend to be more organized and less humorous than defense lawyers. And the women prosecutors tend to be very good. Just look at Marcia Clark or Josefina Baroso.

The state began with the theater manager, whose testimony was matter-of-fact. There was a disturbance outside the theater. A lanky blond-haired boy was cursing at the ticket seller. The boy left and came back half an hour later, at which time he began spray-painting the outside of the theater, first with a drawing of Arnold Schwarzenegger, then the phrase, "*Hasta la vista,* baby." When the manager dashed out of the theater, the boy threw the spray can through a coming attractions display window, breaking the glass. Yes, that boy is present in the courtroom. That's him over there in the Pittsburgh Pirates T-shirt.

That made Kip snicker. "Dork doesn't even know a baseball team from a movie."

I barely cross-examined, except to emphasize that no one was injured.

Next came a policeman who said he found Kip at the scene with blue paint on his hands and an explanation for what he had done. The boy was angry at the cancellation of the film he wanted to see. Again, my cross was concise. I had the officer admit that Kip offered no resistance and told the truth about the incident. That's called putting the best face on a confession. The state rested, and the judge looked at me with raised eyebrows.

"The defense calls Doctor Harvey Kornblum," I announced with a gravity far in excess of my witness's credentials. The bailiff hustled out of the courtroom and into the waiting area. While he was gone, I sneaked a peek at Kip. He was studying a poster on the wall that showed two youngsters, one in a cap and gown, the other behind bars. "School and Job or Jail and Death" read the caption. Subtlety was in short supply in the juvenile justice system.

The bailiff returned with my witness in tow. Dr. Harvey Kornblum might not be the best psychiatrist in town, but he was the cheapest. I choose my expert witnesses based on two qualifications, low fees and a healthy crop of gray hair. The reasons are obvious. Most of my clients can't afford to pay their lawyer and expensive experts, too, so it's easy to see where I'll cut corners. Both judges and jurors like gray-haired doctors, even if they're pompous windbags. Besides meeting my criteria, Harvey Kornblum was also the only shrink who would see Kip on half-an-hour notice this morning and be ready to testify right after lunch.

Dr. Kornblum sat down, unbuttoned his suit coat and let his paunch hang out. He patted his silvery hair and raised his hand to take the oath. I ran through his qualifications as a pediatric psychiatrist, letting him dawdle a bit too long over his internship, his multiple residencies, his fellowships here and there, his long-since outdated papers on bed-wetting and masturbation, and finally, we got down to business.

"Dr. Kornblum, have you had an opportunity to examine the defendant, Sylvester Houston Conklin?"

The witness looked confused until I pointed toward the defense table.

"Ah yes. Kip. I have examined him at some length."

Technically, that was true, the length being twenty-five minutes. "Can you tell the court what your examination revealed?"

Dr. Kornblum opened a thick file that must have contained his autobiography because it couldn't have been the notes of his meeting this morning. He hadn't taken any. The doctor put on a pair of rimless eyeglasses, stared at his file, removed the glasses, and began speaking in deep, magisterial tones. "Kip, er, Sylvester, is a handsome and well-nourished, though thin, lad of eleven years. He has no physical abnormalities and is above average in intelligence, far above average, I must say. Psychologically, I would term him emotionally isolated. He does not know his father. He has, *de facto,* been abandoned by his mother, and is being raised by a woman he calls Granny, though she is not his grandmother."

Dr. Kornblum paused to look at the judge and let the weight of his testimony sink in. Then he continued. "The child spends much time alone, watching television, especially movies. He is not a happy child. Indeed, his reality is one of pain, isolation, and abandonment. For this reason, he seeks escape. His reality becomes the fantasy of movies."

"How important are these movies to the boy?" I asked.

"Very important, indeed. This child doesn't just watch movies. He becomes a character. The movie is real."

"And is there a difference between seeing these movies on television and in a theater?"

"Quite so. For him, seeing a movie on the big screen enhances that reality. In the theater, he can lose himself, can be enveloped in the sheer size of the picture, the depth of the stereophonic sound."

Now we were rolling. "And what happens, Doctor, if someone takes away that opportunity?"

"Clearly, they have stolen his reality. His reaction is far out of proportion to the harm done, at least it would seem that way to those of us for whom movies have not taken on such importance. You see, the boy has his depression under control, in a steel box if you will. He escapes this depression in the movies. Take that away, the depression becomes anger and rage, and the consequence, as we have seen, is an antisocial act in protest of cancellation of his favorite film."

"Would you expect him to repeat this conduct?"

"Most likely not. The conduct was aberrational. It resulted from the highly unusual combination of his high expectations at seeing *Casablanca* in the theater and the unannounced cancellation of the film after he took a bus to Miami."

"Do you see that incarceration would serve any purpose here?"

"No. What the boy needs is a strong male figure, someone he can trust, someone he can look up to. He doesn't need jailers."

"Thank you," I said, nodding to Dr. Kornblum for a job well done.

The state had no questions, and my witness stepped down and took a seat in the front row of the gallery. I could have called Kip to testify, but after his earlier outburst, I didn't think I could trust him. Besides, Kornblum had done the job. I wouldn't have to pay him for his services, but I would defend him *gratis* on his pending DUI charge.

I told the judge the defense rested, and that set T. Bone to mashing his knuckles into his forehead. "Counselor, Ah just don't follow all that psychological mumbo jumbo. You're saying the movies made him do it."

"Not exactly, Your Honor. The deprivation of the movie unleashed his anger at earlier abandonments."

"Well, we can't have him painting up the town every time they change the double feature at the mall, can we?"

It is difficult to respond to a complete non sequitur, so I didn't try.

"Jake," the judge said, his face lighting up with an idea, "do you mind if Ah ask the lad a question?"

I wasn't sure. It wasn't the question that worried me, but the answer. Besides, I wanted to give my closing argument, telling the judge how graffiti has been around since ancient Rome. But all I said was, "Go ahead, Your Honor."

"Son," the judge asked, looking at Kip, "do you remember having done this terrible act?"

"I remember every detail," Kip said. "The Germans wore gray. You wore blue . . ."

"Your Honor, that's from *Casablanca*!" I bellowed.

". . . and orange," Kip continued, looking at the judge's two-tone robes.

"Judge Coleridge," I said, intending to filibuster, just to keep the kid quiet, "it's apparent Dr. Kornblum is correct. The child is bewildered by life and confused by the movies. He doesn't know what he's saying. He's—"

"Clam up, Jake! Now, son, look me in the eye. Help me out here, 'cause Ah don't know what to do with you. Ah could put you on home detention or in community control. Ah could put you in the Crossroads program or in intensive control. Ah could enroll you in the marine institute or maybe the alternative assistance program. Lord knows, we got more programs than a dog's got fleas."

Kip just stood there, a faint smile on his face.

"Son, do you have anything to say to the court?"

Oh no.

"Yeah, Judge. Are you eating a tomato or is that your nose?"

The few spectators, mostly distraught parents, laughed. My eyes pleaded with Kip for a credit line.

"Charlie McCarthy to W. C. Fields in *You Can't Cheat an Honest Man*," he said.

"You see, Your Honor!" I shouted, stepping in front of Kip, as if to shield him from harm. "He can't help it. These words just keep popping out."

Judge T. Bone Coleridge rolled his eyes toward the ceiling, then spun around in his high-backed chair. When he spoke, it was to the wall behind him. "The question for the court is, should this boy be in Youth Hall, where he can learn some discipline and maybe get therapy from left-wing, pot-smoking county-payrolled, thumb-sucking shrinks, or should he be on the streets?"

"Someday," Kip piped up from behind me, "a real rain will come and wash all this scum off the streets."

"What'd you say?" the judge demanded, spinning his chair back toward his supplicants.

"All the animals come out at night," Kip said, a far-away look in his eyes. "Whores, skunk pussies, buggers, queens, fairies, dopers, junkies."

"Your Honor," I leapt in. "I'm sure there's an explanation." I looked at Kip, who rewarded me with a maniacal grin.

"DeNiro in *Taxi Driver*," he said.

"Of course it is!" I shouted triumphantly to the judge, as if Kip had just revealed a major discovery in theoretical physics.

"Skunk pussies?" the judge said, shaking his head.

Thankfully, Kip didn't elaborate. The judge asked if I had anything more to present before he announced his ruling. I declined, and Kip started to say something. I tried to clamp my hand over his mouth, but he wriggled away from me. "Just one thing, Judge. My lawyer's my uncle. He's my uncle Jake."

"What movie's that from?" T. Bone Coleridge asked, wearily.

"None," I admitted. "It's true. Sylvester Houston Conklin is my nephew, my half sister's son."

"Why'nt you say so, first thing, Jake?" the judge demanded. "Hell's bells, where's that low-rent shrink of yours?"

"Right here," Dr. Kornblum called out from the gallery, knowing when his number had been called.

"Did Ah hear you say something about this boy needing a strong male figure, someone to look up to?"

"Exactly, in lieu of a father, he needs . . ."

I knew where this was going, and so did Kip. He was grinning, but I wasn't.

"Your Honor," I said, "if you're thinking that I—"

"Don't tell me what Ah'm thinking. Ah'll tell you, Jake. It's like this. It's either Youth Hall or your house. You heard it yourself, from your very own witness. Ah'm remanding the boy to your custody. You're blood kin, after all. You'll file monthly reports, and if there's any problem, you'll both be back in here." T. Bone cleared his throat, the sound of a shovel digging into gravel, and turned to the young miscreant. "How 'bout it, son? You want to bunk with your uncle Jake?"

"Sure, Judge," Kip responded. "It's like living at the Bates Motel."

"Then it's a done deal. Now, we've got to find a way to keep you out of trouble. You got any hobbies, besides all that movie watchin'?"

Kip shook his head.

"Well, how would you like to play some Pee Wee League football? Your uncle can show you a thing or two."

No again.

"What do you want to do, son?"

"Make movies," Kip said.

T. Bone thought about it a second, then turned to me. "Buy the boy one of those video cameras, and turn him loose. In my day, a boy was rotten, we locked him up and strapped him. Now, we try to let him express himself. Who knows, maybe this'll work. Strappin' never did. Maybe the rapscallion will turn out to be one of your Hollywood moguls."

The judge gave himself a satisfied look. Then he banged his gavel, declared a recess and bolted through the rear door to his chambers, blue and orange robes flapping behind him.

Now what? I hadn't gotten the hang of being an uncle, and I was going to be a father. I looked down at Kip, confused and embarrassed. He had heard me try to weasel out of taking responsibility for him. He was biting his lip.

"Kip. It's not that I don't want you around. It's just that—"

"It's okay, Uncle Jake. Never apologize and never explain. It's a sign of weakness."

I didn't ask, but he told me anyway.

"John Wayne," Kip said, taking my hand and lacing his fingers through mine.

8

Motive, Opportunity, and Means

After court, or *après cour,* as one of my worldly partners insists on saying, I was back in the office, not answering my mail, when Abe Socolow called on my direct line. He barked out his usual greeting, which consisted of my last name in an accusing tone, then told me to get my ass over to Blinky Baroso's apartment. I told him I'd do better than that: I'd bring all of me.

So I abandoned my stacks of opposing lawyers' testy correspondence that begged for even more obnoxious responses. It is a game we play, scrivening abusive letters, insulting the other's client in increasingly harsh terms until one or the other files suit. Once, in a petty dispute over a property line, H. T. Patterson wrote a twelve-page letter, accusing my client of everything from deceit, deception, and duplicity to being on the grassy knoll in Dallas. Pressed for time, I responded simply, "Fuck you; strong reply to follow." As Goethe said, or was it Shula, "When ideas fail, words come in very handy."

Before leaving, I checked on Kip who was installed in the conference room, a splendid place of dark wood, tinted glass and marble, all paid for by grateful, or at least, intimidated clients. Word had gotten back to me that the lad had been videotaping all the female employees in the office, telling them he was the casting director for *Porky's IV*. No one seemed to mind until he asked the receptionist to take off her blouse for her audition. So I grounded him for the day, which he didn't seem to mind, inasmuch as television came with the punishment.

My secretary, Cindy, and two young female paralegals were making a fuss over my ward, who sat in one of the leather swivel chairs, sneakers propped on the marble slab of a conference table, watching a black-and-white movie on the TV tastefully recessed into a teak wall unit. The women were feeding him doughnuts and sodas from the office kitchen and cooing about his blond hair and blue eyes.

"This nephew of yours is the sweetest little thing," said Cindy, who, like her boss, will do anything to avoid sitting at her desk. "He's going to be a real lady killer."

"James Cagney, 1933," the kid said, his mouth covered with powdered sugar.

"Huh?" Cindy looked confused. It was not an entirely unfamiliar expression. She'd been my secretary back in the P.D.'s office and was a tad unconventional for a downtown law firm with offices thirty-two stories above Biscayne Bay. She wore miniskirts and orange lipstick and had three-inch fingernails painted different colors with sparkles embedded in the polish. Her typing sounded like a chef chopping vegetables at a Japanese steak house.

"Look, Cindy, I gotta go. If it's not too much trouble, how 'bout typing some pleadings this afternoon? I'll be back later for Little Lord Fauntleroy."

"Freddie Bartholomew," Kip said, without taking his eyes from the set. "Ricky Schroder in the TV remake."

The Olds was right where I left it, which is always a fifty-fifty proposition in a county where a hundred cars are stolen each day. Some are stripped for parts, some are taken by freighter for sale in the islands, and some turn up, repainted, as local taxicabs. I had parked next to a powder blue SL 300, the Mercedes convertible. My lead gas-guz-

zling monster made the little German car look feminine
and petite.

I eased out of the parking garage and onto Biscayne
Boulevard. It's our showcase downtown street, running
along the bay. There's a wide median with towering palm
trees where hookers, muggers, and transvestites gather,
though they're generally shooed out of there just before
the Orange Bowl Parade. The boulevard intersects with
Flagler Street, which runs due west past the county courthouse and provides an entertaining walk among street ped-
dlers, panhandlers, and tourists chattering in a dozen
languages, none of them English.

Today, I had a short drive north past Bayfront Park,
where the multimillion-dollar Claude and Mildred Pepper
Fountain sits idle and dry because the city can't pay for
the electricity to run it. Just past the park is Bayside, an
outdoor mall of T-shirt shops and rum-punch booths. On
the west side of the boulevard used to be the Coppertone
sign with the dog pulling down the little girl's swimsuit.
It's gone, now, along with the old library they knocked
down to redo the park. Gone too are the Columbus and
McAllister hotels that were bought by some Saudis, then
flattened, and a few other local institutions, including *The
Miami News,* Eastern Airlines, and Pan Am. Things
change, but seldom for the better.

In four minutes I was on the Venetian Causeway, the
bridge across the man-made islands to Miami Beach.
Blinky lived on the first island past the tollgate in one of
those step-back high rises that looks like a pre-Columbian
pyramid. I had been there before, but never with a police
escort. Two uniformed Miami cops were in the lobby. Another stood by the elevator and pushed number ten for me.
Yet another opened the door to the apartment and ushered
me inside.

The apartment was done in white and black. White walls
with postmodern paintings, white marble floor, black furniture. Blinky was smart enough not to decorate it himself,
or it would have tended toward heavy red velvet.

Abe Socolow and his buddy, the Anglo homicide detective, were sitting on a black leather sofa in the living room. Through an open sliding glass door, I saw a woman standing on the balcony, her back to me. I recognized the long, dark hair and angular frame of Josefina Jovita Baroso.

No one was talking. They had been here for a while. It gave off the feel of a homicide scene, and I was sure I'd be ushered into another room for a gander at Blinky's body. The air-conditioning was turned up high, and I shivered in my seersucker suit. Cops sometimes try to chill down homicide scenes. They're not immune to the smells any more than the rest of us. But I didn't detect the sticky-sweet scent of fresh blood or the rot of decaying flesh, and Blinky, I remembered, kept his thermostat at sixty, lest he sweat through his silk undershorts.

Abe Socolow motioned for me to sit down, or maybe recline, in an uncomfortable black plastic chair shaped like a tilde. On a glass coffee table were three stylish candles of different lengths, propped in rough-hewn holders that looked like black granite. Next to the candles was a heavy art book that I was sure had never been opened by Blinky, unless he had started selling fake van Goghs. I eased into the chair without slipping a disk, and Socolow said, "So where the hell is he?"

"Blinky?"

"No, Judge Crater."

"He's not here? He's not dead?"

"I'm going to ask you again. Where is he?"

"Abe, I think we've had this conversation before."

"Yeah, except you left something out." He tossed a leather-bound pocket calendar on the coffee table, then flipped it open. "Go ahead, look at it."

There it was, in Blinky's scrawl, on Sunday, June 26. Yesterday. *10-ish. Meet Jake.*

"Ten-ish," I said aloud. "Sounds like Andre Agassi with a lisp."

"C'mon, Jake. You can do better than that."

Actually, I couldn't. "What're you driving at?"

"You told us you hadn't seen Baroso since Thursday."

"It's the truth."

Socolow cleared his throat. He sounded like a hungry pit bull. "You also told us you weren't expecting anyone last night."

"I wasn't. Not at home, anyway."

The detective stirred on the sofa. "We could bust you right now for obstruction."

"What good would that do?" I asked.

Neither one answered me. They both wanted my help, and jerking me around wasn't going to get it. The detective said, "We sent a squad car over here last night after you called in. No one was home. The security guard says Baroso pulled out of the garage sometime around eight or eight-thirty in his green Range Rover and comes back maybe three hours later. A little while after that, Baroso leaves again, burning rubber pulling out of the garage, nearly sideswiping a car pulling in. We got a search warrant this morning, and here we are."

"What's the charge," I asked, "reckless driving?"

Socolow ignored the crack and said, "Here's how I see it. Baroso and Hornback come to your house, hoping you'll mediate a dispute. Baroso knows Hornback's set to give a statement and he's prepared to pay to keep him quiet. But without you around to referee, the negotiations don't go so well, and Baroso ends up slipping Hornback a Mickey, then strangling him. After stringing him up, Baroso comes back here, gathers whatever he needs and flees."

"Flees," I repeated, because the word always sounded silly to me.

"Take a look around," Socolow said, seeming to wonder if I was mocking him. "Dirty dishes still in the sink. Bedroom's a mess, clothes tossed from the closet, one suitcase opened but not packed. Toiletries are gone from the bathroom, drawers with underwear and shirts mostly empty. And the pocket calendar left behind. Nobody does that unless they're in a hell of a hurry.''

"You're too much," I said. "A guy's a messy packer, and that's your proof of murder. Unless you've got a witness who eyeballed Blinky at my house, you've got nothing, and you know you've got nothing. I'm surprised a judge even gave you a search warrant on all that speculation."

I watched the undertaker's smile form at the corner of Socolow's mouth. He was thumbing through his notes. "You have a neighbor named Phoebe Gethers at the intersection of Kumquat and Solana. That's right across the street from you, isn't it, Jake."

He knew very well it was.

"At about a quarter to ten," the detective said, "she's sitting on her front porch, and a taxi drops off a man at your house. She didn't get a look at him, but we check the cab companies, and a Haitian driver with no work permit positively ID's Hornback from a mug shot. A few minutes later, your neighbor gets some houseguests and goes inside. More guests arrive, and she's back at the front door, letting them in. She puts the time between ten and ten-fifteen, and now there's what she calls a Jeep sitting in front of your house. We show her some pictures, and she ID's it as a dark green or black Range Rover. By the time you show up around eleven-thirty, the Range Rover's gone, and Hornback's strung up with your tie. Basing it on body temperature of the stiff, rigor mortis and livor mortis, the M.E. puts time of death between nine and eleven P.M. Hornback was rendered unconscious with barbiturates, then strangled."

"So where was Blinky between eight and ten?" I asked.

Socolow grunted. "Who knows and who cares! He was at your house when it counted."

"I care because Blinky's not a murderer."

"Jake's right, for once." It was Jo Jo Baroso, coming through the balcony door. Behind her, one of the cruise ships was headed out Government Cut toward the Caribbean. "My brother is not emotionally or physically capable."

The sister to the rescue, I didn't expect it.

"As I see it," she continued, "Luis brought some muscle with him. When Kyle wouldn't agree to whatever deal Luis wanted to cut, the muscle did the dirty work."

Oh boy, with a sister like this, who needs a prosecutor? But then, the sister *is* a prosecutor. I looked back at Socolow and said, "Okay, I get the picture. After ten minutes of detective work, it's the collective wisdom of the police and the state attorney's office that this case is solved."

"Hey, Jake," Socolow said, with a smile I now recognized as a sneer in sheep's clothing, "it wasn't that hard. You know the three elements of every prosecution, don't you?"

"Sure. Perjury, coercion, and pure dumb luck."

"Motive, opportunity, and means," Socolow corrected me. "Baroso knew Hornback was going to flip. There's the motive. We can tie the two of them together in your house, at least circumstantially. That's the opportunity. As Josefina suggests, the means were undoubtedly provided by hired muscle."

"Undoubtedly," I said, with as much sarcasm as possible. "Of course, your security guard didn't see a third party with Blinky, and Phoebe didn't report another car at my house, and even if it was Blinky's Range Rover, you have no one eyeballing *him*, and the three of you are so far off base about the kind of person Blinky Baroso is that I don't even know why I'm arguing with you."

I was getting aggravated, so I stood up and paced. Sometimes, the hardest thing to do is sit still. In court, I have a tendency to prowl when the opposition is doing the questioning. To fight the urge, I imagine myself chained to my chair. Here the chains were broken, but Blinky's living room felt like a cage. Something wasn't making sense, but I didn't know what. After a moment, I stopped pacing and turned back to Socolow. "Why are you telling me all this? What do you want from me?"

"We figure Baroso will contact you," he said.

"Yeah, clients occasionally call their lawyers, so what?"

"When he does, call me."

I started to say something, but Socolow raised his hand as a teacher might to an unruly student. "Now, before you shout attorney-client privilege, hear me out. He killed Hornback, or he knows who did, and either way, I want to talk to him. So, get his story and see if you can bring him in."

I gave Socolow a look that asked what's in it for my client.

"A voluntary surrender and things will go easier for him," Socolow said. "Maybe the muscle was just supposed to muss up Hornback, and he went too far. If your client surrenders, I wouldn't fight a reasonable bail request. If he makes us bring him in, he can sit in county jail until his case is called. He'll have the jailhouse pallor and bum haircut that'll tell the jury he's right out of the can."

"What if he didn't kill Hornback and doesn't know who did?" I asked.

"Then he's got nothing to worry about, does he?" Abe Socolow answered.

Jo Jo Baroso walked back onto the balcony and lit a cigarette. I don't know if statistics bear it out, but it seems more women than men are smoking these days. I'm not sure why, and any speculation would sound like male chauvinism, something I gave up along with bell bottoms and muttonchop sideburns. Male or female, smoking is something I've never understood. Not that I'm a health nut. Sure, I pour skim milk over my granola with mangoes. And I've cut back on the saturated fats and cholesterol, limiting my cheeseburgers (with a chocolate shake, double fries on the side) to days with an "r" in them.

I believe in moderation, not fanaticism. In my younger days, I would close every after-hours bar in the eastern division of the AFC. Yeah, even Buffalo. Some guys work hard and play hard. I played hard and played hard. I was a step too slow and often injured. Coaches, like generals, have great tolerance for other people's pain. In one snowy game against the Patriots, I dislocated a shoulder making a tackle on a kickoff. To pop it back into place, the trainer handed me a cinder block and let go. Gravity and Xylocaine got me back in the game. The shoulder still *clickety-clacks* on the few occasions I comb my hair.

It's the nineties, and recklessness—booze, drugs, and casual sex—is out. Caution is in. I know this is true. There's a chart in *USA Today* to prove it. So now, I don't drink and drive, sleep around, or draw to an inside straight. I'm still not quite housebroken, but I've left some of the wildness behind. I take fewer chances. Where I used to spin the wheel and choose red or black—what difference did it make?—now, I stay out of the casino. I am convinced, you see, that sooner or later, the ball will plop into double zero.

Two policemen I didn't know showed up. Without excusing himself, Socolow, the detective, and the policemen disappeared into a back bedroom Blinky uses as an office. A woman cop in uniform came in from the elevator pushing what looked like a bellman's cart. I heard drawers opening and closing and what sounded like furniture being moved.

I walked onto the balcony, standing to the ocean side—windward—of Jo Jo Baroso's smoke plumes. The bridge was up on the Venetian Csuseway as a forty-something-foot sloop sailed through, heeling slightly in the easterly. Three gulls lazily rode the updrafts, singing their gull songs.

"He's really fooled you, hasn't he?" Jo Jo said.

"Abe?"

"My brother!"

"I just don't think he's capable of murder, in person or with help."

"That's not what I mean. He's charmed you."

"He's a charming rogue," I admitted.

Behind the city, the sky was streaked with scarlet at the horizon, and the sun was setting over the Everglades. "You've gotten him out of trouble so many times, you, of all people must know what he's really like."

"Blinky's a dreamer. You remember the Miami Ski Mountain deal? He ordered three hundred million cubic yards of limestone to build a mountain along Dixie Highway."

"I remember. He tried to sell stock in a ski lift. Even the most gullible figured you couldn't keep snow from melting in the tropics."

"My point is, Blinky believed it. He spent ten grand on the drawings."

"His overhead, just overhead. How could he sucker the rubes without some slick displays?"

"You won't cut him a break will you?"

"He doesn't deserve one."

"You are a tough customer," I told her.

She studied me a moment. Her gaze seemed to look back over the years, or maybe I was imagining it. "You know what infuriates me about you, Jake?"

"Virtually everything."

"Your naïveté. You see life like an overgrown Boy Scout. I bet you help little old ladies across the street."

"Yep, and sometimes tall, young ones." In the blush of the sunset, her dark complexion glowed the color of *café au lait*. I gave her my crooked grin and looked straight in those dark, velvet eyes.

Josefina Jovita Baroso didn't melt. She didn't faint. She narrowed her eyes just a bit to appraise me, and finally said, "You're still a damned attractive man, Jake Lassiter."

Now, that was a switch.

"You have presence," she went on, "and you manage to project strength and warmth at the same time. You have a full crop of hair that looks like a wheat field that needs cutting, a tan that reveals you spend too much time at the beach, and your size is most appealing. Thank God you don't wear those suits with the padded shoulders or you wouldn't be able to fit through doorways.''

I was beginning to enjoy this.

''You are sentimental to a fault, which causes you to have terrible judgment about people. You are bright enough, I suppose, though I doubt anyone ever considered you brilliant, unless it was one of your teammates whose jersey number approximated his IQ. You are a nonconformist, which makes your choice of professions somewhat curious. As far as your lawyering is concerned, while perhaps not technically unethical, it is amoral, at the very least . . .''

Had there been a subtle shift in tone?

''. . . You have a certain easygoing charm and affability. Your eyes crinkle when you smile, and doubtless, there are numerous women who find you irresistible, chief among them I suspect are cocktail waitresses, South Beach models, and bubble-brained cheerleaders.''

Somehow, I heard a ''but'' coming.

''But if you think a smile and a laugh can get you inside my panty hose, you'd better think again, buster.''

''Buster? Whatever happened to *mi corazón*?''

''What happened between us is ancient history. I swear I barely remember it.''

''I don't believe you.''

''Really, what do you remember?''

''A lot of caring,'' I said, ''a lot of moist heat.''

''Anything else?''

''Squabbles, lots of squabbles.''

''That's what I remember, that and your leaving me.''

''I still care for you,'' I told her, the words surprising me as much as her.

Her eyes measured me for just a moment. ''Nostalgia, Jake. Don't get carried away. Right now, you're fantasizing about rekindling something that's been burnt out a long time. It's a way of reliving your youth.''

''I wasn't that young.''

''You were playing ball and having fun, and your future

seemed infinite. Whatever you think you're feeling right now isn't real.''

I tried to examine what I felt, real or not. It wasn't easy. ''What I'm feeling, what I'm wondering really, is if I stuck with your brother all these years just to maintain some connection with you.''

''And now?''

''I'm wondering if you want to give it another go.''

For a moment, her eyes softened. Thoughts seemed to race around in her head, but I couldn't catch them. Her brow furrowed. She didn't smile and she didn't frown. She was processing information, computing what she needed and what she didn't. And then the moment was gone. The thoughtful expression changed. It was almost as if she willed herself not to yield, not to show weakness, which to her, was any hint of emotion, other than one: anger. Her eyes shone with determination, and her voice was fire and steel.

''Never, never, never. As far as I'm concerned, Jacob Lassiter, Esquire, you're just the mouthpiece for that trashy brother of mine. You're no better than he is. You're the enemy, get it?''

Whew! From sunshine to squall in the blink of an eye. The suddenness and the fury shocked me.

''I don't get it,'' I said.

She blew a puff of smoke in my face, which is a good trick against the wind. ''You're hopeless. Why don't you do something useful like find my brother and bring him in?''

Before I could answer, I heard Abe Socolow calling from inside the living room. ''Hey, Jake, c'mere.''

I think Socolow liked bossing me around. Maybe it compensated for the few times I beat him in court. I went back inside to let him insult me some more. Jo Jo followed a step behind, and I made a mental note to check for knife wounds later.

The file drawers from Blinky's bedroom/office were stacked in the living room. Every drawer was open, and the contents were being searched by patient, if bored, cops. In the foyer, an antique milk can, lacquered bright orange, was turned upside down. A dozen carved wooden canes and shillelaghs along with a couple of umbrellas were spilled onto the floor. The canes weren't just for show. Blinky used them after tearing up his knee crawling out of a Dumpster filled with credit card receipts.

Now Socolow marched around the living room, holding a handsome cherry cane with a large polished knob for a handle. The whole thing was fairly phallic, but I didn't bother to share my thoughts with Socolow, who was gesturing at me with the damn thing.

"You know what's in those papers?" he said, pointing in the general direction of the cocktail table where he had spread out several thick, typewritten documents.

"No, Abe. You tell me."

He hunched over the table, leaning on the cane like a pettifogger out of Dickens. He ran a finger along the lines of a page, furrowing his brow.

"You could read faster if you didn't move your lips," I told him, helpfully.

"What the hell is Rocky Mountain Treasures, Inc.?"

"A company Blinky formed," I answered.

"I can see that. What's it do?"

"Hunts for treasure."

Socolow scowled. "Didn't Baroso get indicted for something like that, selling stock in a deep-sea salvage company down in the Keys?"

"Only civil suits, and that involved sunken Spanish galleons," I corrected him. "This is all about gold and silver in the Colorado mountains."

"Yeah, that's what it says here under 'corporate mission.'" Socolow began turning pages, again, reading aloud now. "'The company will use its best efforts and employ the latest sophisticated technology to locate and reclaim one or more of the following: the Arapaho Princess Treasure, the Golden Mummy, the Treasure of Apache Gulch, *La Caverna de Oro,* the Lost Dutchman mine, the

Purgatory Canyon Treasure, Moccasin Bill's Lost Mine, the Lost Gulch mine, the Devil's Head Treasure.' '' Socolow closed the folder and looked up at me. "Hey, Jake, what are you doing involved in this Wild West shit?"

"What do you mean?"

Now he was looking at the corporate minute book. "Says here you're a ten percent shareholder . . ."

"That's right."

"And secretary treasurer of the company."

"What?"

"Plus general counsel."

"What?" I said again.

"You heard me. Your bio is in the prospectus that goes to potential investors. You're described as one of the leading trial lawyers in Florida. Who wrote that, your granny?"

"I don't know anything about it," I said, honestly. "Blinky gave me the stock in lieu of a fee, but I never agreed to be a corporate officer or to let my name be used. You know I'd never subject myself to liability like that."

Socolow was back in the file again, still leaning on his cane. "Blinky's bio says nothing about his criminal record or the lawsuits against him. What do they call that in securities law, Jake?"

"A material omission of fact," I said.

"Right. The feds would be real interested in that, wouldn't they? Maybe a 10 (b) (5) violation. What else do we have here?" He turned over a few more pages. "The corporation issued one hundred shares of stock, twenty to Louis Baroso, ten to Jacob Lassiter, and seventy to Kit Carson Cimarron."

"Who?"

"Just what I was going to ask you, Jake."

"Damned if I know. Sounds like a cowboy."

Socolow closed the folders, looked at the detective, at Jo Jo Baroso, and back at me. He didn't say anything. He was into his genius-at-work mode. He started pacing, the cane *clacking* against the tile. At the moment, he was probably the most irritating person on the planet. He stopped at the sliding glass door to the balcony and seemed to study the smooth waters of Government Cut. To the south, cars were streaming across the newly renovated MacArthur Causeway, and below us, the fronds of the palm trees swayed gently in the breeze. Finally, he turned and faced me. "Jake, I'll bet you all the gold in Apache Gulch that Kyle Hornback was going to sing about Rocky Mountain Treasures, Inc. Maybe it's a little farther from home, but it's just another of Blinky's scams. Now, as for you, I know you step over the line once in a while, but I gotta tell you, I'm real disappointed."

"Abe, listen to me, I—"

"Lemme finish. The way I see it, Blinky figured he'd worn out his welcome down here. Kyle was doing his selling up there, and this Carson probably put up the money and added some local credibility. That left you to handle legal problems."

"Abe, you're not listening. I never agreed to represent the company or be an officer. I didn't ask for the stock, and I didn't write the prospectus. As far as I know, the company's legitimate, but even if it's not, where's the proof Blinky killed Kyle."

"Who's talking about Blinky? I'm starting to agree with you. Baroso's not a tough guy, at least not without someone to back him up."

"Like who, or is it whom?"

"How about the guy who owned the house where the decedent was killed, the guy whose tie was the murder weapon, whose prints are on the body, and who just happened to discover the body and call the cops?"

"Are you nuts? Why would I kill Kyle Hornback?"

"Ah, motive," Socolow said in that infuriating tone intended to indicate his intellectual prowess. "The missing ingredient. If I nailed down the motive, Jakie my boy, I'd be in front of the grand jury quicker than you can say life without parole. But I'm getting warm, aren't I? It's got to do with Rocky Mountain Treasures, doesn't it, Jakie?"

"It's your case, Abe. You figure it out."

"Let's see now. If Kyle had flipped, it wasn't just Blinky who was at risk, was it? What about the company lawyer? Come on, Mr. Secretary-Treasurer and General Counsel. Want to bet that the motive is buried with all that fool's gold in cowboy country?"

He aimed the damn cane at me.

"Abe, I hope you're prepared to use that thing. If not, I may just ram it up your tight ass."

Socolow glared at me, but the detective growled and shifted in his chair. "There's no need for that kind of talk. The state attorney doesn't have to stand for it."

"It's all right, Major," Socolow said, pleased he'd gotten to me. "Jakie seldom hits anyone. Hell, he seldom hit anyone when he played ball."

Still Socolow kept the cane leveled at my chest. He was enjoying this too much. I strained to keep my temper under control, my mind's eye playing a little fantasy involving Socolow's head and a heavy piece of polished wood.

"You see, Major," Socolow said, "I've come face-to-face with every category of miscreant known to the law, but essentially there are only two types, wicked scoundrels and foolish scoundrels. I fear that what you see at the end of my cane is nothing but a foolish scoundrel."

I kept my voice low and didn't raise an eyebrow. "At which end, Abe?"

9

El Amor es Ciego

Sylvester Houston Conklin fell asleep in front of the television, watching Clint Eastwood blast five bad guys in a San Francisco diner. Earlier, Kip had put away a double portion of spaghetti and meatballs and a protein shake. Carbs and protein, I was bulking him up. Yesterday, it was brown rice, broiled fish, and raw vegetables for the fiber. I did the cooking, and he ate it all. As a reward, we split a sixteen-ounce Grolsch.

Now he was sacked out on the sofa, so I carried him upstairs to the second bedroom, his body warm in my arms. I tucked him in, pulling the sheet up under his chin, and pushed the blond bangs out of his eyes. I was starting to feel avuncular, if not downright fatherly.

Kip stirred, half opened his eyes, and said, "Did you really threaten to jam a cane up the state attorney's ass?"

"Guilty."

"He's such a dweeb."

"A major dweeb," I agreed. "You should have seen him prancing around with that cane, putting on a show."

"Like Raymond Burr in *A Place in the Sun* or Everett Sloane in *The Lady from Shanghai*." He reached out from under the sheets and gave my arm a squeeze. "I really like your bedtime stories, Uncle Jake."

"And I really like having you here. Now it's lights out."

His eyes were closing again, and as they did, he pointed his index finger at me, as if holding a gun.

"Go ahead," he said, "make my day."

"Good night, Kip."

He nodded off, and I puttered around in his room, gathering a pile of his shorts, socks, and T-shirts that had been balled up in a corner. Then I padded out, closing the door without a sound. I tossed the clothes into the washer and poured in a double dose of the detergent that is supposed to nuke grass stains into bright, sanitary molecules. Apparently, Kip had accomplished what none of a series of bright and attractive young women could manage: He had civilized me.

Even with the ceiling fan on high and a gentle breeze filtering through the open windows, it was sweltering in my subtropical bedroom. Most nights, I fall asleep to the muted slap of palm fronds against masonry and the occasional blare of a police siren just up Douglas Road in Coconut Grove. I am darn near the last Miamian without central air-conditioning, and I like it that way. The old coral rock house just off Kumquat sits in a neighborhood of delectable street names. Loquat, Avocado, and Cocoanut are just around the corner. My house is positioned on the tiny lot to take advantage of southeasterly winds and is shaded by live oak, chinaberry, and poinciana trees, but still, summer nights are hot and sticky.

I lay on my back, naked, listening to the *whompeta-whompeta* of the fan harmonizing with the *chugita-chugita* of the washing machine, feeling the sweat trickle down my chest. I dozed, dreaming a pastiche of unrelated scenes. An unshaven cowboy in a poncho silently rode a black horse across the high plains. Jo Jo Baroso sat on the black divan in her mother's den, laughing gaily, but the laugh turned sinister and suddenly it was Abe Socolow laughing with all the charm of the Doberman pinscher he resembled.

Somebody said something, but who was it? Somebody complaining. *You gotta do something about your door, Jake.* Sure, sure. I rolled onto my side and tried to chase the dreams. Somebody was smoking a cigarette. Dreaming now in smell-a-rama.

Suddenly, it was daytime, or was it? No, dawn doesn't break with a hundred-fifty-watt blast in the face. I squinted into the glare.

''You gotta start locking your door,'' the voice said. The light clicked off. ''Sorry to wake you, but I'm only out at night.''

''Blinky? Is that you?''

Through a haze of cigarette smoke, a rotund form was backlit by the sodium vapor lights from outside my open window. ''It ain't Dracula,'' Blinky Baroso said.

''You son of a bitch,'' I said. ''You ungrateful, selfish son of a bitch. After all I've done for you . . .''

''Hey, I said I'm sorry. Go back to sleep.''

''I don't care about your waking me up. What the hell were you doing using my name for that treasure company?''

''Jeez, Jake, you're pissed about that?'' he whined, sounding hurt. Like a lot of manipulators, Blinky had the ability to make his victim contrite for hurting his feelings. ''Are you going to hold that against me now? I kind of thought you'd be flattered.''

''Next time, flatter someone else.''

''I meant to tell you, Jake, I really did. We needed to dress up the paperwork a little. I borrowed your good name, that's all.''

''Yeah, I want it back.''

''C'mon, Jake, we'll amend the papers, it's no big deal.''

''Maybe not to you, but the SEC and the Florida Bar might see it differently. To say nothing of Abe Socolow.''

He crushed out the cigarette in a commemorative Super Bowl VIII ashtray and sat on the edge of my bed, moving close to me. ''Jake, I need help.''

"Yeah, me too. Socolow thinks you had me kill Kyle Hornback, or maybe it was my own idea. I can't even follow his reasoning."

"You're joking."

"I'm not, and Abe never does."

"Jeez, you mean *I'm* a suspect."

As usual, Blinky's concerns were about number one. "That's usually what happens when somebody runs from a murder scene," I said. "What the hell were you doing here last night?"

"I tried to get here before you left for the beach. See, I figured my phone was tapped, and whoever was listening would think we'd be on the wall over on Ocean Drive. I started that way, did a U-turn on the Venetian, and came to your place, but I was running late, and you'd already left."

"Who's tapping your phone? What's it all about?"

"I don't know, but before Hornback was killed, I was being followed. I'm sure of it."

In the darkness, I sensed Blinky tremble. "Anyway, I got in, just like now, by putting my weight against the front door. It was dark inside, but I could see something spinning around. I didn't know what the hell it was, so I turned on a light. *Jesús Cristo,* I nearly fainted. Then I nearly puked. I've never seen anything like that, ever. I turned off the light and ran out. I thought the killer might be in the house, might be after me. I went home, grabbed some things, and got out of there. Last night, I slept in the Rover out on Virginia Key."

He leaned closer on the bed, giving me a whiff of cigarette breath mixed with stale sweat. "Jake, who would have done such a thing?"

"Whoa. Back up. What was Kyle doing here?"

"Dunno, exactly. Maybe he was killed someplace else and dumped here, like to implicate us."

"No. A neighbor saw him arrive by taxi. Whoever killed him drugged him first with a fast-acting barbiturate, then strangled him and strung him up."

I got out of bed and pulled on a pair of faded blue gym shorts with the Penn State logo. Then I moved toward the window and inhaled the night air. It was heavy with jasmine, which was an improvement.

"What was Kyle doing here?" I asked for the second time. "Was he coming to see you or me? Did he know you were going to be here, and who else knew?"

"A lot of questions."

"And the big one, who wanted him dead?"

"Besides me?" Blinky asked softly.

I let it sink in a moment before responding. "No, let's start with you."

"Sure, I thought about it, acing him, but it was just wishful thinking, of course."

"Of course."

"I mean, he was going to rat. He had an appointment to see Socolow today, did you know that?"

"I did, but how did you?"

"Kyle told me."

Ah. "When?"

"Yesterday morning."

Blinky seemed to want to say more, but he stopped. Maybe he wanted me to drag it out of him. "Yesterday morning," I said. Sometimes, if you repeat a witness's statement, it's like priming the pump, and the words will just start flowing.

"Yeah," Blinky said. "I was home reading the Sunday papers when he called. He told me he was going in first thing in the morning to see Socolow unless he could get some satisfaction from me."

"Satisfaction meaning bucks."

"*Mucho* bucks. Five hundred thousand of them."

I let out a whistle. "To which you said?"

"I asked him if he'd take a check. Then I told him, '*¡Chingate!* Fuck you and the horse you rode in on.' After I calmed down, I told him I'd get back to him with something, you know, a counteroffer, after I had a chance to think about it."

"And talk to your lawyer," I said, filling in the gaps.

"Yeah."

"And you told him you were seeing me that evening."

Blinky paused before nodding yes. He pulled another cigarette from somewhere and lit it, the tip glowing in the darkened room. "Yeah, I told him. But I never said where, and I never invited him over for espresso and *pastelitos*."

I cocked my head in what is supposed to be an inquisitive, if not accusing, look.

"Honest, Jake. Why would I want him around? I needed to talk to you. Hell, I figured Kyle would be wired the next time he saw me. They'd try to bust me for subornation of perjury or obstruction of justice if I bought him off. I needed some advice from you before talking to him."

We both stayed quiet a moment, and I thought about it. Who wanted Kyle Hornback dead? *Besides* Blinky. And who wanted to frame Blinky and maybe me? The ceiling fan continued its endless circles, slashing the plumes of cigarette smoke like a whirling saber. The washing machine had long since ended its cycles, and outside my window, a mockingbird was singing its early-morning song in the marlberry bush.

"Who's Kit Carson Cimarron?" I asked.

In the gun-metal gray light of a new day, Blinky was smiling a rueful smile. "Now that," he said, "is a long story."

A pink glow was spreading in the eastern sky as we reconvened in the kitchen. I made Blinky *café con leche* and squeezed some fresh grapefruit juice for myself. He asked me to scramble four eggs, and I told him secretary-treasurers of major corporations do no such thing. But I made rye toast, which he wolfed down with cream cheese and guava preserves that Granny had made, or "put up," as she would say. I microwaved last night's spaghetti and meatballs for my breakfast.

"Kit Carson Cimarron," Blinky said, chewing his toast,

seeming to enjoy the sound of the name. "You know how you dumped Josie?"

"That's a little strong," I said. "We split up, that's all."

"Yeah, yeah, you broke up. Well, I was there. You dropped her like a bad habit, not that I blame you. Afterward, she moped around for a year."

"Okay, have it your way. What's that got to do with Cimarron?"

"You ought to ask Josie."

"She knows him? When Socolow mentioned Cimarron's name, Jo Jo didn't blink an eye."

"Yeah, well she isn't about to admit that she was almost Mrs. K. C. Cimarron of Pitkin County, Colorado."

"What!"

"Left her at the altar, or the stable actually, since they were going to get married on his ranch. Broke her heart, Jake, or would have, if she had one. You know, the only two men I ever introduced to my sister are you and Cimarron, and from each of you, she got nothing but pain."

"That sounds like something she would say."

"*Verdad.* I'm just repeating her words."

"Tell me more about him."

"He was rich, but leveraged up to his ten-gallon hat in oil- and gas-drilling loans in the eighties, and when the bottom fell out of the market, he lost everything, except his ranch in Colorado. Anyway, he'd dumped her by then, and there hasn't been anyone else in her life since."

"You introduced them," I said, which was really a question.

"We'd done some business," Blinky continued, "when he still had a seven-figure line of credit. He picked up the financing on the salvage operation in the Keys. Paid for the equipment, the divers, the marketing. I was the brains, he was the bank."

I was about to insult the intelligence of the banker, but Blinky kept talking. "Shit, you should have seen him. He comes down to Sugarloaf Key wearing those hand-stitched cowboy boots and a silver belt buckle must have weighed twenty pounds. He's even bigger than you, and he's got on a black cowboy hat with a feather stuck in it, so with the boots and the hat, he's about seven feet tall, and he's buying the crew drinks with hundred-dollar bills off a wad he carries in his boots.''

"Jo Jo fell in love with this guy?" I said in disbelief.

"*El amor es ciego.* Love is blind, my friend."

"You got sued in the Keys deal."

"Right, but not indicted, thanks to Kit. He saved my ass.''

"What happened?"

Blinky shook his head sadly. "On the Grand Bahama Bank, we found three Spanish galleons loaded to the gunwales with coins and artifacts. Seven million wholesale auction value after expenses."

"What's wrong with that?"

"I had twenty percent of the company, gave Cimarron twenty percent and sold the rest."

"I still don't get it."

"The sixty percent I sold . . . well, I sold it about four times."

"Oh shit."

"Yeah, I had to give up all the promoters' portions to the investors, and Cimarron had to make up the shortfall, about eight hundred thousand, to keep us out of jail." Blinky laughed in disbelief at his own bad fortune at striking it rich. "Who would ever have thought we'd have found the stuff? It was the first deal I ever did that actually worked."

From behind me, a voice. "Just like *The Producers.*"

I turned and there was Kip in his Jockey shorts, his face still puffy with sleep. "Zero Mostel produces this Broadway show he's sure will flop, so he sells it over and over to investors, and when it makes money, he's really fucked."

"Don't say 'fucked,' " I told my ward.

"Right," Blinky said. "Say 'screwed.' 'Fucked' has no

class, and to succeed in business, kid, you gotta have class.''

"Anyway," Kip said, "Mostel's bummed out and he says to Gene Wilder, 'I was so careful. I picked the wrong play, the wrong director, the wrong cast. Where did I go right?' ''

"That's good," Blinky said. "The kid's a regular actor. I could put him into sales.''

Kip grabbed a box of cereal from the cupboard and sat at the kitchen counter, listening. If he paid close attention, he wouldn't need an MBA from Wharton.

"Rocky Mountain Treasures was really Cimarron's idea," Blinky said, turning to me. "Back in the good days, he bought up mineral leases all over Colorado.''

"But how can he finance it? You said he was tapped out.''

"He is. That's why I'm out there selling limited partnership interests. The investors will fund the exploration. But listen, Jake, this isn't a mining operation. Shit, with the price of gold and silver where it is, you can't extract enough to justify the costs. Plus, the environmental rules will tie you up for years before you turn your first spadeful of dirt. But we're after something else. Gold and silver that's already been mined. It's there, Jake, sunk in old mine shafts, hidden in caves, buried under mountains. We've got maps. We've got satellite photographs you can buy from the government. We've got sophisticated sensors and state-of-the-art equipment, and either way, we can't lose.''

"Either way?''

"We hit paydirt, everybody wins and wins big. We don't, Cimarron and I still get management fees from investors' funds. And best of all, it's legit.''

I was watching Kip carefully slice an orange into quarters and nibble at it. "Uh-huh.''

"Okay, so we puffed a little bit where you were concerned, and maybe we didn't give every twist and turn in my biography, but I'm telling you, the business is for real. Honest, Jake. Believe me.''

I thought about believing him, but I was having trouble with it. Sometimes in closing argument, when I'm telling a jury to be cautious of a prosecution witness who's been given immunity in return for his testimony, I tell a little story. I tell about the farmer who found a rattlesnake in the middle of the winter. "Please don't kill me," the snake says. "I'm nearly frozen. Take me back to the farmhouse and warm me up and save my life." But the farmer is worried. "If I warm you up, you'll bite me." The snake wiggles its head and says, "I promise not to bite you." So the farmer takes the snake home, warms it up, and lo and behold, the snake bites him. As he's dying the farmer moans: "How could you do this to me. You promised . . ."

In the story, this is where I pause and give the jurors my steady gaze. "Yes," the snake says, "but when I promised, you knew I was a snake."

Now I looked uneasily at my reptilian client.

"C'mon, Jake, don't you believe me?"

"I believe you," I said, wanting it to be true. "So what did Hornback have on you? What was he going to tell Socolow?"

"It was a bluff. He was selling shares for me, so he just *assumed* it was a scam. Hell, why wouldn't he? Anyway, he threatened to squeal, but he had nothing."

"You know what I do with squealers?" Kip said, a malicious grin on his sweet young face.

"Huh?" Blinky seemed startled.

Kip curled his upper lip into a sneer. "I let 'em have it in the belly so they can roll around for a long time thinking it over."

"What the fuck?"

"Richard Widmark in *Kiss of Death*," Kip explained, "and don't say 'fuck.' "

10

Dead Serious

"When corpses are found out of doors undergoing putrefaction," Doc Charlie Riggs said, sitting erect on the witness stand, "it's quite common to find insect infestation."

"But in a funeral home?" I asked.

Doc Riggs leaned toward the jury box. "Should never happen. Never."

"So in this case, Dr. Riggs, at an open-casket memorial service . . ." I paused for effect just the way they do on TV. "Where mourners saw worms crawling out of the eyes of the late Peter Cooper—"

"Maggots," Charlie corrected me. "Pupa, too. Some intact, some broken, indicating hatched flies."

"Yes, indeed. Maggots. From these maggots crawling out of the eyes of the late Peter Cooper, are you able to form an expert opinion as to the degree of care exercised by the Eternal Rest Funeral Home?"

At the plaintiff's table, from which I had recently risen, my client, Mrs. Brenda Cooper, was sobbing at just the proper decibel level. I always tell my clients that sniffles and whimpers are okay. Wails and shrieks are not, unless I want the jury distracted from the testimony, in which case, caterwauling to the heavens is permitted.

"*Prima facie* negligence, no doubt about it," Doc Riggs announced with authority.

"On what do you base your conclusion?"

That's the lawyer's way of asking "why," but a lawyer will never use one word when seven will do. Charlie Riggs stroked his beard and looked directly at the jury. "Not just from the maggots, alone. No sir. Maggots can emerge from blowfly eggs just a few hours after death. That wouldn't be enough to assign negligence to the funeral home. But as I said before, there were pupa shells, and it should take at least a week for the maggots to go through the stages of larval growth to produce newly hatched blowflies. So obviously, there was complete inattention to Mr. Cooper's body."

As if on cue, Brenda Cooper's sobs grew louder.

Charlie didn't miss a beat. "The eggs would have been clearly visible in his eyes and the corners of his mouth. They sort of look like grated cheese, so I don't know how the attendants missed them."

In the jury box, a woman nervously cleared her throat.

"As I say," Charlie continued, "*prima facie* negligence."

I sat down and let Charlie take care of himself on cross-examination. No one could do it any better.

I was sipping a Cuban coffee in the Gaslight Lounge down the street from the county courthouse, and Charlie was slurping a double order of rice pudding with cinnamon, having already polished off a three-egg western omelet. Testifying about putrefied corpses always made him hungry.

"What's bothering you?" he asked.

"Besides being a murder suspect, not much, unless you count having my name linked to one of Blinky Baroso's schemes, and being forced to revisit my past courtesy of his sister."

"Josefina," Charlie said. "A splendid young woman, though a tad tightly wound, I always thought."

"She says I had a dysfunctional upbringing, what with you and Granny as my role models."

"Do you believe it?"

"I don't know, Charlie. Granny always told me to choose right over wrong, and you taught me how to tell one from the other. If I've failed, it's not Granny's fault or yours."

"For what it's worth, we don't think you've failed. As for your other problems, I don't believe for one minute that you killed Kyle Hornback, and neither does Abe Socolow. He's just trying to pressure you into bringing Baroso in."

"Yeah, maybe, but it's no fun." I looked at my watch. "I gotta go. While you were mesmerizing the jury, Blinky left a message with Cindy that he had something that would blow the Hornback case wide open."

Charlie used his napkin to pry a grain of rice from his beard. "Do you believe him?"

"What a strange question. Why else would he—"

"Your client is a con man, is he not?"

"Yeah. To the world in general."

"*Mundus vult decipi*. The world wants to be deceived. But what about you, Jake?"

I put the top down on the old convertible and swung onto I-95 from the downtown ramp. I passed over the poinciana trees on South Miami Avenue, then swung off the Twenty-fifth Road exit to the Rickenbacker Causeway. Blinky had told me to meet him on Virginia Key, a secluded beach near the Seaquarium on the way to Key Biscayne.

Virginia Key is really just a spit of sand with some pine trees for shade. Because the beach faces due east and there's a reef about a mile offshore to cut down the rollers, it's a great place for windsurfing. To the north is Fisher Island, million-dollar condos surrounded by a moat to keep out the riffraff. Nearby is Government Cut where the cruise ships head toward open water. To the east is the Gulf Stream, Bimini, and the wide expanse of the Atlantic.

To the south is Bear Cut, an open channel through the causeway, and to the west is the city sewage plant. That's right. The city fathers chose an island of unspoiled beauty on which to lace the salt-laden wind with the trenchant scent of human waste. In a way I can't fully explain, Virginia Key seems a metaphor for Miami.

There was a rusted-out Jeep Cherokee up to its hubcaps in the sand. Nearby, an Isuzu Trooper with roof racks and a fine collection of custom-made sailboards was being unloaded by two lean, muscular guys in their twenties. On the water, half a dozen boardsailors were jumping the chop, headed on a broad reach in about eighteen knots of northeasterly breeze. Perfect lines of waves were breaking on the reef, what surfers call "corduroy to the horizon."

I spotted Blinky's green Range Rover parked in the shade about fifty yards from the beach. Long needles, green and fragrant, floated into my convertible from the candles of a slash pine tree.

I got out of the car, leaned on the fender and watched the boardsailors. Even from here, I could hear the sails crackling in the wind. Blinky wasn't around.

I waited five, maybe six, minutes.

Still no Blinky.

Maybe he was collecting pinecones or trying to sell stock in a gold mine to some beach bums.

I looked back at the water, relaxing.

Not thinking anything was wrong.

Why should I?

The ringing phone jarred me. It sounded so out of place here that for a moment I didn't know what it was. It was coming from Blinky's Range Rover. I hustled over and found the driver's door unlocked. Inside, on the passenger's side of the front seat, a cellular phone was ringing, its LCD display reading "CALL" with a blinking insistence.

But I was looking at something else.

A deep black-red stain on the upholstery on the driver's side.

About the size of a salad plate. Still wet.

A spiderweb crack in the front windshield.

But no Blinky.

And still the phone rang and blinked at me. I picked it up and groped for the right button. "Hello," I said, my voice strained.

"Who is this?" A man's voice, strangely familiar.

"Blinky? Is that you?"

"No. Who's this?"

It was coming to me. I didn't know what to say so I didn't say a word.

"Jake," he said. "Jake Lassiter? What the fuck are you—"

But I had hung up.

Now, why did I do that? Why did I feel guilty about being there just now, and why was I wiping my fingerprints off the telephone? I hadn't killed anyone. No one was even dead, right. I mean there wasn't a body. Blinky would be coming out of the woods in a minute.

C'mon, Blinky. Where the hell are you?

I touched the red stain. Still wet. I wiped my hand on the seat but only managed to smear the blood. I opened the glove compartment. There was nothing there, not even gloves.

I was thinking about getting the hell out of there when another noise startled me.

The overlapping whine of sirens. My ass was half out of the Range Rover when three police cars swerved onto the beach, spitting up sand, lights whirling. As they skidded to impressive, cop-style stops, I could no longer see the bright sails or hear the crackling of the wind.

It took Abe Socolow twenty minutes to get there. By that time, a crime scene van was parked in the shade, and a pot-bellied cop was taking plaster impressions of the Range Rover's tires. When he finished, he hauled his little black bag into the van and gathered blood samples, dusted for prints, and used tweezers and a tiny whisk broom looking for who knows what. He had already been through my car, with my consent, since I didn't feel like waiting around for them to bring a warrant. Two uniformed cops were trying to interview the boardsailors, most of whom didn't want to leave the water. When the wind is up, neither shark sightings nor murder scenes will get hard-core boardheads to shore.

I sat under a pine tree whose branches swayed gently in the wind. Three cops stood around me asking questions I wouldn't answer if I could, but they parted when his eminence, the prosecutor, pulled up in his state-owned four-door Chrysler.

"Where the hell is he?" Abe Socolow asked.

I stayed sitting, my back against a tree. Abe looked down at me, his courtroom pallor giving him a sickly look in the open air. "Who?" I answered.

"Don't jerk me around, Jake. Your sleazy client."

"Which one?" I asked, thinking we'd played this scene before, maybe twice.

"I'm losing patience with you. What were you doing here?"

"Waiting for Baroso, or maybe Godot."

"What were you doing in his car?"

I wanted to stand up so I could look down at Socolow who now towered over me, but I sat still, my arms across my knees. I was pulling pine needles off a branch, one by one, a child's refrain popping into my head. *She loves me, she loves me not.* "Aren't you supposed to advise me of my right to counsel and even provide one if I can't pay the freight, which I can't, if it's someone who charges my rates?"

"Why'd you hang up the phone, Jake? You knew it was me on the other end, didn't you? Why'd you do something stupid like that?"

Two could play this game. "Why were you calling here?" I asked.

"My secretary got an anonymous call, male voice she didn't recognize, giving her the number and saying for me to call if I wanted to break the Hornback case.''

''Me, too. I mean, Cindy got a call from Blinky, at least she thought it was Blinky, telling me to come out here.''

Socolow regarded me skeptically. ''Did she now?''

''Call her, find out.'' Socolow was giving me a look that was supposed to make me break down and confess to all manner of felonies and misdemeanors. ''Don't you see, Abe, someone's setting me up? Someone wanted me out here to make it look like I killed Blinky.''

Socolow smiled his *gotcha* smile. ''Who said anything about Blinky being killed?''

''Ah c'mon, Abe, don't play cop games with me.''

''I'm not playing, Jake. I'm dead serious. You know anything about a corpse you want to tell us?''

He looked in the direction of the woods. My mind flashed a picture of Blinky's body half covered by branches, a handful of my business cards clutched in a death grip.

''Like I said before, I came here to meet Blinky. I stood around maybe ten minutes. The phone rang. I went to answer it, saw the blood, heard your voice, froze, and hung up. I don't know why, I just did it.''

''Uh-huh.''

''It's the truth. Look, Blinky's been skulking around because he's afraid someone's trying to kill him. Maybe he was right, but that someone wasn't me.''

''Uh-huh.''

''C'mon, Abe, you can smell a setup. Somebody wanted me out here. Somebody called the cops, somebody called you. Can't you see what's going on? I don't have a motive for killing Blinky.'' I was rambling now, doing just what I tell clients not to do. But it was understandable. I had a fool for a client, and my lawyer wasn't much better. ''Maybe Blinky was mugged. Maybe he's lying in the bushes somewhere. Maybe the blood isn't even his.''

''Oh, I'll bet it is. I'll give you three to one it's type O, weasel. As for your motive, it's tied up with Hornback and whatever you had cooked up with Baroso in the West.''

"That's bullshit, Abe. Blinky was using me. How about looking for this Cimarron character?" I stood up and brushed sand from my navy blue suit pants. "Now, if you don't have any other questions, I think I'll go home. See you in court, Abe."

"As lawyer or defendant?" Abe Socolow asked.

11

Gold Doesn't Rot

There was a NO TRESPASSING sign at the front gate, which hung open. I kept the Olds in second gear and churned up dust on the dirt driveway that wound through the trees. Josefina Baroso lived in what used to be a caretaker's cottage on a tropical fruit plantation just off Old Cutler Road. No one had worked the place for years, and the trees—lychee, Key lime, Surinam cherry, and black sapote—were overgrown with weeds. Gnarled and stunted mango trees surrounded the cottage, the ground covered with rotting fruit, the air heavy with the sickly sweet scent of decay.

It was late afternoon, and gray thunderheads were forming over the Everglades to the west, building into their daily gully washers. I parked in the driveway under a guanabana tree and walked to the front steps. The cracker-style building had walls of Dade County pine, a slanted tin roof with eaves spouts and a brick chimney poking through the top. On the northern, shaded side, there was a small porch, screened to keep out the mosquitoes, fruit flies, and no-see-um gnats. In front was a screen door, latched from inside, a heavy wood door closed behind it.

I knocked on the screen door, and in a moment, the heavy door opened, and Jo Jo Baroso stood there looking at me.

111

"We need to talk," I said through the screen, her face darkened by cross-hatched shadows.

Silently, she unlatched the door, stood back and let me in. It was a small, cool, quiet place furnished in subtle earth tones. She motioned me to a sofa of Haitian cotton, and our eyes met with a knowing memory. The sofa had followed her from that first apartment so long ago. We had lain there in the darkness and exchanged whispers long into the night. We had teased and played and made love there, our limbs locked around each other. And now the faded photographs of memory came back.

Jo Jo broke eye contact first, asked whether I wanted some limeade. I did, remembering she made it with so little sugar it could bring tears to your eyes. She disappeared into the kitchen, a tall, dark, barefoot beauty in pleated, white cotton shorts and orange tank top.

She returned carrying two glasses and a pitcher of limeade on a tray, and I said, "Something may have happened to your brother."

"I know. Abe called me."

"They haven't found a body. I mean, there's no way of telling . . ."

She poured for both of us, handed me a glass, and sat at the far end of the sofa, curling her legs under her. "He's gone. I can feel it, Jake, an emptiness spreading inside me."

There was sorrow in her voice. My look shot her a question.

"He's still my brother, *el es mi única familia.*" She stopped, and we both thought our private thoughts about her brother.

"You know I wouldn't hurt Blinky," I said. It was more of a question than a statement.

"Of course, Jake. I told Abe that, but so far, you're his only lead. Abe has that cop mentality. A shaky case is better than none."

Distancing herself from Abe Socolow, showing affection for Blinky, trusting me, what was happening here?

"I wish everything were different," she said. "With Luis, with you, with me. I wish I could turn back the clock."

Her eyes were moist. It was so unlike her, at least unlike the Jo Jo Baroso of the past decade. How long had it been since I'd seen her display any emotion, other than total indifference tinged with antipathy?

"I tried to change the world and change you, and I couldn't do either one," she said.

"You reminded me of an assistant coach who wanted to move me from linebacker to fullback, even though I couldn't hang onto the ball."

"I don't blame you for leaving me, not anymore."

"At the time, you called me a commitment-phobic coward."

"I was impossible. What we had was real."

Was it?

I didn't know, because I always cut and ran from what was real. *Real* symbolized a mortgage and a pension plan, a morning commute, and evening meetings with the civic beautification committee. *Real* was for suckers, not for me, a guy who could leap tall linemen in a single bound.

As I thought back now, it was such a brief slice of our lives, and our playback equipment shows the past through a soft focus. Days were sunny, winds were cool, a young woman loved me, and the future was without limits. In a sailboat anchored off Elliott Key, we shared a bottle of wine. I remembered the *slipitty-slap* of water against the hull and the scent of salt in the air. I remembered Jo Jo saying she loved me, so why didn't it work?

"Our timing was off," I said. "We always had different goals, or maybe I didn't have any."

"You had potential, Jake."

"Granny always used to say I'd grow old having potential."

It had grown dark outside the windows. The first thunder rumbled in the distance. Jo Jo trembled at the sound. "I wanted you to reach for the stars, and you . . ."

"Short-armed it," I said, using the disparaging term for chickenhearted wide receivers.

She moved closer to me on the sofa, closing time as well as space. "You cared for me, Jake, I know that. But something inside of you tightened up when it came time to show it. Maybe you were afraid that if you cared too much and lost me, you'd be hurt again, like when you lost your father and mother."

Maybe she was right, I didn't know. I've always found introspection to be painful, and analysis from someone else is downright excruciating.

"Why *did* you leave me?" she asked.

I thought about it. Really thought. And it was agonizing. But in the reflected glare of intermittent flashes of lightning I looked at her face and tried to remember what it had been like.

After a moment, I said, "I was a fool. I hadn't grown up. You were right about me, and I didn't like hearing the truth."

"Oh, Jake!" She breathed the words, and in that graceful way women move, she was in my arms. I don't remember turning toward her. I don't remember putting my arms around her, but I held her close, my face pressed to her neck, inhaling the scent of warm flesh, and in a moment, I felt a warm tear trickle from her cheek to mine.

Then, it was just like the old times, or was it? Could it have been, when each of us had traveled so far. Her breath was warm and sweet as I kissed her, cradling her head in my hands. Her full lips parted, and we kissed again. She delicately rubbed her face against mine, catlike, and nipped at my earlobe, then ran a hand through my hair, tugging at it. In a moment, she slipped out of her halter and her shorts, and it was all so familiar. Had it really been all these years?

Her nimble fingers unbuttoned my shirt, and she ran her hands over my chest, tracing figure eights with her nails. Then she unbuttoned my pants, and I fumbled with my shoes, kicking them off, as she tugged at my belt. My hands explored the slopes and curves of her, and she whispered something in Spanish.

A bolt of lightning, followed by the crackle of nearby thunder, lit up the sky and rattled the windowpanes. We changed positions on the sofa, and she emerged on top. The rest was a blur of mouths and hands, the fullness of her breasts, the ripeness of her hips. Again, we tumbled over one another, and this time she was beneath me, our bodies pressed together. When she spoke, her voice was low, the words throaty, "*Quiereme, te necesito!*"

I obliged, and she wrapped her long legs around me. We lay there, rocking in perfect harmony on the sofa like a sailboat in gentle seas, and she exhaled several short gasps, then opened her eyes long enough to let them roll back in her head. "Jake, *te amo,*" she said finally. "*Siempre te he amado.*"

Fat raindrops were plopping off the tin roof now, and driven by the gale, pounding into the windows. Tree branches strained, whined, then snapped and fell against the house. We listened to the wind and the echoing thunder as the storm sat above us. "Thunder and lightning, clouds and rain," she said.

"Are you giving a weather report?"

"With you, Jake, I feel the lightning and the thunder. Then I drift above the earth in the clouds and the rain."

Later, as the storm moved on, we lay there, limbs still entwined, and she said, "I didn't know how much I missed you. We could have been so much to each other, Jake. We could have changed each other's lives."

"Maybe we still can," I said, smoothing her dark hair from her face, not knowing just how true that was.

We were snuggled into a bed a bit too short for me when I said, "Tell me about Kit Carson Cimarron."

I felt her body stiffen.

"What do you want to know?"

"Everything."

In the darkness of the small bedroom, she sighed. Outside the pounding rain had let up, and a light drizzle pinged against the roof. I was on my back, and she lay with one knee over my leg, her head on my chest, breathing in time with my heartbeat. "It was so stupid of me that I'm embarrassed by it, even now. I was so alone then, and he seemed so attentive, so caring. Simmy's a powerful man, very determined, very strong. It's quite a combination, Jake, and I just fell for it, very hard."

"Simmy?"

"It doesn't fit at all. I mean, he's as big as the side of a barn, but I thought I detected a gentle side to him. I was wrong. He's an egotistical manipulator and a master operator. He makes my brother look like the pope. In fact, Simmy is what Luis always wanted to be."

"What about Rocky Mountain Treasures?"

"It's Simmy's deal. He brought my brother in on it."

"Blinky told me it was legitimate."

Jo Jo laughed. "Only in the sense that neither one is likely to go to jail. It's a great, legal scam. You've seen the prospectus. It's got all the exculpatory language: 'Be advised this investment is highly risky, and you may lose part or all of your capital investment.' "

"That ought to keep people out."

I felt her hair swishing across my chest as if she was shaking her head. "You'd be shocked how many people read those clauses and still put money into oil wells filled with sand and mountaintop property with no access roads. People are greedy and gullible. When I prosecuted consumer frauds, I was constantly amazed how easy it was to separate people from their money with a great sales pitch."

"Which is where your brother fits into the deal."

"Exactly. And something I learned from Luis, the more outlandish the promises, the easier the sale."

"I don't get it."

"Neither do I, but it's true. Buried treasure is easier to sell than bushels of apples."

"Wait a second," I said. "Back up. Does Cimarron own these mines or not?"

"Sure, he's got mineral rights to thousands of acres. He bought up hundreds of leases over the past fifteen years or so. He tried mining for gold and copper and silver, and he lost his shirt. Not that he couldn't find the minerals. He could, but the price of excavation and smelting or refining exceeds market price. At the same time, Simmy was always a nut about the old West. He collects the stories—legends really—about the lost gold mines and buried treasures. He can sit around a campfire and tell twenty different stories. There's the Lost Padre in California, the Lost Dutchman in Arizona, the Lost Pitchblende in Colorado. Everything's lost, but none of it's ever found."

"Never?"

"Well, not exactly never. When Simmy was barely out of his teens, he stumbled onto a cache of double eagles. That's what got him started."

"Whoa. Double eagles?"

"Twenty-dollar gold pieces, San Francisco mint, about three thousand of them, worth about one-point-five million today. And he wasn't even looking for them. He was camping out on Devil's Head Mountain in Colorado. He didn't know it then, but there was a legend about a gang that robbed a government train near there in the 1870s. They were chased by a posse and buried the loot at the foot of a towering spruce tree. They marked the tree by sticking a long knife into it, then took off on horseback. Winter came, and the next spring the gang tried to find the tree, but couldn't. After all, the forest probably had fifty thousand spruce trees that looked just alike. They kept looking through the summer. Then a thunderstorm started a forest fire and burned most of the trees to the ground."

"So what happened to the gold?"

"A hundred years or so went by, and Simmy was riding the backcountry by himself, hunting and camping out. The way he tells the story, he was pounding some stakes into the ground to pitch a tent when he hit a rotting old saddlebag that had been brought to the surface by erosion. The wonderful thing is that gold doesn't rot. The eagles polished up just fine, and Simmy had his first nest egg.''

"No wonder he believes in secret treasures.''

"The worst thing that ever happened to him. He got a taste of treasure, and he became obsessed. He was always dabbling in mining, but for the next twenty years, it was buried gold, not mined gold, that consumed him.''

"And you don't believe treasure exists.''

"Look, I've done some reading. Simmy's personal library has just about everything ever written about buried treasure in the West. Four hundred years ago, Coronado set out with five hundred conquistadors and a thousand Indians from Mexico looking for the Seven Cities of Cíbola. What they found were Zuni Indians growing corn in a dusty village in what is now New Mexico. Then an Indian guide tells Coronado of the fabulous city of Quivera where the streets were paved with gold, and a marble palace was hung with golden bells, and the royal canoes had oarlocks of solid gold.''

"Gold seems to be the operative word.''

"Right. It drives men mad. All Coronado had to do was take his men north, the Indian tells him. Of course, the Indian just wanted to get Coronado the hell out of New Mexico where he was taking slaves and doing the traditional macho conquistador stuff. So Coronado falls for it and sets out with his army in plumes and shining armor with a thousand mules to carry back the loot.''

"That's optimism.''

"*Verdad,* or stupidity. Anyway, they get all the way to Kansas, and all they see are hot, dusty plains. But Coronado believed till the day he died that there were cities of gold out there somewhere.''

"And Cimarron does, too. Is that what you're saying?''

"Who knows? He studies mining claims and trappers' maps as if they're holy works. He's bought diaries from the families of frontiersmen and borrowed family Bibles with crude drawings of mines and graveyards. He's scoured the files of newspapers from western towns that don't even exist anymore. He's spent months in museums, and he's filled a hundred notebooks with his plans. He's not willing to admit he's chasing legends. He figures if one in twenty is legitimate, it's still worth the search.''

"So he believes in Rocky Mountain Treasures. To Cimarron, it's not a scam."

"Either way, it's a good deal for Simmy. He's got all these leases, and other than the ranch, that's about all he's got left. It doesn't make any sense to dig for gold that costs more to extract than to sell. But they can form a company with suckers' money, take fees as consultants and managers, and sell Simmy's maps to the company at a price they set. If they find the *Caverna de Oro* of Marble Mountain, then everybody's happy. If not, Blinky and Simmy still make money. Unlike Coronado, it's a no-lose situation.''

I was dreaming of conquistadors in heavy armor and helmet plumes when I awoke suddenly without knowing why. Next to me, Jo Jo was breathing deeply, a slight whistling sound accompanying each exhalation of warm breath. Outside, crickets made their night music, and overhead, a lone jet made its way toward the airport. I looked at the digital clock and watched 3:13 magically become 3:14.

Before we turned in, I had called Cindy, my loyal secretary, and asked if she would extend her baby-sitting through the night. She whined and said she was meeting Dottie the Disco Queen at a South Beach bar, and I told her to take Kip along but make sure he got home by one A.M., because I promised he could watch Burt Lancaster in *The Killers* on the all-night classics channel. How's that for parental guidance?

Now I was awake, and Burt Lancaster had long since been plugged by William Conrad, and I hoped Kip was sleeping soundly and Cindy was sleeping alone.

I lay there a moment, wondering why I had awakened. No indigestion, despite putting away three plates of Jo Jo's *picadillo*. Cooking was not a skill passed down from her mother. Jo Jo dried out the ground beef, and the raisins were as moist as BBs. The flan was fine. It came from a local bakery.

And then I remembered why I woke up. The groan of the pine floor planks did all the remembering for me.

Someone was in the house, someone besides the sleeping woman and me.

In the depths of sleep, I had heard a noise, and there it was again. Or was it? Old houses are full of sounds. Pipes clang, walls moan, floors . . .

Creak.

Again, the sound. It seemed louder, or was it my imagination?

I swung out of bed, my bare feet touching the cool floor. The rest of me was bare, too, and it did not inspire the fighting parts—arms and legs, hands and feet—to know that another part of me was exposed to the air, useless and vulnerable. I tried to take a step without making a sound, but it didn't work. The floor gave under my feet, too, with what sounded to me like a wail, but was probably no louder than a yawn.

I stopped and listened again.

Silence.

Except for me. My breathing chugged like a locomotive. My heart was running a marathon.

I tiptoed toward the closed bedroom door. No light shone from beneath it. The night had cleared, and moonlight streamed in from outside the window, casting my shadow across the floor and up the door. I took another step toward the door, heard a sound from the other side . . .

I spun backward.

Not of my own accord. The door had opened with a rush, catching me across the shoulder, surprising me, bouncing me, hop-skip-lurch toward the window. My knee sideswiped the dresser, and when I was off-balance, teetering like a drunk, an anvil caught me on the side of the head, just above the right ear. Okay, so it wasn't an anvil, but a fist that felt like iron, and it dropped me to the floor.

I yelled something unintelligible, and Jo Jo woke up

screaming, and then I tried to get to my feet, but a knee came up and just missed my dimpled chin and caught me on the shoulder. It did no damage, but set me down again.

I came off the floor, adrenaline flowing. Before I could get off a punch, he threw a looping left hook. I blocked it with my right forearm, and he came at me with a right. Now I was in the defensive position of the double forearm block, sort of like Floyd Patterson's peekaboo defense. His punches kept coming, landing like concrete blocks on my triceps and forearms, and so far, I hadn't even swung.

I backed up a step and tossed a jab. So did he, and his reach exceeded mine. He peppered my face with two more stinging straight lefts. I wanted to get a clear shot at him, but unlike almost any brawl I'd ever been in, he was bigger and stronger, and for all I knew, could beat me in the forty-yard dash.

I feinted with the left, came across the top with a right and hit him on the side of the nose. I heard cartilage splinter, and I was showered with blood. His eyes would be closed and watering now, so I came in close, tucked my head into his chest, and shot upward, butting him under the chin. I heard a snap and hoped I broke his jaw. He grunted and gagged.

I took a step back and went for his chin again, this time with a long left hook. I had a lot of hip behind it, but I was too slow. Story of my life.

He stepped to his left and hit me squarely in the solar plexus with a short right I never saw. I doubled over and fell to the floor, gasping for breath that wouldn't come. I dipped a shoulder and rolled into him just as he lifted a foot to kick me. The foot was encased in pointed burgundy cowboy boots that shimmered in the moonlight. The toe skimmed the top of my skull, and the heel slammed me in the forehead. Still, the weight of my body pinned his other foot to the floor. I kept rolling, trying to hyperextend his knee and tear his anterior cruciate ligaments into strands of spaghetti. It would have worked, too, if he hadn't had the legs of an ox.

I weigh two hundred twenty-two pounds, and I didn't budge him. This left me at his feet. He locked his hands and brought them down hard on the back of my neck, and I saw the Milky Way and Orion, with Betelgeuse particularly bright. I reached into the dazzling light to fight my way into the next galaxy, but just floated for a while. I tried to grab him behind one knee and buckle his leg, but I couldn't have squeezed the breath out of a kitten.

I heard Jo Jo screaming. "*¿Qué demonios haces aquí? Vete ahora mismo!*" She came off the bed at him, but he lifted her effortlessly and tossed her across the room.

I was on my knees, now, vaguely aware of a voice above me and warm blood dripping onto me. "Where is he?"

I was dazed and didn't get it. "Who he?"

He grabbed me by the hair and pulled my head back. "Where's Baroso? Where's the little son of a bitch?"

"I don't know. Hurt, dead, I don't know."

He yanked harder on my hair. "The two of you screwed me good, didn't you, lawyer?"

"I don't know what you're talking about."

He dropped my head and called out, "Josefina, where's that low-life brother of yours?"

She was huddled on the bed, crying. "I don't know. Leave us alone." She gathered herself up and threw a pillow at him. It did about as much good as my left jabs.

I was on all fours now, trying to get up, expecting another blow, but it didn't come. From above me, a booming voice: "Stay out of my affairs, lawyer! Stay out of my affairs, or you're a dead man. Do you understand?"

I must not have, because he lifted up a foot and stomped my right hand. I heard the knuckles fracture—the sound of a cue ball on a break—long before I felt the pain.

12

A Bumpy Night

Kip watched in silent fascination as Doc Charlie Riggs mixed water with plaster for the cast.

"Does it hurt much?" Kip asked, gently touching my swollen hand.

"Only when I play 'Dueling Banjos.'"

"Out of the way, Kip," Charlie advised, approaching with a strip of gauze soaked in dripping plaster, some of which had become affixed to his bushy beard. I was sprawled on the sofa in the pit—not a conversation pit, just a pit—of my living room, my arm slung onto the sailboard coffee table.

"You ever do this before?" I asked the doc, who was leaning over me, squinting through his lopsided eyeglasses.

He harrumphed. "You'll be my first patient who lived."

"Don't make promises you can't keep."

Kip leaned close as Charlie began wrapping my hand. "What's AMAL YNOT?" the kid asked.

I peered at the back of my hand through a nearly closed eye. The hand disappeared under the wet gauze. "The lasting impression of a Tony Lama boot, size sixteen, quadruple E."

"Bummer," Kip said. "The dude went ballistic, huh?"

He ran a finger over bruises the color of ripe eggplants on my bare arms.

"Third and fourth metacarpals fractured, ligaments stretched, but not torn," Charlie Riggs announced. "Tylenol with codeine for the pain." He studied me a moment. "How do you feel?"

"Like I was blindsided by a Mack truck. Next time I run into that cowboy, I'm going to tear his heart out."

Charlie gave my hand a gentle squeeze and a jolt of electricity shot up my arm. "Not for a long time, my friend."

Charlie poked around for a while, shining a light in my eyes to check pupil dilation, taking my blood pressure, pinching and poking this part and that. When he was done, Kip nudged me and whispered, "You didn't thank the doc."

He was right. I was beginning to take my friend for granted, another of my failings, right up there with my inability to ward off bedroom attackers. My self-esteem was taking a beating, along with my body. "Thanks, Charlie. You're always there for me, and sometimes I don't show my appreciation."

He dismissed the idea with a wave of a pudgy hand. "*Tacent satis laudant*. Silence is praise enough."

Codeine took the pain away with a drowsy, cloudy half sleep. I awoke with a throbbing hand and a head filled with bowling balls that rolled whichever way I tilted. It was dark outside, and the mockingbird in the chinaberry tree was whistling for a mate.

Which made me think of Jo Jo Baroso. What did it mean, the friction of body parts and remembrance of old times, so rudely interrupted? I took two pills and started to drift off again, vaguely aware that Kip kept opening my bedroom door, looking in at me, during breaks between TV movies.

"Want to split a beer, Uncle Jake?" he asked during one of my periods of semiconsciousness. The aroma of home-delivery pizza entered the room with him. I thought he was doing well in the self-sufficiency department. Kids left on their own somehow manage. I ought to know.

I shook my head, and the effort made my head pound with a pain that kept time with my heartbeat. Kip came over and put a hand on my forehead, and for some reason I couldn't explain, tears came to my eyes and then sleep overtook me.

"You look like death warmed over." She opened the blinds with an irritating *clackety-clack,* and bright sun slanted through the window and across the bed. "Lord-y, you look even worse in the daylight."

I pried my eyes open and squinted into the glare, finding a silhouette of Granny Lassiter leaning over me. "Good morning to you, too, Florence Nightingale."

Granny clucked her disapproval and began straightening up the room, picking up perfectly clean T-shirts that happened to be crumpled into piles on the floor. She rearranged my stylish collection of Dolphins commemorative Super Bowl ashtrays, ran a finger over a chest of drawers, leaving a trail in the dust. "Brought you some white lightning," she said, hoisting a wicker picnic basket onto the bed. She pulled out a mason jar filled with a liquid that could power a Saturn rocket. "It'll stop the pain dead in its tracks."

"So will a coma," I said.

I took a sip and grimaced. Granny slipped downstairs into the kitchen, and at lunchtime reappeared with a bowl of steaming conch chowder and some grouper fillets cooked in coconut milk and lime juice. I ate, then dozed off again, just after she told me she was going to give Kip a haircut since I apparently hadn't thought about it.

It was late afternoon when two more visitors squeezed into my little bedroom. One had been there before. They both wore navy blue business suits, but the lady looked better in hers.

"Hello, Jo Jo," I said. "Abe, what brings you here? Find another corpse in my house?"

"Nah, but if *you* looked any worse . . ."

Just then, Kip stuck his court-ordered video camera through the open door. "I told John Law he couldn't come in without a warrant, but Granny said it was okay. Did I do right, Uncle Jake?"

"You done good, kid," I said, trying to sound like Jimmy Cagney, "but next time, give him a fatal case of lead poisoning, see?"

Kip lowered the camera, winked, and shot a pretend gun at Abe Socolow, who seemed distressed at my felonious advice. Jo Jo came over to the bed, leaned down and kissed me on the forehead, or rather, on a purple welt on my forehead. Kip walked in and sort of hung around in the corner, taping the scene for a documentary, *My Uncle, the Punching Bag.*

"I brought you something," Socolow said, tossing a bag onto the bed.

I smelled the garlic bagels before I opened the bag. "Thanks, Abe. Better than serving an indictment. I guess you believe me now."

"About what?"

"That I didn't kill Hornback or Blinky. That crazy cowboy Cimarron did, and he tried to kill me, or at least, threatened to."

Socolow reached into the bag, pulled out one of my bagels and started chewing. "Doesn't fit. If Cimarron killed Blinky, why'd he ask you where he was?"

I shot a look at Jo Jo.

"I'm sorry, Jake. I gave a statement. I had to tell Abe what Simmy said."

I turned back to Socolow. "I don't know why he asked. Maybe it doesn't make any sense, but look at the facts. There are four people involved in Rocky Mountain Treasures. One is dead, one is missing and presumed dead, one just got the crap kicked out of him by the fourth one. C'mon, Abe, it doesn't take Sherlock Holmes . . ."

"Maybe you're right, but maybe not. You know as well as I do that when you're dealing with circumstantial evidence, you've got to rule out the possibility of any other set of facts. Who's to say that you and Cimarron aren't involved in a power struggle for that treasure company? Maybe the other two just got in the way. Or maybe Hornback sided with Cimarron, and you had him taken out, and Blinky sided with you, and Cimarron took him out. Or vice versa, or a hundred other scenarios I haven't thought of."

"Abe! I'm not in a power struggle with the cowboy. I never even knew the guy existed. I never asked to be in that company. I was just dragged into it."

Socolow seemed to think about it. He gave the impression of engaging in quiet, deductive reasoning, but after a moment, he said, "You got any cream cheese?"

"No. Abe, you're giving me a headache. What are you doing about Cimarron?"

"No way we can charge him with murder, but if you and Josefina give a sworn statement, we'll file a direct information for aggravated assault and trespass. You want us to charge him?"

"Yes," I said.

"No," Jo Jo said.

"Well, I'm sure pleased the two of you are back together," Socolow said. "Just like old times. Maybe I ought to leave the room and let you hash this out." He stood up and started for the door. "You think your granny brought any of that Key lime pie with her?"

When he was gone, Jo Jo shot a nervous look toward Kip, who was sitting in the corner.

"It's okay," I said. "Kip and I are covered by the uncle-nephew privilege."

"There's no such thing," she told me. Turning back to the kid, she said, "Would you turn off the camera please?"

"I will if you say, 'Fasten your seat belts. It's going to be a bumpy night.' "

She looked puzzled.

"An audition," I explained. "He's looking for a new Bette Davis."

"Jake," she said, giving me a no-nonsense look I remembered so well, "this is serious."

"Okay, Kip. It's a wrap. I'm closing down production. You can stay and listen but keep quiet."

He grumbled but turned off the camera.

Jo Jo waited a moment, then said, "Simmy called me this morning."

"Great, where is he?"

"Didn't say. He apologized, said he lost his head, but it was a combination of things. Jealousy at finding you in my bed, anger at Luis, frustration with the company."

"Okay, he's got problems, and he works them out by using my head for punting practice. I hope you told him that the next time I see him, I am going to even things up."

"No, I didn't tell him that," Jo Jo said, evenly. "Mostly, I listened. He kept repeating what he said the other night, that Blinky had double-crossed him, and you must have been in on it. Then, he told me he wanted me back. He didn't realize it before, but he wants to start again."

"Yeah, well tell him to take a number. I'm first in line."

"Oh, Jake. I don't know what to do. I really don't. A week ago, I had no one, and now, two men want me."

"Like Katharine Hepburn in *The Rainmaker*," Kip said.

"Hey, kid," I said, "how 'bout going downstairs and keep an eye on the D.A."

"Why? Is this where it gets X-rated?"

I shooed him out, and we were alone. "Jo Jo, my head is spinning when it isn't throbbing. Two nights ago, we made love, and it was a ten on the Richter scale. We turned back the clock. Then we get a visit from a maniac the size of a missile silo, a guy who may have killed your brother, and now you're telling me you're thinking about going back to him. Is that what I'm hearing?"

Her dark eyes were moist. "I don't know, Jake. I just don't know. It's so much more complicated than you realize. Luis didn't tell you everything, and neither did I."

"I'm listening," I said.

But she wasn't talking.

"Jo Jo!"

"I'm so sorry Luis got you involved in this. Maybe it's not too late to get you out. Please, Jake, let it drop. Let me handle it. I have things I've got to do. Don't follow me. And someday I hope you'll forgive me."

She bolted from the room, and I heard her blue patent leather pumps beating a staccato retreat down the stairs. I wanted to chase after her, but I couldn't. I wanted to call out to her, to ask her more questions.

Starting with one . . .

Forgive you for what?

And backing up a bit . . .

Follow you where?

And maybe most important . . .

Get me out of what?

Which was the most difficult of all, because if you don't know what you're involved in, how the heck are you going to get out?

13

A Dozen Deadly Thoughts

I went back to work, shuffling papers, pleading out first-timers for stern lectures and probation because the prisons were too crowded to house my fallen angels. Weeks passed with no news. Metro police could not find the moose disguised as a cowboy and finally asked for help from the sheriff's department in Pitkin County, Colorado, on the theory that Cimarron had gone home.

Our local cops seemed to be happy to lateral the ball. In a county with a murder a day and a hundred stolen cars a week, arresting a guy for assault was not the highest priority. Especially when the word I was getting from the state attorney's office was that Socolow considered the whole thing a lovers' triangle where nobody got killed. In other words, no big deal, a couple of guys trading punches over a woman. I didn't see it that way, but then I was the guy whose ears rang for a week.

Maybe the case embarrassed Socolow. After all, Jo Jo Baroso was on his staff. Who needs the sly remarks and elbow-in-the-ribs jokes about the lady prosecutor *con dos amantes* in the bedroom?

Anyway, that's what I was thinking because Socolow was more aloof than usual. He stopped returning my calls. He let it get around town that I was either a witness or a suspect in more cases than I was a lawyer. Then I noticed a gray Dodge behind me on the way home from the office, and again the next day on the way to the courthouse. I wouldn't have paid attention, except each day, the Dodge changed lanes suddenly to keep me in sight. Two men were in the front seat, but I couldn't make out their features. On South Miami Avenue headed north from Coconut Grove, I pulled into the Vizcaya parking lot and let the car go by, checking the license number. As I figured, state-owned. Either Socolow had me under surveillance, or the governor was tracking me down to offer a judgeship.

Abe Socolow.

We had known each other since I squeaked through the bar exam and landed a job in the P.D.'s office. He was a young assistant state attorney, whose enthusiasm had not yet been sharpened into cynicism. He prosecuted shoplifters, check bouncers, and drunk drivers with equal vigor, and I defended them with creativity. He usually won, but that's the way it works in the den of iniquity (and inequity) of the Metro Justice Building. Other defense lawyers considered Socolow dour and mean-spirited. I always liked him, admired his fighting spirit, even found him funny in a hard-assed way. Years ago, in an arson case, I asked for a continuance because my client was in the hospital.

"What's wrong with him?" the judge asked.

"Probably smoke inhalation," Socolow said.

Socolow worked long hours, took on difficult cases, and his career soared. Felony division within a year, major crimes the next, public corruption unit, then capital cases. He became state attorney by default when Nick Wolf, his predecessor, took a fall for playing footsie with drug dealers.

My career was different. It started slow, then tapered off. When I realized that virtually all my clients were guilty—though not always with what they were charged—some of the air went out of me. If I was going to rescue the flotsam and jetsam of the sewage pipe we call the justice system, I might as well get paid for it. I went downtown to Harman & Fox, an old-line firm that represents insurance companies and banks. The crusty coots there wanted someone who could try a tough case without peeing his pants, and as a concession to my past, allowed me to handle criminal cases, though I suspect they wish they had a back door for my clients to enter and leave.

So Abe Socolow was an old foe. Strange that I had begun to think of him as an old friend. Is my life so empty that I concocted a kinship out of an adversarial relationship? Maybe, but what a depressing thought.

Now what was Socolow doing? He was a real pro who wouldn't let old times get in the way of a case. He could bring me bagels one day and have me tailed the next.

And on the third day, maybe get a warrant to tap my phones.

And on the fourth day, get the grand jury to indict me for murder.

And so on until he rested. At which time I'd have to present my case.

So here I was sinking into paranoia, shooting glances at my rearview mirror, listening for buzzes on my phone line. There is no worse fear for a defense lawyer than to believe the government is listening to his telephone calls. Well, maybe one. A few years ago, the feds tried to seize lawyers' fees on the theory they were clients' ill-gotten gains, something that shook the defense bar down to its Gucci loafers. The lawyers weren't concerned about their fees, of course. No, not at all. As I recall the high-falutin' argument, my brethren were all lathered up about the government tampering with the constitutional right of counsel. And if you believe that, I'll sell you some of Blinky Baroso's waterfront property.

The state has awesome powers when it decides to use them, and right now, it was using the power of intimidation. I wouldn't talk to my clients on the phone, except to remind them of the importance of testifying truthfully.

Even when clients came to the office, I was worried they

might be wired. A carelessly misspoken line could be interpreted as suborning perjury or obstructing justice.

So I was testy, suspicious, and tweaked out, to use Kip's phrase. Mostly, though, I couldn't focus. It didn't help that Jo Jo Baroso failed to return my phone calls for a week. When I tried the state attorney's office, I got her voice mail. At her cottage, the answering machine kept picking up.

On a hunch, I had Cindy call *The Miami Herald* as one Josefina Jovita Baroso, asking why her paper hadn't been delivered. Because, the circulation clerk said, the computer said you stopped the paper indefinitely three days ago.

Okay, she has a right not to read the paper.

Or to leave town.

Maybe a quick vacation. And what right do I have to complain, just because we had a quick roll in the sack?

I kept telling myself these things. Then I asked Cindy to run to the courthouse and check out the property tax rolls, a task that conflicted with an appointment to dye her hair the color of blue steel .38. She came back with information on a twenty-seven-acre parcel just off Old Cutler Road that years ago was a tropical fruit plantation and now is zoned for three-acre homesites, though the only building is a former caretaker's cottage. The owner, according to the computer printout, is one K. C. Cimarron, Roaring Fork Road, Basalt, Colorado.

Oh.

So the tough guy is her landlord.

And former lover.

Who wants her back.

And she's gone to who knows where.

I left the office and put the top down on the Olds 442. In late afternoon, the sun was slanting hard from a cloudless summer sky, and the breeze was a blast furnace of noxious fumes. I headed down U.S. 1 to LeJeune, took a left, passed Merrie Christmas Park, rounded the circle with the statue honoring the Barefoot Mailman, and drove under an umbrella of banyan trees down Old Cutler Road, a winding two-lane strip of asphalt that hugs the shoreline of Biscayne Bay.

I got to the plantation around six o'clock. The same No TRESPASSING sign at the front gate, the same stunted trees and rotting fruit, the same cottage, this time dark and empty.

I went around to the back and tried the porch door. Nothing doing. I circled the cottage, nudging the windows. Still nothing. The screen door in front was locked with a simple hook from the inside.

Strange.

That could only be done if you're in the house. Once you leave, the screen door stays unlocked.

My first thought was one of sheer terror. Images of the strangled Kyle Hornback, the missing Blinky, the attack by Cimarron.

A dozen deadly thoughts ricocheted through my mind. Jo Jo must be inside the house, her body broken and bloodied. What a fool I had been. I hadn't protected her from Cimarron, and now I was overcome with equal portions of dread, grief, and guilt.

I yanked open the screen door, tearing the hook out of the soft wood. My hand was still in the cast, but my shoulder was fine, except for old scar tissue. I knocked the door off its hinges in three tries.

Inside it was hot, stuffy, and silent, except for a lone horsefly that buzzed and banged against a window. There were women's magazines on the wicker coffee table. In the kitchen, a clean cup and saucer sat in a drying rack in the sink. In the small bedroom, all was neat and tidy, the bed made, the pillows fluffed.

There was no body, of course.

The porch door was locked. I knew that. I had tried it from the outside. I looked out the window at the tire tracks in the brown grass in the shade of a Key lime tree. *That's* where Jo Jo parked her car. I knew that, too. But I had forgotten, or hadn't put it all together. A stupid little mistake, leaping to conclusions. Jo Jo left the house by the porch door, leaving the front screen door locked. What was wrong with me, anyway? I was jumpy, irrational, using bad judgment.

I was getting ready to leave, figuring I could call a carpenter to replace the door, when I saw the answering machine with its little green light. Seven calls, according to the digital message counter. I hit the playback button.

Three from me, the first one and the last two.

Two from the state attorney's office: Call your secretary.

One from a solicitor for a charity.

And one from Gables Travel, the second message, which I figured to have come three or four days ago. "Your ticket will be waiting at the Continental desk at the airport tomorrow. Flight four-fifty-eight, Miami to Denver. Open return."

I slept restlessly, dreaming of snow-covered mountains filled with buried treasure. I awoke early, squeezed a Key lime onto a fresh mango for breakfast, then drove to the office. I called my loyal secretary into my office, something that interfered with the filing of her three-inch stiletto-blade fingernails.

"Cindy, help me."

She waited.

"It's Jo Jo."

Cindy stopped chewing her gum and twirled a finger through a knot of hair. "A cool customer. She was always one step ahead of you, but maybe that's not saying much."

"What would it mean if, after she and I . . . ah . . . reacquainted ourselves—"

"You mean you jumped her bones, boss. C'mon, everybody knows you two were playing hide the sausage when her ex-dude showed up from the O.K. Corral."

"Yeah. Anyway, what would it mean if she doesn't return my calls and then leaves town."

"She tell you where she went?"

"No."

"She make any effort to hide where she went?"

"Not exactly."

"Then it's a toss-up. Either she doesn't want anything to do with you, or she wants you to follow her."

"No. She told me *not* to follow her. I didn't even know she was going anywhere, but that's what she said. 'Don't follow me.' "

Cindy laughed. "That's the clincher. She wants you on her trail. Otherwise, why would she say not to, I mean, you wouldn't have known to follow her, unless she told you not to."

"I don't get it. I really don't."

"You don't have to, just trust me."

"Look, Cindy, she must have gone back to Cimarron. So what you're saying doesn't make any sense. She wouldn't want me around if she's with him."

"*Jefe*, what you don't know about women would fill Biscayne Bay. Women don't communicate the same way as men, but of course, men don't communicate at all. Even strong career women like Josefina Baroso don't necessarily come out and say what they mean."

"Cindy, that's downright sexist of you."

"No, it's not. We've been taught how to act and how to speak. If we're too direct, we're ballbusters. If we don't say a word, we don't get anything. And where relationships are concerned, a woman falls back on her feminine wiles. If she just said, 'Jake, I love you, I want you forever,' what would you do?"

"Did you say 'forever?' "

"That's what I mean. Your palms start to sweat. But if she let you know she was going back to an ex-lover, somebody you thought was bad news, what then?"

"You tell me, Cindy. You're the one who takes the tests in *Cosmo* when you're supposed to be typing writs of replevin."

"Well, either you'd go home and drink a six-pack of that Dutch beer and maybe put your fist through the plaster, or you'd hop the first plane to go get her."

"How does she know which it is?"

"She doesn't. It's a test. For both of you. She may be headed back to the cowboy, but she's not sure about it. She wants you to go up there and drag her out by the hair. She wants you to stop her, to fight for her."

"I did that once and got my bell rung."

"You know what I mean. If the cowboy is professing his love, maybe she wants you to do the same thing, then she can choose."

"If that's it, why not just say—"

Just then, the phone rang on my private line. Abe Socolow got right to the point. "We found Cimarron."

The way he said it, my first thought was another body. There I go again. Why was I so morbid these days?

"He's sitting fat and happy on his ranch," Socolow continued.

"Great. Have him arrested."

"Yeah, well, the sheriff's deputies up there didn't serve the arrest warrant. They just called him up and told him about it. Seems he's a big deal in town. Anyway, he picked up the phone and called me. Says he'll gladly face assault charges, or if you want, Jake, maybe go another couple of rounds."

"To hell with that. Next time, I'll just shoot him in the kneecaps."

"Uh-huh. Well, he says he wants to file a complaint against you with my office."

"What for? I scuff his boots with my head?"

"Grand larceny. Claims you and Blinky conspired to defraud him and the third-party investors in that treasure company. Something about selling the stock three or four times. Diluted his stock, claims Hornback was going to blow the whistle on both of you."

"I don't know anything about it, Abe. If you've got proof, go ahead, take your best shot."

"Nah. I don't believe it. Just want you to know. I figure you can explain everything."

I didn't like the way he said 'everything.' "What's that supposed to mean?"

"You still bank at Southern Federal, right?"

"Yeah, what about it?"

"We served a subpoena on their records custodian about an hour ago, so I gotta ask you about a cash deposit of seventy-five grand to your account last week."

"That's got to be a mistake."

"Hey, Jakie, I'm looking at a photocopy of the deposit slip. Seventy-five thousand in cash last Thursday."

"Abe, stop and think about it. If the money was dirty, would I put it in the bank?"

"How should I know? The only times I ever saw seventy-five grand in cash, it came from bad guys. Drug dealers, bookies, tax evaders. But maybe you're only half-bad, Jake. Maybe you were going to declare taxes on it, claim it was a legal fee, so why not put it in the bank? Besides, I long ago gave up figuring out why you guys do what you do . . ."

You guys?

". . . We've still got burglars going into tented homes being fumigated. Come morning, they're just as dead as the termites. Last week, another Seven-Eleven robber shot himself in the dick. You'd think by now, these wise guys would stop shoving their guns down the front of their pants when they get outside. You know how much pressure it takes on the trigger to fire a cocked nine-millimeter?" Socolow barked his unpleasant laugh. "Is that what you did, Jakie. Shoot yourself in the dick?"

"Abe, we've known each other a long time. You ever know me to steal anything?"

"Don't pull any of that *auld lang syne* shit on me. It doesn't work."

"You didn't answer my question."

The line hummed, and I pictured Socolow scowling into the phone, his feet propped on his state-issued, green metal desk. "No, Jake. I've never known you to steal. Up till now. Or to kill, either, for that matter."

"What's that supposed to mean?"

"The grand jury meets this afternoon on the Hornback case." He dropped his voice to a whisper. "You didn't hear it from me, but here's the evidence that'll be presented. On Sunday, June thirteenth, Kyle Lynn Hornback, a white male, age twenty-seven, was found swinging from a ceiling fan in a house belonging to one Jacob Lassiter, who reported the crime. From body temperature, livor mortis and rigor mortis, the medical examiner places the time of death between nine and eleven P.M. Mr. Lassiter was home early in the evening, but cannot account for his presence between ten and eleven-thirty, having claimed to be on Ocean Drive during that time, but there are no alibi witnesses, not even Kato Kaelin. Cause of death was asphyxiation as Mr. Hornback was strangled with a silk tie belonging to Mr. Lassiter. Toxicology showed a substantial quantity of phenobarbs in Mr. Hornback's blood, and he may have been unconscious when strangled. The methyl methacrylate test revealed latent fingerprints on the face, neck, and arms of the decedent, and the latents matched those of Mr. Lassiter. You follow me, Jake?"

"Like a shyster behind an ambulance."

"On Monday, June fourteenth, Mr. Hornback was scheduled to appear before the state attorney to give a statement that would have implicated Mr. Lassiter's client in a fraudulent investment scheme. That client has now disappeared, and based on evidence obtained from his vehicle, he may also have been killed. The only person known to have been at that scene is Mr. Lassiter, who answered a phone call from the state attorney, then hung up without identifying himself, and apparently was intent on fleeing at the time officers arrived."

"Is that it?"

"Not quite. A witness, a ranch owner from Colorado named K. C. Cimarron is prepared to testify that Mr. Lassiter's client, apparently with Mr. Lassiter's advice, knowledge, and assistance, engaged in a scheme to defraud investors of a closely held company called Rocky Mountain Treasures, Inc. Mr. Cimarron claims that at least one hundred fifty thousand dollars in corporate funds are missing, and Mr. Lassiter has no explanation for a seventy-five-thousand-dollar deposit to his bank account last week. Additionally, the stock subscription to the company was apparently sold several times over.

"Mr. Cimarron is the last living witness who can testify to these matters. About five minutes ago, Mr. Lassiter threatened to shoot Mr. Cimarron in the kneecaps. About two weeks ago, Mr. Lassiter threatened to tear out his heart. The remark was made to the retired coroner and repeated innocently to the state attorney, as the retired coroner was afraid for Mr. Lassiter's well-being, and also allowed as how his old friend was acting strangely."

"Hey, Abe. I once punched out a tight end for the Jets. Drew a fifteen-yarder for unsportsmanlike conduct. Why not introduce that to the grand jury?"

"This isn't a joke."

"You're telling me. Abe, listen for a minute. I'm going to confess. I confess to hating K. C. Cimarron, and you're right, if I see him again, I may just tear him apart. But I didn't steal from him or anybody else, and if you don't know that, I'm really disappointed in you."

"Not half as disappointed as I am in you. Jake, I'm not going to insult you by telling you I'm only doing my job, because it's never been just a job to me, and you know it. If you're dirty, I take it as a personal affront. I take it as a rejection of everything I stand for, and it makes you the lowest of the low. I'm champing at the bit to get a piece of you, fellow, but I'm gonna play it by the book. If the grand jury thinks we submitted enough evidence to establish probable cause, you'll be indicted for the murder of Kyle Hornback. Maybe you'll be convicted and maybe you won't. That's not for me to say. As for Baroso, we don't have a body, and the state can only fry you once, anyway."

"Anything else, Abe, or should I get my papers ready to sue you for malicious prosecution? You're going to look like a fool, Abe. I'm going to end your career, old buddy."

"I'll ignore that for now." He paused and the line buzzed with static. "One more thing. Don't leave town. If they indict, I won't send out the deputies. You can come in with your lawyer, and I'll handle the booking myself."

I placed the phone down on the desk.

"Jake." I heard the voice, faint now, as I slipped my suit coat on. "Jake, are you there?"

I always keep an overnight bag in my office. It contains a toiletry kit, a pair of jeans, sneakers, a T-shirt, and a warm-up suit. I grabbed the bag from behind the credenza.

"Jake." Barely audible now. "Did you hear me? No tricks, no funny stuff."

And then I was gone.

14

Continental Divide

I grabbed Kip from the conference room and told him we were taking a little trip. He'd been pestering me about going to Universal Studios near Disney World, so he figured we were headed to Orlando. I reluctantly promised we would another time, and on the way to the airport, gave him my sermon about the paving over of Central Florida, a land of motels, alligator shows, pancake houses, shell shops (with imported shells), go-cart tracks, miniature golf courses, T-shirt shops, and medieval castles made of plastic. Call me a curmudgeon, but I just don't go for prepackaged, no-surprise, sterilized "attractions." I'd rather take the kid fishing.

So I told Kip where we were going and added that he'd better tie the laces of his high-top sneakers, and he began asking the first of six hours of questions. "But why are we going out west, and why couldn't we get my clothes first?"

"We're going because the state attorney here thinks I killed someone, and a dangerous guy there thinks I double-crossed him."

"Broly! Just like *North by Northwest*."

"Huh?"

"The cops think Cary Grant killed this guy at the UN,

but it was really an assassin hired by James Mason, who thinks Cary Grant is someone else, and—"

"Kip, this is real life."

"I know, but you can learn things from the movies."

"Yeah? Like what?"

"Like, if you see a crop duster flying real low, you better duck."

"Okay, got it. As for your clothes, I'll get you duded up when we get there."

He made a face. "Duded up? Uncle Jake, that's totally geekified. I mean, nobody talks like that, not even Pee Wee Herman."

On the expressway, just before the airport exit, a blond woman in a red Porsche cut me off, changing lanes. I gave her a friendly honk-honk, and she responded with the middle finger of her left hand. A bumper sticker on the Porsche read: "I still miss my ex, but my aim is improving."

From a phone on Concourse E, I called Charlie Riggs to tell him what I was doing. "Are you going because of the girl or to get yourself out of a jam?" he asked.

"I don't know," I answered, honestly.

At the other end of the line, Charlie seemed to think it over. After a moment, he cleared his throat with his genial harrumph. "Plautus probably said it best."

"He usually did," I agreed.

"*Ubi mel ibi apes*. Honey attracts bees."

"I know what you're saying, Charlie. Be careful of that other bee, the one with size-sixteen cowboy boots."

"Surely, but be careful of the honey, too, my friend."

The flight to Denver was uneventful, unless you count the look the flight attendant gave me when Kip asked whether they had Dutch beer instead of that canned piss supposedly made from Rocky Mountain spring water. I made a mental note to watch my language in front of the lad, maybe get some advice from Granny, who would probably hoot and offer us both some moonshine.

I tried to nap, but my hand, out of its cast, began throbbing, maybe from the cabin pressure, maybe from the task of opening all those little brown bottles with Mr. Daniel's name on them.

We had ice-cream cones at the new Denver airport, and I bought Kip a Broncos sweatshirt, which matched his Day-Glo shorts and his orange sneakers. We rented a Mustang convertible, and top down, headed west on Interstate 70, the summer sun hotter than in Miami.

"Where's the snow?" Kip asked.

"Off yonder," I said, pointing straight ahead at the unseen mountains.

I told him everything I knew about Colorado, which wasn't much. Just before I retired from pro football, which sounds better than saying I was put on waivers and twenty-five other teams didn't notice, I had gotten friendly with three of the Packers defensive players. They kept bugging me to come skiing at the end of the season. When I finally gave in, I discovered that skiing was a lot like windsurfing, the combination of recklessness and gracefulness, although I always had a lot more of the former.

After that, I'd meet the guys each January, usually during Super Bowl week, so we could forget we weren't there. We'd team up with a few guys from the Vikings and Bears, rent a couple of houses within snowball range of each other in Aspen or Crested Butte or Vail or Telluride, ski all day and play poker and drink bourbon most of the night. One of our number eventually made it to the Hall of Fame—football, not skiing—and all of us gathered in Canton, Ohio, for the ceremonies. Nobody, least of all the honoree, was sober, which may explain his emotional speech, which began, "I want to thank everyone responsible for my being indicted."

Our gang was not the most skilled of skiers, what with creaky knees wrapped and braced against the torque, and our penchant for dueling with ski poles on the way down the slopes. We wore torn jeans and mismatched gloves and women's stockings over our heads instead of ski masks, and we grossed out everyone with our sweatshirts, which had cute slogans, including, "Who Farted?" and "How's My Skiing—Call 1-800 EAT SHIT."

We didn't always follow etiquette on the slopes or in the coffeehouses, tearooms, and chichi, wood-beamed creeping-ferned restaurants that abound in such places, and in general, we were as welcome as a Christmas week thaw. We did manage to avoid arrest and deportation, but not for lack of trying. We were remarkably unsuccessful with women, especially in the tonier places like Aspen where they talk about *après* ski, causing me to coin any number of phrases, such as "*Après* ski, I'm gonna take a crap."

I had never been here in the summer, and I had never chased a woman here, if that's what I was doing now. I thought about it. The grand jury would have already met, and the foreman would have signed an indictment with my name on top. Sure, Charlie, I was here for Jo Jo, but I was here for me, too.

I was squinting into the late-afternoon sun, and the air was getting cooler. We passed Vail and got off the interstate to head south on U.S. 24 to Leadville, the old silver mining town. Kip had fallen asleep, and I woke him so he could see Mount Elbert and Mount Massive, both over fourteen thousand feet. Kip thanked me by growling and curling up again, his head in my lap.

We kept going south along the Arkansas River, then hung a right at Twin Lakes and up two-lane Route 92 toward Independence Pass. By now, it was downright cold. The top was up, and Kip was awake, reading the fine print on a tourist brochure we picked up at a gas station. We wound up the mountain road, slowed to near stops on a variety of hairpin turns, and below us, where we had been, was now a darkened, faraway valley.

"When they were looking for gold, the first miners traveled on burros in the winter over Independence Pass," Kip informed me, reading aloud in the dying light. "They went through thirty-foot snowdrifts." He looked out the window. "Hey! There's snow! Stop the car!"

I did, and Kip got out. Just before dusk, and the wind

was howling. Bright wildflowers, blues and reds and yellows, grew out of a moist topsoil, and nearby was a patch of wet, melting snow tinted reddish-brown by the blowing dust. Kip leaned down, gathered up a handful, and patted himself a soggy, misshapen snowball.

"Hit me with that," I said, "and you can take a burro over the pass yourself."

He aimed at a road sign but didn't come close. "I never saw snow before. Bitchin' stuff!"

"Totally," I agreed.

He grabbed his video camera from the trunk and began recording the flowers, the snow, and every rock and shrub within eyesight. Then, we both started shivering, so I hustled him into the car. In a few moments, we passed the lookout point, driving through low-hanging clouds, a fine mist glistening in the headlights.

"That's the Continental Divide," I told my nephew, spotting a tourist information sign, but sounding as if I were an old Rocky Mountain hand.

"I know," he said. "It's a movie with John Belushi as a newspaperman who doesn't like nature 'till he gets out here."

We began the long descent into the next valley, and just then the mist turned to rain, and in a moment, chunks of ice fell from the sky, pinging off the hood and plopping onto our canvas top.

"Jeez! What's that?" Kip was wide-eyed.

"Hail, my boy. And not little pebbles, either."

"What a racket. Yikes!!"

I rounded a curve a bit too fast, then hit the brakes, just like you're not supposed to do. The Mustang's rear end skidded toward the darkness of a sheer drop-off. I let up on the brakes and swung the wheel back the other way. Too hard. We fishtailed toward the mountain side, nearly slamming into a boulder the size of a house. Again, I whipped the wheel the other way, and we skidded toward the black abyss. This time, I gave it some gas, tugged the wheel gently toward the mountain, and we straightened out, but I was in the left-hand lane, and a Jeep was headed toward me, headlights flashing, horn honking. I spun the wheel once more, and we skidded onto the gravel on the mountain side.

A long-lost word popped into my head. *Makua*, the Hawaiian word meaning "toward the mountain." It came from a trip to Maui, and a deadly drive down Crater Road on the slopes of Haleakala. I'd gone after a woman then, too. What was the other word? *Makai*, "toward the sea." If you're going to go off a mountain road, choose the *makua* side. Always take a ditch or even a boulder over a two-thousand-foot drop.

I fought the skid and the urge to stomp on the brakes. The Mustang thudded to a stop and stalled in a shallow ditch. The hailstones, more like slabs of ice, clanged off the car with a frightening noise and stuck to the windshield in frozen sheets. Steam rose from under the hood. I sat there with both hands on the wheel, my heart pounding. Then I turned to Kip and tousled his blond hair, giving him a forced smile that said Uncle Jake had everything under control.

Our breath and body temperature was fogging the inside of the windshield. In front of the car, shrouded by our man-made fog and the frozen windshield, the mountain towered over us.

"You okay?" I asked Kip.

"Sure."

"You're kind of quiet."

"Uh-huh."

"What are you thinking, young man."

"Nothin'."

"You sure?"

"Yeah. It's just, I guess . . ."

"Go on, Kip. Tell me."

"Toto, I have a feeling we're not in Kansas anymore."

I gave Kip his first driving lesson. It consisted of my standing in the ditch up to my ankles in slushy mud, bracing my arms against the trunk of the car and pushing as if the two-ton chunk of metal were a blocking sled. All the time, Kip was supposed to be gently giving it gas. Except he wasn't so gentle. The rear wheels spun and splattered me with mud. I was just happy he didn't throw it into reverse.

The hail stopped and was replaced by a fine cold mist. I tried to wipe off the mud, but it was everywhere, including in my right ear. I rested a moment and checked out the car. There were a few dents on the right side where we'd sideswiped a boulder shaped like a tombstone, but otherwise, we were fine. In a few minutes, Kip got the hang of it, and together we rocked the car out of the ditch.

Kip took a long look at me when I slid back behind the wheel. "Yuck!"

We started down the mountain toward Aspen. I was cold, filthy, and exhausted and now, on this narrow, slippery road, I began to wonder again just what I was doing. I didn't know the territory. I didn't know if Jo Jo wanted me to follow her. I didn't know how to clear my name.

I had just traveled two thousand miles, but I didn't have a plan. Where to begin?

With Jo Jo? With Cimarron? I decided to take one step at a time. It's the way you build a case in the courtroom. The big picture is sometimes too complex, too daunting. So first, figure what you need to prove, then take a small step in that direction.

Kip flicked on the inside light and buried his head in the tourist brochure.

I kept thinking. And driving. I'm not sure I could have chewed gum too.

Inside my head I was pacing. Socolow thinks I killed Kyle Hornback. Cimarron thinks I defrauded him. Covering up the fraud was the motive for the murder. So, if I can prove I didn't defraud Cimarron . . .

Right.

That's thinking like a lawyer. Building my case, chipping away at the other guy's, proving I had no motive to kill, maybe proving that somebody else did.

Which made me think of Kit Carson Cimarron again, which in turn, made me flex my right hand. Clenching the fist was fine, but spreading the fingers caused the hand to flare with pain. If I hit anybody tougher than the Pillsbury Doughboy, it would hurt me more than him.

Kip turned off the map light and looked toward me. "You know why they call it the Continental Divide?"

"Something to do with the way the water flows," I said, remembering a tidbit of lost information from a long-ago geography class.

"Right. It's the part of the Rockies that divides the continent, east from west. On the Leadville side, the Arkansas River flows east. On the Aspen side, the Roaring Fork and the Frying Pan flow west, eventually reaching the Pacific. Do you believe that, Uncle Jake? I mean, if the wind is blowing one way, or if the raindrop hits this rock or that one, it determines whether the drop goes to the Atlantic or the Pacific Ocean?"

"Sure. It's just like with people. Little things push us one direction or the other. But we're not drops of water, Kipper. We've got free will, and the power to act, to change course. Trouble comes when we see that shallow reef dead ahead, and we plow right along, damn well knowing that any moment we'll hear the crunch of coral against hull."

That quieted him for a moment, but not much longer. "Is this one of your lessons about life, Uncle Jake?"

"Yep."

We were slowing down again as the two lanes seemed to narrow, and we crept along mountainside cliffs cut deep by torrents of water that tumbled into channels alongside the road.

"I get it," he said. "That's the reason we're here, right? Like you could stay in Miami and get scorched by that goober, Mr. Socolow. But you've seen the reef and decided to change course, right?"

"Something like that."

"Totally excellent. I'll help you steer, Uncle Jake."

15

Birds of Prey

An owl sat on a fence post eating a skunk.

The owl's legendary eyesight is apparently keener than its sense of smell.

"Kip, that's a great horned owl," I said, with authority, having been told as much by the fellow at the front desk of the Lazy Q ranch.

"Yuck. I think I'm gonna blow chunks."

"*Whoo*," said the owl, between bites.

The skunk didn't say a thing.

I didn't want to stay at any of the hotels in town. If Abe Socolow thought about it, he probably would figure I followed Jo Jo or Cimarron, or both. So the Hotel Jerome, the Little Nell, and the Ritz-Carlton were out, it being damn near impossible to check into a decent hotel under a phony name these days. Having to surrender your credit card takes care of that.

I hate credit cards. I hate leaving a trail of where I've been, what I've eaten, how I've shopped. A credit history these days is a life story. Where would divorce lawyers and other snoops be without the computer printouts of hotel rooms, jewelry stores, and weekend flights to Nassau when the business meeting was in Tampa? Government at every level, companies that employ you and companies that choose not to, every school you've attended, and every liquor store you've frequented maintain a cradle-to-grave digital trail of facts and figures about you. The data—some mundane, some striking at the core of intimate privacy—is never discarded and never fades into yellow clippings. Ask not for whom the computer chimes. It chimes for thee.

I chose a ranch located just off Maroon Creek Road outside Aspen. It had nine wooden cottages that were a tad too primitive even to be called rustic. My skiing buddies and I had stayed here once after we'd been thrown out of an Aspen condo complex for staging diving contests into the swimming pool.

In January.

The pool was filled with five feet of powdery snow, and nobody got hurt, but the building manager was screaming about his insurance rates until I dragged him up the three-meter board and tossed him in. His belly flop sounded like a whale breaching.

The lodge of the Lazy Q was an A-frame made of logs with a Ben Franklin stove, a moth-eaten bearskin rug, and what I took to be the antlered head of a deer on the knotty pine wall, but it could have been an elk or an orangutan for all I knew. Behind the counter was a skinny clerk in faded jeans, scuffed boots, greasy hair with long sideburns, and a cigarette jammed into the corner of his mouth.

"Dork thinks he's Harry Dean Stanton," Kip whispered to me.

"Hush." I shooed the kid away, and he wandered around the one-room lodge, pausing in front of a wall calendar featuring cowgirls wearing nothing but boots and hats. When he was done with July, he studied August and September, too.

The clerk said his name was Rusty or maybe Dusty. He handed over a key to number seven and told me about the great horned owl that called the fence post home.

"Got a golden eagle, too, in the blue spruce trees out back. Come daylight, you'll get a gander at him if you want. Got a set of talons could tear your head off. Son of

a gun dives after mice. Clocked that sucker with a radar
gun at a hundred fifty miles an hour in his dive. Can you
beat that?''

"Not on my best day," I said.

"Got a couple little falcons out there, too. Called kes-
trels around here. They'll eat whatever the eagle misses.
Raptors, that's what the fellow called them. Birds of prey,
flesh eaters." He studied me a moment. "Will you be
wanting binoculars, or you got your own?"

I didn't know what he meant.

"We got people come out here to ride the horses, some
to see the birds. Which is it with you, Mr. Lassiter?"

I might have been bleary-eyed and muscle-cramped
from the trip. I might have had jet lag and a sour stomach,
but I knew the answer. "The raptors," I said. "I came for
the birds of prey."

"I'm *ow-dee*," Kip said.

"Huh?"

"*Ow-dee*, like outta here." Kip gestured around the
small cottage. "What's missing from this picture?"

I looked around. Two single beds whose springs had
sprung. A nightstand with a two-bulb reading lamp. A couple of ersatz Frederic Remington prints of cowboys busting
broncos and branding steers. A porcelain sink stained or-
angish-brown under the faucet, a shower and toilet tucked
behind a partition.

"I don't know, Kip. I'm going to sleep."

"A TV! Uncle Jake, there's no TV!"

I was already peeled down to my Jockey shorts and was
stripping a paper-thin brown blanket off the bed. "We've
had enough entertainment for one day. Lights out, Kip. Go
to bed."

"Without a TV! Without dinner! I'm hungry, Uncle
Jake. We haven't eaten anything since the pork rinds and
root beer at the gas station."

"There's a machine with peanut butter crackers at the

lodge. If that's not enough, ask the horned owl to share his dinner with you.''

He said something to me, probably some eleven-year-old sassified backtalk, but I was falling toward the squashed pillow, already drifting off to dreams of mice and falcons, wondering which I was.

The Pitkin County Courthouse is a hundred-year-old red-brick building that sits formidably on Main Street. Court-house architecture is intended to represent strength and permanence and a certain majesty of the law that mortar and stone can convey better than the weak-willed Homo sapiens who ply their trade therein. This one was a solid building that would be considered squat, if not for a faintly baroque tower that might have been the battlement of a castle. The American and Colorado flags flew atop the tower, crackling in the early-morning breeze.

Rosebushes crept up a knee-high iron fence that surrounded the building, and spruce and aspen trees provided a measure of shade. On the lawn was the obligatory statue honoring local lads who died in various wars, and above the entrance was Lady Justice.

Inside were plaques naming 4-H champions, old black-and-white photos of cowboys, miners, and farmers at work. The local police and county sheriff's offices were in the basement, the county treasurer, the county commission, and tax assessor's offices were on the first floor. Hardwood stairs with a polished balustraded railing led to the court-room on the second floor, but my business wasn't there.

I went into the tax assessor's office where a pleasant young woman in jeans and a cotton sweater hoisted a ledger book off a shelf for me. The book had the musty smell of age and the heft of a decent-sized barbell. The walls were decorated with framed deeds from the 1800s, plat maps, and the other official memorabilia of the town.

Before opening the book, I studied a framed map of what looked like the town maybe a hundred years ago. There was the courthouse, just where it is now, at the corner of Main and Galena. But there was something odd.

"What are those lines going through the streets?" I asked the woman, who sat nearby, using a fountain pen to make entries in another ledger.

She followed my gaze to the framed map. "Mines."

I read some of the names aloud. " 'Durant, Little Nell, Enterprise, Little Mack, Pride of the Hills, Mollie Gibson, Copperopolis, Esperanza.' I thought the mines were in the mountains, but some of the tunnels go right under Main Street."

"That's right," she said. "The shafts generally were up on the slopes of the mountains, but once they got as deep as they were going to go, the tunnels started branching in all directions, like the streets of a town that hasn't been planned too well. We've got some right below the courthouse here. Some old-timers say you could get from Smuggler Mountain over to Aspen Mountain and never see the light of day. Just go down the Mollie Gibson shaft, take the right tunnels and come up the Compromise. The skiers on Aspen Mountain don't know it, but underneath all that snow are dozens of shafts and tunnels. They're still there, maybe some filled with water, some with rotting timbers, but there are locals hereabouts who own the claims and are just waiting for the price of silver to rise."

"And if it does?"

"Well, wouldn't it be interesting if the ski companies could make more money leasing the land to miners, instead of hitting up tourists for fifty bucks a day for the lift?"

While I pondered that, I opened the plat book and thumbed some pages until I found K. C. Cimarron's parcel, all properly described in the arcane language of metes and bounds and "running thence" of the property rolls. This little side excursion might not have been necessary if I hadn't botched it with the clerk at the ranch this morning. While Kip was eating some dry corn flakes from the box, I asked the skinny clerk, who must have worked all night, if he'd ever run across my buddy, Kit Carson Cimarron.

"You a friend of that big ole hoss?" he asked, dropping

ashes from his cigarette onto the scarred counter.

His tone was neutral, giving nothing away. Cimarron could have been his cousin or someone he hated, or both.

I put on my amiable, out-of-towner face. "Yeah, I met him back in my skiing days."

He exhaled a puff of smoke at me. "Never heard of him skiing. Horses, sure. 'Course, ole Kit needs one about the size of an elephant."

Ole Kit. Maybe these two guys skinned mules together, whatever the hell mule skinning was.

"No, *I* was skiing. He was ranching and, as I recall it, always talking about buried treasure, or some such stuff."

That loosened up his face a bit. "Yeah, that's ole Kit. The dreamer, that's what we call him. Spent a fortune, hell two fortunes, on wild-goose chases. Years ago, I remember the town offered a five-thousand-dollar reward for anyone who could find the Silver Queen. Ole Kit musta spent a hundred thousand hunting for her, but the damn thing hadn't been seen since the Chicago World's Fair of 1893. I could understand it if ole Kit could profit from it, but hell, she would have gone to the town."

"The Silver Queen," I said. It was more of a question, but what I was really thinking about was the clanging dissonance of Kit Carson Cimarron, the civic booster and historical preservationist, and Kit Carson Cimarron, the coldly efficient mugger and partner of Blinky Baroso.

"A statue made of silver from the biggest damn nugget ever found," the clerk continued, "more than a ton, damn near a hundred percent pure. The mining folks got together and made this silver lady, had some gold and diamonds in her too, and some crystals and precious stones for her eyes, the way I hear tell. Anyway, they took her to the World's Fair, but she disappeared, and ever since, the town wants her back."

"Sounds like some wise guys may have melted her down for the metals and stones."

"Sure does, and everybody in these parts knows it, except ole Kit. That's what I mean, a dreamer."

"Yeah, that's him," I agreed. "Anyway, I don't see his name in the phone book, and I was wondering where I could find him."

The clerk squinted at me. If Kip hadn't been scarfing down a second box of corn flakes, he would have said ole Rusty/Dusty was into his Clint Eastwood mode. "Same place as always," the clerk allowed.

"Same place as always," I repeated, as if savoring rich memories. "The old ranch, I suppose."

"Well, not the old ranch off Frying Pan Road just over the Eagle County line. That was Kit's daddy's, and they lost that, oh hell, thirty years ago."

"Well, the new ranch, then," I said.

"It ain't hardly new," he corrected me.

"Not hardly," I acknowledged.

"Nice piece of property though, what with Woody Creek and all."

"Mighty nice," I concurred.

I stopped asking questions, and he stopped not answering them, and then I came to the courthouse, dropping off Kip in a video arcade in the middle of the town. I had checked a map and found Woody Creek, the town, plus Woody Creek, the creek, plus two other streams, Little Woody Creek and Dry Woody Creek. Which is why I needed to see the property records.

And there it was. K. C. Cimarron, the fee simple owner of the Red Canyon Ranch, about six hundred acres not far from where Woody Creek and the Roaring Fork River meet. He was up to date on his taxes, and checking the lien ledgers, I saw he owned the land free and clear. In another office, I found he was a registered voter, independent, and hadn't missed an election in over ten years.

An upstanding citizen, this K. C. Cimarron. At least in these parts. But we know differently, don't we, ole Kit? I forced myself to remember everything about him. I didn't get a good look at Cimarron on that dark, dreadful night, but I remembered the mass of him, the sheer raw tonnage. And I remembered his voice.

"Where is he? Where's Baroso?" That's what he said first, and I remembered the deep, gravelly tone of a big man with a deep chest. It was a voice that demanded attention, and attention was surely paid to such a man.

I had answered that I didn't know, and then he had asked Jo Jo the same question. Which meant Socolow was right about something. Either Cimarron didn't kill Blinky, or he was going to a lot of trouble to make it look like he didn't.

Then, just before he stomped my hand, he said something that wasn't a question at all. "Stay out of my affairs, lawyer! Stay out of my affairs, or you're a dead man."

Just like in school, my memory was pretty good, but I wasn't great at following instructions.

It was a five-minute walk from the courthouse to the arcade, where I picked up a juvenile delinquent who was banging away at a video game where steroid-pumped wrestlers removed each other's spines. I dragged him out, and he responded by saying I was a "goober-throwing major tude," which I took as a compliment and thanked him.

"Where we going?" Kip asked. "I was just about to pin the Mountain Man."

"We're going to visit a cowboy."

"Oh, the one who stole your babe."

"I beg your pardon."

"Granny told me. When you were spaced out on the medicine, Granny told me about the lady lawyer you've got the hots for, but this dude swooped her away. So, when you said we were coming out here and you were going to switch courses, I knew the babe figured into it."

"You're a pretty bright kid, aren't you?" I asked, as we reached our car, parked in front of a shop where mannequins in mink coats smiled regally at us from the display window.

"It runs in the family," he said.

No wonder I liked this kid.

We got in, and I aimed the rental convertible northwest on Route 82. The air was cool and dry. The sun was shining, plump white clouds were scudding by, and the meadows were filled with bright wildflowers. It seemed like a fine day to see if Mr. K. C. Cimarron was as good as his word.

16

🐚

Fool Me Twice

There were red bluffs along the winding dirt road that led from the entrance to the ranch house. There were rolling fields of scrawny cattle. Along the road, a narrow stream gurgled and tumbled over black and brown boulders. But as far as I could tell, there was no canyon at the Red Canyon Ranch.

A short, swarthy woman in a starched white dress and a red apron opened the door. She was wiping flour from her hands onto the apron. "*¿Lo puedo ayudar?*"

"*Por favor se encuentra el Señor Cimarron,*" I said, exhausting my extensive Spanish vocabulary.

Behind her, I could see a foyer of red Mexican tile. A buffalo head was mounted on the far wall, and beneath it, two crossed rifles with a vaguely antique look were enclosed in a glass case. Just off the foyer was a living room with a brick fireplace and a bearskin rug in front of a sofa carved from heavy logs. A nice place if you're into southwestern postmodern macho.

"*Señor Cimarron, está en el establo,*" she said, indicating the direction with a tilt of the head.

She spoke deliberately, either because she figured me for the gringo I was, or because Mexican Spanish is slower than what I'm used to in Little Havana.

I gave her my best *gracias,* then Kip and I walked along a flagstone path from the main house to the barn, a huge weathered structure up a small incline. Twenty yards away, I heard what sounded at first like a muffled gunshot. Instinctively, I moved in front of Kip, shielding him with my body. "Get real, Uncle Jake," he said, darting by me.

Another muffled *whomp,* and then two more at regular intervals, maybe three seconds apart. A whinnying horse, then another *whomp, whomp.*

A door wide enough to accommodate a tractor trailer was open, and we walked in. Smells of moist hay and creosote, the tang of molasses feed mixed with manure. A buzz of horseflies, a bank of stalls, horses pawing the dirt floor, tails swishing. Weathered saddles, harnesses, and saddlebags hung from wooden pegs in the walls. Blankets and feed bags were stacked in neat piles. A ladder led to a loft sagging with bales of hay. And on a wooden stepladder against one wall, a man with his back to me, a man in boots, dirt-stained jeans, a wide leather belt, a red plaid shirt with sleeves rolled up the elbows. A man who, on the third step of the ladder, looked about ten feet tall and as wide . . . well, as wide as the broad side of a barn.

With his left hand, he was bracing a four-by-eight-foot piece of three-quarter-inch plywood against a window frame. With his right hand, he was holding a stud gun. Maybe it wasn't as impressive a feat as say, tossing a shotput with one hand and dunking a basketball with another, but it showed strength and a certain agility. *Whomp.* Another nail jolted into the plywood and wall beneath. The stud gun did not seem to recoil, but stayed firmly planted in his meaty right hand.

With his back still to me, he said, "You're Lassiter, aren't you?"

"Guilty as charged," I said.

He turned around and we studied each other. He had a bushy mustache that reminded me of Buck Buchanan, an old defensive lineman for Kansas City. His hair was long and gray and swept straight back, falling over his ears, and curling up slightly at the nape of his neck. The overall impression was of a gunfighter from the old West, Kirk Douglas maybe, but twice as big.

Our chemistry was as immediate as the mongoose and the snake. We hated each other. He had inflicted a great deal of pain on me. This morning, in the early chill, my hand had been stiff, a reminder as sure as a dueling scar of the searing eternity of personal violence. This man, this towering menace of a man, had bruised and dented me.

Which was also why I was here, I now knew. Sure, clearing my name had something to do with it, and so did coming after Jo Jo. But there was something else too. I needed to prove to myself that he hadn't broken me. So I stood there in khaki slacks and Top-Siders without socks and an old Penn State sweatshirt looking at this big galoot who happened to be holding a lethal weapon, making me wonder why I chose a day when he was nailing instead of painting.

"Ever use a stud gun, Lassiter?"

"Nah. I usually just drive nails with my forehead."

"I don't doubt it." He turned away and resumed working, but it didn't keep him from talking. "When my daddy built this barn, he framed the first floor with concrete beams. Not concrete blocks, mind you, but solid poured concrete. That's how my daddy was, and that's how I am. Do you follow me?"

"Sure, some guys got shit for brains. You got concrete."

"You trying to rile me?"

"No, I'm trying to insult your intelligence, but it's a daunting task."

He was still on the ladder, so I couldn't get a precise idea of his height, but he had to go six seven, maybe six eight. As for his weight, it probably wasn't more than your average side of beef. If you want to judge a man's mass, look at his wrists or ankles. It'll tell you the size of the frame. I couldn't see his ankles, but the wrists were telephone poles attached to forearms cabled with veins, forearms bigger than most men's biceps. The shoulders were no larger than a double-wide mobile home, the chest a rain barrel. He had the look of brawny muscle built by hard work, not by pumping iron. The only thing that detracted from the look of complete physicality was his belly. It had grown over the top of his silver-and-turquoise belt buckle. Grown big, not soft. There is a difference.

If I were to guess, I would say that ten years ago, he was an extremely fit and dangerous two hundred eighty pounds, and now he was about three ten, and still dangerous.

Whomp.

"Damn," he muttered. "Out of bullets. Now, you got your stud guns that work off an air compressor and a clip that holds forty or fifty nails. But like I said, this is solid concrete, so I use the gun powered by .27-caliber bullets. Clip only holds ten bullets, and you got to put each nail in separately, but I don't mind. Whatever it takes, however long it takes, do the job right. That's how I live my life, Lassiter. How do you live yours?"

"One day at a time."

He gestured in Kip's direction. "Who's this, your bodyguard?"

"My nephew," I said.

"When you grow up, you gonna be a piss-ant lawyer like your uncle?" he asked.

"No," Kip answered, "I'm going to be an entertainment lawyer. Beats the hell out of being a shit-kicking cowboy."

Now where did he learn to talk like that? I'd have to bring it up with Granny.

Cimarron slipped a clip of bullets into the stud gun, took a nail from his pocket and shoved it into the barrel. "Josefina told me I should be expecting you. Said you'd cause trouble but that I shouldn't start anything. I promised her I wouldn't unless you asked for it."

"Where is she?"

"In town at the music festival. Spends all day there.

They got more concerts in that little town than a dog's got fleas.''

Cimarron turned back to the plywood, whipping the heavy nail gun as if it were a revolver, and added a *whomp*, either for extra stability or to deliver a message. "Damned hailstorm broke three windows, scared the shit out of the cattle and the summer tourists. Not that it bothers me when the tourists get caught in the rain or avalanches for that matter. Are you one of those assholes who straps boards on his feet, races down the mountain, then waits for a ride back up so he can do it all over again?''

"I was, until my third knee operation.''

He came down from the ladder and walked toward us, the nail gun still in his hand. "Skiers!" He spit into a stall and an Appaloosa gave him a dirty look. I tried to imagine Jo Jo with this guy, but it just didn't compute.

"What a waste of time, what a piss-poor use of our resources," he was saying. "You know what's under the ski slopes on Ajax, what you tourists call Aspen Mountain?''

"Shafts and tunnels," I said, displaying my knowledge so recently gained. "Silver mines crisscrossing under the town from one mountain to the other.''

He nodded and seemed surprised. "Right. That's our history, the history of the West. Mines and small towns grown big with gold and silver. Now what do we have, million-dollar condos and music tents and jugglers and little red wagons selling crepes with cinnamon and bananas, and traffic jams because assholes from Miami and Beverly Hills have taken over.''

"The Silver Queen," I said. "That's part of your past, too.''

His eyes narrowed just a bit. "What do you know about it?''

"Enough. You spent some money trying to find her, a statue that disappeared from a World's Fair a hundred plus years ago. It was made from a pure chunk of silver that weighed over a ton.''

"The nugget was taken from the Mollie Gibson on Smuggler Mountain. Hell, it was more like a boulder, weighed twenty-one hundred fifty pounds and assayed out at ninety-six percent pure. Never been anything like it ever, before or since. The town fathers commissioned the statue for the Chicago World's Fair as part of a lobbying effort to keep Congress from demonetizing silver, but it didn't work. The Sherman Act was passed, and that was the end of the silver boom. So the Silver Queen is the perfect symbol of a lost era. Can you understand that?"

"Sure, what I don't understand is you. I didn't figure you for a historical society type."

"There's a lot you don't understand." He put the nail gun on a table of plywood supported by two sawhorses. "How about the two of us have a drink and talk?"

It wasn't quite noon, but Cimarron was pouring bourbon from a cut-glass decanter into crystal tumblers. "What's the little tyke want?"

"Gimme a viskey, ginger ale on the side, and don't be stingy, bay-bee," the little tyke answered.

"What?"

I gave Kip the crossed-arms signal for declining a penalty. "He doesn't care for your Garbo, kid, so play it straight."

"Okay, Liberty Valance, gimme a Grolsch," Kip ordered.

We had taken the stone path back to the house, walked through the foyer past the buffalo and the antique rifles, through the living room, around the bearskin rug, and were in a room with a green felt pocket billiards table, and old, cracked leather chairs.

"Will a root beer do?" the big man asked.

Kip grimaced. "If that's all you've got, bartender, make it a double."

I took a hit on the warm bourbon. Cimarron didn't offer ice, and I didn't ask. He racked the balls, offered me a choice of cues and games. I chose eight ball.

''What should we play for,'' I asked, ''money, stock . . .
Jo Jo?''

''She said you make lousy jokes, and she was right. Or
maybe I don't have much of a sense of humor. I don't joke
about Josefina.''

''What *do* you joke about?''

''There isn't much I find funny.''

''Maybe you should loosen up,'' Kip said.

''What's that supposed to mean?'' Cimarron asked. We
were double-teaming him. If it got rough, maybe Kip could
bite him in the ankle.

''Nothing,'' Kip said, trying to suppress his malicious
grin, ''except you're so tight, if you stuck a piece of coal
up your ass, in two weeks, you'd have a diamond.''

''What the hell!''

''It's from a movie,'' I explained.

''*Ferris Bueller's Day Off,*'' Kip said.

Cimarron was shaking his head. Then he looked at me.
''I know all about you. You're a trivial man. You couldn't
appreciate a woman of substance like Josefina.''

''Yeah, so what happened to the two of you?''

''That is none of your concern, but the life I can give
her is of far greater significance than what you can do. For
most of your life, you played a game, a *game*! Do you
even have a philosophy?''

''Sure. I try to go through life doing the least damage
possible. Having fun without hurting anyone, maybe doing
a little good along the way, but without taking myself too
seriously.''

''Having fun! I don't know what Josefina ever saw in
you . . .''

Funny, that's what I was thinking about him, but now,
he was starting to sound like her. Maybe they had more
in common than I thought.

''. . . unless it was the chance to reform you, make you
over, but it didn't work, and you ended up in cahoots with
her worthless brother.''

He chalked a cue stick, leaned over the table and broke,

sending balls ricocheting with a *crack* like a rifle shot. The fourteen ball plopped into a corner pocket.

"High balls," Cimarron said, a little like the way we played the game at home. Without looking at me, he knocked in the ten, fifteen, and nine, the last on a nifty bank shot that threaded the four and the seven. He lifted his head from the table and gestured with the cue stick toward a black-and-white photo on the far wall. "There she is, part of our legacy."

I walked over to the wall and studied the Silver Queen. The lady wore a crown and looked a little like the Statue of Liberty, but she was riding in a chariot with giant wheels. The front of the chariot resembled the prow of a ship, and two little Greek god types ran alongside, wearing what looked like diapers. They carried cornucopias that seemed to be overflowing with coins. The queen held a scepter topped by a star and a gigantic silver dollar. Under the photo was a glass-enclosed clipping from the *Aspen Times* dated March 1893. It was a review of the sculpture. "A noble work of art, majestic in proportions . . ."

I turned around in time to see Cimarron whack the thirteen ball into a side pocket, stopping the cue ball just short of dropping in.

"It's big," I said, after a moment. "Big and gaudy. It would be hard to say beautiful."

"Victorian style, a symbol of the end of that era, too," he explained, patiently. "Eighteen feet high. The face, bust, and arms are of solid silver. The drapery is studded with precious stones. Her hair is glass. The chariot is finished in stripes of dark minerals and crystals. The two winged gods represent Plutus, carrying riches. One horn overflows with gold, the other silver. The pillars are made of burnished silver, crystals, and a mosaic of minerals."

"What's it worth?"

Cimarron laughed, bent low over the table, and sent the eleven ball careening into the four—one of mine—which ended in a side pocket. "Damn."

I chalked a cue stick while he talked. "Who knows what

it's worth? Who cares? It's the history of this town, this state, and I wanted to find it, preserve it."

I hit the cue ball too high and knocked it and the six into a corner pocket. "How could it disappear from the World's Fair?"

"It didn't. That's one of the misconceptions. The Queen came back from the fair and was put on display at the Mineral Palace in Pueblo, which was eventually torn down. Nobody knows what happened to the silver lady. She just disappeared."

Cimarron ran out the rest of the high balls and was focusing on the eight.

"I still don't get you," I said. "I mean, what are you doing as partners with Blinky Baroso?"

He lifted his head and looked at me with one eye squinted shut. "What are you doing as his lawyer?"

"That's different."

"Hah!" He nailed the eight on a line and clunked it into a corner pocket.

Kip made a sucking sound on the straw in his root beer. "You shoot a mean game of pool, fat man."

Cimarron turned toward him, either puzzled or angry, I couldn't tell which.

"Paul Newman," Kip explained.

"My first deal with Baroso was strictly legitimate," Cimarron said, turning back to me. "Sunken treasure in the Keys. There was no need to oversubscribe the stock. Hell, I'd been the majority shareholder in the company that had located the wrecks. I'd been to the old naval library in Madrid, had examined the manifests of the ship. I knew every gold bar on her, every piece of jewelry. But we ran out of cash before we could salvage. It was so damn foolish of Baroso, but he just didn't believe we'd find her. I would have never done business with him again if I hadn't gotten involved with Josefina."

Funny. I probably would have stopped representing Blinky except for her. "She encouraged you?"

"Josefina thought I could straighten him out, just like she thought you could."

"That was a long time ago."

"Maybe so, but I went back to Baroso when I needed to raise cash for the new operation up here. I've got land, and I've got maps and claims, but I needed the start-up money. I told him, no funny business, and he said not to worry, he'd get his lawyer to handle the money. He wouldn't make a move without his lawyer, good old reliable Jake Lassiter, that's what he said."

"Good old reliable Nathan ... Nathan, Nathan Detroit," Kip sang out.

"Well, that's news to me," I told Cimarron, ignoring Kip. "I defended Blinky in his criminal cases, but I never had anything to do with the business. You could have called me. You could have checked it out."

"Sure I could have done a lot of things, but I wanted the deal. I told myself I did it for the money he could raise, but lately I think I did it for Josefina. Anyway, that's what happened. I checked you out with her, and she said you were all right. I didn't even mind the fact that the two of you had a past. With me, business comes first. Anyway, my lawyers here set everything up, reasonable finder's fees for the promoters, stock subscription agreements, two million dollars' key man life insurance on Baroso and me, restrictions on selling any of our shares, except to each other. Everything was in order."

"For what, to find buried treasure? To chase stories told by drunks and braggarts. If your maps were real, these mountains would be crawling with technicians from major companies. The place would be swarming with helicopters and laser beams."

"Are you calling me a fool?" His voice had lost its hospitality.

"No, I just think when you stumbled over a bag of twenty-dollar gold pieces, it addled your brain. This new project will turn out just like the Silver Queen. These poor slobs who bought shares would lose their money either way, whether Blinky stole it or not.''

"You know, once in a bar down in Carbondale, a man called me crazy. I was standing there having a beer, minding my own business, and this fellow—drove a semi for a living—came up to me. 'You're that big bastard chasing after Coronado's gold, ain't you?' I just ignored him, but he kept coming after me, pointing at me, telling his friends I was the biggest fool in the county. He was about your size, maybe a little smaller through the shoulders. Finally, I just picked him up by the collar and lifted him off his feet. Had a ceiling fan in there, and it bashed him across the ear. 'Course the blades stopped then, so I let him down, then hoisted him back up, about a dozen times till he had blood running out his nose and each of his ears.''

"You're partial to ceiling fans, aren't you, Cimarron? You ever tell Abe Socolow that story?''

"What's that supposed to mean?''

"Kyle Hornback.''

"You think I killed him?''

"Well I know *I* didn't.''

"Think about it, Lassiter. Hornback came clean with me. Admitted they'd been selling the same stock three or four times. Why would I kill him?''

"*That's* why.''

"No, you got me wrong. I was indebted to him. By nature, I'm not a violent man.''

"You could have fooled me. What the hell were you doing in Jo Jo's house when you tap-danced on my forehead?''

He didn't answer for a moment. "Have you ever been so angry you could have killed someone?''

I didn't think he wanted an answer, so I didn't disappoint him.

"Anger beyond anything you'd ever known,'' he continued. "I was enraged at Baroso, at Josefina, at you, a man I'd never seen. And at me, too. I'd been taken by that slippery son of a bitch the second time. You know the expression 'fool me once, shame on you.' "

"Fool me twice, shame on me," I said.

"No. Fool me twice, you're dead. I'd been made a fool by Baroso and you, and there you were with Josefina. Like I said, Hornback told me what they'd been up to, and I advised him to go to the authorities. Send Baroso to jail, let the chips fall where they may."

"So who killed him?"

"I figured you did. You're the guy who cooked the books. Your dick was on the chopping block."

"Cimarron, let me try this one time in simple, straight-forward English. I'm Blinky's lawyer, that's all. I didn't cook the books, hoodwink the investors, or steal the money. And I sure as hell didn't kill anybody."

"So you say, but your client sold the outside stock three times over, and the money is missing. There's a hundred fifty thousand in money I put up that was taken from the company account the day before Baroso disappeared. So-colow tells me half that amount showed up in your bank account in Miami."

"Like I told Socolow, I don't know anything about the deposit, except I didn't make it."

"Who did?"

"Probably Blinky, but if he's dead, we may never know."

"I'd bet you a hundred head of Hereford he's sitting by a swimming pool somewhere with about one-point-nine million of investors' money. I figure the two of you plan to split it."

"You're wrong again," I told him.

"That's what Josefina tells me, and so far, I've been listening. That's why I didn't throw you in the Roaring Fork when you showed up here. I've been listening real good 'cause I love that woman and respect her, too. I'll be honest with you. She doesn't know what to do. She's been sleeping in the guest room, and we've been like brother and sister since she got back. She wanted to see if we could be friends first, then lovers again. But she's got you on her mind.''

"I knew her before you did.''

"You lost her. She came to me. She's mine.''

I laughed at him, and he didn't like it. I didn't care. "Maybe the word hasn't gotten all the way to the Rockies, but a woman's not a mining claim. You don't own her.''

"She belongs here just like my heifers and my horses, and I'm not going to lose her.''

"Hey, pal, that's her choice, not yours.''

"That's right, but she's going to make that choice without any interference from you.''

"What's the matter, can't stand the competition?''

"Lassiter, I promised Josefina I wouldn't hurt you if you showed up here, even though you stole my money and tried to steal my lady.''

"Hey, I didn't—''

"Shut up, lawyer, or football player, or skier, or whatever other fool thing you are. I've fulfilled my promise. I told Josefina I'd offer you a drink and have a little chat and not muss up your hair, though if you must know, I've got an itch to kick your face in. Now, here's the way it is. You're going to get the hell off my property, and out of Pitkin County, and out of the state of Colorado because—''

"This territory ain't big enough for the two of us," Kip chimed in.

"Because if you don't," Cimarron said evenly, "I'm going to bust you up.''

"If that's supposed to scare me, you better try again," I said. "We're all going to die, and soon, in a celestial blink of an eye, so there's no use being scared. You come at me, and I'll do what I have to do. I'll chop you in half with an ax if I have to.''

"I'm only going to tell you this once, Lassiter. You come sniffing around Josefina, I mean if you're in the same area code, I'm going to break you like a twig.''

With that, he split his pool cue in two. He didn't break

it across his knee or muscle it with two hands. He just held it in one hand, his thumb straight up the shaft, and he snapped it clean in two.

Like a twig.

17

All Angered Up

"I'm confused."

"Why, Uncle Jake?"

"Coming up here, I thought Cimarron was either a thief or a killer or both."

"Yeah?"

"Well, he's rough around the edges, all right, and he's got a temper. But he's not the thug I thought he was. He's Kiwanis man of the year or something, and he really believes this buried treasure stuff."

"So?"

"Whoa! Is this thing rocking or what?"

"Take it easy, Uncle Jake. It's just the wind."

"There it goes again. Hey, I even close my eyes on a ski lift."

We were riding to the top of Aspen Mountain—or Ajax, if you prefer—on the Silver Queen gondola. Yeah, that's the name, in case I wasn't already dwelling on Cimarron's stories. Suspended from a cable, our enclosed car was a good fifty feet above the top of a strand of healthy spruce trees that were a good eighty feet tall themselves. Strong wind gusts pushed us from side to side. Below, some hikers took the hard way, straight up the steep face of the ski slopes, now green with thick grass and spotted with yellow sunflowers. Behind us, the town of Aspen faded away. To our left were the snowcapped mountains leading to the Continental Divide.

"We should have gotten some aerobic exercise by hiking up," I said, gripping the handrail with whitened knuckles.

"Uncle Jake, are you afraid of heights like Jimmy Stewart in *Vertigo*?"

"I wouldn't say afraid. More like concerned. I'm concerned about heights."

We were slowing down, approaching the port at the top of the mountain. "Something else, too. Cimarron *really* thinks I conspired with Blinky to defraud him."

"How do you know?"

"I can tell, Kippers. This is what I do for a living. I ask questions and listen to the answers, and I watch. Boy, do I watch. There are some very good liars and some people who can delude themselves into believing anything they want. They're hell on polygraphs, juries, and spouses. But this guy didn't tell a fib, not one I could catch."

The gondola bucked into a V-shaped catching device, slowed down, and the door automatically slid open. We stepped out, and a middle-aged couple bundled into ski jackets climbed in. It had been sunny and in the mid-seventies in town. It was still sunny up here, but a stiff wind was blowing, and the temperature had plummeted twenty degrees.

I followed Kip, who can sense the proximity of food, and we headed to the snack bar where he ordered a hot chocolate and a cheeseburger. We sat at an outdoor table, looking down into the valley.

"The other thing, unless he's the world's greatest actor, Cimarron really thinks I killed Hornback."

"So what? You didn't, did you, Uncle Jake?"

"Of course not. But what it means is that Cimarron didn't kill him, either."

"So who did? And what happened to Mr. Baroso?"

"Kip my boy, that's what we're going to find out."

While Kip was chomping his burger, I found a pay phone and dialed a familiar number, putting the charge on a credit card. When he answered, barking his last name, I said, "Hello, Abe, coerce any confessions today?"

"Jake! Jake, goddamnit, where are you? No, strike that. I know where you are. You're harassing my witness. Cimarron called me less than an hour ago. What do you think you're doing?"

"Seeking the truth, Abe, just like Charlie Riggs always taught me."

"No, you're not. You're a fleeing felon, evading arrest, surreptitiously departing the jurisdiction after I cut you a break. You're obstructing justice and threatening witnesses."

"That's bull."

"Yeah, on this very day, did you or did you not threaten to take a hatchet to my last living witness?"

"I think I said ax."

"Damn you! Do I have to put guards around Cimarron?"

"Nah, he does a pretty good job of protecting himself."

Socolow snorted, the wet sound of a dolphin clearing its blowhole. "Jake, you know I'm sitting on a sealed indictment, naming you for the murder of Kyle Hornback."

"I figured."

"I can courier it to the Aspen police. We'd have you extradited in a week."

"Give me a couple of days, Abe. I'll call you."

"What! You think this is like scheduling lunch? You've been indicted for murder one, a capital fucking crime. It took the grand jury about fifteen minutes. Can you get that through your thick skull?"

"Listen to me, Abe. I'm standing on top of a mountain at maybe eleven thousand feet. In the winter, it's one of the best ski slopes in the country. In the summer, it's filled with hikers and picnickers. Abe, have you ever seen a columbine?"

"A what?"

"A wildflower that grows up here. Some are yellow, like buttercups. Some are lavender. Anyway, the mountain is blazing with wildflowers now. In the winter, there's six feet of snow, and under the ground, winter or summer, under my feet right now are mine shafts and tunnels. Dozens of them, hell, hundreds of them, and there's still silver in there, and maybe buried treasure and who knows what?"

"Jake, what the hell are you talking about?"

"I don't think Cimarron killed Hornback."

"Neither do I. Neither do twenty-three members of the grand jury. So now, it's unanimous."

"But it's so screwy, Abe. Cimarron's the one who had the motive. Hornback and Blinky cheated him, and the guy's got a fearsome temper. I've got a couple of mending metacarpals to prove it. Blinky cheated him twice, and Cimarron told me he'd kill a man for that. Something else, Abe. Cimarron and Blinky had two-million-dollar key man insurance policies on each other's lives. That would just about cover the amount of money Cimarron thinks Blinky stole."

"What are you saying, that Cimarron didn't kill Hornback, but he killed Baroso?"

"He had the motive, but I still don't think so. I just have this feeling about Cimarron, that he really sees himself as the victim and Blinky and me as the bad guys. I don't think he killed anyone."

"You're not helping your case any. If Cimarron didn't do it, who did?"

"I don't know, but whoever's setting me up has got to be the one . . ."

A thought was racing around the perimeter of my brain. I struggled to get a rope around it and bring it in.

". . . Abe, that deposit into my account, where'd it come from?"

"Wire transfer from the Rocky Mountain corporate account at Florida Southern Bank."

"Who authorized it?"

"You did, dummy! That's the nail in the coffin."

"I didn't. I couldn't have. I had no signatory powers over the account. I never even knew what bank it was in."

"Nice try, Jake, but you filled out a signature card when the account was opened, and the signature on the wire transfer request matched."

"Abe, I'm telling you I never signed any card or transfer request or anything. If they match, it's only because the same forger did them both. I was set up the day the Rocky Mountain Treasures bank account was opened."

"Pretty farfetched, Jake."

"Who opened the corporate account?"

I heard a rustling of papers at the other end of the line. "Louis X. Baroso, last December nineteenth."

"Blinky. Of course, who else would it be?"

"A week later, he mailed in a signature card signed by Cimarron and you."

"No, *forged* by Blinky."

"So you say. Well, we can have a handwriting expert take a look at it."

I was still chasing the shadow of an idea. "They still needed my bank account number."

"What?"

"Abe, the night Hornback was killed, Kip said someone came up to my bedroom."

"Right. That's where they got your necktie."

"They got more than that. There's a desk in my bedroom by the window. In the middle drawer, along with last year's Christmas cards, is my checkbook. Abe, I want you to dust for prints. There shouldn't be any latents, except mine."

"You expect to find Blinky's greasy thumb? Did he kill Hornback, too? As I recall, you're the one who said he wasn't capable."

"Abe, this is really getting complicated."

"You're trying too hard. Come on in, Jake. You're just going to make it worse for yourself."

"Worse! How?"

There was a faint buzzing on the long-distance line. "I don't know," Abe Socolow said, "but I'm sure you'll find a way."

The ride down the mountain seemed to take longer, but that's always the way it is when you're in a hurry. I had parked the car on Durant Street near the Little Nell Hotel, and I told Kip to hustle. He did, and we both hopped into the rental convertible without opening the doors.

I drove north on Spring Street to Main, turned left, passed the courthouse, the old Hotel Jerome, the Sardy House, and the Christmas Inn, turned right on Third Street and parked just behind the music tent. It hadn't taken five minutes, one of the joys of small towns.

"What's up?" Kip asked.

"A little culture for you, my boy."

There were maybe eight hundred people half filling the place. We took seats in the rear, near the main entrance, Kip pausing long enough to fill his pocket with candied throat lozenges thoughtfully provided at the door.

"What is this?" Kip asked.

I looked toward the stage. "A couple of women playing violins," I said, providing expert commentary.

"A violin and a viola," whispered the man next to me. He had silver hair, a matching mustache, and wore a tweed sports jacket with elbow patches. His eyes were closed, and his head swayed gently to the music.

"That's what I meant," I whispered back. "We miss anything?"

He didn't speak until the music stopped and people applauded, and the violinists—or is one a *viola*-ist?—took slight bows. "I should say so," the man said, eyes open now. "You missed all of Mozart's K. 423 in G, and quite marvelous it was, filled with contrapuntal ingenuity, enhanced by double stops, a wonderful piece of didactic, étudelike virtuosity."

"It's one of my favorites," I allowed.

"Well then, you will appreciate K. 424 in B-flat. It's next."

In a few moments, they started playing again, and in my expert opinion, they sounded swell. I walked down the aisle, crossed in front of the stage, and up another aisle. I caught a few stares, but most people seemed entranced. Finally, halfway up on the right-hand side, there she was.

Jo Jo Baroso was wearing jeans and a long-sleeve green cotton blouse covered by a red Mexican serape. She wore no makeup, and her dark hair was pulled straight back. She would have looked about eighteen years old, but there were dark circles under her eyes and her face, even in quiet repose, seemed to convey a profound sadness.

I slid into the seat next to her. "I'm partial to violas, how about you?"

A tremor seemed to go through her body. She reached for my hand, the healing one, and pressed it to her cheek, which was cool to the touch. She just held my hand there, letting it gently caress her face. In a moment, twin tears slid down her granite cheekbones. She lowered my hand, leaned close to me, and softly kissed me on the cheek.

"Oh, Jake," she whispered, now grasping my hand with both of hers. "I'm frightened. So much is happening. Simmy has flipped out over all of this. I just don't know what to do."

"Go home with me. Help me prove I didn't kill anybody."

"Is that all?"

"No. Be with me."

"I want to, at least I think I do."

From behind us, a loud *shush*.

"Go now, please," she whispered. "I'll call you later and tell you everything."

"Call me? Why don't we meet somewhere?"

"No, Simmy's watching me like a hawk. I ride every night before dinner. I'll call you from the barn just before dark. Please, trust me."

I told her where we were staying and promised to be in

the room for her call. Then I gathered up Kip, who was dozing peacefully just as the violin, or maybe it was the viola, got to one of those parts of didactic, étudelike virtuosity.

I was sitting in the little cottage at the Lazy Q, waiting.

Thinking.

Worrying.

I thought I heard the floorboards creak on the front step. I opened the door and looked outside.

Nothing.

Getting paranoid.

I shouted to Kip, who was across the road in a grassy field with two kids from a neighboring cottage. Kip was fooling around with the video camera, trying to get some shots of the golden eagle. He waved to me, one of those I'm-having-fun, I'm-not-hungry, don't-bother-me kind of waves.

I went back into the cottage and sat on the sagging bed. Something was nagging at me, something besides the fact I was wanted for Murder One, to say nothing of transporting a juvenile delinquent across state lines. There was an itch I couldn't scratch, a feeling of dread I couldn't contain or even describe.

I had made a mistake with Blinky Baroso. I had gotten too close to him, forgetting he was just another client, and let's face it, a born loser. I had let my guard down because he was Jo Jo's brother.

Pathetic.

Such bad judgment.

Jo Jo had been right about him all along. And right about me, too, I suppose. Just what was the social utility of keeping that crumb out of jail. What was my thanks, anyway, getting set up for murder?

Louis X. Baroso. What a waste. He could have been successful in a legitimate business, but that held no thrill for him. Risking it all and losing it, that was Blinky's style. He was like the slots player who hates to hit the jackpot because it takes so long to put the quarters back in.

Now, who had killed him? If he really was dead. Socolow had told me the blood in the Range Rover was Blinky's, but they never found a body or a trace of other evidence. None of the surf bums saw or heard a thing. Blinky had disappeared, bloodied but seemingly invisible.

And here I was, trying to figure it all out, coming up empty, but filled with a sense of foreboding.

The phone rang, startling me. It took two rings for me to even realize what it was. Get hold of yourself, boy.

"Oh, Jake! Thank God you're there." Her voice was desperate.

"What is it? What's happened?"

"He hit me. Oh God, just like before. He used to knock me around, Jake. He's got such anger in him. I thought it was my fault then, and finally, I couldn't take it anymore. That's why I left him, but he's changed, or I thought he had."

The fury began as a ball of fire in the pit of my stomach and moved up, thickening my chest, constricting my throat. I could barely speak. "Did he hurt you?"

"No. He just does it to inflict pain, to humiliate me. If he ever let loose, I'd be dead."

"Where are you?"

"In the barn. Somebody saw us together at the concert. Either that, or he's having me followed, because he knew I kissed you. It set him off. He threw me across the barn. Jake, I must have flown thirty feet. Thank God for the hay, or I would have broken my neck. Then he lifted me up and slapped me, back and forth, again and—"

"I'm coming over. Wait there."

"No! Please, Jake! I don't want you to see me like this. My face is puffy, and I'm . . . I'm so filthy."

"What?"

"Oh, darling, I didn't want to tell you. He forced me. He tore off my clothes, just ripped them to shreds with his hands. He was crazed, his eyes wild like a rabid animal. He took me, then left me here, filthy and naked and freezing.'' She started to say something else but was racked with sobs. I waited, the heat spreading to the back of my neck, sweat pouring off me. ''Oh, Jake, I feel so stupid, so ashamed.''

''Wait there! Don't move. I'm coming over.''

''No, don't!''

''Jo Jo, I swear I'm going to tear him apart, and when the doctors put him back together, we're going to prosecute.''

''Jake, no! You don't understand. It's more complicated than you realize.''

''I know. You said that before. You said you hadn't told me everything, you were sorry Blinky got me involved in it, and you hoped I would forgive you. When I get there, you can tell me everything.''

''I'll tell you now, darling, but you've got to calm down. I'll be all right. You can't come out here. Simmy's in the house. If he—''

''Don't move,'' I told her again. ''Wait for me.''

I flew out the door, running for the car. Kip was videotaping a mangy dog urinating against a tree. I don't know what I looked like, but Kip turned, at first puzzled, then fearful as he watched me. He left the dog there and raced toward the car.

''Uncle Jake, what's wrong? Your face is all angered up.''

''Huh?''

''That's what Granny says about you. That you're sweet as mother's milk, but watch out if you ever get all angered up.''

From the neighboring cottage, the father of the two boys wandered out, pulling up suspenders over plaid Bermuda shorts.

''Kip, I'm in a hurry, and I don't have time to explain. Stay here.''

I hopped in the car, and as I started the engine, Kip tossed the camera in, then vaulted over the passenger door, just like I taught him. ''Nothin' doin', pardner. Granny also told me that when you're like this, you don't think clearly. You make mistakes, and my job is to help you stay cool.''

''C'mon, Kip, out! This is serious.''

The car was moving, and Kip was buckling his shoulder harness. ''I'm not letting you head into Shinbone all by your lonesome. I'm riding shotgun, Uncle Jake.''

I was aware of Bermuda Shorts watching us argue. ''Kip, this isn't a movie. Now, for the last time, get out!'' I started to unbuckle him.

''I'll scream child abuse,'' Kip said, ''so you might as well gun it before knock-knees there throws himself in front of the car.''

''Kip!''

''You promised never to leave me alone again. Last time—''

''I remember last time,'' I said, hitting the gas.

We tore up clouds of dust as we headed toward the Red Canyon Ranch and what would be my third and final meeting with the last living witness.

18

A Tooth for a Tooth

Granny taught me right from wrong.

I didn't have a father or a mother around, and I didn't pay a lot of attention to teachers, ministers, or United Nations ambassadors. I hung around Key Largo and Islamorada with the kids from the trailer parks. Their idea of fun was to throw rocks at tourists' cars coming down U.S. 1, maybe jimmy Coke machines in their spare time. Their dads—the ones who had them—worked on shrimp boats or road crews, if they worked at all.

For a mentor, it was either Granny or the guys who loafed at the 7-Eleven on Little Pine Road, the place I started drinking beer when I was about Kip's age.

Thank God it was Granny.

She taught me not to cheat, not to steal, and not to hit anyone who hadn't hit me first. She taught me to avoid cruelty in words and deeds. She taught me that black and brown folks were as good as white folks, and many times, a damn sight better.

And when I was a little older, she taught me never to raise a hand to a woman. "Only the lowest kind of trash hits his woman, and don't you fergit it. Only a sniveling weakling, a bottom-feeding gutter rat will ever strike a woman, and no Lassiter ever done it or ever will. You understand?''

I told her I did, and if I ever saw a man abusing a woman, I'd step in and put an end to it right then and there.

"Another thing, too, Jacob. No real man ever forces a woman to do what she don't want to do. A woman who don't want to be touched is *not* to be touched."

I understood that, too. The thought of a man doing violence to a woman, any woman, is repellent to me. The thought of it happening to Jo Jo Baroso filled me with rage.

Another memory came back to me on the drive past Woody Creek. In my first year as an assistant public defender, I was handling domestic violence cases. One of my first clients was a grinning yahoo who had tossed a frying pan filled with sizzling bacon at the woman who lived with him. The grease left a ridge of scar tissue from one eye diagonally across her nose to her upper lip.

"Bitch deserved it," he told me, a cigarette flapping out of the corner of his mouth. "If I told her once, I told her a hundred times to have two six-packs in the fridge, cold and ready. A man comes home from pouring tar on roofs in August, a man is thirsty. She's there making BLTs and she says, 'Sorry, honey, there's only one can left, but you took the car, and I couldn't carry beer, what with the eggs and bread and what all.' So I chugged the can, smashed the empty on her forehead. Bitch just smiled at me, so hell, I picked up the frying pan."

Then he grinned, looking for approval from his state-appointed counsel. Just a couple of guys who understand you have to smack them around once in a while, let them know who's boss.

I'm not real proud of what I did. He was small and wiry and sun-browned from his outdoor work, with a creased face and dumb, blank eyes. He was expecting to cop a plea, maybe get probation, go out drinking with the boys, brag about teaching the bitch a lesson. He wasn't expecting his lawyer to be crazed on the subject of men beating women.

"I'd like you to put out your cigarette," I told him.

He looked around. "Don't see no ashtray."

"I want you to swallow it," I said, placidly.

He gave a nervous little smile, wondering if I was joking. I let him wonder a moment, then came around my desk and yanked him out of his chair by the scruff of his neck. The cigarette fell from his mouth, but I caught it, remembering even now the singe of hot ash in the palm of my hand. His eyes were wide and fearful. I let go of his neck, and with one hand, pinched his jawbone hard, forcing his mouth open. Then, I jammed the cigarette in, hit him under the chin to close his mouth, and yanked back on his neck to tilt his head toward the ceiling.

"Swallow!" I yelled at him. "Swallow, you worthless piece of slime."

I watched his Adam's apple work the butt down his throat, then I let go of him.

The punk filed a complaint, and I was suspended for a month without pay, forced to undergo psychiatric testing, then counseling, then a program called Alternatives to Violence, which, ironically, was intended for abusive husbands and boyfriends. When I came back to work, I was reassigned to zoning cases, where I defended a Santería priest for sacrificing live goats in neighborhoods usually reserved for drug deals.

It was years later in private practice that I crossed paths with another of those cowardly cretins. This one was a yellow-haired, blue-eyed devil in a padded-shoulder, double-breasted suit, a guy Granny would say considered himself the last Coke in the desert. He was a rich man's son, driving a Porsche, living in a high rise on the Intracoastal, sharing his chrome and glass bachelor pad with a flight attendant who eventually grew tired of his two-timing. When she moved out, the blond boy's ego was hurt, and he asked her to return his Christmas presents. She thought he was joking—the presents were the crowns on her front teeth—but he took them back anyway. With pliers.

"Can we, like pay a fine, and go home?" he asked, slouching in the cushioned client chair in my office.

I couldn't help it, but I kept looking at his smile. "You have nice teeth."

"Huh?"

"They all real?"

"Yeah, sure. What of it?" He self-consciously licked his lips and forced the smile closed.

"Does it bother you when I look at your teeth?"

He shook his head and shot nervous glances around the office. Except for a full-size cardboard cutout of Joe Paterno, we were alone.

"Nice teeth," I repeated.

I riffled some papers, finding the A-form and the dentist's report. "Two incisors, two canines, upper and lower. Eight in all. That right?"

"Huh?"

"The crowns you repossessed."

"Yeah, I guess. I dunno. What difference does it make? I mean, how much is it going to cost?"

"Eight teeth," I said, and then I counted aloud from one to eight, trying to imagine the pain and the terror he had caused. He watched me as if he had a lunatic for a lawyer. He did.

"Stand up, shithead!" I ordered him.

"What?" Confusion. The beginning of fear.

"A tooth for a tooth."

He bolted from the chair and started for the door. I jumped up, danced around my desk, caught him by a shoulder and spun him around. He screamed before I could slug him, and the sound, a high-pitched girlish squeal, threw me off. I swung high, glancing an overhand right off his nose, which nonetheless squirted blood and closed his eyes. The next shot was on target. I came up from below with a left that connected flush on his mouth, splitting his upper lip and breaking off two incisors right at the gum line. I felt a stinging in my hand and looked down to find the teeth embedded in my knuckles. I still have tiny scars to prove it.

He was wailing, blood pouring from his nose and gurgling from his mouth, and looking far worse than he was.

"Six more to go," I told him, but by now, my office door had flown open, and crowding inside were three of my partners, my secretary, a paralegal, and, mouth agape, the general counsel of an insurance company we were trying to woo. I decided to regain some sense of decorum, so I chose that moment to extract the two teeth from my knuckles and toss them into my wastebasket where they *ping-pinged* to the bottom.

"My client," I said to the crowd, as if that somehow explained everything. Then I turned to the insurance company lawyer, trying to salvage the moment. "You ought to see what we do to the opposition."

So it was not without some history that I approached the ranch of K. C. Cimarron this cool summer night in the high country.

Light spilled across the countryside from a three-quarter moon. Cattle stood motionless in fenced fields, and as we slowed for a curve, a deer bolted in front of our headlights, prancing out of our way. We followed the dirt road as it wound toward the Red Canyon Ranch. I parked the car outside the gate, pulling off the road into some sagebrush, where we began walking the mile or so to the barn. By daylight, the barn was a faded red. At night, it was the black maroon of dried blood.

"Kip, there's a lesson about life I need to give you now, I hope you'll remember as you get older."

"Oh brother."

"Listen up. You never strike a girl. Never. You never touch—"

"I know, Uncle Jake. Granny told me all that."

"Already?"

"Yeah, plus, I shouldn't cheat or steal or say nasty stuff."

"You got the whole course. Anyway, I'm glad you're here. I want you to videotape Jo Jo."

"For my movie?"

"No, for evidence. I'll interview her on tape. I want visible proof of her injuries. It'll help prosecute Cimarron and might help in my defense if he claims I assaulted him."

"Are you going to pick a fight?"

"I'm going to tear him into little pieces."

"Uncle Jake."

"Yeah?"

"He's too big. He's the only man I know who's bigger and stronger than you, and in the mean department, he's got it all over you."

"Don't underestimate your uncle when he's all angered up," I told him.

The barn door was open, and inside, in the darkness, I could make out the shadows of horses in their stalls, a saddle sitting astride a railing, bales of hay silhouetted against a corncrib by the moonlight streaming in a window. Kip reached for my hand and stayed close. I was aware of the sound of my breathing, of the rumbling exhalation of one of the horses, the caw of a nighttime bird in the distance.

"Nobody's here, Uncle Jake," Kip whispered.

"Shhh."

A few more steps. Then, "Jake. Is that you?"

It was her voice, coming from above.

"In the loft. Up here." She flicked on one of those lanterns that runs off a nine-volt battery but is made to look like an old kerosene lamp.

I scrambled up the ladder to the loft, Kip right behind me. Jo Jo was huddled in a corner, wrapped in a blanket. Her face was smudged with tear-streaked dirt. Her eyes were puffy. The beginning of a bruise was apparent on one cheek, and an angry red scratch was visible on her neck.

I crouched down next to her and reached out, but she dug herself deeper into the corner like a frightened animal. When I gently touched her cheek, she trembled.

"Jo Jo. I'm here for you."

"Oh, Jake, you shouldn't have come. And the boy, what's—"

Kip was already shooting, using the hand focus ring, rather than the automatic. "Light's a little low," he said, "but this lens has tremendous sensitivity. Plus, the mike is incredible. This baby can pick up a rat farting at fifty yards."

"No, Jake, please. I'm so ashamed. The boy shouldn't be here."

"Uncle Jake, please, you're cutting off the angle." The temperamental director was pouting. "I want to zoom from medium close up to extreme close up."

"Jake, no! Haven't you done enough to me already?"

Now what did that mean? I was trying to help her. She seemed on the edge of hysteria. I turned to my nephew. "Okay, Kip. Cut! I've got enough."

He shrugged and clicked off the camera.

"Now, head back down the ladder and wait until I come get you."

He frowned but took off.

Jo Jo huddled under the blanket, and when I reached for her hand, she let go. The blanket fell away, revealing bare shoulders and breasts.

"He threw my clothes in one of the filthy stalls and told me that sluts sleep with the horses. He was so hateful, so ugly. Oh, Jake, I've made such a terrible mistake coming back here. I knew from before what he was like. It's almost like he has a split personality. He can be so good, so kind and caring, and then, if something goes wrong with a claim or the leases, he becomes . . . I don't know . . . irrational, unhinged, violent."

"I'll take care of him, but first I want to make sure you're all right."

I moved close to Jo Jo, and she wrapped her arms around me, the blanket slipping farther away, her breasts pressing against me.

"Oh, Jake. I must smell like a horse."

"Hush. You're as beautiful and sweet and precious as the day we met."

"*Mi ángel*. So long ago. I've changed so much."

"No you haven't. Maybe you're not as sure about everything as you were then, but that's natural. The young know it all."

She was crying again. "I was always too hard on you. I shouldn't have tried to change you, but I could never accept things the way they were. It was the same with Luis."

I pressed my face against hers, and her arms tightened around my neck. I kissed her, softly, and her lips yielded, and for a moment it seemed her breathing had stopped, but then she sighed, a long vast release of tension, and her body molded itself to mine.

I reached out and clicked off the lamp. Shafts of moonlight filtered into the loft through cracks in the plank walls of the loft, dust motes rising in the creamy glow. Somewhere in the distance, a dog barked, and the chilly nighttime breeze made the old barn groan and shudder.

And *crack*.

The sound startled me. Like the rung of a wooden ladder splintering under a heavy foot.

I sat up, and Jo Jo gasped, clutching at the blanket. Another sound, maybe the shuffling of feet. In the darkness, I couldn't pin down the direction. I rolled to one side, grabbing the lamp, and came up in a crouch, keeping my back to the wall. I flicked on the lamp, blinked and looked around.

Nothing but shadows.

And a voice. "That's better. Natural light just wasn't doing it."

I looked up. In the rafters above the loft, Kip was aiming his video camera at the two of us.

"Out of here, Kip! Now!"

"Okay, okay, I don't want to lose my PG-13 rating, anyway."

He scrambled down from the rafter and climbed back down the ladder. I turned out the light again.

"Just hold me, Jake," Jo Jo said.

I did, and a thousand memories flooded my mind. I thought again of the day so long ago in her mother's backyard. I thought of the good times, and the bad, and no times at all. I thought of Blinky and what he had gotten me into, and what was it Jo Jo was keeping from me, and was this the time to ask?

We lay there on our sides, her bare body warm even in the chill of the unheated barn. She coiled her legs around mine and buried her head against my chest. I could hear her heart beating.

"Jo Jo, tell me all about it. What's going on? Whatever it is, we can work together."

"All right. I owe you that. I owe you the truth. I've been so unfair to you. The night Hornback was killed, you went to meet my brother . . ."

"Go on," I said.

Then, the unmistakable *creak* of a foot on the ladder to the loft.

"Kip, c'mon now!"

Another *creak*.

"Cut your uncle a break."

No sound at all.

"Kip! You're starting to bug me. I've got some business to finish here."

Then a sound like a muffled voice.

I untangled myself from Jo Jo, and in the darkness, found the lamp once again, clicking it on.

Kip was there all right, but a large hand was clamped over his mouth, and he was tucked like a bedroll under a heavily veined arm that could have been sculpted from stone.

"Fool me twice," said Kit Carson Cimarron, "and you're dead."

19

The Stork and the Snake

"Let the boy go," I said, getting to my feet.

Cimarron dropped Kip to the floor.

"I tried to yell." Kip was on the verge of tears.

"It's okay," I said.

"I tried to warn you, Uncle Jake, but the big bastard just sneaked up on me. If I'd have seen him, I'd have kicked him in the nuts." When scared, some people clam up. Others just babble. Kip was a babbler. "I mean, he's uglier than Mike Mazurki in *Some Like It Hot,* and—"

"It's okay, Kip. Now, get out of here."

"... bigger than Richard Kiel with those steel teeth in *The Spy Who Loved Me,* and meaner than Alan Rickman in *Die Hard.*"

"Now, Kip!"

Kip scrambled down the ladder. Cimarron hadn't moved. He wore jeans and boots and no shirt, his chest and shoulders throwing a huge shadow against the far wall. Next to me, Jo Jo was clutching the blanket to her throat.

"Josefina," Cimarron said, "what the hell's going on here?"

"Simmy, he forced me," she said, her eyes moist, her voice choking.

What!

"He hit me, just like he used to." Now the tears were gushing. "He tore off my clothes and just forced me."

Who he?

"You knew what he was like," Cimarron said, his voice devoid of emotion. "You told me yourself. Whatever possessed you to let him get close?"

It couldn't be me they were talking about.

"I don't know, Simmy. I thought he'd changed. He made promises to me. Oh, I feel so stupid, so filthy . . ."

So ashamed. She left that one out.

"Wait a second!" I turned to Jo Jo. "I don't know what game you two are playing. Maybe you get your kicks this way, but I don't. Now, tell Wyatt Earp the truth. Tell him why I came here."

"Jake wanted to take me back to Miami. He wanted me to leave you and go back with him, but I wouldn't, Simmy, and he became enraged. He hit me and called me names, and then he . . ."

"This is crazy!" I shouted. "You're both crazy. Every which way I turn, I get set up. Jo Jo, what the hell are you doing?"

"Shut up, lawyer." Cimarron's expression hadn't changed, and his voice had a touch of sorrow, of sad inevitability. "My woman goes out to the barn to polish up her saddle, and she doesn't come back. I mosey over, and I find you. First, you steal from me. Then you trespass on my land, and now you violate my woman."

He seemed to think about it a moment, then began speaking again, even softer, as if discussing an idea with himself. "No one could blame me. No, it would be understandable. I warned you. I told you what I would do, and you flouted me. My woman on my own property. How much can a man take?" He turned to face me head-on, his eyes drilling me. "I'm going to inflict some pain on you, partner, and when I'm done with you, there won't be enough left for a buzzard's midnight snack."

He moved toward me, slowly, methodically, with a

sense of purpose. No excitement, no urgency, no flooding emotions to drain energy and detract from the business at hand. With his bushy mustache and bare chest and belly bulging over long pants, he reminded me of one of those bare-knuckled fighters of a century ago.

I put my arms up in a defensive mode, remembering the last time with Cimarron. At least now, I had my clothes on. "She's making a fool out of you, Cimarron."

"Now why would she do that, lawyer?"

I didn't know.

He stayed an arm's length away and threw two quick left jabs. They bounced off my shoulder, but not without reminders they'd been there. I feinted with a left and threw a straight right hand that he blocked with his left forearm, and it hurt me more than it did him, my supposedly healed knuckles flaring with pain.

He was a bigger, stronger man with a longer reach. Usually, that was me. I would have to maintain space—the outfighting range—then come right at him with direct frontal attacks. A tall, powerful fighter concentrates on offense and doesn't worry about defense. He uses the reach advantage to work over the opponent from a safe distance. A shorter, smaller fighter needs to infight, defend, and counterattack by shortening the offensive space and lengthening the defensive space.

He came at me again, and I sidestepped, glancing a left off his temple as he came by me. I fought the urge to throw a combination and waited for a chance to counterattack. I didn't have long to wait.

He turned and came back squarely. I spun around to get more room behind me and retreated in the peacock style of kung fu. Cimarron lunged at me with a looping left, the weakest punch he had thrown, and I stepped inside and peppered him above the eye with a right and then a left hook aimed at his chin that caught him on the neck.

I jumped back again and let him advance.

"Chicken shit," he called out. "What's the matter, you afraid?"

"Go fuck a sheep." My wit knows no bounds.

This time, he stayed out of my range, feinted a left, and shot a foot at my groin. It lacked the speed of the *Mae kekomi* front thrust kick, and I avoided it by taking a step backward. He nearly lost his balance, and I was tempted to step forward, but I resisted, and he caught himself, cursed, and came at me again while I circled, keeping him from pinning me against a wall.

He tried another kick, this one shorter. I was in a praying mantis defense, and I hooked his heel and spun him off his feet. He landed with a thud on the wooden plank floor, and again, I fought the urge to attack. Get tangled up wrestling on the floor with him, and I wouldn't have a chance.

He got up and approached me warily. This time I was holding my own. I had hung around enough gyms to pick up the odds and ends of the manly art of self-defense, and at the moment, I was using the womanly art of Wing Chun. It's designed to help a woman fend off a man, and I wasn't so full of machismo that I missed its relevance here. The object is to wear down a larger attacker by making him miss. My strategy was to infuriate him, make him lose his patience. At the same time, I was testing his endurance. With him chasing me, throwing punches would deplete him.

There's an analogy in the animal kingdom. A stork attacks a snake with its beak, but the snake darts away, then lunges for the stork's head. The stork deflects the counterattack with its wing, and the whole process starts again. Whoever wears out first will likely lose an eye or suffer a fatal bite. If both are exhausted, they withdraw and live to fight another day.

Right now, a draw sounded just fine. I had come here, adrenaline flowing, wanting to inflict serious damage. I had felt strong, my confidence fueled by virtuous anger. Now, I was merely defending myself, having been wrongfully accused. The power of righteousness resided in K. C. Cimarron's meaty fists.

This time, he faked the kick, and I dropped a hand to

deflect a foot that never came. He hooked me in the ribs, either with his right fist or a sledgehammer, I couldn't tell which. I used my right hand as a claw, the *kumade* in karate. I went for his eyes and ended up sticking two fingers in his nose. I was too close inside, and he wrapped his left arm around my head. He cocked his right hand to smash me in the face, and I pulled back with all my strength, flexing my knees, twisting my torso, trying to break free. My movement threw him off, and his punch landed on my forehead, but he never let go.

We moved like that, back and forth across the loft, a couple of drunken sailors trying to dance. He was puffing hard now. Big, but not in shape. I caught the whiff of sour mash whiskey on his pained breaths. As we struggled in each other's grip, feet scuffling along the wooden floor, I found a point of leverage, planted my feet, pivoted a hip and swung him backward into the wall. His head *thunked* off a wooden plank, causing more damage to the wood than his skull. When he came off the wall, his knees seemed to buckle, and I went at him.

Mistake.

He was playing possum. I threw a left, which he ducked, and then he came inside and doubled me over with a short right to the gut. I gasped and he moved behind me, slipping an arm under my chin and across my neck. I flailed away at him, but caught only air, and his grip tightened, squeezing off my air.

Still choking me, he slammed me headfirst into the wall. This time, the plank cracked, or maybe it was my skull. I heard Jo Jo screaming. "No, Simmy! You'll kill him! Don't!"

How thoughtful.

How considerate.

How late.

I was about to black out, but just then the pressure eased around my neck. I opened my eyes, but I was dizzy, and Kit Carson Cimarron seemed to be spinning around me. I lifted an arm to fend him off, and he grabbed me by the wrist, twisted it behind my back and spun me into the wall again. This time, I hit it with my full weight, and the plank tore loose and fell to the ground outside. I am wider than the plank, or I would have gone with it, which would have been fine with me.

I bounced off the wall, and he grabbed me by the same wrist, twisted it behind my back again, and whipped me the other way where I smacked into a wooden railing that looked over the stalls. Maybe the railing had termites, or maybe the equation of my mass times my velocity was too much energy for the old wood. Whatever the reason, the railing split and I fell through open space.

I landed with a thud on a thousand pounds of Appaloosa. It was moving, and making noise, and I slid to the floor, where it stepped on me and kicked me. I covered my head with my arms, and rolled over, spitting out blood and dirt and straw, trying to focus my eyes. Above me, half a ton of horseflesh was baring its teeth, stomping its feet, and loudly complaining about sharing its stall.

I was aware of voices. Jo Jo was shouting, but I couldn't make out the words. Kip was out there somewhere, too, saying something, and suddenly, I was worried about him. If Cimarron killed me, what would he do to the little witness?

I tried to clear my head. I heard footsteps on the ladder. Heavy footsteps. I hoisted myself to my feet, grabbing the mane of the horse. If this were a movie, when I fell, I would have landed astride the mighty steed without doing any damage to my private parts. I would have whispered some magical incantation in the great beast's ear, and he would pound down the door to the stall. With a Hi-ho, Silver, I would have scooped up Kip, and we would have galloped out of the barn and into the moonlight, the evening breeze tousling my hair.

But this wasn't a movie, and I could barely see, and as best I could tell, my head was covered with a mixture of blood and horseshit.

The stall door swung open, and I heard his voice.

"C'mon out, lawyer. I'm not through with you."

I eased back to the wall, behind the horse, where they tell you never to stand. I smacked him on the rear, and he bolted through the open door, with me right behind.

K. C. Cimarron was not born yesterday, and he had a lot of quick for a big man. He stepped to one side and did not get trampled or even brushed by the horse, but at least I had a moving pick bigger than Charles Barkley, and it got me out of the stall without being clobbered.

The horse bolted for the open door, and I stepped that way, but Cimarron anticipated the move. He blocked me, and I raised my hands in surrender. "Enough. I've had enough."

He stood there watching me.

"Simmy!" Her voice came down from the loft. Shrill and hysterical. "Simmy, he raped me! Are you going to let him go?"

Wait a second. Didn't she just try to stop him from killing me? Just what the hell *was* going on here?

"No," he said, stepping to the wall and pulling down a bullwhip from a wooden dowel peg. "He's not going anywhere. I'm going to flog him. I'm going to leave scars he'll remember till the day he dies."

The yell came from my left. Cimarron and I both looked that way.

"*I* am Spartacus!" With that, Kip charged him, a five-pronged pitchfork aimed at the big man's groin. Cimarron pivoted to one side, reducing the target to his flank. The blades glanced his leg, and then in one smooth motion, Cimarron grabbed the pitchfork just where the wooden pole met the steel fork. He *did* have a lot of quick.

With a flick of the wrist, he lifted boy and pitchfork, Kip hanging on, as if practicing his pole vault. Cimarron shook the pitchfork and Kip tumbled to the floor.

"Next time," I said to my nephew, "don't yell first."

"No need for this," Cimarron said, cocking his arm, and sailing the pitchfork over my head. I ducked anyway, and it landed with a thud in the far wall, where it sunk in and vibrated like a tuning fork.

"Now, boy, you git out of here," he said to Kip, who hesitated.

"I'll be all right," I lied, and Kip headed for the open barn door, looking back at me with sadness and fear.

"Now, you," Cimarron said. "Let's finish this."

We stood maybe fifteen feet apart, facing each other. "I've never touched a woman against her will in my life," I said. "She's lying to you. I don't know why. I don't know who killed Hornback, or what happened to Blinky, or why Jo Jo came up here, or even why I followed her, but I know I didn't touch her."

Cimarron brought his right hand up behind his ear and snapped his wrist forward. The bullwhip flicked toward me unseen, and cracked, the tip catching me on the shoulder. I thought I'd been stabbed. I backed up, trying to get out of range, and Cimarron advanced, lashing the whip at me, coming up short. He lowered his arm, flicked his wrist, and this time, the tip caught me on the thigh, sending a stinging pain down my leg.

He had cut off my path to the open door, and now I hobbled toward a window, but this was one he had boarded up after the hailstorm. Two steel support posts supported the loft here, and I squeezed between them to block the oncoming whip. Cimarron still tried, though, snapping the leather against the steel posts with the sound of ricocheting gunshots.

After three or four tries, he dropped the whip and just came after me. I backed farther along the wall, studded with dowels hung with bridles, reins, and blinders. Still facing Cimarron, I moved backward, my hand feeling along the wall, until my fingers wrapped round the cold metal of a bit and bridle.

He was on me then, reaching for me with open palm, trying to grab me around the neck. As he did, I swung the bridle, and the bit cracked his front teeth and sunk between his jaws. I kept pushing and he gagged, his tongue stuck under the bit. I had his head bent back, and still I pushed, cutting the sides of his mouth, his tongue and gums, forcing his mouth open, farther still.

Then he bit down.

He clamped the metal bit between his jaws and stopped my movement. Both my hands were on the bridle, and both his hands were free. He boxed my ears with a thunderous double punch. I sank to my knees, my head ringing, and he kicked me in the solar plexus. I pitched forward, heaving, and he grabbed my hair and knocked me over backward. I stumbled back two steps, tripped over a two-by-four railing and tumbled into a corncrib. I was on all fours, gagging, staving off the urge to vomit, trying to catch my breath.

Cimarron stood watching me, his eyes blazing with hate. His tongue flicked the corners of his mouth, where blood trickled down his chin. I tried to get to my feet, but the corncobs rolled under my feet and I fell. When I looked up, Cimarron was pointing something at me. At first, I thought it was a gun.

I blinked twice.

"Don't move, lawyer, or I'll nail you to the barn wall. I'll crucify you, and no court in the land would convict me. Even the Lord would understand."

I was trying to get up again.

"I mean it, lawyer."

"Jo Jo," I called out. "Where are you? Tell him the truth. Tell him how you got me out here. Tell him that you told me he beat and raped you."

I heard the floorboards creaking overhead and caught sight of her coming down the ladder. In a moment she was beside Cimarron, clutching the blanket at her throat, looking small and vulnerable. "He raped me, Simmy, and then attacked you. And you're right, no one would blame you. You'll never even be charged. I know. It's what I do for a living. You were protecting a loved one and defending yourself. It's justifiable homicide."

"She's lying," I said, my voice weak and unconvincing. "She's lying about everything."

I was half crouching, half standing, like some prehistoric ape-man, ancestor to us all. He aimed the stud gun at my chest, then carefully lowered it toward my groin, then lowered it an inch more.

"You're bluffing," I said. "It won't fire that way. The barrel has to press against the target . . ."

Whomp. A carbon steel nail ricocheted off an ear of corn beneath my feet.

". . . unless you modified it," I said.

Cimarron slipped another nail into the barrel, raised the gun, aimed at the center of my forehead, then turned his wrist a fraction of an inch.

I felt the whistle of the nail by my ear and heard it *whomp* into the wall. Again, he slipped a nail into the barrel. *Whomp*, into a cross-hatched beam just above my head.

When I looked back at him, he was aiming at my midsection. *Click*.

"Damn. Josefina, there's a full clip over by the sawhorse."

Cimarron stood ten feet away. I could launch myself out of the corncrib, lower a shoulder and send him flying. I could fake and juke and zig and zag and get the hell out of there. Sure, and I could fly to the moon, but at the moment, I couldn't lift one leg. Exhaustion and fear had paralyzed me.

I saw Jo Jo hand Cimarron something, heard the sound of metal sliding against metal. He was pointing the stud gun at me again. "A fellow could grow tired pulling this trigger all day. Gives you respect for roofers and carpenters. I've got some pretty strong wrists, and already I'm getting tuckered out. Maybe I should just end the game."

He aimed at my heart, lowered to my groin, moved down to my knee, then back to the heart. "Bang," he said, then laughed as I winced.

He quickly moved the gun to a point high over my head.

Whomp. Another nail into the barrel. *Whomp.* Again, a high shot. Just what the hell was he doing?

I heard a tearing sound and looked up in time to be hit in the face with a dozen ears of field corn, kernels hard as pebbles, cobs heavy as nightsticks. And then another dozen, and then a deluge. Down they poured through a mesh screen at the bottom of the silo torn open by the nails.

I tried to scoot on hands and knees, but I slipped again, and the corn continued to fall. I raised my arms above my head, but I was knocked off-balance and buried, facedown, as still it poured over me.

Air.

I couldn't breathe.

I tried to inhale, but the weight of an elephant pressed down on my back. I wriggled to one side and took in a breath.

Dust.

I coughed and sputtered and struggled to gulp in air.

From somewhere I heard his muffled voice. "Lawyer eats all my corn, the animals will starve this winter."

I squirmed some more, managed to take one breath, then was conscious of movement. Mine. I was being pulled backward by my ankles. Then I was hoisted up and over the crib railing and tossed to the floor. I was flat on my back, and in a moment, Cimarron was on top of me, sitting on my chest pinning my arms down at the wrists. He didn't weigh any more than the Appaloosa. Then he released one of my wrists and slapped my face with an open palm, and then the back of his hand, his huge knuckles hitting me hard across the bridge of my nose.

He dug into his shirt pocket and pulled out a handful of nails, placing them in his mouth. He loaded one into the gun, reached around my head and pulled at the top of my sweatshirt. I felt the cold metal of the gun barrel against my neck.

Whomp. A nail tore through my sweatshirt and into the floor.

"Maybe the lawyer needs a haircut." He loaded a nail, placed the barrel at the top of my skull, then slid it over the skull. *Whomp.* A nail skimmed my head and sunk into the floor, giving me a new part in my hair. He slid off me and placed the gun just below my crotch. Another nail in the barrel, another shot into the floor, close enough to make various parts of me retreat northward.

The rest was a blur. A nail that just missed my kneecap, another alongside my foot. One alongside each temple, the noise deafening. Finally, a last shot between my splayed fingers. Then he dropped the gun into the straw.

"Josefina," he called out. "I'm gittin' tired of this. The fireplace is lit in the house. Take one of those branding irons in there and heat it up good. I'm going to show this fellow what we do with rapists out here."

Her voice was a whisper. "Simmy, why not just finish it?"

He was sitting on my chest again, and I felt him turn to face her.

"I don't know about that."

I stretched my right arm out as far as it would go. Beneath my hand, I felt something metallic.

"I want him to suffer for what he did to you, but I'm not going to kill him. Scar him, maim him, put the fear into him so he never bothers you again, but I've never killed a man, and I won't start now."

"If he lives and starts talking, it'll just complicate things," she said. "Keep it clean and simple."

My hand had worked itself around the metallic piece, which was hot to the touch. I hadn't used one since Hurricane Betsy lifted the shingles and tar paper off Granny's roof with 140-mile-per-hour winds when I was still a kid. I was going to use it now. I didn't know if the clip had a bullet left or if there was a nail in the barrel, but I had very little to lose in finding out.

I made a show of moving my left hand, just to distract Cimarron. He saw the movement and used his right hand to pin down my left. Then he smacked me in the face again with his free hand. In that instant, I came up with the stud gun.

Heavy sucker.

It took me a long second to get it pointed at his chest. Too long.

His hand grabbed it underneath and swung it up. It was just passing his forehead when I squeezed the trigger. At the same moment, his left fist smashed straight into my chin. I wanted so to hear the *thunk* of carbon steel into flesh and bone, but all I heard was a metallic *click* followed by the crash of surf against rocks and the volcanic roar of exploding pain.

My last conscious thoughts were merely a series of sounds.

The sounds were far away and dreamlike, echoing against the dented tinplate of my skull. The world was spinning on a wobbly axis. Everything seemed so slow, except the hot ice pick of agony that flashed from jaw to brain.

Did I really hear anything through the fog? Yes, there it was: a thud, a grunt, a muffled *whomp,* and as I slipped into the cool quiet darkness, a hazy image of Blinky Baroso floated high above me, laughing, calling me something, a lousy judge of character. Finally, his voice faded, and I was swept away by a feeling of ultimate and unyielding dread.

20

Do, Re, Mi

Jail food is to food as military music is to music.

Hard biscuits and fatty bacon and greasy meats. Maybe the idea was to induce cardiac arrest and save taxpayers money. The jailer was a potbellied, slack-jawed man of sixty who looked as if he'd been eating the jail hash for thirty years. He was a football fan, and when I told him I had chased the oblong spheroid for a living, he treated me with kindness and respect and brought me pizza and beer. Then I made the mistake of telling him I was now a lawyer. He shook his head sadly, spat on the floor, and said no wonder I ended up here.

Or was I a lawyer?

The Florida Bar had begun disbarment proceedings.

Judge T. Bone Coleridge had ordered me to show cause why Kip shouldn't be transferred to the custody of the state H.R.S., and when I didn't appear in court (having been unavoidably detained, as they say, in Colorado), he adjudged me in contempt of court. Actually, contempt was too mild a word for how I felt about the courts.

I was under indictment in Miami for first-degree murder of Kyle Hornback, local securities dealer. Yeah, that's what the paper called him. It sounded better than con man, flimflam artist, swindler, extortionist, or racketeer. In death, we are all judged more kindly. The crueler the death, the kinder the obit.

I was under indictment in Aspen for second-degree murder in the brutal slaying of Kit Carson Cimarron, ranch owner and civic activist, according to the local weekly.

Civic activist? I suppose they'd call Bonnie and Clyde interstate bankers.

Completing the list of my legal troubles, I was also being dunned by a record club for three CDs I had never ordered. I wrote a couple of letters telling them what they could do with *The Best of Jim Nabors,* but their computer kept threatening my credit rating, heaven forbid.

Okay, so I was a little bitter, sitting in the Pitkin County Jail. Florida and Colorado were drawing straws to see who had the pleasure of providing me with room and board for the next twenty-five years or so, and in Florida's case, maybe causing a brief power shortage in the immediate vicinity of Raiford Prison. Right now, Colorado had dibs on me under the ancient legal maxim, possession is nine tenths of the law. This was a matter of great consternation to Abe Socolow, who pointed out to a Colorado judge in typical lawyerly fashion that (a) I committed my vile deed in Florida prior to coming to Colorado; (b) Florida had charged me with an even more serious crime; and (c) Florida had indicted me first.

He really said *a-b-c* while making his argument. Lawyers tend to argue in threes, building to dramatic conclusions. Some lawyers get confused and say *a-b-3.* Once in a while, just to see if a judge is listening, I'll sing out *do-re-mi.*

But now, I was just a spectator, wearing jail coveralls, sitting on a hard bench in the county courthouse, trying to listen to words like venue and jurisdiction and equity and conservation of judicial resources.

Florida, said Abe Socolow, representing the people of that great state.

Colorado, said Mark McBain, prosecutor in these here parts.

Florida versus Colorado. It sounded like an old Gator Bowl between the runners-up in the SEC and Big 8. I wouldn't have minded being sent back to Florida. After all, I hadn't killed Hornback, and I did kill Cimarron. At least, I thought I did, though I didn't have a recollection of actually rocketing a nail straight into his right ear and out his skull just above the left ear, spraying bone and blood and gray matter over a fine English riding saddle that was now marked state's exhibit twenty-three. In fact, the last thing I remembered, the stud gun didn't fire. I think.

When I woke up in the hospital with my ankle shackled to a bed, a sadist posing as a doctor was shining a light into my eyes and poking me here and there. My ears were ringing, and he was saying something about a concussion, some tenderness in the area of the liver and minor internal injuries that reminded him of a head-on car crash. In the next twenty-four hours, I discovered the rest without any help. Bruised ribs on the left side where Cimarron had hooked me, welts on my forehead, scratches and scrapes on my face where I landed squarely against the side of the barn, red blisters every place the bullwhip kissed me, plus a collection of abrasions and contusions just about everywhere else.

Still, I seemed to be doing better than K. C. Cimarron. A cop whose name I didn't catch sauntered in and told me Cimarron was dead and that anything I said might be used against me. Did I want a lawyer. Hell no, I didn't even want to *be* a lawyer.

I was bleary and had a splitting headache but was semi-happy to be alive, and when local prosecutor McBain strolled into my hospital room, brown leather satchel in hand, I didn't have the presence of mind to clam up. When he turned on his tape recorder and asked whether I wanted to make a statement about splattering Cimarron's brains on the barn wall, I told him it was the first time I ever drove a nail straight in my life. McBain nodded appreciatively at such candor and asked how many men I had killed over the years, and I decided it might be a good idea to either get counsel or plead insanity on the spot.

Jail time.

Except for the food, it wasn't so bad. I had my own cell, part of the status derived from being a crazed killer.

I wasn't bored. Not with the parade of local lawyers who were itching to represent me. There was one barrister who was a part-time ski instructor, another a part-time wilderness guide, yet a third who was a part-time white-water rafter. There was a woman lawyer who piloted hot-air balloons in her spare time and another who took off Wednesdays to ride in amateur rodeos in Snowmass. I'm all for Renaissance men and women, but at the moment, I wanted a hard-boiled, do-or-die, go-for-the-jugular lawyer who would bleed for me, not leave me naked and alone in the dock on the first day of trout season.

One day, a local chap named DeWitt Duggins stopped in to see me. We sat across an old wooden table from each other in the visitors room. He was a short, trim man in his mid-thirties with shaggy brown hair and John Denver granny glasses. He had just finished a case in Mesa County in which his client pleaded guilty to killing three elk, and like lawyers everywhere, he wanted to tell war stories.

"Caused quite a stir over in Grand Junction," Duggins said, proudly, impressed with the enormity of it all. "After all, three slaughtered elk."

"A serial poacher," I responded gravely.

"A first-spike bull, a five-spiker, and a cow."

"Get him a good deal?" I asked, hopefully.

"Nine-thousand-dollar fine, ten years."

"Probation?"

"Prison."

"Ten years in prison! What do they do if you kill a human up here?"

"Don't get that many murder trials. They're treated rather special, I'm sorry to say."

"Okay, let's say I hire you. How would you handle my case?"

"Holistically," said DeWitt Duggins.

"What are you, a chiropractor?"

He took off his glasses, one wire temple at a time, and breathed on the lenses. "Entities are really more than the sum of their parts."

"What?"

"Gandhi was a holistic lawyer, you know. He once wrote that the true function of a lawyer was to unite parties riven asunder."

"Sounds like law for the wimp. I want a lawyer with buckskin and cowboy boots, someone who'll spit in the eye of the prosecution."

"That may be what you want, but introspection is what you need. Healing inner conflict."

Duggins wiped his glasses on his red plaid shirt, put them back on, and pulled a stick of sugarless gum from his pocket. He unwrapped it, slowly, ever so slowly, giving the impression that holistic lawyers aren't real busy. He popped the gum into his mouth, carefully folded the wrapper into a little square, which he put back in his pocket.

"Gonna recycle that?" I asked him.

"Confrontation solves nothing. Perhaps I could have suppressed the evidence of the elk carcasses. Sure, I could have cross-examined the game officer, tried to establish he was lying about the carcasses being in plain view in my client's pickup."

"And you didn't?"

"What would it have solved? My client might have gone free, but would he have dealt with his inner demons? Do you understand what I'm saying?"

"Sure, you want me to plead guilty."

"It would be your first step to recovery."

"Your first step is out of here before they indict me for a second murder. Or actually a third."

"Peace," he said, smiling pleasantly and wisely leaving.

Outside my jailhouse windows, green Aspen leaves fluttered in the wind. White puffy balls from cottonwood trees tumbled along the gutter, gathering at storm drains into globs the size of pillows.

Two weeks went by, and the judge served up a dose of home cooking, ordering the first trial in Colorado. Kip spent three nights in the custody of state welfare workers until Granny arrived, wearing lace-up army boots, a Mexican poncho, and cussing out every government official in the county. She brought me a basket of Key limes, carambolas, and guanabanas, told me I looked penitentiary pale, and wondered aloud if I'd come down with rickets or scurvy. She rented a double-wide trailer downvalley and said she was staying for the duration, come hell, high water, or first snow.

More lawyers trooped in, and I sent them home. Wearing a backpack and looking like a Boy Scout, Kip took a bus to visit me. He brought a mango nut cake Granny had baked. It was made with walnuts, and I half expected to find a file inside.

"I'd really like to see your cell," Kip said. "Is it really funky, like Spencer Tracy's in *Twenty Thousand Years in Sing Sing*?"

"Kip, I've been meaning to talk to you about reading more, and watching fewer movies."

He took a folded newspaper from the backpack. "I've been reading this."

It was the local paper, and it must have been the Kit Carson Cimarron memorial edition, because the entire front page was devoted to his life and tales of his forebears. The story continued on page three, and altogether, I counted eleven photos, though my favorite was one of Cimarron astride a white horse. Cimarron wore weathered chaps and a red bandanna was slung around his neck, and he was smiling from beneath his bushy mustache. The horse looked like it was about to have a stroke.

The story detailed the long history of the Cimarron family in Pitkin and Eagle counties. Kit's great-grandfather worked the Montezuma silver mine in Ashcroft and later the Spar and Galena on Aspen Mountain. He toiled at all the dirty jobs, driller and mucker, trammer and timberman, cageman and nipper. Saving his money, he filed his own claims, working them alone.

He found silver, but not long after he did, the crash of 1893 gutted his claims. Luckily for future generations of Cimarrons, he believed in land as well as holes in the ground. He had bought, free and clear, six thousand acres near Basalt. His son had tried ranching, farming, and apparently drinking, and the third generation—K.C.'s father—lost the spread to unpaid taxes. K.C. ended up with the more modest digs near Woody Creek.

I read aloud to Kip. " 'Mr. Cimarron died apparently without leaving a will. So far, no one has claimed to be the intestate beneficiary, and no living relatives are known to authorities. If none are found, Cimarron's assets, including the ranch and mining claims, escheat to the state.' "

"So what?" Kip asked.

"*Cui bono?* Who stands to gain? That's what Charlie Riggs always asks when someone is killed. But the estate doesn't give us any answers."

I skimmed more of the story, then read aloud again. " 'Although prosecutors refuse to confirm it, well-placed sources indicate that Mr. Cimarron was killed attempting to protect Ms. Josefina Baroso from sexual assault. Ms. Baroso, an assistant state attorney in Miami, Florida, was Mr. Cimarron's houseguest, and the pair were frequent companions at local social events several years ago. Ms. Baroso is expected to be the key prosecution witness. Her whereabouts are currently as big a secret as the location of the Lost Dutchman's Mine.' "

A little local wit there, I suppose.

Sexual assault. That would make me real popular with the local jury pool. In my experience, jurors don't mind murderers all that much, but rapists and child molesters are dog meat.

"If I were you, Uncle Jake, I'd go into that newspaper

office and kick some butt. You remember Paul Newman in *Absence of Malice*?"

"Hush. I'm still reading."

There were some pictures of old smelters and railway cars filled with ore and a brief recitation of Cimarron's collection of mining claims and maps of supposedly buried treasure. The head of the historical society had fond memories of the late Mister Cimarron, who would sit for hours in the library poring over old diaries, family Bibles, maps, and deeds. I learned more than I needed to know about the Treasure Mountain hoard, millions in gold buried near the top of Wolf Creek Pass. If a man could only find a grassy mound and stand on it at six o'clock on a September morning, he could dig for the gold buried under the shadow of his head.

Then there were the prospectors who used a cave near Dead Man's Creek to wait out a blizzard in 1880. Inside the cold, dank cavern, they found five human skulls and hundreds of gold bars hidden in the rocks. After the storm, they took five bars back to their camp and returned with wagons, hoping to bring the rest out. But they never found the cave entrance again.

"Hey, Kip, get a load of this. 'K. C. Cimarron was a larger than life romantic figure, a man of vision, a combination of Indiana Jones and Errol Flynn.' "

"Errol Flynn was a Nazi, Uncle Jake."

"Good point."

The newspaper story concluded by calling Cimarron a "throwback to Pioneer days, a big, hearty son of the West."

Son of a bitch was more like it.

At the bottom of page three was a sidebar in a box. There was a photo of a mean-looking lug with a threatening scowl. He had two black eyes, a swollen lip, and a thoroughly disagreeable countenance. Wait! That was me. The photo was taken in the hospital at a time I was not prepared to receive guests. In fact, all I was prepared to receive was codeine.

The alleged killer of Saint Cimarron, according to the story, was one Jacob Lassiter, a Miami lawyer facing disbarment, a man accused of a second murder in Florida. Then they repeated the "sexual assault" on the angelic Ms. Baroso.

"Hey, Kip, get a load of this. It says here I'm facing additional charges for contributing to the delinquency of a minor."

"It ain't true," he said. "I was a delinquent before I met you."

"With all this pretrial publicity, maybe I should ask for a change of venue."

"Yeah, like to Samoa."

I needed help. Granny could only do so much. Charlie Riggs wrote me inspirational letters with moral support. Britt Montero called from the *Miami Daily News,* either to wish me well or to get an exclusive interview, I couldn't tell which. We went out a couple of times years ago, but Britt always found triple homicides more interesting than my description of a bull rush past the offensive tackle.

At the moment I needed a lawyer more than friendly chitchat. So when Kip headed back for his bus, his eyes wet as I hugged him good-bye, I used the jail phone to make a collect call to an old friend and sometimes adversary.

H. T. Patterson was in Aspen the next day and had a bond request filed the day after that. The state attorney worked up a sweat arguing against any bond, but the judge set it at a cool million dollars. Granny and Doc Charlie Riggs pledged all their assets, as did I, but we were still short, and not even close at that. One more phone call and Gina Florio came up with the rest, only her name was Gina de la Torre now, married for the time being to Carlos de la Torre, sugar baron. When I knew her, she was a Dolphin Doll, shaking her booty for fifteen bucks a game, and we lived together for a while, but that's another story. Thanks to Gina, we had enough collateral to spring me, and as long as I showed up at trial, they'd get their money back, minus ten percent which I promised to repay, even if it was out of my prison salary. I was ordered not to leave the county or attempt any contact with Ms. Baroso, or bond would be revoked.

The day I got out, I assembled my team. Granny, Kip, H. T. Patterson, and I met at the Woody Creek Tavern. Granny had bourbon, H.T. an iced tea, and Kip and I split a Coors, the world's most overrated beer.

"You sure you want me to try the case?" H.T. asked. He was wearing a blue denim suit with red piping and red leather cowboy boots so new he must have bought them at the Denver airport. He looked like a very short and very black John Wayne.

"Why wouldn't I? You're a real lawyer. You got bond issued in the blink of an eye."

"I merely pointed out your clean record of never having been convicted of a felony, though you do seem to have a history of contempt citations and occasional misdemeanor assault. But the fact remains that I am not . . . shall we say, demographically correct for this case?"

"Why?"

"This ain't exactly Malcolm X country. You're not likely to get even one dark complexion on the jury, unless it's pasted on at the tanning salon."

"I don't care. I need you. I'm facing a lifetime of sleeping with a cork up my ass—"

"But you're innocent," Granny interrupted. I didn't correct her.

"Guilt or innocence isn't always black or white," I said in my lecture tone I must have learned from Doc Riggs. "It's more of a continuum. Somewhere in the middle is not-so-guilty bucking up against not-so-innocent. The state has to prove guilt beyond a reasonable doubt. Apparently, they can prove I fired a nail through Cimarron's brain. Hell, I can't even deny it, 'cause I don't remember. But it was justifiable if I was acting in self-defense. The problem is that Jo Jo Baroso is going to weave a web for the jury that makes me the attacker. That's why I need you, H.T.''

"You think I can break her?"

"I don't know, but you're a great lawyer. Hell, when we oppose each other, you always convince me you're right.''

"Jake, I've never known you so accommodating and amiable, so considerate and cooperative as when you're under indictment. In any event, I thank you for the gracious compliment.''

"I mean it. You remind me of Bum Philips's line about Don Shula. 'He can beat your'n with his'n or his'n with your'n.' H.T., I'd take you on either side of a case.''

"Well then, let's get to work,'' Patterson said. "Start by telling me everything that happened that night. Take it slowly, try to remember every word spoken, every move made. Don't leave out anything, no matter how seemingly insignificant. I'll take notes, but you might want to write everything down yourself. It helps jog the memory.'' He looked at Granny and Kip. "You two will have to take a walk.''

"No,'' I told him. "They stay.''

"The privilege, Jake. We lose it if—''

"I know, I know, and I don't care. They stay.''

So I rehashed it, everything I could remember. Jo Jo Baroso's pleas for me not to come to the barn, my trotting out there anyway like a good little puppy.

"Women!'' Granny huffed. "Following a woman will get you in Dutch every time.''

I told Patterson of Jo Jo's puffy eyes and bruised face, and then Cimarron dropping in. "At first, we sparred, mostly. He slung me into the walls a few times to see whether my head was harder than his lumber. Then he dropped me into a pile of horseshit. Once he chased Kip out, it was just the two of us.''

"And Ms. Baroso,'' H.T. reminded me.

"Yeah, and Ms. Baroso. At first she was in the loft, but she came down to join the fun.''

Patterson turned to my nephew. "And where did you go, young man?"

"Out toward the main house, along a stone path. I was yelling for help, but there wasn't anyone around. I came back when I heard the nail gun. It's so loud, I thought it was a real gun."

"It is," Patterson said. He thumbed through some documents the state gave him in pretrial discovery. "Powered by a .27-caliber charge, it can drive a carbon-steel nail through solid concrete."

"Or a mushy brain," I added.

Patterson gave me a raised eyebrow.

"I wasn't trying to kill him," I said.

Now he arched both eyebrows.

"Okay, I went there meaning to do him some serious harm, but after Jo Jo accused me of assaulting her, I realized she was lying about being beaten by Cimarron. That took the stuffing out of me. But by then, I didn't have a choice. Cimarron wanted to maim me and was doing a pretty good job. At first, I just wanted to defend myself, so I went into a Wing Chun defense because Cimarron was bigger than me."

"Just like Bruce Lee did to Chuck Norris in *Return of the Dragon*," Kip added, helpfully.

"What gets me," I said, "is how Jo Jo played me for a fool. I thought her brother was a great con artist, but you should have seen her. She fooled me, and then she fooled Cimarron. She had me hating him, and then had him hating me, and when he hates . . ."

I let it drift off, realizing he isn't hating anymore.

"Why would she have done it?" Patterson asked. "What's her motive?"

"I've been lying awake nights on that one. Only thing I can figure out is that she wanted me dead."

"What makes you say that?"

"Are you kidding, H.T.? She set me up so Cimarron would kill me."

"But that isn't what happened, is it?"

"No, *I* killed him. So?"

"So what makes you think that is not precisely what Ms. Baroso intended?"

21

Accurate Lies

Summer became fall, and the aspen trees turned their shimmering gold. Football season began, and locals at a basement sports bar saluted the Broncos' early success, all the while bitching about how they would fold in the playoffs.

Trial was set for the first week of December. Patterson had completed his pretrial discovery and arranged his documents in color-coded files. Unlike Florida, Colorado law did not give us the right to take pretrial depositions, a severe handicap in trying to peck away at a criminal case. Although we didn't have a chance to cross-examine their witnesses before the trial, we knew what they would say on direct examination. The state gave us their sworn statements and grand jury testimony, and so far, no one, including Josefina Jovita Baroso, had a kind word to say about me.

I was in a daze.

I tried to focus on the trial but felt like I was swimming through Jell-O.

My concentration was off. My nerves were shot. I consumed too much Grolsch, and when that left me without a buzz, I switched to Finlandia straight out of the freezer. *Kippis,* as they say in Helsinki, which made me think of

Eva-Lisa Haavikko, a good woman who died needlessly, but that, too, is another story.

Occasionally, I came up with slightly inebriated ideas for my defense, and I shared them all with H. T. Patterson. Sometimes, just after Jay Leno didn't put me to sleep, I called Patterson with strategy for impeaching Jo Jo's testimony. With the two-hour time difference, it was two-thirty A.M. or so in Miami, and I would awaken H.T. from a sound sleep, but he never complained.

"You interrupted a dream," he mumbled groggily one early morning.

"That some day all men will be brothers?" I inquired.

"No, that Gwendolyn was taking me to her bosom."

"Gwendolyn, from Jamaica? Judge Ferguson's secretary?"

"One and the same, a woman of charm and grace, intelligence and beauty, righteousness and rectitude."

"So what's she doing with you, Henry Thackery?"

"She's not, my felonious friend. It was, after all, a dream."

Lawyers hate for clients to call them at home. There is always an emergency that, in the client's mind, cannot wait until morning. By the harsh light of day, the crisis will be shown to have existed solely in the client's mind. But H. T. Patterson tolerated my late-night calls because he was a friend. And he understood. No, check that. He nearly understood. Until you are asked to rise in the courtroom and identify yourself as the defendant, you cannot understand. Send in the clichés, which are clichés, after all, because they are true: A lawyer is a mouthpiece, a hired gun; have briefcase, will travel; have mouth, will argue; another day, another dollar.

But if you're the defendant, it is different. It is real, and it is forever. Win, lose, or draw, the lawyer will walk out of the courthouse and enjoy supper with family and friends. The day may end for the defendant with the echo of a steel door *clanking* shut with absolute finality.

*   *   *

A chill bit through the air. It rained and became colder, and the trees lost their leaves. Snow began to fall. H. T. Patterson had flown up for a pretrial conference with the judge, and Granny asked him to stay for Thanksgiving dinner. Granny cooked a turkey with chestnut stuffing, wild rice with bacon and brandy, and corn pudding. She baked a pumpkin pie and an apple pie, there being a scarcity of mangoes and Key limes in the Rocky Mountains. She prowled through the kitchen of her double-wide, more cantankerous than usual, grumbling about the altitude as she tried to bake honey wheat bread.

"Yeast rises quicker here than a skeeter draws blood. Ye gods, I'll never get used to this. Water boils at a lower temperature, so you got to boil longer, increase heat for baking, use more liquids but decrease the baking powder and sweeteners. What a damn fool place."

The bread turned out to be soggy, and Granny said to hell with it, we could have eggnog with bourbon if we wanted. I told her to skip the first half of the recipe.

After the last slice of pumpkin pie, served hot with vanilla ice cream, and ample quantities of liquid refreshment, my lawyer and I took a walk. Snow flurries whipped around our bare heads as we trudged along a muddy trail that would soon be used for cross-country skiing. In the distance, the snow-covered peak of Mount Sopris rose high above the valley.

"Jake, you ever represent any lawyers?"

"Sure, a few." It is a matter of some pride to be a lawyer's lawyer.

"What kind of cases?" Patterson asked.

"The usual. Divorce, disbarment, money laundering."

"How were your clients to work with?"

That made me laugh. "You know lawyers. Always wanting to be in control. Terrible witnesses, either arrogant or condescending, and they always talk too much."

"All in all, tough clients?"

"The worst, H.T. They confuse their roles. They're sitting in the second chair, wishing it's the first."

"I see."

He studied me through a blur of snowflakes. A hardy jogger in shorts and a windbreaker chugged by us.

"I get it, H.T. You want me to stay out of the way. Hey, don't worry. I'll be the perfect client. I won't sneer at the prosecutor or wink at the stenographer. I won't chew gum in court or toss paper airplanes at the jury. I'll write you discreet little notes on my legal pad and sit quietly while the wheels of justice turn ever so slowly."

A snowflake caught him in the eye and melted into a tear. "You pulling my chain, Jake?"

"Hell no. You're the boss. I'll be the client I always wanted to have."

The week before trial, the local paper was drumming up so much publicity you'd have thought they were selling tickets. "GREED, LUST DROVE LAWYER TO MURDER," one headline read. Another story called Jo Jo the "linchpin of a love triangle that turned deadly."

Kip read the story aloud to me, then wrinkled his freckled nose. "A triangle doesn't have a linchpin," he said. "It has a hypotenuse if it's a right triangle. It can have an acute angle or an obtuse angle. It can be isosceles or equilateral, but it can't have a linchpin."

I decided to give Kip a lesson that had nothing to do with geometry. "Let me tell you something about the news media."

"I know, Uncle Jake. They lie through their teeth."

Amazing, the process of generational osmosis. *He's lying through his teeth* was one of Granny's expressions. We influence our children in so many subtle ways. I made a mental note to never again drink directly from the milk carton, curse moronic drivers, or pee in the shower.

"Not exactly," I said, "but the news is often accurate without being truthful."

"Whadaya mean?"

"Reporters rely on what people tell them. A woman claims she was the lover of a president. The story is accurate, because she *said* it, but where's the truth? A spokesman for the tobacco industry claims there's no proven link between smoking and lung cancer. Religious fanatics ignore all science and maintain that the Earth is only six thousand years old. So rule number one, the news is filled with accurate lies.''

"How come the newspapers print what they know is false?"

"Our system has faith in citizens' ability to weigh conflicting evidence and reach the truth."

"Just like jurors are supposed to do."

"Right, and if newspapers print only what is undisputably true, there'd be nothing to read but yesterday's box scores."

"But in the stories about you, only the prosecutor and the cops are talking."

"Prosecutors mouth off to the media to get the jury pool thinking their way before the trial begins. Usually, the defense keeps quiet because you can't take a public position that may have to change with the ebb and flow of the trial. Most times, you don't even know if your client will testify until you hear the state's case."

"Are you going to testify?"

"It's up to H.T. But if I don't, there'll be no one to rebut Jo Jo's perjury."

"There's me, Uncle Jake."

"I'm keeping you out of it. Besides, you're not exactly impartial, so the prosecutor would cross you on how much you'd like to help your uncle out of a jam and how you'd do anything for me. Besides, you weren't even in the barn when the real action took place."

"I could lie."

"Forget it."

"Okay, what else?"

"Rule number two about the news media. The more you know about a subject, the less truthful the story. Most stories are equal parts crude approximations, unfiltered information, rough summaries, and educated guesses, all strung together with random quotes chosen for maximum impact, not substance. If the story is about troop movements in Manchuria, you're not going to know whether it's even close. But if you're a CPA and the story's about the new tax code, you can pick apart every mistake.''

''And if the story is about you and Jo Jo and that big cowboy, *you* know the truth.''

''That's a funny thing, Kip. We each see the truth through our own clouded lens. Our perceptions are always skewed. When we're excited, when our adrenaline is pumping, even more so. Put four people in a room—''

''Or a barn.''

''Yeah, and each one will have a different version of what happened.''

''Like *Rashomon*,'' my nephew said.

The day before jury selection, it snowed two feet. A blizzard so hard and thick and gusty, it closed the ski lifts and the gondola for three hours. The morning of the trial, the redbrick courthouse looked like a Christmas decoration, puffed up with virgin snow, the spruce trees bent low under all that white.

I entered the old brick building from the Main Street side under a statue of Lady Justice. Inside, all spit and polished was an old steam engine that once ran a saw that cut timbers for the mines. I passed grainy hundred-year-old photos of cowboys, miners, and farmers at work and climbed the stairs to the second floor. The courtroom was a cathedral of dark wood, the jury box on a raised platform, the gallery a series of church pews. On the walls were photos of judges who had presided here, from the days of silver mining to high-tech skiing.

From a window, Main Street looked like the small town of a kid's toy train set, all decorated with cotton-ball snow and miniature Christmas wreaths. To the south, Aspen Mountain was deep with fresh powder, and under a blinding blue sky, the Monday morning skiers were carving their signatures on the slopes. For some reason, I thought of the shafts and tunnels so far below the snow.

"All rise!" the bailiff yelled. "The Ninth Judicial District Court, in and for Pitkin County, Colorado, the Honorable Judge Harold T. Witherspoon presiding, is now in session."

The judge was gray-haired and lean, with cold blue eyes. He sternly read preliminary instructions to the jury pool, whose members sat stiff-backed in the gallery waiting to be called forward.

H. T. Patterson wore cowboy boots below a double-breasted black wool suit. His tight little smile reflected the expression of quiet confidence we use to mask opening-day jitters. I had a fresh haircut that clipped my shaggy hair from over my ears and trimmed it to a half-inch everywhere else. No longer sun-bleached from windsurfing, my hair was darker, and I was paler than I had been since my last winter as a student-athlete in the Appalachian mountains of central Pennsylvania.

I wore a shapeless dark blue suit, a white shirt, and a striped tie. My shirt collar seemed unusually tight. I felt pasty, out of sorts, awkward. That morning, as I was staring at myself in the mirror, my nephew announced his ratings: two stars for my suit, half a star for my haircut, and two thumbs-down to the little white handkerchief I stuck in my suit coat pocket, trying to give off the aura of a small-town banker.

"Uncle Jake, you look like a major dweeb," Kip said.

"It's a ploy to make the jury think I'm lovable and innocent."

"With that haircut, you look worse than Kevin Costner in *The Bodyguard,* though not as bad as Harrison Ford in *Presumed Innocent,* when he was on trial for killing Greta Scacchi."

I thanked him for his support and drove myself to court.

Mark McBain, the prosecutor, started *voir dire,* asking perfunctory questions about family backgrounds, run-ins with law enforcement, and whether any of the prospective jurors knew any of the principals. No one knew me, but three were excused because they knew Cimarron, another two because they had formed opinions of my guilt based on newspaper accounts and swore they couldn't shake those opinions. A few others were sent home for various personal reasons, including sick relatives, sick cattle, or just plain sick of lawyers.

I watched the jurors file in and out of the box for most of the day, and for no rational reason, I started hating them. Who *were* these people to judge me? They didn't know me. They weren't there. They can't know what happened. How would we ever tell them so that they would know?

I felt out of place. Distant. At times, I listened to the jurors' answers but never heard a word. I felt I was drifting over the courtroom, looking down at the proceedings. Other times, I wasn't there at all.

Once in a while, H.T. would ask for my opinion of one of the panel, but I just waved him off. Let him decide who to challenge and to seat. I was in no condition to help.

Just after four o'clock, H. T. Patterson nudged me. We had a jury of shopkeepers, ranchers, homemakers, a bartender, a waitress, a woman schoolteacher, a mechanic, and a student. They sat in a raised box of varnished walnut, seven men, five women, ten Anglos, two of Mexican descent. Just before they took their oath, I studied their faces, and they studied mine.

Who was this man, they seemed to ask, and what has he done?

And for a moment, looking back, I didn't know the answer to either question.

Mark McBain was a nuts-and-bolts prosecutor. Gray suit, gray eyes with, dark pouches underneath, and a little soft through the middle. He had no desire to be governor, senator, or Santa Claus. He had attained all his goals by dogged persistence and hard work. Unlike Abe Socolow, who bled out his guts to win each case and left a piece of himself on the courtroom floor, with McBain, it was all in a day's work. No flash, no dash. Paint the jury a picture by the numbers. Nothing unnecessary put into evidence, nothing important left out. No pomp, no pageantry, and no nonsense. No ghastly blunders either, just the plain, unembellished, unsentimental facts. A D.A. from the old school.

A prosecutor is a stolid carpenter who patiently hammers his wood into place as he builds a house, one board at a time. A defense lawyer is a nihilistic vandal who finds the support beam and pulls down the house before it's complete. Or if you want to get high falutin' about it, imagine prosecutors and defense lawyers as great painters. The former would be Winslow Homer realists, the latter Man Ray cubists.

At the moment, Mark McBain was leaning on the balustraded railing of the jury box, beginning his opening statement by methodically telling what he expected to prove. "Imagine a trial as a book and opening statement as the table of contents."

He droned on in a monotone, unfolding his case, witness by witness, using the time-honored phrase, "The evidence will show . . ."

He talked about my past with Ms. Baroso, my decade-long involvement with her brother, the convicted felon, my position in her brother's company which I systematically looted of funds advanced by Mr. Cimarron, the decedent. He told the jurors that they would hear from the medical examiner, the investigating detective, an expert on power tools, and from Ms. Baroso herself, the sole eyewitness to the murder. "Ms. Baroso is the only one who can tell us exactly what happened that night. She has no ax to grind. She is a professional woman of impeccable background and credibility, a woman embarrassed by her brother and . . ."

He turned toward me, all twelve jurors following his gaze.

". . . embarrassed by her past involvement with this criminal lawyer from Miami."

He made "criminal lawyer" sound redundant, and the

way he said "Miami" left the impression of Sodom-by-the-Sea.

"I am not going to steal these witnesses' thunder," McBain continued. "You will hear the testimony from each of them, and when you do, I am convinced that you will determine that the state has met its burden of proving beyond and to the exclusion of every reasonable doubt that the defendant is guilty of murder in the second degree."

H. T. Patterson smiled, rocked back and forth in his cowboy boots, and told the jurors that it was an honor to stand before them, the people who can put an end to a grave injustice that has befallen his client. He reminded them of their promise this very morning that they would wait until all the evidence was in before reaching any conclusions. He told them that the state's burden to prove guilt beyond a reasonable doubt was the highest standard of proof known to our system of jurisprudence. Without his nose growing a millimeter, he told the jury that my character was unblemished, and a string of witnesses from Florida, including football coaches, judges, and lawyers would attest to that.

Moving close to the rail, Patterson raised his voice a notch. "Ms. Baroso's testimony is subject to cross-examination, and it is on cross-examination that you will judge whether the evidence meets this burden of proof. It is not true that she is the only eyewitness. No, Ladies and Gentlemen, Mr. Lassiter was an eyewitness, also, and you shall hear from him. I submit that you will find Ms. Baroso's story to be ambiguous and improbable, dubious and doubtful, and when you do, the state's case will fall. It will fall like a house of cards. It will collapse like—"

"Objection, Your Honor." McBain slowly got to his feet. It was the quietest objection I'd ever heard.

"Sustained," the judge said. "I don't know how they do it in Mia-muh, but up here, we save closing argument till the evidence is in."

Patterson thanked the judge with a gracious smile as if

he had imparted the wisdom of the Holy Grail. Patterson summed up with the usual platitudes about our by-golly best system of justice in the world. He thanked the jurors in advance for their rapt attention, though two were already looking out the window, and another was catnapping. Then he sat down, and Judge Witherspoon gave the jurors a little speech about not reading the newspapers or discussing the case among themselves.

I leaned over to my lawyer. "H.T., what's going on? You promised I'd testify. Isn't it a little early to—"

"Already decided. You have to."

"Okay, but then, why no mention of self-defense? If I'm going to testify, it's my only way out."

"Self-defense admits you killed Cimarron."

"Of course it does!" My whisper was a little too loud, and one of the jurors looked over, just as the judge explained he would work them nine-to-six and get them out of here by the end of the week. "Jo Jo will testify I put the stud gun to Cimarron's head and pulled the trigger."

"But you can't remember that?"

"Not exactly, no. I mean, I remember pulling the trigger, but I didn't think it went off."

"And Ms. Baroso lied to you about Cimarron beating her?"

"Yes."

"Then lied to Mr. Cimarron about your having assaulted her?"

"Of course."

"And lied to the police about who attacked whom?"

I threw up my hands in disgust. "Yes. She fooled me. She fooled Cimarron, and she fooled the police."

"Don't look so glum, Jake," H. T. Patterson said. "She hasn't fooled me."

22

🐎

Mobile, Agile, and Hostile

Sheriff's deputy Clayton Dobson testified that he was the first officer on the scene where he found a woman who identified herself as Josefina Baroso. When he first saw her, she had a blanket covering her. She was disheveled and emotionally distraught. She led him to the body. Two bodies really.

The man who was alive was semiconscious. Kind of moaning, lying on his back in the straw. Yes, sir, I do see him in the courtroom. That's him sitting right over there, the big fellow in the blue suit.

The victim, one Kit Carson Cimarron. Recognized him, knew this was his ranch. Knew his daddy, too.

Called for homicide and an ambulance. Took a statement from Ms. Baroso who said—

Objection, hearsay.

Sustained.

Secured the scene and turned it over to Detective Racklin when he arrived twenty, maybe twenty-five minutes later.

Homicide Detective Bernie Racklin was perhaps the only male in Pitkin County who didn't wear cowboy boots. He was short and pudgy, in his mid forties, with a receding hairline. He wore khaki pants, a blue blazer, and scuffed cordovan penny loafers. Racklin looked familiar, but I couldn't quite place him. He, too, took a statement from Ms. Baroso, who apparently had plenty to say and told the same story every time. Racklin puttered around the barn for several hours, along with a crew of crime scene technicians dusting for prints, shooting photos, swabbing up drops of blood, slipping nails and chips of wood into little evidence bags.

"What was Ms. Baroso's condition when you interviewed her?"

"She was upset and had been crying. She displayed bruises on her ribs she said came from—"

The prosecutor held up a hand. "Just give us your observations, please."

Thanks, McBain. I appreciate that.

"She was bruised about the torso. Her face appeared to have been struck as she had the beginning of a black eye. The injuries did not appear to be serious, and she was lucid, alert, and aware of her surroundings."

With the prosecutor's assistant displaying a series of photos blown up to poster size, Racklin spent the next hour describing what seemed like a twelve-round championship fight.

"Photo number one represents what, sir?"

"This is the loft of the barn. This is where the defendant first attacked the decedent."

Whoa! He wasn't there. He was relying on Jo Jo's statements.

"Based on the physical evidence, were you able to determine what occurred in the loft?" Mark McBain asked.

"Yes. The floor is wood. There are scuff marks from the decedent's cowboy boots consistent with a struggle occurring there. He would have been dragged across the floor . . ."

Cimarron dragged? With what, a crane?

". . . There were no scuff marks from the defendant's footwear."

Of course not. I was wearing sneakers. I just hate pseudo-scientific evidence from cops.

"We inspected the wooden planks that make up the walls of the loft. Close examination revealed the presence of human hair embedded in the rough splinters. The hair matched that of Mr. Cimarron, and scuff marks on the floor near the wall are consistent with Mr. Cimarron having been thrown into the wall with great force."

He paused a moment while the prosecutor handed him an enlarged photograph showing a cracked wooden plank.

"Looking at what's already been marked as state's exhibit twelve, can you tell us what that photo shows?"

"Yes, that's the plank. As you can see, there is a fissure in the area from which we extracted Mr. Cimarron's hair. That was an area of the plank seventy-seven inches above the floor. Mr. Cimarron was a very tall man, six feet seven, even taller in boots. Further, there was an abrasion on the back of Mr. Cimarron's head, and indications of a heavy blow, serious enough to cause a concussion."

Bull! He did more damage to the wall than it did to him. I'm the one who had a concussion. He never even blinked.

"Based on your investigation and the physical evidence, what did you conclude concerning the activities in the loft, as pictured in photo number one?"

Hey, H.T., do something. Anything.

I squirmed in my seat, and Patterson placed a calming hand on my arm. Damn lawyers!

"Mr. Cimarron was attacked by the defendant, who though not as large, is quite a physical specimen. He is a former professional football player who is still in good condition, better in fact than Mr. Cimarron . . ."

That's for sure. Mr. Cimarron is stone-cold dead.

"It would appear that the defendant dragged Mr. Cimarron around the loft. They might have been locked up as wrestlers sometimes do. Then the defendant swung Mr. Cimarron into the wall, where he struck his head with great force. Frankly, I'm surprised it didn't knock the man unconscious at the time, though it surely stunned him. Then, the two tussled some more. Somehow, the defendant fell through the railing depicted in photo number two and into the stall below, as shown by the third photo.''

''Are your conclusions consistent with the statements provided by Ms. Baroso?''

Oh brother, talk about getting hearsay in the back door.

I shot a look at Patterson, who hushed me with a whisper. ''Stifle yourself, Jake. She's going to testify anyway. No use making it look like we're afraid to hear it.''

He had a point, though I could have done without hearing her lies twice.

''Yes, consistent in every material respect.''

McBain walked his witness through more exhibits and more description of the brutal beating administered to poor, fat, Kiwanis Man of the Year Kit Carson Cimarron by a weight-lifting ex-football-playing flatlander from a godforsaken place where they don't hardly speak no English.

Detective Racklin testified that the defendant continued his assault upon Cimarron on the ground floor. There was evidence the defendant attempted to impale Mr. Cimarron with a pitchfork, four superficial stab marks in the thigh matching the prongs precisely.

Well, that was close, as close as a nephew of the first degree of consanguinity.

No, there were no usable fingerprints on the pitchfork handle, but that's not unusual. They could have been smeared, or the pitchfork could have been held in a way not to leave prints.

Mr. Cimarron defended himself with a bullwhip, and subsequent examination of the defendant's wounds revealed Mr. Cimarron scored some defensive strikes.

Defensive? I'd like to show Detective Racklin some defensive strikes.

So the two behemoths continued to slam each other around, falling into the corncrib, Mr. Cimarron defending himself, as always, and landing some punches, too. They were both physical men, and they did damage to each other.

"Then what happened?" McBain asked.

"Apparently, the defendant got hold of the nail gun, and—"

"Objection!" Patterson was on his feet. "Evidence is not based on what *apparently* happened."

"Sustained."

"Let me ask it this way," McBain said. "When you arrived in the barn, what did you observe concerning Mr. Cimarron."

"I observed that he was dead."

In the gallery, a couple newspaper reporters tittered, but the jurors were ominously serious.

"Go on," McBain prodded.

"He was lying on his left side on the floor. A pool of blood extended from his right ear in a circular pattern surrounding his head. There was a small amount of blood appearing in his right ear in what was clearly an entrance wound, very small. There was a smudge of grease or dirt on the ear itself that could have come from the muzzle of a gun. Examination revealed an exit wound in the skull above the left ear. It was about the size of a quarter. My first impression was that Mr. Cimarron had suffered a gunshot wound to the head at close range."

"Did further inspection change your opinion?"

"Yes. Lying approximately three feet from the body was a nail gun, or stud driver as they're sometimes called. It had a clip of live ammunition—a plastic strip of .27-caliber bullets—sticking out the top. That's how they're loaded."

"What else did you observe in the vicinity of the body?"

"Approximately eight feet away, in the direction of the exit wound, there was a leather saddle on top a sawhorse. Embedded in the saddle just under the horn was a nail that was bloody at its point and along its shaft. Adhering to the underside of the nail's head were fragments of bone and skin and what may have been brain tissue.''

One of the jurors, a middle-aged woman schoolteacher, put a lace handkerchief to her mouth. The others sat at rapt attention.

''From your experience as a homicide detective, what did you then conclude?''

''Mr. Cimarron had been shot in the right ear at point-blank range by a nail from a stud driver powered by .27-caliber bullets. The nail exited Mr. Cimarron's head through the skull just above the left ear and continued until it struck the saddle.''

''Was this conclusion consistent with Ms. Baroso's statement?''

Cute. Speculation corroborated by hearsay, but H.T. didn't want to make a fuss.

''Yes, it was consistent.''

''We'll learn more about the fatal shot both from a tools expert and from the medical examiner,'' Prosecutor McBain told his witness, but the statement was intended for the jury.

McBain looked through his notes, made a series of check marks on his legal pad, took a sip of water, and started off in a different direction. ''Did there come a time when you had an opportunity to question the defendant?'' McBain asked.

''In a manner of speaking, Mr. McBain. I accompanied you to the hospital the next morning, and we spoke to Mr. Lassiter there.''

Right. I remember the guy now, somewhere in the fog.

''Tell us what transpired.''

Patterson shot me a look. No lawyer likes surprises, and though I had remembered the prosecutor, I forgot about talking to the cop. Now what the hell did I say? Whatever it was would be admissible as an admission by a party.

''I told the defendant I remembered him from his pro football days. I recalled a game against the Broncos where he had a couple of sacks and a fumble recovery . . .''

Great. Five mediocre seasons, and this guy has to remember my best game.

". . . so I complimented him on that."

"And what did he say?"

"He sort of spoke in an exaggerated Southern accent and said he always aspired to be mo-bile, a-gile, and hostile, but all he could manage was the last of the three."

Oh shit.

"Anything else?"

"Yes, sir. You informed him of the cause of Mr. Cimarron's death, and he said . . ." Racklin made a production of thumbing through his notes. " 'It's the first time in my life I ever drove a nail straight.' "

"Your witness," McBain said pleasantly, allowing himself a little smile. If the smile could talk, it would have said, take your best shot, sucker.

H. T. Patterson nodded, as if thanking his adversary for a great favor, and stood to address the witness. "What was my client's physical condition when you first saw him?"

"I'm not a doctor."

"Oh come now, Detective Racklin. Long before you were a homicide detective, you were a patrolman, were you not?"

"Yes, sir."

"And you testified many times in auto accident cases as to physical condition?"

"Yes, sir."

"And in criminal cases, too?"

"Yes."

"And were my ears deceiving me, or did you this very morning describe Ms. Baroso's physical condition when asked to do so by the prosecutor?"

"I suppose I did."

"Then why be so reluctant to describe Mr. Lassiter's condition?"

"I just—"

"You just didn't want to tell the jury that Jake Lassiter was beaten to a pulp by Kit Carson Cimarron."

"Objection! Argumentative."

"Sustained." Judge Witherspoon looked at Patterson and instructed him gently, "Please confine your questions to . . . well, to questions."

"Isn't it true that Mr. Lassiter was beaten to a bloody pulp?"

"I don't know if I would characterize it quite that way."

H. T. Patterson was good. Damn good. As soon as he saw Racklin was defensive, he would pour it on. Trying to hide the obvious when the truth won't hurt is a common cop mistake. If I attacked Cimarron, it didn't matter if he ran over me with a steamroller defending himself. So a smart prosecution witness would just shrug and say, yeah, ole Kit got in a few licks. But Racklin was trying too hard to help the prosecution, something that's almost always a mistake.

"Well, Detective, how would you characterize a concussion, multiple lacerations and contusions of the torso and all four limbs. How would you characterize bruised ribs, strained ligaments, blackened eyes, blurred vision, a dislocated shoulder, and numerous scars from a bull-whip?"

"I'd say your client bit off more than he could chew when he jumped K. C. Cimarron."

Ouch.

"Really? Did you see Mr. Lassiter do just that? Did you see him jump Mr. Cimarron?"

"No."

"Because you weren't there."

"That's right."

"So your testimony is dependent on what Ms. Baroso told you?"

"That, and from my independent investigation of the scene."

"Your in-de-pen-dent in-ves-ti-ga-tion," Patterson drawled, as if the two-bit words weren't worth a nickel, "began after you took a statement from Ms. Baroso, did it not?"

"I don't follow you," the detective said.

"It is not necessary that you do, but I would appreciate it if you would answer the question. Isn't it true that you first spoke to Ms. Baroso, and after getting her tearful version of the events, you proceeded to in-ves-ti-gate?"

"Yeah, it's true. I had to start somewhere, and your client was unconscious."

"So he was, having been beaten into that state by Mr. Cimarron, correct?"

"Yeah, he got hit. I said that."

Patterson's voice grew louder. "And thereupon, having been told what supposedly happened by Ms. Baroso, you began to in-ves-ti-gate, or shall we say, you began to gather evidence that would corroborate and confirm, exculpate and exonerate this attractive young woman from any and all suspicion?"

"The lady was never under suspicion."

"What!" thundered Patterson, as if the answer was the biggest shock since the Jets beat the Colts in Super Bowl III. "You never even considered that Mr. Cimarron had been dispatched into the hereafter by . . . the *lady*?"

Racklin sighed with exasperation. His look to the jury said *these fucking lawyers are a pain in the ass.* "Ms. Baroso identified herself as an assistant state attorney in Miami, and then—"

"Did she show you her badge and ID?"

"Yes, as a matter of fact, she did."

"So here is one dead body on the floor and another man lying unconscious with multiple injuries, and once you learn that the third person on the premises is a fellow law enforcement official, you immediately conclude she is a mere witness and not a suspect, correct?"

A good question on cross-examination must be answered yes or no. And if the cross-examiner is really sharp, the question asks whether the witness has stopped beating his wife. If Racklin answered yes and admitted that he immediately concluded Jo Jo was free of suspicion, H.T. made his point: It was a hasty call by the cops. If Racklin answered no, then he knew the next question would be: *When* did you conclude she wasn't a suspect? And on and on.

"I've been doing this a while, and I concluded she was not a suspect. I considered her a witness. She seemed credible and—"

"She *seemed* credible! I suppose Jeffrey Dahmer seemed like a good prom date."

"Objection!" Now McBain was on his feet. "Counsel keeps arguing with the witness."

"I withdraw the question," Patterson said, graciously.

"What question?" McBain muttered under his breath.

Ramrod straight, pulling himself up to his full five feet six inches, cowboy boots included, H. T. Patterson strutted to the clerk's table and picked up the report compiled by the crime scene technicians.

"Now, Detective Racklin, you have testified that Mr. Cimarron died of a nail wound to the head . . ."

"No, I didn't. I said I observed a head wound. I believe the deputy medical examiner will testify as to cause of death. That's how we do it up here."

Oooh. Racklin was no dummy. He was telling the jury to keep an eye on this slick-talking stranger.

"Yes, thank you so much for that clarification. Did you observe any nails other than the one you described as having been embedded in the saddle?"

"I believe the technicians came up with some in the corncrib. It's in their report. You'll have to ask them."

"I see." Patterson came back to the defense table and was thumbing through his notes. You like to conclude cross-examination with a bang, but H.T. seemed to be out of bullets, or nails, as the case may be. Just then, one of Charlie Riggs's old lectures popped into my head. Something about the four manners of death. Natural, accidental, homicide, and suicide. I wrote a single word with a question mark on a yellow pad and slipped it to Patterson.

My bantam rooster of a lawyer nodded and turned his

attention to the witness stand. "Detective, when did you conclude the death was a homicide?"

"Upon being shown the body by Deputy Dobson who responded to the call."

"*Prior* to taking Ms. Baroso's statement."

He thought about it a moment. "Actually, Deputy Dobson was telling me what the lady said, as he led me to the body."

"So you knew Ms. Baroso's version of events even as you looked upon the body for the first time?"

"That's what I just said, yes."

"And you concluded it was a homicide."

Racklin smiled a crooked smile. "It didn't look like a heart attack or a fall down the stairs."

"Or a suicide?"

That stopped him a second.

"Did it *look* like a suicide?" Patterson asked. "Yes or no?"

A perfect question. It's fun to watch someone good at his work, whether it's Marino finding the open receiver or Perlman plucking the right string.

"No, not exactly," Racklin said quietly.

"So you never contemplated the possibility of suicide?"

Another problem for the detective. If he did contemplate the possibility, when and why did he rule it out? If he didn't contemplate it, why not?

Racklin tried to hedge his bets. "Not in any great detail," he answered, but the look on his face said he'd never even considered it.

"In what detail did you contemplate the possibility?"

"I can't recall."

"Isn't it true you never considered the possibility of suicide?"

"I can't recall spending time considering it. Like I said, it didn't look much like a suicide."

"Did you fail to consider the possibility because it didn't *look* like a suicide or because you immediately accepted Ms. Baroso's version of events?"

Racklin's pause said he was trying to figure out the ramifications of each possible answer. "Both, I suppose."

"But you have testified previously that the wound initially appeared to have been caused by a gunshot fired at point-blank range, correct?"

"Yes."

"You have witnessed many such wounds, have you not?"

"Some."

"Some? Let's see, in your years as a homicide detective, first in Denver and then here, how many such gunshot wounds have you investigated, confining ourselves to those gunshots fired at point-blank range into the temple or ear?"

"I'm not sure."

"Five, fifty, a hundred, a thousand?"

"I'm not sure. More than five, less than fifty. Say nine or ten."

"And in those dozen gunshot wounds, how many were homicides and how many were suicides?"

He paused and gave the impression of honestly trying to remember. "One was Russian roulette. I suppose that was an accident. Maybe two were gang killings. The rest were suicides, as I recall."

"But you never considered that possibility here because you immediately accepted as true Josefina Baroso's version of events, isn't that correct?"

Trapped. He'd already said it. Not that we could prove Cimarron killed himself. But there were two living people in that barn, and it damn sure helps a reasonable doubt case if the cops were too quick to grab one of them.

"Yes, that's right," the detective said, just wanting to end the agony.

H. T. Patterson told the judge he had nothing further and gave the witness back to the prosecutor, who didn't want him. Judge Witherspoon allowed as how it seemed like a good time for lunch, and no one disagreed.

*   *   *

By the middle of the afternoon, half the jury was dozing or looked as if they wanted to. Two crime scene technicians and a lab worker identified little bags filled with odds and ends, none of which you'd want in your refrigerator. The blood, skin, bone, and brain matter belonged to K. C. Cimarron. Fingerprints on the stud gun were smudged, and the handle may have been wiped with a cloth, but there were still latents on the barrel identified as belonging to Cimarron and me. A partial of a third person's print was picked up there, too.

"Do you have any idea who this final fingerprint comes from?" McBain asked on direct examination.

The prints guy, a bookworm type with a laboratory pallor, looked at the jury as he was doubtless instructed and said, right on cue, "All I can say is that it isn't from Mr. Cimarron, Mr. Lassiter . . ." He paused for effect, "or Miss Baroso."

McBain smiled at Patterson, and just in case anybody missed the point, he repeated it. "Not Ms. Baroso's prints?"

"No, sir."

The other technician, a dark-haired woman in her thirties, testified about picking up the stud gun and delivering it to a Douglas Clifton who would perform certain tests on it. This was just chain-of-custody material, so the gun could be admitted into evidence. When she picked up the gun from the barn floor, or in her words, when she "secured the apparent weapon," there was no nail in the barrel, but there was a plastic clip with nine .27-caliber bullets remaining in the gun.

The nail pulled from the saddle was three inches long, made of carbon steel, and fit perfectly into the gun. The head of the nail contained a small amount of gunpowder residue in addition to the gunk from Cimarron's skull. Actually, she didn't say "gunk." She called it brain tissue, and the schoolteacher juror with the lace handkerchief squeezed her eyes shut.

*   *   *

It was a few minutes before six o'clock, and all the technical talk was over, so the judge sent the jury home with the usual admonition against forming opinions or discussing the case with the neighbors, and added the friendly advice about driving carefully with all the tourists in town.

As he stuffed his files into cardboard boxes for the night, H. T. Patterson asked me, "Can I buy you a drink?"

"Is the law an ass?"

We walked out of the stuffy, overheated courthouse and into the bracing air of dusk in the Rocky Mountains. Snowflakes whirled in a crisp breeze, and a three-quarter moon hung low over Smuggler Mountain. Cars crunched through a new snowfall on Main Street, and exhausted, happy skiers headed back to their hotels, condos, and chalets. I was struck by the utter beauty of the coming night, but at the same time, was overcome by a profound, nameless melancholy, a sense of approaching doom, and an unshakable conviction that I was powerless to affect my own destiny.

23

Where Light Meets Darkness

If you are charged with murder and plead not guilty, you have several choices. You can simply try a reasonable doubt case. Don't take the stand, but cross-examine the bejesus out of the state's witnesses. Magnify inconsistencies, exaggerate sloppy police work, and ridicule the prosecution. With some luck, you might get an acquittal, or at least a hung jury.

Or, if you have evidence the victim attacked you first, plead self-defense. But that admits you did the killing, and you'll be convicted unless you can convince the jury that you had reasonable ground to believe your life was in danger when you struck back.

Or, you can bravely confront the state head-on. Take the stand and swear you didn't do it, pure and simple. Well then, jurors might ask, if this rascal didn't, who did? In which case, it's useful to have a straw man. Or woman, as the case may be.

Which is what H. T. Patterson wanted to talk about after court. Once the jurors were sent home, promising not to read the newspaper or chat about the case, oaths broken more frequently than marital vows, H. T. Patterson bought me a beer at a local pub not frequented by the chichi Beverly Hills ski crowd. The place didn't have a view of the ski slopes, and it didn't have a burning fireplace. It sat in a warehouse/office center across Route 82 from the airport and had dim lighting where even accused murderers could enjoy draft beer in peace. We sat at a round wooden table scarred with cigarette burns, sipped our brews and ate boiled peanuts.

"I want you to watch your demeanor in court. Don't be so despondent and dejected, depressed and discouraged. The jury's going to conclude you think they're going to convict you."

"I do."

"Well, don't show it. It's a self-fulfilling prophecy. It also makes you look sorry for what you did. It's a face for sentencing, not for trial."

"Okay, from now on, I'll laugh uproariously at every objection."

"Don't be difficult. You know what I'm talking about."

"I know. Never let them see you sweat."

"Right. You ever hear the story of the two generals watching their forces battle the enemy?"

"No, but I have a feeling I'm going to."

"One general is wearing a bright red cape, and the other asks him why such an outfit on a day of battle. 'Because, if I'm wounded, my troops won't see the blood, and they'll fight on.' The first general thinks about it and calls to his aide, 'Fritz, bring my brown trousers.' "

That made me laugh, and my laughing made Patterson beam. "Good, much better. Now, you ready to play some poker?"

"Deal."

There weren't any cards, of course. It was a joke that went back to our first case together. Patterson had cleaned my clock in a civil suit in which I had sued a striptease joint where my client, a soon-to-be-groom, pulled a groin muscle in a hot-oil wrestling match with noted stripper Wanda the Whirling Dervish. It was my client's bachelor party, and Wanda thought it would be fun to see how far apart his legs could spread in a hold called "make a wish." I don't remember what damn fool mistake I made in closing argument, but Patterson came up to me afterward and said, "Lawyering is playing poker with ideas, and you just drew to an inside straight, sucker."

Now he looked at me as a more or less equal. "How do you like the jury?" Patterson asked.

"I don't know. I suppose if we had six blacks and six Hispanics, all of whom had been wrongfully arrested and distrusted the cops, I might feel better. But we've got a white bread and mayonnaise crowd. You'd never see this in Miami. You remember the jury when the judges were tried in Operation Court Broom?"

"Sure do. Ten blacks, one Hispanic, one Anglo."

"Yeah, wouldn't that be wonderful?"

"Miami's different," Patterson said.

"I know. Exotic and yet so close to the U.S. of A. I remember I was trying a case during the Persian Gulf War, and I had a witness flying in from Topeka or Omaha or somewhere normal. Anyway, he takes a cab from the airport straight to the courthouse, and when I meet him, he says how great it is to be in a city where everyone is so patriotic. I figure he's mistaken some Santería ceremony for a marching band, so I ask him what he means, and he said that in every neighborhood he passed, people had strung up yellow ribbons for the troops."

"What'd you tell him?" Patterson asked.

"The truth. I said those aren't yellow ribbons. Those are crime scenes with their perimeters taped."

"A common mistake," Patterson agreed.

"So what do *you* think of our jury?"

"They're bourgeois and banal, common and conventional, the worst imaginable collection of middle-class, mundane white folk this side of 1950s television. Cimarron was a local lad, and even though he was considered something of an oddball, he's become a mythic Western hero in his death. Our problem is that his halo now shines on Ms. Baroso. When she accuses you, she speaks for him."

"So, what do we do?" I asked without much enthusiasm.

Patterson drained his beer and patted his mouth with a paper napkin. "Destroy her, of course."

"She's very smart, H.T., and very convincing."

"So am I," my lawyer said.

I started to order another beer, then thought better of it. I was working evenings, sketching outlines of questions, reviewing notes.

"Now let us assume we convince the jury Ms. Baroso is lying about your alleged assault," Patterson said. "What have we accomplished?"

Lawyers just love rhetorical questions. "We've discredited her. If a witness lies about one material fact, all the testimony is in doubt."

"Including who attacked whom, and more important . . ."

"Who killed Cimarron."

Patterson smiled at me and waved at the waitress, holding up one finger and pointing to his glass, the international symbol for another drink, *s'il vous plaît*. "So you understand, my large lugubrious friend?"

"You're saying we're not arguing self-defense. I fought back, okay, and maybe I tried to kill Cimarron, or maybe I was just fending him off. Who knows? I certainly don't. But I didn't put the nail in his head . . ."

"Go on."

"Jo Jo did."

"It is a plausible version of events, is it not? She encouraged you to fight him, provoking you with the tale of her beating. When you failed to dispatch him, she expedited the process."

"Great theory, H.T. How do we prove it? I can't testify that she told me to attack Cimarron. Hell, she told me *not* to come to the barn. She tried to stop me."

"Really? And did you pay attention to her words or to the pain in her voice, to the choking sobs with which she enticed you?"

"Okay, I get it, but will a jury believe Jo Jo set me up to kill Cimarron?"

"Or him to kill you."

"What?"

"She egged him on, but from what you said, he resisted. Oh, he was going to do plenty of damage but stop short of killing you. That's not what she wanted. She needed you dead."

"Wait, you're losing me. I thought she wanted him dead."

"Either way, Cimarron would be out of the picture, wouldn't he? If you were dead, she could go back to story number one. Cimarron beat her, you tried to help, he killed you. He gets convicted of murder. If he's dead, well that's even better, and if Jake has to take a fall, too bad."

I chewed that over with some boiled peanuts, then said, "No way a jury will buy it. I don't even buy it. I mean, why did she want Cimarron dead or convicted of murder?"

"How should I know? I'm just playing poker with the cards dealt to me. You've got to figure the rest out."

"But you want me to say Jo Jo killed him?"

"As I said before, it's a plausible version of events, and the only explanation I have for her goading first you, then him, into a brawl."

I sat quietly a moment, trying to think like a juror and follow the twisted path of our defense, as just outlined by my lawyer.

Too complex, too weird.

Besides, I couldn't swear I didn't fire the shot, if you'll pardon the double negative.

Another thing, I didn't see Jo Jo shoot anybody.

And finally, if you're going to accuse someone else, you better show a motive for the crime. If Jo Jo had a problem with Cimarron, she didn't have to kill him *or* have him charged with murder. She could have just gone home. After all, she came to Colorado to be with him.

Patterson said, "Just so the record is straight, Jake, I am

not encouraging you to tell a version of the story that is less than the truth. I am only asking you to search the depths of your subliminal memory, that shadowy territory where light meets darkness, where conscious thought gives way to clouded, obscured vision. Perhaps if you search those dim perimeters of the mind, either by intense concentration or by hypnotic trance, your recollection will be enhanced.''

In other words, H.T. was telling me, I could make it up, but that was my decision entirely.

I thought about it some more, then said, ''I can't do it, old buddy. I can't do it because that's not what happened, and I can't do it because it wouldn't work anyway.''

Patterson nodded gravely and signaled the waitress for the check. ''I understand, Jake, but just out of curiosity, would you do it if that's not what happened, but it would work?''

On Wednesday morning, a fellow in a cardigan sweater took the stand. He told the jury his name was Don Russo, and he was director of products safety for Toolmaster Inc., a Delaware corporation that was a wholly owned subsidiary of a Japanese conglomerate with factories in Indonesia and Taiwan. Don Russo knew everything you ever wanted to know about the Masterjack Stud Driver 500.

''That's our top-of-the-line powder-actuated power-load stud driver, or what you folks might call a nail gun,'' he told the jury.

Russo was a pleasant man with clear-rimmed eyeglasses, and he reminded me of the enthusiastic clerk in the hardware store who knows just what grade of sandpaper you need for every imaginable job. Russo usually testified in civil cases where a hapless amateur carpenter put a nail through his hand, trying to cock the gun with his palm over the muzzle and his finger on the trigger.

Now Russo stood in front of the jury box, holding state's exhibit nine, a red evidence tag tied around its rubberized handle. ''I always advise folks to treat the

Masterjack as they would a rifle. Heck, they don't understand, just because the bullet's got no projectile, that
doesn't mean it's not powerful. It's really much more powerful than small arms ammo of the same caliber.''

We learned how the powder explodes, sending expand-
ing gas against a captive piston, which slams into a pin
that shoots a nail out the barrel into what Russo called the
working surface, which in this case was K. C. Cimarron's
skull. We learned not to use nails that are too long, because
they may fishhook in concrete and come back out at you
like a boomerang. We learned the importance of keeping
the breech wiped clean and we learned that someone, pre-
sumably Mr. Cimarron, had disengaged the safety device
which was intended to prevent discharge unless the muzzle
was pressed against the working surface. Russo tut-tut-tut-
ted at that and said the gun is perfectly safe unless mis-
used.

"The stud driver is really for the professional, but every
once in a while, we get somebody trying to hang a picture
on the wall of his apartment and he ends up nailing his
neighbor to the sofa in the next apartment.''

"In short, Mr. Russo,'' McBain asked in summary, "is
exhibit nine a deadly weapon?''

"If used as such, yes.''

"And the firing of such a gun into the ear of another is
an act calculated to cause death?''

Ah yes. The issue of intent.

"Objection.'' Patterson got to his feet. "Invades the
province of the jury and not subject to expert opinion.''

Judge Witherspoon seemed to think about it.

"This witness cannot ascertain the state of mind of my
client,'' Patterson continued.

"I don't believe that's what the question called for,''
the judge said. "Overruled.''

"Yes, I should think so,'' Russo responded. "Anybody
who sticks a stud driver in somebody's ear and pulls the
trigger . . . why, there's only one thing that can happen,

and I guess every red-blooded American boy's gotta know that.''

The coroner was an Asian-American woman in her forties who was the only trial participant shorter than H. T. Patterson. She approached the witness stand with dainty steps, sat down, and looked the jurors straight in the eye. She wore black flats and a white lab coat that came to her knees. A touch of purple eye shadow was her only makeup.

She took the oath, told us her name was Dr. Ivy Chin, with degrees from Berkeley and Harvard Medical School, internships and a residency at Mass General, plus extensive training in pathology at a variety of big-ticket hospitals. For the past five years, she'd been the chief deputy medical examiner for Pitkin County.

"Did you have occasion to perform an autopsy on the body of Mr. Kit Carson Cimarron?" McBain asked.

"Yes.''

Dr. Chin first saw the body in the morgue, cowboy boots hanging over the end of the steel tray. "I observed a major head wound, which I ultimately concluded to be the cause of death. There was what appeared to be an entrance wound in the area of the right ear and an exit wound in the temporal bone just above the left ear. From outward appearances, it had the characteristics of a gunshot to the head.''

"What did you do then?''

"I ordered X rays of the head to determine if any projectiles were inside the skull. There were none. With scalpel, I refracted the scalp which was bloody underneath. Then I sawed through the skull front to back and removed the skullcap. I noted lacerations in the dura, both subdural and arachnoid. Additionally, there were multiple hemorrhages and disruption of the brain tissue. Near the exit wound, there were fractures radiating throughout the skull.''

"At this point what had you concluded?''

"That a projectile had entered Mr. Cimarron's right ear and exited the temporal bone of the skull above the left ear."

"Then what did you do?"

"I removed the brain and did the usual."

Easy for her to say.

"Yes, Doctor, and what was that?"

"Well, I examined the brain, of course. It was quite sodden with blood. I weighed it and replaced it in the skull."

McBain ran through a series of photographs, trying to get Cimarron's bloody brain on display in front of the jury. Patterson objected, and the judge, bless his heart, sustained on the ground he'd already let in a police photo of Cimarron lying in a pool of blood, and his rule was one gory photograph per trial.

Dr. Chin identified a nail in a little Baggie that the police had given her. It had been removed from a saddle and had been admitted into evidence when the crime scene technician testified. Dr. Chin's tests revealed the presence of Cimarron's blood, tiny fragments of his skull, and chunks of his gray matter, though it actually looked tan. She concluded that the nail had, in fact, been the projectile.

"What did you do next?"

"I completed an autopsy of the entire body."

"Any other abnormalities?"

"Some coronary atherosclerosis, but that's not what killed him."

"And what did kill Mr. Cimarron, Dr. Chin?"

"A three-inch steel nail fired from a power tool directly into and through Mr. Cimarron's brain."

"This nail?" McBain asked, holding up state's exhibit seventeen.

"It would certainly appear so."

"To a reasonable medical certainty?"

"Yes, in my opinion, to a reasonable medical certainty."

Patterson was brief. There was little to be gained, and

it doesn't do you any good to get whacked twice.

"Dr. Chin, other than what you have described, were there any other injuries to the head?"

She put on a pair of glasses that dangled from a chain around her neck and took a moment to review the autopsy report.

"On the back of the skull, there was swelling that was evidence of trauma with a blunt object."

"Based on your examination, can you tell us what caused that trauma?"

"An object made of wood. We removed several splinters that were embedded in Mr. Cimarron's hair and scalp."

"Can you tell us the severity of the blow?"

"Not precisely."

"Well, can you tell us whether the blow was severe enough to fracture Mr. Cimarron's skull?"

"The skull fracture I described radiated from the site of the exit wound and was caused by the projectile. The blow to the back of the head did not cause it."

"Would the blow to the back of the head have been sufficient to render Mr. Cimarron unconscious?"

Dr. Chin closed her eyes and thought about it. "It could have, but that is not to say that it did."

"I understand," Patterson said, nodding.

I was glad someone did.

"Anything further?" Judge Witherspoon asked. "The jury looks hungry."

Me too. Autopsies do that to a guy.

Patterson allowed as how he was finished. McBain had no redirect examination, and everybody gathered up their coats, scarves, and gloves and left for the lunch recess.

Edie Laquer was thirty-eight, suntanned, and athletic. She worked as an assistant vice president at Southern Federal in downtown Miami. Her job this week was to fly to Houston on Continental, change planes, fly to Denver, take a commuter flight to Aspen, get a cab to the Little Nell Hotel at the foot of Aspen Mountain and check into a four-hundred-dollar-a-night room. The next day, she had eggs and a bagel at sunrise, rode the lift to the top of the mountain and skied until noon, then changed clothes, walked down Spring Street, past Le Tub, a bicycle shop, Wienerstube German restaurant, past Hyman Avenue and Hopkins to Main Street, where she turned left and continued two blocks to the courthouse. Edie Laquer carried a thin file of documents to the second floor, where she spent approximately ninety seconds on the witness stand authenticating my banking records. Whatever the glories of our justice system, efficiency is not among them.

Judge Witherspoon admitted the records into evidence, so the jurors would have documents showing that seventy-five thousand dollars was deposited into my account. When I testified, you could be sure the prosecutor would have a few questions about the transaction.

Edie Laquer left the courthouse, and the wheels of justice continued to turn. Housekeeping is what lawyers call it. The official seal of the secretary of state of Florida was emblazoned on the certificate of incorporation of Rocky Mountain Treasures, Inc. The shareholders' agreement also came into evidence, as well as the prospectus, and various books and records.

As a case builds, you get the drift of where the state is going. The prosecutor was taking no chances on the issue of motive. It wasn't just the lust for Cimarron's woman that drove this brutal man. It was greed for Cimarron's money, too. Already, I was imagining McBain's cross-examination.

So, Mr. Lassiter, correct me if I'm wrong, but didn't you embezzle seventy-five thousand dollars from Mr. Cimarron's company and thereafter stalk Ms. Baroso to Colorado where she was visiting him, trespass on his property at night, sexually assault Ms. Baroso, then viciously attack Mr. Cimarron, finally killing him by shooting a steel nail through his brain?

Yes, it's true! All of it! And not only that, I also picked protected wildflowers on state-owned lands.

My mind does that in trial sometimes, takes flight on winged journeys. Now, everything seemed so ludicrous it would be funny if it weren't so damn real. What had happened? A few months ago, I was a moderately successful trial lawyer doing his best in an imperfect world. Now, I was caught up in . . . what did Patterson call it last night? A Kafkaesque tragedy.

Right. One of the few books I read in law school that wasn't filled with legal citations and jurisprudential mumbo jumbo was *The Trial*. To this day, I can remember the first line. "Someone must have been telling lies about Joseph K., for without having done anything wrong, he was arrested one fine morning."

Hey, Joseph K., this is Jacob L.

Me too.

24

Who Dropped Whom?

"How long have you known the defendant?" Mark McBain asked.

"Years," Abe Socolow said. "Ever since he started practicing law. He was an assistant public defender, and I was an assistant state attorney."

"You know him well?"

"Yes."

"Both in and out of court?"

"Yes."

"The two of you speak freely with each other?"

"I like to think so."

"Now, Mr. Socolow, did there come a time when you and the defendant had an occasion to discuss Mr. Cimarron?"

"Yes. About six months ago, the two men had an altercation in Miami."

"Please tell the jury exactly what you said to the defendant and what he said to you."

Socolow sighed and glanced at me. He didn't want to be here. He looked as out of place on the witness stand as I did in the client's chair. We had been adversaries for a long time, but there was always a certain amount of respect. Now he was being asked to tattle. His long, lean frame hunched forward. His complexion was more sallow than usual. He looked as if he hadn't gotten much sleep last night. Good, that made two of us.

"Jake . . . Mr. Lassiter wanted to press charges against Mr. Cimarron for a fight that took place in the home of Josefina Baroso. In fact, Mr. Lassiter swore out an affidavit so that Mr. Cimarron could be arrested for assault and battery. I contacted Mr. Cimarron who said he'd be happy to—"

"Objection, hearsay!"

"No!" I tugged at Patterson's sleeve. "Let him answer."

"Why?"

"Trust me."

The judge cleared his throat, *ah-hem,* and looked at us with the same bemusement one might have when watching a dozen clowns tumble out of a car at the circus. "Is there an objection?"

"Objection withdrawn, Your Honor," Patterson said, graciously.

"You may continue, Mr. Socolow," the judge said.

"Mr. Cimarron said he'd be happy to return to Miami and face assault charges, or if Mr. Lassiter wanted, the two of them could go another couple of rounds."

A couple of the jurors looked surprised, and I winked at Patterson.

"And what did Mr. Lassiter say?"

"He said, 'To hell with that. Next time, I'll just shoot him in the kneecaps.' "

Damn, I'd forgotten that.

The lady schoolteacher gasped. The judge shook his head. A reporter for the local fish-wrapper scribbled away in the front row of the gallery. Next to me, Patterson turned, shielding his face from the jury, and gave me a withering look.

"In the kneecaps," McBain repeated, as if once weren't enough.

"Yes, that's what he said."

"Are you aware of any other verbal threats made by the defendant?"

"Yes. About two weeks before my conversation, he told Dr. Charles Riggs—"

"Objection, hearsay." Patterson rose halfway out of his chair. "In fact, hearsay within hearsay."

"Not so," McBain responded. "Mr. Lassiter is here and can refute the statement if he so wishes. Additionally, he can call the doctor to testify if he denies the statement was made."

"You're both barking up the wrong tree," the judge said. "Send the jury out for a short break."

The bailiff escorted the jurors into their little room, and the judge turned to McBain. "I assume your witness is going to testify that the doctor told him Mr. Lassiter threatened Mr. Cimarron."

"That's it, Your Honor. We attempted to serve a subpoena on Dr. Riggs, but he avoided service. In fact, he nearly ran down our process server in his pickup and screamed gibberish at him."

That wasn't gibberish. It was Latin, Marcus Ineptus.

"Mr. Socolow," the judge said. "Was the defendant present when the doctor told you of his threat?"

"No, Your Honor. I did repeat the statement to him, however."

"And did he respond by denying he made the threat?"

"No, Your Honor, he did not."

Patterson was prancing in front of the bench. One of my threats was quite enough for the jury's ears, and Patterson knew it. Experienced lawyers know what points are worth fighting for, and this was one of them.

"Your Honor, a man has a right to confront his accusers," Patterson said, "and when he's faced with hearsay, he is deprived of that right. This testimony is highly prejudicial, inflammatory, and if I may say so, might well be grounds for reversal if a conviction results."

Judge Witherspoon narrowed his eyes at my bantamweight lawyer. I've never met a judge yet who likes to be reminded of his fallibility. "That's what we've got appellate courts for, Mr. Patterson. Please feel free to appeal me on anything you like."

"Your Honor," McBain began, "the statement is not hearsay . . ."

"Yes, it is," the judge said, "but when it was repeated to the defendant by this witness, who is available for cross-examination, and the defendant did not deny making the statement, it becomes an exception to the hearsay rule as an adoptive admission. Bring in the jury."

I sunk lower in my chair, and Patterson slowly returned to the defense table. It was the first time I'd ever seen his shoulders slump in a courtroom. Usually, it's the lawyer who gives pep talks to the client, but just now Patterson was the one who needed cheering up. We had made a big deal out of trying to keep my statement out of evidence, and the jury knew it. We had lost, so my twelve peers would be keenly interested in what we didn't want them to hear.

The judge turned to the stenographer, a young woman in a pantsuit and cowboy boots. "Please read back Mr. McBain's last question."

The stenographer riffled through her accordion stacks of paper and read, " 'Are you aware of any other verbal threats made by the defendant?' "

Socolow nodded. "About two weeks before the conversation I earlier related, he had a conversation with Dr. Charles Riggs, retired coroner. I wasn't there, but Dr. Riggs repeated it to me, saying he was worried about Jake, who was acting strangely. I asked what he meant, and he answered that Jake was enraged with Mr. Cimarron and had threatened to tear his heart out."

"Tear his heart out," McBain echoed, shaking his head, sadly. "Were those his exact words?"

"I don't know if they were Mr. Lassiter's exact words, but they were Dr. Riggs's words, verbatim."

"Did you repeat Dr. Riggs's statement to the defendant?"

"Yes, in the same conversation I spoke about earlier."

"The one in which the defendant threatened to shoot Mr. Cimarron in the kneecaps?" McBain asked, in case the jurors had forgotten.

"Yes."

"And did the defendant deny threatening to tear out Mr. Cimarron's heart?"

"No, he did not."

"Did he say he was only joking?"

"No, he did not."

"What did he say?"

"First, he said something about once punching out a tight end for the Jets and drawing a penalty. Then he said he hated Mr. Cimarron."

"I see. So in the course of one conversation, the defendant threatened to shoot Mr. Cimarron in the kneecaps, and when reminded of his earlier threat regarding tearing Mr. Cimarron's heart out, he concluded by saying he hated the man."

"Yes, that's just about it."

"And what did you say to him?"

"I told him I wanted him to come into the office after the grand jury—"

"Objection!" Patterson pounded the table so hard, it woke up the bailiff. "Your Honor, this is the subject of our motion *in limine.*"

The judge called the lawyers to the bench for a sidebar conference. He had already indicated he would prohibit any mention of the indictment against me in Miami for Kyle Hornback's murder. I couldn't hear the whispers at the side of the bench, but in a moment the two lawyers, the stenographer, and the judge were back to business.

"Mr. Socolow," McBain said, "without telling us the surrounding circumstances, did you give Mr. Lassiter any advice regarding Mr. Cimarron?"

"Yes. I suppose you'd call it advice. I told him to stay away from Mr. Cimarron."

"Anything else?"

"I advised him not to leave the state because of certain
. . . ah . . . potential court proceedings in Miami."

"Did he follow your advice?"

"Apparently not."

"Thank you, Mr. Socolow. Your witness."

H. T. Patterson was in a bind. If he brought out the
mutual respect Socolow and I shared, it would help polish
my tarnished image. It would also show the jury that Socolow, this good, decent state attorney, had concluded his
old buddy had sunk so low into depravity he would now
testify against him.

Patterson stood at the lectern a respectful distance from
the witness stand.

"Now, Mr. Socolow, you never thought Mr. Lassiter
intended to shoot Mr. Cimarron in the kneecaps, did you?"

"No, sir."

"Or tear his heart out?"

"No, sir."

"We all say things in the heat of passion that we don't
mean?"

"Yes, sir."

"Mr. Lassiter was upset at the time of these statements?"

"He seemed to be."

"Was he, in fact, recuperating from injuries inflicted by
Mr. Cimarron?"

"Yes, he was."

"A fight in which Mr. Cimarron was the aggressor?"

"That was Mr. Lassiter's position. It was not shared by
Mr. Cimarron."

"And Ms. Baroso?"

"Mr. Lassiter wanted her to press charges against Mr.
Cimarron. She declined. Frankly, I don't know who did
what that night."

"But Mr. Lassiter suffered serious injuries?"

"I believe he broke his hand and had a number of
bruises and scrapes, that sort of thing."

"You've known Jake Lassiter a long time. Have you ever known him to provoke violence?"

Socolow wrinkled his high forehead. He didn't want to answer. "I'm not sure what you mean. Once, in a trial, he provoked a witness into a fistfight, but it was a ploy, a strategy to show the violent streak of the witness."

"They must do things differently down in Miami," the judge said, and a couple of the jurors smirked.

H. T. Patterson had heard all he wanted on that subject and sat down. "Nothing further."

"Redirect?" the judge asked.

McBain stood and buttoned his suit coat. "Are you saying, Mr. Socolow, that you didn't take Mr. Lassiter's threats seriously?"

"No, sir."

"What are you saying?"

"I didn't take them literally. I didn't think he intended to shoot Mr. Cimarron in the kneecaps or tear his heart out."

"I suppose not," McBain said, already easing back into his chair. "I suppose he just intended to shoot a nail through the man's brain."

"Objection," Patterson yelped.

"Withdrawn," McBain said, sitting down.

The judge called for the noon recess, and not a moment too soon. Socolow walked by my table, clasped me on the shoulder, and left without a word. The jurors filed out, then the judge, and then the spectators. The prosecutor and his assistants hitched up their pants and walked out, too.

Patterson and I were alone.

"H.T., you look a tad peaked."

"What?"

"You look pale."

"That's impossible, I assure you."

"Okay, then you look stressed out. Hey, it's still the top of the first inning. We haven't been to bat yet."

He forced a smile, but his eyes were glazed over and distant.

"H.T., I think you need to drink some lunch."

"Demon rum won't cure what ails me."

"Counselor, you're a little rattled, that's all."

He looked at me with sorrow in his eyes. "It's hell to represent a friend, Jake. It's so much easier to take a fat fee from a stranger and give it your best shot. You win, you lose, you go on. Hell, we're not paid to win, right, just to force the state to prove its case. But now, with you, I care. I want to win, but I don't know how. They've got us outflanked on self-defense, and there's no way to pin this on Jo Jo or anyone else. I lie awake at night trying to come up with theories and I don't have any. Oh, I can cross-examine until the snow melts, but once the state rests, we've got to put on a case, and there isn't a thought in my head."

"Okay, I get it. We need to brainstorm. Just tell me what can I do to help?"

His smile held more sadness than joy. "Fetch me my brown trousers, Fritz."

Sergeant Kimberly Crawford was assigned to something called the Spousal Abuse Unit. She took the third statement of the night from Josefina Baroso, driving her back to the station after Sheriff's Deputy Clayton Dobson and Detective Bernie Racklin did their work. Defense lawyers love to get prosecution witnesses on the record as many times as possible to ferret out contradictions. We had copies of all three statements, and there wasn't an inconsistency in the bunch.

Sergeant Crawford took photos of bruises on Jo Jo's thighs and ribs, and a shot of the face revealed a black eye. Jo Jo looked appropriately distraught, helpless, victimized.

Yes, Ms. Baroso was crying and moaning.

No, not about her injuries. Poor Simmy is dead. Poor Simmy is dead. That's what she kept repeating, rocking back and forth in a chair down in the station, right here in the basement of the courthouse.

The photos were passed out to the jurors, who appeared more upset with Josefina's black eye than Cimarron's gray matter splattered in the straw.

The woman cop was on and off the stand in fifteen minutes, and the judge asked the prosecutor to call his next witness. I thought McBain looked a little too smug when he sang out, "The state calls Josefina Baroso."

The bailiff hustled into the hallway and called her name. The jurors had been waiting for this. McBain was no dummy. Most prosecutors would have started their case with her. She could tell the story chronologically, and that always makes it easier for the jury. You also want to create a good first impression, and Jo Jo could surely do that. But if you're clever and subtle, it's a neat trick to save your star witness. Build the jurors' interest with hints and clues and let them wonder. Who is this woman who launched a thousand fists? What does she look like? Is she worth dying for?

Even before I saw her, I knew. "Ten to one, she's wearing black," I whispered to Patterson. In her own cases, Jo Jo dressed her witnesses for maximum sympathy. Pluck the jurors' heartstrings with a grieving widow and all the kids. When her witnesses gathered for lunch in the Justice Building cafeteria, it looked like an Italian funeral.

The heavy door swung open, and Josefina Jovita Baroso walked into the courtroom. She wore a flared black wool dress with gold buttons from its high neck to its hem, which stopped halfway down her black, knee-high crushed leather boots. The dress concealed her womanly curves and, combined with the sophisticated look of hair pulled straight back and a light dusting of makeup and lip gloss, spoke volumes of who she was, or rather, who she appeared to be. Her dark eyes were bright and intelligent and avoided mine as she strode on long legs to the witness stand. She nodded to the jurors, looked the clerk in the eye as she took the oath, smoothed her dress, and sat down.

I studied her. Now, here was a total woman. Here was a woman who had been assaulted, who had witnessed a savage crime, and who was ready to do what had to be done to right those wrongs. She was attractive without being seductive. She was purposeful without being pugnacious. She was here, not because she thirsted for vengeance, but because she sought justice. She was, in short, the perfect witness, which was precisely the image she had worked so hard to create.

Jo Jo recited her name, her address, and her profession.

"So you have the same job I have?" McBain asked.

"Yes," she said.

Bonding with the witness, telling the jury: If you like me, you'll like her.

McBain had her run through the life and times of Jo Jo Baroso, beginning with her family fleeing Castro's Communist island when she was still an infant. Her father lost everything in Cuba and never adjusted to life in the States. He turned to liquor and gambling and eventually left her mother who raised a son and daughter by herself. She met the defendant while she was still in college, and he was a pro football player.

Yes, she became romantically involved with the defendant. "I was so young then," Jo Jo said, almost shyly.

Making me sound like a cradle robber.

"How did the relationship end?" McBain asked.

"Rather badly," she said. "I always pushed Jake to be better, to make something of himself."

True, true.

"He went to law school, and I like to think I had something to do with that . . ."

Okay already, you saved me from a life of selling insurance.

"But I always believed in public service. I wanted to repay this country for what it gave me, a home, freedom . . ."

Arroz con pollo in every pot. Talk about laying it on thick.

"And I don't think Jake could relate to that. He had so much, and everything came so easy to him."

Wait one gosh-darned second. I'm the one without a daddy or mommy.

"I wanted him to do something meaningful with his life, but he preferred hanging around with swindlers and con men, including, I am sorry to say, my brother, Luis, or Louis, as he preferred to call himself. They hatched schemes together, and Jake would defend him when things went bad. I was just devastated that my brother and my ... my lover were involved in activities that ran counter to everything I believed in, so I cut myself off from both of them. It was the hardest thing I ever had to do."

"You terminated the relationship with the defendant?"

"Yes, I dropped him."

Hey, who dropped whom?

"Did you lose touch with the defendant?"

"Yes, for several years. Oh, I'd see him in the Justice Building once in a while, walking some three-time loser out of court, but we no longer had a relationship. Then, I ran into him when he was defending my brother in a fraud case. After the trial, I learned how they ingratiated themselves into Simmy's ... Mr. Cimarron's venture."

"You're talking about Rocky Mountain Treasures, Inc.?"

"Yes. It was Simmy's dream. Buried treasure. I know it sounds foolish, but it was part of his love of the old West. He knew most of the legends were just that, but he believed some were true, and he wanted to explore. He had studied the old maps and diaries, and he would talk about it for hours. It was my brother's idea to raise money through a public sale of stock. Unfortunately, he and Jake embezzled money from the cash Simmy put up."

"Objection!" Patterson thundered. "There's been no predicate laid for such a conclusion. The testimony is prejudicial and inflammatory and should be stricken."

"Sustained. The jury will disregard the last remark of the witness."

Sure. Just try.

"What did Mr. Cimarron tell you concerning the stock sale and Mr. Lassiter's involvement?"

"Objection, hearsay!"

"Not at all, Your Honor," McBain replied. "It's not coming in for the truth of the statement. Perhaps Mr. Cimarron was wrong about Mr. Lassiter. It doesn't matter. The statement is coming in to show what Mr. Cimarron believed, and once that belief was communicated to Mr. Lassiter, it is relevant to the issue of Mr. Lassiter's intent to commit the homicide."

"Respectfully, Your Honor," Patterson said, "Mr. Cimarron's state of mind is not at issue here. It doesn't matter what he—"

"Overruled. I'll give the state some leeway here."

"Simmy said that Jake stole seventy-five thousand dollars from him, but even worse, he helped my brother in the stock scam. They defrauded investors and threatened the existence of the company."

"Were you present at a conversation between Mr. Cimarron and Mr. Lassiter to that effect?"

"Yes. Last June, in my house in Miami."

If that was a "conversation," Ali versus Frazier was a tea party.

"And what transpired?"

"Simmy and Jake exchanged words . . ."

To say nothing of fists.

"Simmy accused Jake of stealing. Jake hit Simmy, but Simmy is . . . that is, was . . . quite large and very strong. He got the best of Jake that time."

Her voice cracked on the last words, and her eyes teared.

Judge Witherspoon was looking at his watch, and McBain was thumbing through his notes. It was a few minutes before six and had been a long day, at least for me.

"Perhaps this would be a good place to recess," the judge said. "Your witness can resume at nine in the morning."

"Just one more question, Your Honor."

A lawyer promising to ask only one question is like a kid promising to eat only one jelly bean.

The judge nodded, and McBain came closer to the witness stand. ''Ms. Baroso, I seem to have quite forgotten to ask something. What was your relationship with the deceased?''

Her voice was as soft as a fluttering snowflake. ''He was my hus . . .''

That's funny. For a second, I thought she said ole Kit was her . . .

''Please keep your voice up for the jury, ma'am.''

''Kit Carson Cimarron was my husband,'' she said, in a strong, proud voice. ''I am his widow.''

25

Your Money and Your Wife

My brain trust couldn't agree whether to lather the margarita glasses with salt, so how could I expect coherent advice on cross-examining Josefina Baroso? We were in the kitchenette of Granny's double-wide, the four of us scrunched onto stools at the Formica counter.

"That girl's lying through her teeth," Granny said, as she squeezed limes the old-fashioned way, in her clenched fists. "She never got hitched to that cowboy, or Jake would know about it."

"McBain showed me the marriage certificate," Patterson said, glumly. "A civil ceremony in Nevada six years ago. Uh, no salt on mine, please. Watching my blood pressure."

Granny growled and kept squeezing. "Six years! Criminy, Jake, you been sniffing after a married woman." Now she poured tequila into the juice. "You like yours with a dash of Triple Sec or Cointreau?"

"The bottle of tequila will do just fine, Granny, and I broke up with her before she met him. It just beats me why she kept the marriage a secret."

"Maybe the cowboy was already married," Granny said conspiratorially.

"Yeah," Kip chimed in, digging into a bowl of chocolate ice cream. "Maybe he was a bigamist, like Clifton Webb in *The Remarkable Mr. Pennypacker.*"

"Nothing so sinister," Patterson said. "He wanted to live out west and dig for Coronado's gold. She wanted to prosecute criminals in Miami. They tied the knot but didn't tell anybody. She kept her name and her job. For the first couple of years, they'd fly back and forth every few weeks, but that got old. They began to see each other less. I suppose you could say they separated, except they did that right after the honeymoon. But they kept getting back together over the years. Essentially, what you had were two strong-willed people who were drawn to each other, but neither one would budge on geography or lifestyle."

"So why'd she invite me to her bed in Miami six months ago?"

"It never happened," Patterson said.

"I need that tequila, right now, Granny." I turned back to my lawyer. "What's that supposed to mean?"

"When the widow lady testified today, did you hear anything about her exchanging bodily fluids with you?"

"No, she just said I was at her house, and Cimarron and I had a conversation. Then I hit him but lost a fistfight, something like that."

"And you want me to get her to admit on cross that she was in bed with you when Cimarron broke in?"

"Of course I do, and for lots of reasons starting with destroying her credibility. She's going to testify I sexually assaulted her in the barn, right?"

"About a dozen hours from now."

"Well, why would I have to attack her if she was a willing bedmate?"

"You wouldn't, so she must deny the sexual interlude ever took place."

"Well, I'll say it did," I said, somewhat petulantly.

"Did Josefina ever tell Socolow that Cimarron rousted you from her bed?"

"No, I don't think so."

"Did you?"

"No. I don't kiss and tell, but I figured he knew what was going on."

"Yet, he cannot dispute her testimony, can he?"

I didn't answer, so he asked another question. "How did Cimarron get into the house?"

"I don't know. I was asleep at the time. There was no sign of forced entry."

"Well then, I'll tell you," Patterson said. "He had a key. Always did. Had it on his key chain the night he died. As you know, he owned the house in Miami. Josefina knew he was in town. He was, after all, staying there with her. Now, you're going to ask the jury to believe she invited you to spend the night when she knew her husband would be coming home."

"So what the hell *was* I doing there?"

"According to Josefina, discussing Blinky and Rocky Mountain Treasures, waiting for Cimarron to show up for a meeting."

"That's crap! We were fastened onto each other like—"

"Jake!" Granny gave me her steely stare. "There's tender ears on the premises."

"Where?" Kip asked. "Hey, Granny, I saw *Basic Instinct* where Sharon Stone crosses her legs and puckers up—"

"Hush!" Granny commanded.

Patterson drained his margarita. "Jake, it doesn't matter what the two of you did because I can't prove it. You want to testify that you bedded her down in Miami, you'll come off as a boorish lout who's accusing the grieving widow of infidelity."

"Infidelity? Who gives a flying fandango? She's accused me of murder!"

"And I'm trying to keep you from proving her case."

I took a hit on the tequila straight out of the bottle. It was intended to make me think more clearly, but it made my lips feel like rubber worms. Still, the outline of a thought was forming. "H.T., maybe it's starting to make sense, now."

"What is?"

"What you were saying the other day. She set me up, all right, starting with that night in the cottage."

"Keep talking," he said.

"At the time, I thought she craved my body. Desire under the mangoes."

"Elms," Kip corrected me. "Sophia Loren and Anthony Perkins."

"Boy am I stupid!"

"Don't state the obvious," Patterson said. "Get on with it."

"Just like you said, she knew Cimarron was coming over. Coming home, in fact. She *wanted* me in her bed when he showed up. She wanted me to fight him. Who knows, maybe Cimarron would be carrying a gun and one of us would buy the farm right there. If not, there's always a second chance after she got me to chase her to Colorado. H.T., you've been right all along."

"I have been, as surely as God makes little brown babies, but what am I to do with it? I can't prove a word of it. I guarantee you that no member of the jury will buy it."

Here I was getting pumped up, and my lawyer's defeatist attitude rankled me. "Hey, Counselor, whose side are you on?"

Patterson looked hurt.

And must have been.

He didn't ask for a refill. He just grabbed his wool ski cap, put on his orange parka, and headed for the door. "We're all a little tired, Jake. I'll see you in court."

I didn't tell him good night.

Now Granny was scowling at me. "You know, Jake, you're a fine specimen of a man."

"What's that supposed to mean?"

"Well, you got about an acre of shoulders, a bushy head

of hair, all your own teeth, and a by-God full allotment of mouth.''

"Okay, okay, I was a little tough on H.T., but I'm getting so frustrated, I feel like hitting someone.''

"Don't worry, Uncle Jake," Kip said, his upper lip coated with a chocolate stripe. "If that woman's saying bad things about you, no one will believe her. No one could believe you did anything bad.''

"Kip, I love you, do you know that?''

"Sure.''

"I'm sorry I haven't been able to spend much time with you.''

"It's okay. I like it here. The snow and all, it's like *Dr. Zhivago.*''

"You been making any movies?''

"Can't." He looked into his bowl of melting ice cream. Granny said, "He's been afraid to tell you. In all the commotion, moving around and all, he lost the camera.''

"I'm sorry, Uncle Jake. I just don't know where—''

"Hey, it's okay. When's the last time you had it?''

"That night in the barn. Maybe the cops took it.''

"I don't remember it on the inventory," I said, consigning the information to the repository in my brain where I store odds and ends that don't fit anywhere else.

"I know this sounds ridiculous," Josefina Baroso said, "but to this day, I don't know if it was rape. It's so difficult to explain. Jake forced himself on me, but . . . I didn't fight back. He hit me. He had before, so that was nothing new. He tore at my clothes. He told me he would have me whether I wanted it or not. He used to get like that, so full of anger, so violent. He just wore me down, and I let him. I just let him.''

With that, a tear tracked down a sculpted cheekbone. I felt my face heat up. The jurors were riveted to their chairs. No darting eyes, no coughs, no fidgeting. They just watched Josefina Baroso with empathy and concern for this brave woman. She was so damn good. She gave the appearance of trying to be fair. No, she can't call it rape. Of course not, she never told the cops she'd been raped. A physical exam would have disproved that lie.

It was a flaw in her story, at least until she explained it away with her sob story about not knowing whether it was rape at all. Still, Patterson could cross-examine as to why she didn't tell the cops the whole story.

McBain anticipated the question on cross-examination and defused it. "Ms. Baroso, you never told Sergeant Crawford that the defendant forced you to submit to sex, did you?"

"No . . . I couldn't. I was so ashamed. I blamed myself for it. Maybe I should have fought back, but I was afraid Simmy would hear. I was afraid someone would get killed."

Josefina Baroso had spent four years on the sexual assault team in the state attorney's office, and it showed. She knew what worked, and what didn't, and when she spouted clichés, they sounded heartfelt.

"Now, Ms. Baroso, what happened after the defendant forced you to submit to him?"

"I was lying there crying, and Simmy came into the barn looking for me. Jake said something about wanting to thank him."

"Thank him?"

"Yes. He turned to Simmy and smiled, a really vicious smile, and said, 'Thanks, cowboy, for your money and your wife.' "

In the jury box, it looked like 12–0 for stringing me up right there.

"Then what happened?" McBain asked.

"I was crying, but somehow I told Simmy what happened. He stayed calm. He was breathing hard, and he told Jake to leave or he'd take him apart. Jake laughed and said, 'Try it.' Simmy came at him, I'm not going to deny that. He wanted to throw him out of there so he could take care of me. But Jake was on him so quickly, tossing him into the wall, hitting his head. Jake is very strong, and even though Simmy was big, he wasn't quick enough.''

Then she told the story, blow by blow, and it matched everything the jury had already heard. So warm and comforting for the finders of fact. They'd heard the story in McBain's opening statement. They'd heard it again from the three police officers. Now, the eyewitness tells it one more time. Anticlimactic but reassuring. Lawyers like to say they tell jurors what they're going to hear, then tell them, then tell them what they've told them. That's what McBain was doing, and he'd recap it in closing argument.

So I sat at the defense table, a miscreant with curved horns and hairy ears, as my hellish deeds were recounted. I heard how I slammed Simmy around, stabbed him with a pitchfork, laughed in the face of the bullwhip, tackled him in the corncrib, and eventually put a nail through his head. I heard every agonizing, perjurious detail, hoping for inconsistencies, but there were none.

She took the better part of the day, stopping several times to wipe the tears. As the afternoon wore on, the windowpanes of the courtroom shuddered with an approaching storm. Outside, the sky darkened, and snow cascaded from the sky. Inside, it was stuffy and the air so dry, the skin on my knuckles was splitting. I longed for the heat and humidity of home, for a gentle easterly, warm as a baby's breath, as it crossed the Gulf Stream.

What was I doing here? I fought the urge to stand and run, the courtroom door banging behind me. My arms tensed. Would the bailiff stop me? No, he was asleep, waiting for his Social Security check.

Where would I go? An island, maybe. Barbados, Aruba, Curaçao. I yearned for sunny days and wide beaches, and most of all, freedom. How far would I get? They would hunt me down. They would compare me to Ted Bundy, who crawled out a window in this very courthouse, before going on a rampage of rape and murder in Florida.

I'm not sure what my face showed, but Patterson put a calming hand on my shoulder. I forced myself to concentrate on a spot on the wall just above a line of old photographs of judges who presided here. And I thought about where we were and where we had to go.

McBain had done his job, and Jo Jo had done hers. It was all wrapped up neatly and tied with a bow, an early Christmas present for the jury. I was jotting down notes as the prosecutor was winding down his questioning.

"Ms. Baroso, please forgive me for asking this, but did you love your husband?"

"So very much. It was an unconventional arrangement, I know, but it worked for us. He had his ranch and his dreams of buried treasure. He was out here, in the country he loved. I had my career, contributing to society in the best way I could. In my heart, I know we loved each other as much as any other couple."

"Did you intend the defendant to follow you to Colorado?"

"No. I didn't even tell him I was coming here. He admitted to me he broke into my house and listened to my answering machine to find me." A look of sadness for the pathetic, obsessed stalker seemed to cross her face. "I thought he had gotten over me, but once he began representing my brother again, something happened. It started all over again, and he began pursuing me."

The poor woman. How could anyone blame her for all this?

"So, in summary, Ms. Baroso, the defendant followed you to Colorado without your knowledge or consent, confronted you in the barn on your husband's property, struck you and forced you to submit to sexual intercourse . . ."

I tugged at my lawyer's sleeve, but he waved me off.

". . . and when your husband found you, disheveled and beaten, the defendant taunted him, beat him, and finally shot a nail through his brain, killing him?"

"Objection, leading," Patterson said, quietly.

"Granted. The jury will disregard the question . . ."

It didn't matter if they disregarded the question. They already knew the answer.

"Mr. McBain," the judge said, "do you have anything

further, because the bailiff tells me the weather is deteriorating, and I believe I'm going to let these good folks go home early today.''

''Just about finished, Your Honor.''

''Ms. Baroso, is there anything else you wish to say, anything you've left out?''

She didn't even have to think about it. You don't have to when you've rehearsed the closing line. ''If only you could have known him,'' she said, turning toward the jury. ''Such a fine, decent man, so full of life. I loved him, and I miss him so.''

The judge cleared his throat and banged his gavel, telling everyone to be back at nine in the morning.

My eyes were still on Josefina Jovita Baroso, as she walked gallantly out of the courtroom. I thought about what Kip had said this morning, that nobody would believe her. My lovable nephew was wrong.

I can read their faces, Kipper. I can read their minds.

They believed her and were ready to convict. Hell, if I'd been on the jury, I would have convicted me, too.

26

A-Thousand-One,
A-Thousand-Two

I didn't go to Barbados, Aruba, or Curaçao. Instead, I said good-bye to Patterson, slogged through the snow, and got my rental car from the garage at the foot of Galena Street. There were no beaches or bikinied lasses along the way. There were boots and gloves, scarves pulled tight against the cold. Before coming here, the last time I saw a ski mask, it was being introduced into evidence against my client who wore it when pointing an Uzi at a convenience store clerk in Hialeah.

My car yawked and hawked and sputtered like an old codger clearing his throat. I nearly flooded the carburetor but finally got it to turn over and cough itself to life. I pulled onto Main Street and turned left, for no good reason, it could just as well have been right. Clouds hung low, shrouding the town in a gray mist, obscuring the surrounding mountains. There was no wind, and the snow fell straight and hard, as if dumped from a celestial truck. I used to ski on days like this, the visibility so poor you had to guess where the next mogul would pop up. But then, I windsurf in thunderstorms, too.

I drove slowly, politely yielding the right of way a cou-

ple of times. Traffic was heavy, the Volvos and Jeeps,
Range Rovers and Land Cruisers heading home, ski racks
laden with equipment. Hey, fun seekers, I envy you, muscles stretched and lungs expanded. Load up with complex
carbs tonight, stretch out with someone you love—or at
least like—in a hot tub, and be back at it in the fresh
powder tomorrow. Me, I think I'll just visit the courthouse
and let them call me a rapist and murderer all day.

I drove aimlessly and found myself heading east out of
town. I turned left and started up a gentle rise on the lower
slopes of what was probably Smuggler Mountain. I was
lost, but what did it matter? I had nowhere to go and lots
of time to get there. Suddenly, from behind, a black Dodge
Turbo Ram pickup with dual rear wheels pulled out and
passed me, its oversize tires chomping through the fresh
snow. Through its steamy rear window, I caught sight of
a long spill of dark hair. I squinted at the personalized
Colorado plate as the truck sped on. "Aurum." I didn't
have to call Doc Riggs for the translation. I remembered
it from high school chemistry, right along with dropping
a dissected frog down Joan Wooldridge's blouse.

Aurum is gold.

She was driving Cimarron's truck. Hers now, I supposed. I gave the rental some gas and followed the taillights up the hill. She turned right, and so did I. She turned
left, and I followed. Hey, this was fun. We went about a
mile, made a couple more turns, and she slowed. I hung
back, watching, waiting.

I tuned the radio to an oldies station and heard the Beat-
les longing for yesterday. Me, too. I listened to my wipers
clackety-clacking and had a conversation with myself.

Just what the hell was I doing?

Following Jo Jo Baroso.

Why?

Because, like Everest, she's there.

What does that mean?

It means I don't know why. Maybe I want her to testify
tomorrow that I'm still stalking her, turn up the heat some

more. Maybe I'll run her car into a ditch, grab her and make her eat a handful of snow. Or maybe I just want to know why she's driving up Smuggler Mountain in the middle of a blizzard. Maybe I figure there's an answer out here, because there sure as hell isn't one anywhere else.

Through the gray haze and falling snow, I didn't see the fork in the road. She turned left smartly. I hit the brakes and tried to follow but spun out. I whipped the wheel back, let up on the brakes, then kissed them gently. The car straightened and came to a stop. I had missed the turn. I started up again, threw it into reverse, tires spinning, got back to the fork, and took the turn ever so slowly. The taillights were gone. Half a mile up the road was another fork. I took the low road and never saw the pickup again.

I kept going because I had nothing better to do. I listened to the Rolling Stones complain about getting no satisfaction. I took another turn onto what seemed to be a gravel road, though under a cover of snow, you couldn't tell. Then I figured out it wasn't a road at all, but a private drive. I hit the brakes and slid to a stop in front of a black, wrought-iron fence. A cemetery. How appropriate.

I got out of the car, tromped through the snow, opened a gate and walked in. The headstones were topped with snow and weathered from the years, but the vertical ones could be read. Many dated from the mining days. Beneath a marble figure of a child asleep on a pedestal, the inscription: "Mabel Garnett Asbell, December 12, 1888, one year and four days."

I thought about the winter of 1888 and the girl's parents, burying their child, and it made me think of Kip and suddenly I was filled with sorrow. If I was sent away, what would become of him? What a strange thought. A year ago, I didn't know of his existence. Now, my first thought about my future, or lack of it, was of him. So that's what love is all about.

Other questions plagued me. How long will Granny be around? Who will take care of her?

A statue of a lamb guarded the grave of another child.

"Our darling Mallory." A white marble headstone, July 28, 1898, for "Little Dale, ten months and fifteen days." Nearby, the headless statue of a woman in the Greek style stood guard over a grave surrounded by a rusty iron fence. The woman wore a flowing gown, and her right hand held a garland of granite flowers.

I stood there, bareheaded in the falling snow, overcome with a sadness such as I've never known. Tears flowed down my cheeks. I turned and started to run, slipping in the snow and falling, legs splayed. I got to my feet and hurried to the car in a crablike crouch, a foolish figure of a man frozen to the core, not with cold, but with fear.

The Jack Daniel's warmed me, comforted me. The bottle sat between my legs under the steering wheel, and I'd already put a good dent in it. From the liquor store, I headed west out of town for the same reason I earlier had headed east: none.

When I got to the turnoff to Red Butte, I swung right, fishtailing in the snow. I missed the road to Woody Creek, did a U-turn, barely avoiding a ditch concealed by snowdrifts, and slowly began climbing the hill past fenced fields covered with virgin snow. I knew the way, though I had been here only once before.

The front gate was chained and padlocked, and the county sheriff had posted a NO TRESPASSING sign. Not enough to stop a man overcome with lust and greed, a man with a thirst for violence, or whatever McBain would say in closing argument.

I was wearing my trial suit and a wool overcoat and felt out of place in the broad expanse of the frozen ranch. I climbed over the gate, my wing tips crunching into the snow of the driveway. I sunk to my knees with each step. It was a laborious walk, and I began sweating. Cold on the outside, steaming inside. Halfway up the road, I turned back to look at my tracks. I thought of an animal, chased across the fields by hunters.

The house was quiet and dark, no cars outside. Wher-

ever Josefina was staying, it wasn't here. That was smart.
She might have figured I'd come looking for her.

But that wasn't why I had come to the Red Canyon
Ranch.

I hadn't known it while driving here, but I knew it now.
I came because it was time to act more like a lawyer and
less like a client. As a lawyer, I always visited the site,
whether it was an auto accident or a murder scene. Sure,
I used investigators, and in discovery, I'd get the state's
evidence. But there is no substitute for being there, even
if you've been there before. After I hired H. T. Patterson,
we came here under the watchful eyes of a police escort.
I had walked him through it, but now, cold and alone, I
would do it again. Instead of a briefcase, I carried a bottle
of Jack Daniel's.

The barn door was unlocked. I flipped on the lights. The
horses were still in their stalls, oats freshly poured. Muddy
footprints led to the feed bags and back to the stalls. A
neighboring rancher must have been helping out. I said
hello to the horses, and one of them said something back,
his breath visible in the cold.

I retraced my steps of that night. The night in question,
as lawyers like to say.

Up the ladder to the loft. I remembered Jo Jo flicking
on a lantern, the shadows creeping up the wall. What had
she said?

Oh, Jake, you shouldn't have come. How true. What
else? Think now. How did she look? Remember that face.
She had seemed surprised Kip was with me. And upset
about it.

The boy shouldn't be here.

Why not?

Because she didn't want him, or anyone else to witness
what would happen. Right, but how did she know what
would happen? What was her plan? That I kill Cimarron?
That he kill me? And why?

Motive, motive, motive.

I walked the circumference of the loft, making a trail in

the straw. Snowflakes drifted through the wall where the plank had been removed. I looked around, but I didn't know for what. I saw the railing, or what was left of it, where I had broken through before landing in a stall.

I went down to the first floor, but this time took the slow route of the ladder. Accurately re-creating the scene has its limits. I opened the Appaloosa's stall, walked inside, and my shoes squished in a steaming pile of what had been oats only a day before. The horse seemed to smile at me.

I left the stall, straw sticking to my shoes. For a while, I fiddled around, tinkering with this and that, touching the rough wood planks, trying to divine some message that had to be there. I went into the corncrib, still overflowing with ears that had tumbled down the silo. I stepped out of the crib and wandered in a circle, first clockwise, then counterclockwise. I kicked at bales of hay and feed bags.

What was missing? A saddle with an embedded nail, a plank from the wall with Cimarron's hair embedded in it. The bridle and bit I had used to get Cimarron off me. The nail gun. Now all tagged and marked as state's exhibits.

I took a hit of the bourbon to fend off the chill and kept looking. There were no surprises. No revelations. No clues, at least none I could see. Just the crisp air and sweet smells of horse feed mixed with the musky tang of manure. Just a nondescript barn where a man had died a gruesome death.

I pulled two blankets from a railing and put them around my shoulders. I sat down in the straw and made myself comfortable. I sneezed, maybe from the dust, or maybe from the cold. For medicinal purposes, I guzzled some more bourbon, liquid *aurum* to warm the throat. I leaned back and tried to concentrate on words like "evidence" and "proof" and "reasonable doubt," but my mind was a battery running out of juice. I couldn't concentrate and after a while, I didn't even try. I listened to the snorts of the horses and the shuffling of their hooves. Outside, an owl hooted. I hummed a song to myself and dug deeper into the straw, a babe in the manger, finally closing my eyes and burying myself under the warm velvet blanket of sleep.

I don't know if it was the morning sun or the cold that woke me. The sun slanted through the open slat in the wall and struck me squarely in the eyes. Dust motes floated in the light, and the cold bit through me to the bone. I tried to stand, but every joint was locked into place. I felt like the tin man in *The Wizard of Oz*. It took several moments to work out the knots and kinks in my back. I felt an urgent need to pee and a secondary need to brush my teeth. A cup of coffee and a Danish wouldn't have hurt anything, either.

I needed to get back to my apartment, shower and change for court. I started walking out when something caught my eye. The shaft of sunlight crossed the barn floor and ended barely two feet from where I had slept. There, in a depression I had made in the straw, the sunlight caught the reflection of a wedge of glass that twinkled back at me. I followed the sunlight four paces, bent down and dug into the straw. Up came Kip's video camera, lens pointed to the sun.

It was clear and cold, the sky a bottomless blue. Light snow was falling, puffy, dry flakes unlike what I was used to in the five winters I spent as a student-athlete in the hills of central Pennsylvania. Yeah, that's right. It took five years, but I got my degree. I remember those ice storms, including one during a game against Notre Dame. The referee fell on his ass flipping the coin, and the rest of us could barely break a huddle without skating like Dorothy Hamill on LSD. My fingers were numb by the end of the first quarter, but I refused to wear gloves or a second pair of socks. Let the sissy wide receivers keep their pinkies toasty. I played with short sleeves and a cutoff jersey that stopped right above my navel. After missing a tackle on the opening kickoff, I slid halfway across the field on my belly and ice water sloshed down my jock. I can't remember if we won or lost, but I seem to recall spending Sunday through Thursday in the infirmary with the flu.

That was then. This is now.

Here the snow was dry and powdery, just like the travel posters show, and the roads were already clear, snow piled high alongside. I wasn't as polite driving back into town as I had been getting out. I honked at tortoiselike tourists. I skidded around one corner and ignored every posted speed limit I could find.

Back in town, I stood ten minutes in the doorway waiting for the camera store to open. The female clerk gave me a curious look. Maybe it was the wildness in my eyes, maybe the smell of straw and manure. After a moment, she found the battery I needed and an earphone, took my cash, and watched me leave, the bell attached to the front door tinkling merrily.

When I had picked up the camera in the barn, I muttered a private prayer to whatever God protects the semi-honest man who doesn't strangle kittens or litter in public parks. The prayer was answered when I found the on button engaged. The battery, of course, would be dead. It was. So far, so good.

A silent thank-you.

Through the Plexiglas cover, I saw the tape was three-quarters unwound. A couple of hours had been recorded before the battery gave out. With any luck, it would all be there.

Not the video, of course, once Kip left the loft. The camera had been buried in the straw. But the sound. The audio would be there. What had Kip told me? *This baby can pick up a rat farting at fifty yards.*

I was back in the car, parked at the curb, engine running, heater on, my heart thumping as the tape rewound. It was one of those Super-8 formats you don't need a separate VCR to show on your TV. I rewound to the beginning of the tape, fighting the urge to see the middle first. I attached the earphone jack to the camera and watched through the viewfinder as I hit the play button.

The first shot was a speck against the sky. The lens zoomed. A bird. The frame jumped around as Kip tried to steady the camera. "Lord of flight," Kip said into the microphone. "A golden eagle. Last of a breed. Mighty predator." Kip went on for a while, sounding like a pint-size Marlin Perkins. The bird disappeared into some spruce trees and Kip said, "Shit, where'd he go?"

Next, a shot of the kids from the neighboring cabin at the Lazy Q. Then, a dog urinating against a tree. Then, there it was: a darkened room, growing lighter as the lens opened wider. The nine-volt lantern cast half of Jo Jo's face in a white, bleaching light, the other half in darkness, but I saw her, huddled under a blanket.

"No, Jake, please. I'm so ashamed. The boy shouldn't be here."

The camera jiggled and seemed to adjust itself to the light. "Uncle Jake, please, you're cutting off the angle. I want to zoom from medium close up to extreme close up."

He did, and Jo Jo's face filled the screen, tear-streaked cheeks and puffy eyes. But close up, the eyes revealed something else altogether. That blazing intelligence, that quick mind, that total control.

Her forehead was wrinkled in thought. She wasn't in shock. She wasn't in fear. Her brain was in overdrive. Why didn't I see it at the time?

"Jake, no! Haven't you done enough to me already?" She buried her head in her hands.

I didn't say, "What's that supposed to mean?" I didn't say, "What the hell are you talking about?" I didn't say anything. But then, I thought she was talking about old times, or that she was confused. Hell, I don't know what I was thinking, but I sure didn't think she had it all figured out, that the prosecutor lady knew the tape might just pop up as evidence and it might be nice to show the All-Pro pervert had a kid videotaping his evil deeds.

"Okay," I said on the tape. "Kip. Cut! I've got enough."

Was it my imagination, or was there an unnecessary harshness to my voice. The screen faded to black.

Oh, Jo Jo, you are one bright, evil-hearted woman.

The screen flashed on again. Too dark to make out anything. Then, the lantern came on, and Kip's voice: "That's better. Natural light just wasn't doing it."

I shooed him out again, and the screen went dark. But I knew there would be more.

The camera would be off now. No telling how long.

The screen lightened, then twirled upside down. A rustling sound through the earphone. An *oomph* that might have come from Kip. "Put me *dow-nk.*"

The camera must have been dropped or thrown, Kip's thumb plopping the record button. The auto focus was trying to sharpen the picture, but all I could see were fuzzy, thickened pieces of straw, now covering the lenses. The camera had fallen.

Show time. Again, I said a prayer.

Another muffled *oomph,* fading away. Kip was being carried up the ladder, a hand over his mouth.

The voices were indistinct from the loft. But the footsteps pounding the boards were picked up clearly. Heavy feet. Soft words, "Quiet down, boy."

Then, my voice calling out to Kip, when I thought he was playing games again. "Kip! You're starting to bug me. I've got some business to finish with the lady."

Was that me? It sounded not like the fellow I know so well, but the goat-man I'd heard described all week in court. Another moment passed, then the unmistakable voice of Kit Carson Cimarron, "Fool me twice, and you're dead."

The audio was clear. Better than I could have hoped. I kept listening.

"Simmy, he forced me."

Damn. Even her lies are consistent.

"He hit me, just like he used to do. He tore off my clothes and just forced me."

Then Cimarron's voice, calm and dispassionate. "You knew what he was like. You told me yourself."

I heard myself shout, "This is crazy!"

But who would believe me? Don't all criminals deny their crimes?

Cimarron's voice grew louder. "First you steal from me. Then you trespass on my land, and now you violate my woman."

Why don't I just hand the tape to McBain? He can play it for his closing argument. What else does he need?

When Cimarron started flinging me into the walls, the audio captured every thud.

"No, Simmy! You'll kill him! Don't!"

She seemed to mean it. But then, if H. T. Patterson was right, she wanted me to kill him.

A *cr-ack,* the rail splitting, and the noise of the horse snorting and stomping its feet as I landed on its back and slid into its stall.

"C'mon out, lawyer. I'm not through with you."

No, he wasn't. I listened to the rest, so familiar and yet so unreal. There was Kip crying out he was Spartacus, Cimarron taking away the pitchfork, Kip dashing out of the barn. There was the first shot from the nail gun, then Cimarron telling Jo Jo to reload a clip for him. The muffled *whomp* of another shot and then another. The noise from the corncrib, the sounds of two big men crashing into each other and whatever else got in the way. More *whomps* of steel into wood, and finally, after a pause, the last shot straight into the meat of a man's brain.

I hit the stop, then rewound to the beginning and played it again. Something was bothering me, but what? I listened more carefully when I knew it was near the end, but still, it seemed out of sync. The timing of the last shot was off. I needed to count the seconds.

Again, I rewound the tape and listened. This time I closed my eyes and saw the scene. I was on my back, my hand curling around the nail gun and lifting it toward his chest. I remembered his hand grabbing it and my pulling the trigger, hoping for the blast and hearing nothing but a . . .

Click.

Then the sound of my own head being snapped against the floor by Cimarron's fist.

A *thud* like a baseball smacking into the catcher's mitt. Followed quickly by a grunt.

I couldn't place the sounds. I would have been already close to unconsciousness. Seconds passed. What was happening?

Whomp.

Silence.

I stopped the tape, rewound just a bit, and played the last few moments yet again.

I counted, a-thousand-one, a-thousand-two, a-thousand-three. From the time I was hit, three seconds, then the *thud* and grunt. Seven more seconds until the final *whomp.*

Ten seconds from the time I was hit! I couldn't have fired it. At the time, I was drifting toward dreamland, having been battered into a fair-to-middling concussion.

I tried to figure it out.

Ten seconds.

What happened when I was sailing somewhere between pain and coma?

I was still thinking about it as the tape ran on. This time, I didn't stop it.

Then I heard the voice.

And I knew.

27

A Lousy Judge of Character

I didn't have time to shower and change. I rushed to the sheriff's department in the basement of the courthouse and found Detective Racklin at his desk. I told him what I needed.

"A dummy?" he asked.

"Two dummies, like they use in the crash tests."

"What for?"

"Come to court, and you'll see."

I barged through the courtroom door carrying a brown paper sack from the City Market, and everyone turned toward me. Why were they looking at me that way? H. T. Patterson stood at the lectern, peering over his shoulder. Jo Jo Baroso was on the witness stand, and the jurors were in their places. The clock said nine-forty.

"Ah, here you are," Judge Witherspoon announced from the bench. "I was about to issue a bench warrant, but if you'll take your seat, Mr. Lassiter, perhaps we can continue. Next question, Mr. Patterson."

"No!" I called out, plowing through the gate that separates the spectators from the gladiators.

"I beg your pardon," the judge said.

"I mean, no, Your Honor. Respectfully, may we approach the bench?"

"*We,* as in the lawyers and *you*?"

"Yes, Your Honor. I'm an attorney duly admitted to the Florida Bar, attorney number 163327. Additionally, I believe I have a constitutional right to be heard in my own defense. I wish to be associated as co-counsel."

Patterson hustled over and grabbed me just above the elbow. He had a good grip for a little guy. "Jake," he whispered, "what the hell are you doing?"

"Trust me."

"Trust you? You have straw in your hair, you look like you slept on a park bench . . . and what's that on your shoes?"

I looked down. Oops. Never wear wing tips in the morgue or a horse barn.

"Gentlemen," the judge called out, a note of irritation creeping into his voice. "Would you please step forward?"

I put my paper sack on the defense table and joined Patterson, McBain, and the stenographer on the side of the bench away from the jury.

"Your Honor," I began, "I wish to take over the cross-examination of Ms. Baroso."

The judge wrinkled his forehead. "Surely you know the old saw about a man representing himself having a fool for a client."

"This is different, Your Honor."

"Why?"

"Because there are only two people in this courtroom who know what happened in the barn that night. One is sitting on the witness stand, and the other is me, and I only learned it this morning."

"That's not good enough. The client always knows more than the lawyer about the case. I'll give you fifteen minutes to consult with Mr. Patterson, then we continue."

"No, Your Honor. I have to do it myself. I'm the only one who can."

The judge studied me a moment, his jaw muscles tightening. "I am cognizant of your right to defend yourself, but I have a duty to protect defendants from themselves." He seemed to ponder the question of my competence, then sniffed the air, before turning to the clerk. "What is that godawful smell? Would someone ask the bailiff to check on the furnace?"

H. T. Patterson cleared his throat. "For the record, Your Honor, I have no objection to Mr. Lassiter joining as co-counsel, although I do not join in his motion."

In other words, don't blame your lawyer if you screw it up.

"What about you, Mr. McBain, any objection?" the judge asked.

"Yes, sir. Yes, indeed. Cheap theatrics and a trick for the appellate court. Mr. Lassiter sees which way the wind is blowing, and he's trying to build error into the record. He's going to take over, and when he's convicted, claim ineffective assistance of counsel. If he loses the appeal, he's got a federal constitutional claim for habeas corpus. It's all a ruse, Judge, a slick ploy."

"But if I deny the request, that's an issue for appeal, too," the judge mused, smiling ruefully.

He thought it over some more, and I remembered one of my first clients in the P.D.'s office. He insisted on representing himself, but he had no legal training, so the judge appointed me to sit as co-counsel and offer advice, none of which was taken. The client was cross-examining a man he supposedly mugged in a dark alley. "How can you identify me when I knocked you cold from behind?" the budding barrister asked.

Finally, Judge Witherspoon shrugged and said, "Well, I'm going to let you have a go at it, though I wonder if you might show the court some respect by pulling your tie up to your collar before you address the witness."

I grabbed a yellow pad and a pen just to look official, adjusted my tie, ran a hand over a two-day growth of beard and got as close to the witness stand as I could without asking for permission to get closer.

"Good morning, Jo Jo," I said.

"Good morning, Mr. Lassiter," she replied.

"*Mr. Lassiter.* Yesterday, it was Jake. And a few months ago in Miami, it was *mi ángel,* was it not?"

"No. That was a long time ago."

I gave her a little smile. "It must have been before I started stealing, raping, and killing?"

"I don't know when your life swerved off its path."

"Nor I, yours."

"Objection, argumentative!" McBain stayed on his feet. He didn't want to waste time leaping up for the next objection.

"Sustained. Mr. Lassiter, you know better than that. I caution you to adhere to the rules of evidence, or you may resume your seat."

"Ms. Baroso, or should I say, Mrs. Cimarron?"

"Either one."

"But you obviously prefer Ms. Baroso, correct?"

"That's what I go by."

"In fact, you never told anyone you were married, isn't that right?"

She paused, then nodded and said, "That's right."

"Except your brother, Luis, who prefers to be called Louis, and is known affectionately throughout the justice system as Blinky?"

I was smiling at her confidently, and for the first time, her look changed. Just the first hint of apprehension. She knew me well enough to know my sarcasm usually preceded the baiting of a trap. Her look seemed to ask: *What does he know?*

"Let me think," she said.

"Think? You need to think whether you told your only sibling you were married?"

"I believe I did tell Luis," she said, a bit too quickly.

"So you did tell someone?"

"Yes, I suppose I did."

"Then a moment ago you were mistaken when you said you never told anyone?"

"I suppose I was."

"Ever tell anyone else?"

"No."

"So you never told me, did you?"

After all of that, she had to say no.

"No," she said. "I never told you."

"Not when you and I were alone in your house in Miami last June?"

"No."

"Not when your husband showed up that night?"

"No."

"And not when you say I attacked you in the barn?"

"No."

"You didn't say, 'Jake, please, I'm a married woman, and my husband is in the house over yonder?' "

"No."

"You didn't think that information was important?"

"I didn't think it would stop you."

Ouch. I had committed the cardinal sin on cross, one question too many. It was the equivalent of the "why" that will always burn you with a smart, hostile witness. Time to move on.

"Mrs. Cimarron, what were the terms of your late husband's will?"

"Objection," McBain said, still standing at the prosecution table. "Irrelevant."

"He wouldn't say that if I was the beneficiary," I told the judge. "Relevant to the issue of who wanted the decedent dead."

Motive, motive, motive.

"Overruled, but move it along, Mr. Lassiter."

"Simmy left no will," Jo Jo said. "He died intestate."

"So as the surviving spouse, you receive one hundred percent of the estate, free and clear of all federal taxes?"

"I really don't know the law in that area."

"Oh come now, Mrs. Cimarron, you're a lawyer."

"I've spent my entire career prosecuting criminals, not writing wills."

Gonna wing it now. "But surely you have retained probate counsel and have prepared to file the appropriate papers with the state."

Her eyes flickered almost imperceptibly. "Yes, I've retained a local probate lawyer."

"Who explained to you that you were the sole beneficiary and would receive one hundred percent of the estate, free and clear of federal taxes?"

"I believe it was mentioned."

"So the ranch goes to you?"

"Yes."

"And all personal property?"

"Yes."

"And the mining claims, the treasure maps, the artifacts and products of Mr. Cimarron's years of work?"

"Yes."

"Life insurance?"

"No."

"But there is a policy, isn't there, with two million in death benefits?"

"I believe my brother is the beneficiary, just as Simmy was the beneficiary of Luis's policy."

"Ah yes, your brother. Where is he?"

"Nobody knows."

"When did you see him last?"

She studied me a moment before answering. The jurors were watching her, so I risked a little smirk. *What does he know?* "In June, just before he disappeared."

"And you're sure you haven't seen him since?"

"Objection, repetitious as well as irrelevant." McBain didn't have the slightest idea where I was going, but he would soon.

"Your Honor, I'll tie it up shortly."

"All right, overruled."

"I'm sure I haven't seen him," she answered.

I paused to make a note on my legal pad as if this was

testimony of great import, and of course, it was. Then I told the witness to take us through the events that night, and she did it all again, starting with my tearing off her clothes, and ending with my plugging Cimarron.

"Was anyone else in the barn besides your husband, you, and me?"

"Yes, the boy, your nephew, but he ran out when the fighting began. I've already testified to that."

"No one else?"

"No, Mr. Lassiter. No one else."

"My nephew. What did he have with him?"

"What do you mean?" A look of uncertainty in her eyes.

"Did he have a video camera?"

She paused a moment. *What does he know?* "Yes, he did."

I went to the defense table and pulled opened the paper sack. "This camera?"

"I don't know. It could be."

"Your Honor, I've taken the liberty of asking the bailiff to bring up a video monitor from downstairs. It's in the corridor and can be brought in now. At this time, I'd ask that this videotape be marked for identification, and then I'd like to ask Mrs. Cimarron some questions about its contents."

The judge glanced toward the prosecution table. "Counsel?"

"We object, of course. We've had no notice."

"It's impeachment material," I responded, "and no notice is required."

At the word "impeachment," I thought I saw Jo Jo flinch. The judge overruled the objection, the clerk tagged the tape, and the bailiff wheeled in the monitor.

"Now, Mrs. Cimarron. I've cued the tape to what we might call Round Two. Mr. Cimarron and I are struggling on the ground floor. You recall that?"

McBain was on his feet again. "Your Honor, we request

that the tape start at the beginning so that the jury gets the full picture.''

"Denied. You can do it on redirect. I don't like to fuss with lawyers on cross.''

I was starting to like Judge Witherspoon. He came from the diminishing number of judges who let lawyers try their cases.

"Mrs. Cimarron, just sit back a moment,'' I told her gently. "Let's close our eyes and listen.''

Jo Jo's eyes remained open. Wide open.

The television flicked on with the sight of out-of-focus straw. The first sound was the whinny of a horse, then hoofbeats.

"Simmy! Simmy, he raped me! Are you going to let him go?''

I kind of liked that as an opening line. On direct examination, she never mentioned goading him. She had said she tried to stop us from fighting. Out of little inconsistencies does cross-examination grow.

The sound of the bullwhip, a whistle and crack of the leather sharp as a bee sting. The sound of feet shuffling again, close to the microphone, my hand scraping the wall, coming off with the bridle and bit, smashing Cimarron in the mouth, then a gasp and gagging—mine—as he kicked me in the gut.

The jurors strained to listen. If you hadn't been there, you couldn't tell who was doing what to whom. That's okay. At the end, I hoped, it would all be clear. For now, so strange, listening to my own labored breathing, remembering the pain and the fear.

"Don't move, lawyer, or I'll nail you to the barn wall.''

The words stabbed me, even now, recalling the terror.

I heard myself calling out to Jo Jo to tell him the truth. Again, she accused me of raping her and egged him on.

I heard the first *whomp*, the nail hitting at my feet. Another that buried itself in the wall. The *click* of the empty gun.

"Damn. Josefina, there's a full clip over by the saw-horse."

I stopped the tape. "Let's pause here for a moment. Did you reload the stud gun?"

She thought about it before answering. Surely, she knew there would be more sounds of the nails thunking into wood. "Yes, I believe I did."

"Once or more than once."

"Just once."

"With a clip of ten bullets? I believe Mr. Russo testified each clip had ten .27-caliber bullets."

"Yes, that's right."

"And after you reloaded, Mr. Cimarron continued to fire nails at me, didn't he?"

"Not at you, near you. He just wanted to frighten you, to teach you a lesson. You wanted to kill him, and you did."

"How did I manage to get the stud gun away from him?"

She didn't want to answer. Get her off the script, she isn't ready. "It's all so confusing now, and listening to this, hearing his voice, it's all so very upsetting." Tears welled in her eyes.

"Your Honor," McBain said. "It might be a propitious time for a recess."

"No, Your Honor! It's a propitious time for the prose-cutor to coach the witness."

McBain puffed out his chest. "I resent that, Mr. Lassi-ter. We don't insult lawyers like that in Pitkin County."

"In Miami," I told him, "that'd be considered a com-pliment."

"All right, you two, that's enough." Judge Witherspoon was pointing at me and glaring at McBain, an evenhanded way of getting order, sort of like throwing a flag for un-sportsmanlike conduct on both teams. "I don't like to in-terrupt the flow of a lawyer's cross-examination. Let's proceed."

"Now, Mrs. Cimarron, so that the jury is clear on this

issue, you only loaded one clip into the stud gun?''

''Yes, I just said that.''

''Did Mr. Cimarron ever reload?''

''No.''

''Did I?''

''No.''

''Okay, I'm going to start the tape again, and this time, let's count. Each time we hear a nail shot, I'm going to keep track right here.'' I positioned a blackboard in front of the jury, grabbed a piece of chalk, and nodded to Patterson, who hit the play button.

''Bang,'' said the voice of Kit Carson Cimarron. The jury looked puzzled, but I remembered his taunt, pretending to shoot me while pointing at my heart.

Whomp, a pause, and *whomp* again. I put two vertical lines on the chalkboard, and on the tape, the sound of the corn crashing onto me. A moment passed. Indistinguishable sounds. I heard myself grunt. Cimarron had dragged me out of the corncrib and was sitting on my chest. He jammed the stud gun along my neck, and I felt a chill now, remembering . . .

Whomp. A nail pinned my sweatshirt to the floor.

''Maybe the lawyer needs a haircut.'' Another shot skimming my head. Another I remembered just below my crotch, and I winced now with the sound of it. Now, I had four vertical lines and a diagonal one crossing them.

Another shot by my kneecap, one by my foot, one alongside each temple, as he outlined me, like the silhouette of a body at a homicide scene. Then one last nail between the fingers of my hand. Five more lines. I stopped the tape.

''How many shots is that?''

''I counted ten.''

''Ah, our numbers coincide. I guess the gun is out of bullets, is it not?''

She knew where I was going. ''You must have reloaded.''

"*I* must have? A moment ago, you said I didn't. You told this jury that no one reloaded."

"I must have been wrong."

"Let's see what else you were wrong about. Now who was shooting at whom in the little exchange we just heard?"

Again, she sensed where this would lead. "Simmy was shooting, but you must have gotten the gun away and . . ."

"And what?"

"I don't remember."

"Well, maybe this will refresh your recollection."

I nodded to Patterson who started the tape.

Cimarron called out to Jo Jo to bring the branding iron.

"Simmy, why not just finish it?" she said, and in the jury box, no one moved.

Cimarron told her he wanted me to suffer, "but I've never killed a man, and I won't start now."

"If he lives and starts talking," she said, "it'll just complicate things. Keep it clean and simple."

There was the sound of grunting and great, husky breaths. My hand had found the stud gun, and we were grappling for it. I remembered lying there on my back, his weight pinning me down, my raising the gun.

Click.

Again I stopped the tape.

"What was that?"

"You tried to shoot him."

"Right. But there were no bullets. So what happened?"

"As I said before, you must have reloaded, then shot him."

"Now, on direct exam, you testified that immediately prior to firing the fatal shot, I was fighting with Mr. Cimarron?"

"Yes."

"We were both on the floor, with Mr. Cimarron pinning me down?"

"Yes."

"So, how did I manage to shoot Mr. Cimarron? Did I

ask him to get off me and wait a moment while I walked to the sawhorse, calmly found a new clip, inserted it, found another nail, loaded it, then asked Mr. Cimarron to please put his ear up to the muzzle so I could shoot him at point-blank range?''

"I don't know. I was under great stress and frightened. I just know you shot him."

"Was I conscious at the time I allegedly shot him?"

"Of course."

"And did Mr. Cimarron strike me after he was hit?"

Her eyes darted from me to the jury. "Of course not. He died instantly."

"You heard the testimony of Sheriff's Deputy Dobson that I was unconscious when he arrived."

"Yes."

"What rendered me unconscious *after* I supposedly shot Mr. Cimarron?"

No answer.

"Isn't it true, Mrs. Cimarron, that the *click* we heard on the tape came when your husband and I were struggling for control of the stud gun, and immediately thereafter, he hit me with such force that my head bounced off the barn floor, knocking me unconscious?"

"No. You shot him before you passed out."

"How! With an empty gun?"

"I don't know how. I can't be expected to remember every detail." She turned to the jury. "You can't know what it was like, seeing your husband butchered. You can't get everything straight."

"Well, let's see if we can re-create what it was like." I walked to the defense table and whispered a request to Patterson. In the back row of the spectators' gallery, I saw Detective Racklin. Patterson got up and headed into the corridor, returning a moment later with the bailiff and two life-size dummies. I placed one on its back and struggled with the other to get it sitting on the first one's chest.

"Now, Mrs. Cimarron, do these dummies accurately

represent the situation with your husband pinning me to the floor?''

"Yes, I suppose."

I got the stud gun from the evidence table and removed the clip. Then I put in on the floor next to the two dummies.

"And your testimony is that somehow, from that position, I put a nail through his ear, though you don't recall my reloading the stud gun?''

"It happened. You shot him. Only you know how."

"Now where were you standing in relation to the two of us?''

She pointed to my left.

"Please answer audibly,'' the judge told her, his voice seeming to startle her.

"Close, maybe five yards away."

I stepped back several steps. "Here?"

"Yes."

"And where was the sawhorse with the clips of bullets and the nails?''

She pointed to the end of the clerk's table. One step from where I stood.

It would work. I knew it now. The timing was perfect.

I picked up a nail and a plastic clip from the evidence table and placed them where she indicated. "Okay, let's back up the tape a few seconds, start it again and see what happens. And Mrs. Cimarron, if you'll bear with me, for purpose of this demonstration, please pretend I'm you.'' The jurors' eyes never left me. They expected magic, and I intended to deliver. I nodded to Patterson who hit the rewind button, then the play.

Again Jo Jo told Cimarron to keep it clean and simple. Again the sound of our grappling, then the *click* and the *clunk* of my head against the floor. *One-thousand-one*. I picked up the wooden plank from the evidence table, *one-thousand-two*, came up from behind the Cimarron dummy and swung at the back of its head.

Thud. The plank hit home and the dummy toppled forward onto the Lassiter dummy. A millisecond later on the tape, *one-thousand-three, thud.*

Then a grunt that had to be from Cimarron on tape, because the dummy didn't say a word.

One-thousand-four.

I dropped the plank, took two steps to the clerk's table, *one-thousand-five,* picked up the clip and a nail, *one-thousand-six,* walked back to the dummies, picked up the stud gun, *one-thousand-seven,* calmly inserted the clip and the nail.

One-thousand-eight.

The Cimarron dummy's head was leaning, chin down, on the Lassiter dummy's chest. I leaned over and jammed the muzzle of the stud gun into its ear.

One-thousand-nine. I pulled the trigger.

Whomp. The sound shuddered through the courtroom.

Whomp. More muffled perhaps, but the same sound on tape.

The nail tore through the dummy's head, traveled on an upward path, and embedded in the wall of the courtroom just below a photograph of an 1890s judge with full chin whiskers.

"Mr. Lassiter!" The judge rose from his chair. I stifled him with a "shusssh."

The tape was still running.

The only sound in the courtroom was sand trickling onto the floor from what had been the dummy's plastic skull.

"Shit."

Who said that? The jurors were confused. No one in the courtroom had said a word.

"Shit," again on the tape. It was Jo Jo, and the jurors knew it. They looked at her. Not accusing. Not yet. Just intense curiosity. *Shit* is fine if you've hit your thumb with a hammer, but it isn't the most eloquent lament for a lover slain. She sounded exasperated. Not angry, not mournful.

"That's not the way it was supposed to go," she said.

Now the jurors looked at each other. Who was she talking to?

"No." It was a male voice, and it hadn't been heard on the tape before. "*No, seguro que no*. Jeez, I hate violence."

"For a while," Jo Jo said, "I couldn't decide which way it would go. I thought Jake could handle him. I mean, either way, it would work, though this way is better."

"Much better," the man said. "Besides, Jake's not a killer. He doesn't have it in him."

"Funny, that's what he said about you."

"Yeah, and he thought you were too good for him."

"Jake's always been a lousy judge of character," Jo Jo said, and they both laughed.

I nodded, and Patterson stopped the tape.

"Mrs. Cimarron, who was that man?" I asked.

She didn't answer. Her eyes were closed, and she rocked slowly back and forth.

"If you wish," I suggested, "we could run voiceprints on the tape and compare them with your brother's early radio commercials for the gold bullion business."

Still no answer.

"Or we could ask Abe Socolow to fax your brother's fingerprints up here and draw a comparison to the unidentified latent on the gun barrel."

She was sobbing now.

"Isn't it true that the man in the barn was your brother, Louis Baroso, and that the two of you conspired to murder your husband and did, in fact, kill him?"

She didn't answer.

"Which one of you killed him?" I asked.

"I didn't kill Simmy," she said through trembling lips.

"Even though he beat you?"

Again, she didn't answer.

"What you told me in the barn was true, wasn't it? He had beaten you."

Her head slumped forward.

McBain was on his feet. "Your Honor. Perhaps . . ."

"Sit down," the judge commanded.

"He began hitting me just after we married," she said.

"That's why I left him. So many times, he begged me to come back. So many times I thought I could change him. He could be so wonderful, but he could be someone else, too, someone violent and evil."

"You could have divorced him."

"He would have killed me. He threatened to, and he boasted that no jury in Pitkin County would convict him. He let me move away, but he wanted me back. That's why he came to Miami in June. I just couldn't go back to that. Jake, you saw what he did to me . . ."

"You thought I'd kill him, didn't you? You thought I'd kill him because he broke my hand and beat you up?"

Silence except for her sobs.

"You set me up to kill him, and when I didn't or couldn't, you and your brother finished the job."

"Luis was right. You don't have it in you to kill a man."

"He was right about something else, too. I'm a lousy judge of character."

28

No Way to Treat a Lady

I was the first one out the door. Ignoring protocol, taking advantage of the confusion and cacophony, I raced from the courtroom, ran down the carpeted stairs and out the front door beneath old Lady Justice and onto Main Street. I jogged to the parking garage on cleanly shoveled sidewalks, got the rental, its fenders caked with dirty snow, and headed east toward Smuggler Mountain.

The last two minutes in the courtroom had been chaos. H. T. Patterson pounded the table and demanded the state immediately dismiss all charges, and if not, he beseeched the court to do the job. "In the name of Jefferson and Madison, in the memory of Marshall and Brandeis, for the reasons blood was spilled at Gettysburg and Bull Run, Iwo Jima, and Normandy, this man should be set free without further ado . . ."

I was all for skipping the ado.

". . . Let the state move to right its wrong. Let this man pick up the pieces of his shattered reputation, and let him do it with dispatch. Let the bells of equity and justice toll for him. Yea, if liberty be thy name, let justice be done."

It was good to hear Patterson preaching again, his voice hitting the high notes with that Holy Roller cadence.

The prosecutor pleaded with the judge to delay a ruling

until he had a chance to meet with Ms. Baroso and determine if her testimony was simply the product of posttraumatic stress syndrome and whether she could be rehabilitated on redirect.

Translation: I just got run over by a cement truck. Give me till morning to count the broken bones.

Pretty fair ad-libbing, I thought. I admire lawyers who, like captains of sinking ships, refrain from leaping overboard, but instead appear on deck in their dress whites with the polished brass buttons. Judge Witherspoon listened stoically, occasionally banging his gavel at the spectators whose behavior was worse than New York Jets' fans at old Shea Stadium.

As the door closed behind me, the judge declared a recess until nine the next morning, when he expected the prosecutor to announce whether he wished to proceed. If he did, the judge broadly hinted, a defense motion for a directed verdict would be looked upon with favor once the state rested.

"Mrs. Cimarron," the judge said. "You are free to go, but I admonish you against leaving Pitkin County pending the outcome of tomorrow's hearing."

I didn't think Jo Jo was leaving town. Not just yet. I figured she was keeping her brother apprised of each day's events. Today would be a hell of a briefing.

I'd love to be there. In fact, I was doing everything I could to be there.

It took just a few minutes to find the road where she lost me the day before. I coaxed the rental car around the turn I had missed, then pulled as far off the road as I could without sliding into a snowdrift. The branches of a fir tree weighted with snow hung low and shielded my car from view. Especially from someone with a lot on her mind.

I didn't have long to wait.

The Dodge Ram dual-wheel pickup roared past me and headed up the road. I eased out from under the tree and hung back, catching sight of the pickup's taillights as it took the fork that led up the mountain. Yesterday, I took the wrong turn. Today, I just followed her. From here, it was easy. Unless she doubled back, she was headed straight to the top.

I stopped the car along the road at the last bend, got out and walked the rest of the way, a quarter mile or so. It was one of those bright, cold, dry winter days, the sun glaring off the snow, the temperature in the high twenties.

There was a chicken-wire fence around the property. Fastened to an iron gate with an unlocked rusty latch were two signs, your standard hardware store NO TRESPASSING and a piece of rotting wood crudely painted DANGER, BLASTING, which was older than Granny.

I opened the latch and walked through the gate. The pickup was parked a hundred yards up the hill. Next to it was a Jeep Wrangler with a canvas top. Narrow-gauge railway tracks emerged from a tunnel cut into the rock and led to a small building of unpainted wood with a tin roof. The building had a wooden chute that emptied into a railway car twenty feet below. Other sheds in various states of disrepair sagged into snow-covered piles of dirt and debris. An elevator cage of rusted iron stood idle and filled with snow. All around the site, like the fossils of dinosaurs, the evidence of extinction. A fallen building of charred timbers, rusted boilers and compressors, winches and furnaces. I pictured the scene a century ago, the sky blackened with fires from sawmills and smelters. I thought of Cimarron's great-grandfather and the other drillers and muckers, a mountainside crawling with grim-faced, wiry men whose hands would never scrub clean.

The entrance to the tunnel was framed by three wooden timbers, two vertical, and one horizontal connecting at the top. Rusty nails held a metal sign to the horizontal timber. SILVER QUEEN, TUNNEL NO. 3, 1888.

I expected to see the tracks of a woman's stylish high-heeled boots in the snow, but the imprints were of wide, plebeian work boots. The tracks went from Jo Jo Baroso's pickup straight into the tunnel. Okay, she had changed shoes. Always prepared, that Jo Jo. It wouldn't surprise me if she had a hard hat, a flashlight, and a pickax, too.

I headed into the mine. Bare electric lightbulbs were strung along the rocky ceiling, laced to old timbers. Canvas air chutes ran along the walls. The bulbs were lighted, and even after the tunnel took a gentle, rounded turn to the right, cutting off light from the entrance, visibility was fine. It was warmer inside, probably in the fifties, but dank. Water dripped down walls of rock stained purple and yellow from whatever minerals had been locked inside by volcanic explosions a thousand millennia ago.

I had walked maybe half a mile when the tunnel opened into a cavern, a ballroom-sized chamber with fifty-foot ceilings. Inside, where I imagined a thick, rich vein of silver was found, now were only empty ore carts and wooden crates that may have once held dynamite or tools. On the ground, a broken bottle of thick, brown glass, the remnants of a miner's beer break. I took off my topcoat and tossed it into one of the ore carts and kept going. At one end of the chamber, there was a ladder of steps cut into the mountain itself. It only went one way, down.

I started the descent, slowly at first, the way lit by the overhead bulbs. Timbers stained black from thousands of hands provided a railing. Perhaps fifty feet below, another horizontal tunnel connected with the downward shaft. I kept going. Another tunnel connection, then another. Deeper still, I paused and listened. The steady *thumpeta-thumpeta* of machinery, a pump maybe. It came from below. I descended farther, counting eleven tunnels at different intervals before running out of ladder in a narrow, darkened tunnel. I paused on the last step. No lights here, but the sound of the machinery was louder. A steady *whirring* and a combustion induced *chugging*, joined the *thumpeta-thumpeta* machine.

I took the last step and splashed into a puddle of icy, black water. At least I thought it was a puddle. I slogged two steps into the darkness. Then two steps more. It wasn't a puddle. More like a river. The floor of the tunnel was covered by a foot of water. I was sweating, but my feet were freezing.

I had no idea how far I had descended. Five hundred feet, a thousand? I waited a moment for my eyes to get adjusted to the light. They didn't, because there wasn't any.

I started my way along the wall in the direction of the sound. I was moving away from the mountain and back toward the town. If I walked far enough, I'd probably be right under the courthouse.

Ouch! My forehead cracked hard into an overhead timber. I'll bet miners a century ago weren't six feet two.

Now, I hunched forward and scuttled along, my hand trailing over the ragged walls. Ahead of me, a sound of rushing water, like the rapids on a shallow, rocky stream. I kept wondering where the sound was coming from until my foot stepped into space and I fell forward into the torrent. The drop-off was only two feet or so, but the landing was hard, facedown. I tumbled ahead, water pouring over me from the ledge I just stepped off. Soaking and freezing, I got up, spitting out cold, filthy water, feeling for sensation in my right shoulder. It still had a stainless steel pin inside, and it didn't take kindly to surprises.

I kept going, splashing along until I saw the light, a yellow glow from an opening at the side of the tunnel. I cautiously inched ahead. Suddenly, a blinding flash turned the black water a bright orange, illuminating stalactites overhead—or stalagmites—who the hell can remember the difference? The flash was followed by a dull *thudding* explosion, and a wave of dust rolled down the tunnel from the direction of the light. Overhead, timbers creaked and groaned.

With the explosion still bonging in my ears, I hurried my pace. If I couldn't hear my splashing, I figured no one else could, either. In twenty seconds, I was at the opening. It was a rough rectangle in the limestone walls, perhaps four by six feet, beginning a few feet off the floor of the tunnel. Three steps were cut into the rock wall and ended in a ledge, which led directly through the opening and into another cavern, higher and drier than the tunnel. From inside, voices echoed off the walls. I crept closer.

As dust rolled out of the opening, I heard a man cough. "¡Jesús Cristo! Too much dynamite. We'll be buried here along with this silver-dollar *puta*."

Blinky's voice, no mistaking it.

"How else do you propose we get it out?" Jo Jo Baroso asked.

"The same way they got the bitch in if we could find the old shaft."

I lay flat on the ledge and peered through the opening, trying to keep out of view. Inside, a gasoline generator chugged away, powering spotlights mounted on two aluminum poles. One of the lights shone directly in my eyes, and I couldn't make out my favorite team of siblings.

"There isn't time." She sounded exasperated. "There wasn't before, and there surely isn't now. I'll be lucky if I'm not charged with perjury. If you're found, you'll be charged with murder."

The sound of a shovel scraping against rock, then gravel clattering against metal.

"Like I told you before," Blinky said, from somewhere behind the glare, "Jake bluffed you, and you fell for it. The prints will never match up, 'cause I never touched the barrel. All they can prove is that I was in the barn, but that's no case for murder. And when's the last time *anybody* got prosecuted for perjury. I'm sorry you got embarrassed, Josie, *me da mucha pena, pero,* I'm glad Jake's gonna be okay. He never fucked with me, and I didn't want to sandbag him this way."

"Thanks for the testimonial, Blinky." Shielding my eyes from the glare of the spotlights, I slid off the ledge and into the cavern, my wet shoes squishing on the hard rock. Blinky wore a red plaid shirt under coveralls and a hard hat and was tossing a shovel full of rocks into an ore cart. Next to him was Jo Jo Baroso with rubberized boots sticking out incongruously from her long, fur-trimmed coat. "What are you doing, kids, building a clubhouse?"

"Jake, *mi amigo,* I've missed you so much." Blinky leaned on the shovel and smiled at me. He seemed genuinely, weirdly, happy to see me. "You got no idea what it's like to go underground. Hey, that's a pun, isn't it?" He allowed himself a short chuckle. "You give up all your friends, you gotta move around. Hell, I even gave some blood, which you found in the Range Rover. What a pain in the ass. Never again."

"Blinky, you'll forgive me if I don't throw my arms around you, but I'm—"

"Don't say it, Jake. We did you wrong. We never should have set you up. I said to Josie, let's cut Jake in for a full share, let him figure out a way to just steal the *maldita compañía* from Cimarron, but she said, no, you'd never go along with it. She was right. I knew that as soon as you raised a stink when we left a few things out of the prospectus. You just didn't want to play the game."

"Not your game, Blinky. Not the con."

"Yeah, well this wasn't a con. For once it was real. Really real and really big. That's why we had to get Rocky Mountain Treasures back from Cimarron. Why give seventy percent to that *condenado*? Was that fair? Hell, if I hadn't raised the money, he never could have found her. I asked him to renegotiate, but he said no and called me a door-to-door salesman in patent leather loafers. Hey, Jake, I never sold door to door, and you know it. This was his life, he said, everything he'd worked for, and a deal's a deal, so I was stuck. So the little sister and me, we decided to get the company back, but that cowboy was smarter than—"

"Shut up, Luis!" Jo Jo was glaring at him.

"*Hermanita,* I'm gonna do the talking for once. Jeez, she even bosses me around down here. I learned this shit from Cimarron. How to drill the holes in a round pattern, put different length fuses on the dynamite so it explodes just right and the rock falls the way you want it. There's a science to it, if you want to knock a hole in the rock without blowing yourself up. Jake, you wouldn't believe it, but I like this shit. I really found myself down here.''

"I'm not surprised. You've got a great future breaking rocks.''

"C'mon, Jake, don't be pissed. It's time to make amends.''

Next to him was a wooden crate with sticks of dynamite poking out of the top. A fuse was attached to each stick.

"Okay, Blinky, so now you've gone straight. You're a miner, right?''

"Yeah, sort of, and Josie thinks she's the foreman of the crew. Some things never change, right? I always put up with it because she gave me the skinny on the state's cases against me and my friends. She'd tell me when investigators were sniffing around, and we'd close up shop and head to another jurisdiction. When I got arrested, she'd pull stuff out of the files. Why do you think you had so much success on my cases, Jake? It wasn't just *buena suerte*.''

I turned toward Jo Jo. "So it was always an act, how much you detested your brother?''

She didn't answer, and for a moment, the only sound was the whirring generator and the thumping pump.

"Nah,'' Blinky said, waving his shovel. "She still ain't president of the Louis Baroso fan club, but blood is thicker than water. At first, she tried to get me to go straight, but then, I started carving out a piece of each deal for her. Hey, the state attorney's office pays peanuts. Pretty soon, she's my partner. Hey, Jake, I learned a long time ago it's easier to get an honest person to steal than to get a thief not to. Anyway, where was I?''

"Something about how smart Cimarron was,'' I helped out.

Blinky used the back of his sleeve to wipe streaks of dirt-stained sweat from his forehead. "Yeah, smart enough to know when he's getting taken for a ride. He was pressuring Kyle Hornback, who didn't know jackshit about the oversubscription of stock, but had some photocopies of bank transfers that would have told Cimarron everything I didn't need him to know. Cimarron was in town and was gonna see Hornback when Socolow was done with him.''

''Why'd you try to pin it on me?''

''Josie's idea, entirely.''

''Luis!''

Blinky shrugged. ''Well, it's true, and I suppose it had to be done. Cimarron had to think you were in on the scam, that you were stealing from the company, and you were banging Josie, too. If he didn't hate you, it would never have worked.''

Jo Jo Baroso had turned away so that I could only see her in profile under the glare of the spotlights. ''So that's what it was from day one, Jo Jo. Including that night in your house. The only reason I was in your bed was to bait the trap.''

''Don't tell me you're hurt, Jake,'' she said, still not looking me in the eye. ''Don't give me that sophomoric how-could-you-do-this-to-me-when-I-really-cared-for-you bullshit.''

''But I did!''

''You dropped me, Jake. You dumped me. Do you know what that's like?''

''Is that what this is about, you getting even with me for that?''

''No, it was just business,'' Jo Jo said.

I shivered, either because I was soaking wet, or from her cold-bloodedness.

''C'mon, Jake, don't be sore,'' Blinky said, annoyed that I objected to being set up for murder. ''It isn't like we knew what was going to happen. In the beginning, we didn't even plan on killing Cimarron.''

''What did you plan?''

''We wanted him to come after you, but we knew you wouldn't kill him. That night in the house, we sort of hoped you'd kick some butt, soften him up, and then we'd renegotiate from different positions. It hurts a man's pride to be beaten.''

"I know."

"But anyway, *he* stomped you pretty good, and that shot the plan all to hell. Then, everything got out of hand. I mean, Josie said she was afraid Cimarron was going to kill you, and I said too bad it can't be the other way around, what with me being the beneficiary of his life insurance and Josie as the sole heir of the estate. So we kept talking about it. What if, this. What if, that. How can we get all of her? Finally, it was a no-brainer. After all, if Cimarron died, we'd get her all. I figured you'd follow Josie up here, and I knew you'd come to the rescue if you saw Josie all black and blue."

I turned to Jo Jo. "But Cimarron did beat you, didn't he? You weren't lying about that."

"Yes," Jo Jo answered. "I told him I saw you at the music tent, and you wanted me to come back to Miami with you. He hit me, Jake. Time and again, just enough to cause pain without knocking me unconscious or leaving scars. He was a master at it. Can you blame me for wanting him dead?"

"No, but I blame you for setting me up."

Blinky leaned on his shovel as if it were a cane. "We figured you'd be so mad about what he did to Josie, and remembering what he did to you that you'd grab a pitchfork and make shish kebab out of him. At first, we planned to have Josie back you up, claim it was self-defense, keep you from ever getting charged."

"Why didn't you, Jo Jo? Even after killing Cimarron, you could have told the truth, that I was defending myself. It *would* have been justifiable homicide if I had killed him."

She didn't answer, but Blinky did. "Once we had to give you a little help in the barn, the script changed. Josie got worried. What with her history with you, it would have looked like the two of you conspired to kill him. It was a close call. Hell, we almost went that way, but in the end, we figured the truth wouldn't wash, and you'd both be indicted. Trying to get you off would make her look like a two-timing slut, but blaming you made her look like a grief-stricken widow, at least that's the way we figured it.''

"So I was just a fall guy to get the insurance and the stupid treasure claims?''

"Not so stupid," Blinky said. "Not when you're talking about all of her.''

"Her? That's the third time you've talked about getting all of her. The mine?''

"No, the Silver Queen.''

"That's what I said, the mine.''

Blinky was puzzled. Then he figured it out. "No, not *that* silver queen. This one.'' He grabbed one of the light poles and swung it around, tossing the beam to a position directly behind him. It illuminated a lady of silver nearly twenty feet high. She looked a little like the Statue of Liberty, except this lady sat on a throne in a half chariot, half ship.

"Ain't she something?" Blinky asked. "I been studying up on her. I read all of Cimarron's newspaper clippings from a hundred years ago." Blinky lowered his voice into a Miami con man's imitation of a Lowell Thomas newsreel. " 'The queen reclines with the voluptuous grace of a Cleopatra in her Egyptian barge.' ''

I walked over for a closer look. The chariot sat on a pedestal trimmed with a drapery of silver, gold, and what looked like ebony. Leading to the throne were steps inlaid with silver dollars. On the risers, the words "Silver Queen" were raised in letters of solid silver. The background was a mass of brilliant colored minerals, and the borders were white crystals. The words "Aspen, Colorado" appeared on a lower panel of the pedestal. The letters were formed from broken pieces of silver on a background that looked like pure white sugar. I moved closer for a better look.

"Diamond dust," Blinky said.

Six pillars of burnished silver and crystals inlaid with mosaics of different ores rose from the pedestal and supported the throne. The wheels of the chariot were four feet high and made of solid silver. A canopy of minerals and crystals covered the queen's head. Her hair was made of glass, and the drapery across her Rubenesque bosom was adorned with bright minerals I couldn't identify. In her hand, she held a silver scepter that must have been ten feet long. It was topped with a silver dollar a foot across and a five-pointed silver star. Two Greek gods ran alongside the chariot carrying cornucopias filled with gold and silver coins.

"Her head and body are carved from from the biggest, purest silver nugget ever mined," Blinky said, "more than a ton, and it came from this mountain." There was a note of pride in his voice, as if he had made the damn thing. "What do you think of her, Jake?"

"Let me try to find the word. How about tacky? Gauche? Overblown? Laughable? Kitschy, if there is such a word."

"Yeah, well I know it ain't too subtle. Cimarron called it one of the last purely Victorian pieces, but who gives a shit if it ain't a da Vinci? See, Cimarron figured it out. Its got historical value plus the value of the minerals and the fact there's never been anything like it, before or since. After the World's Fair, the lady had been sitting there at the museum over in Pueblo, but they were going to tear down the place. The guys who owned the mines and contributed the minerals were mighty pissed and wanted her back, but the museum guys were going to send her to the Smithsonian or maybe New York, so the mining guys just stole the damn thing. Brought her here on a freight car and lowered her back into the ground from whence she came. The mine was petered out by then, and the bottom tunnel flooded. They wanted to put the lady on display for the local folks, but they had lost their minerals claims to the banks, and they had more to worry about than museums and such. Luckily for the lady, she sat up here where you see her, good as new, or she will be once we polish her up. We got the patents and the mineral rights to this mine, and the big queen is made of minerals found herein."

"What are you saying, that you *own* this thing?"

"Free and clear, and I got the paperwork to prove it." In a singsong voice, Blinky intoned, " 'Know all men by these presents that Rocky Mountain Treasures, Inc. has located and claimed by right of discovery and location, in compliance with the Mining Acts of Congress approved May 10, 1872, and all subsequent acts, and with local customs, laws and regulations, seventeen hundred and fifty linear feet and horizontal measurement on the Silver Queen, No. 3, with all its dips, angles and variations as allowed by law, and all veins, lodes, ledges or deposits, and surface ground within the lines of said claim,' blah, blah, blah. What I'm saying, Jake, is we got one hundred percent legal title to a fat lady worth millions."

"*We?*" I said. "As in you and your sister."

"No, we, as in you and me. You got ten percent of the company, remember."

"What about Jo Jo?"

"You tell me, Counselor. She killed Cimarron. She hit him with the plank, then put a nail through his big fat, head. I oughta know. I handed her the nail gun, but I never touched the damn barrel."

"You're going to give up your sister?"

"After today, they gotta go after somebody new, so I say throw her to the fucking wolves."

"Luis! Have you gone mad?" Jo Jo's face was a mask of anger, but anger without fear.

"Nah, I'm just doing what's got to be done."

"Blinky, what about Kyle Hornback?" I asked. "You killed him."

"No fucking way. I'm sitting with that *chi chi cabrón* on your sofa, which I'd be embarrassed to give to the Salvation Army, and my little sister gives him a drink with enough barbs to knock out a cow. In about two minutes, he's slobbering on my shoulder, and Josie goes up to your bedroom and brings down a tie your grandmother must have bought you."

"Luis! *¡Cállate la boca!*" Jo Jo's forehead was tight-ned into vertical lines, and a vein throbbed in her neck. 'Do you think I'm going to let you get away with this?''

He turned toward his sister. "C'mon, it's true. You trangled the *hijo de puta* with Jake's tie. Hey, Jake, I hought that tie looked bad on you. You should have seen t on Hornback with his tongue sticking out.''

"I did.''

"Yeah, that's right, I forgot.''

"Who strung him up on the fan?''

"That took both of us, and it wasn't easy 'cause Kyle idn't help any.''

"Is that right, Jo Jo? Is that the way it happened?''

But she wasn't talking.

"The failure to deny the accusation is admissible,'' I aid. "What's the fancy name Judge Witherspoon gave it, n adoptive admission?''

"Go to hell, both of you,'' said my former love.

"I'm home free, and she takes the fall,'' Blinky said. 'My holier-than-thou sister who always put me down. Vell, let me tell you something. I never killed a man. I'm ist a thief, but she is heartless and bloodless and soulless. was there, man, and I tell you I nearly puked on your oor when she did Hornback. She never blinked an eye. Ie could have been a cockroach. With Cimarron, same hing. Mostly, she was pissed you didn't do the job. here's a name for what she is. A psycho or something.''

"A sociopath,'' I said. "And as for you, Blinky, you're learly an accessory to Hornback's murder and probably a onspirator to Cimarron's. Or maybe it's the other way round, I could never tell the difference.''

"So what, they got nothing on me.''

"Maybe they can piece it together. For starters, every-ing you've said to me is admissible against you.''

"Are you *loco*? You can't testify against me. You're ay lawyer. I got the whatchamacallit, the privilege, and esides, I want you to represent me, not rat on me. You're ie best, Jake, and more important, you're *mi amigo*. For n percent of the silver lady, plus a bonus, you can take

care of it. Get me immunity up here if there's any ris]
they'd try to indict. I'll tell 'em what I saw. I'll take
polygraph.''

"No dice. I'm through with both of you."

Blinky's expression changed. "Then what am I goin;
to do with you?"

He raised the shovel as if to take a swipe at me.

I flexed my knees and let my arms dangle loosely at m
sides. "Go ahead and try, Blinky. I'll ram it up your ass.'

While he was thinking about it, Jo Jo Baroso took tw
steps to one side, reached inside her coat, and came ou
with a handgun. She pointed it at Blinky, then at me, the
somewhere between the two of us.

"All right, both of you," she said, waving the gun i
the air. "Jake, move away from the ledge. Luis, move nex
to Jake."

It was a Smith & Wesson Bodyguard .38, the airweigh
model with the two-inch blue steel barrel. At less tha
fifteen ounces, just dandy for a lady's purse.

"I'll bet Abe Socolow gave you that thing the day yo
got your badge and promised to uphold the Constitution,'
I said.

"Shut up, Jake, and do what I say."

"Most prosecutors can't shoot a lick."

"Try me."

"Where you going to go, Jo Jo? After today, there'
nowhere to run."

"That's enough, Jake. Just move."

"You going to shoot us?" I persisted. "Your brothe
and the man who loved you."

"If you loved me, you would never have left me. A
for Luis, his loyalty has just been demonstrated. This i
the last time I'm asking. I want both of you back by th
statue."

Blinky started walking in that direction. I took one ste]
leapt to the right and grabbed the aluminum pole with th
spotlight, crashing it to the ground. The spot broke, an
we were in the shadow of the Silver Queen, a second spo

light still shining fifteen yards away. A gunshot ricocheted off the rocks above my head. Not even close. I was on the hard, cold floor of the cavern.

Another shot, again wildly above me. I heard Blinky scrambling on all fours and saw him duck behind an ore cart.

"C'mon out, you two!" she yelled.

I kept down, and Blinky got up, put a shoulder to the cart, and using it as a shield, began pushing it toward his sister. It gave me a chance.

I lunged toward the wooden crate and grabbed three sticks of dynamite and a handful of foot-long wooden matches. I turned in time to see Jo Jo deftly step to one side and Blinky crash the ore cart into a rocky wall. The impact sent his head into the side of the cart, and he reeled backward, collapsing on the floor. Jo Jo turned the gun on him, then swung it toward me.

Two more steps and I dived for the other aluminum pole, taking it down with me, crashing the spotlight.

Total, blinding darkness broken by a flash of orange, a gunshot missing me but *pinging* off the Silver Queen.

"That's no way to treat a lady," I said. In the darkness, I picked up a rock and tossed it one direction while I crawled in another. Another stray gunshot just after the rock hit the far wall.

I crept behind the Silver Queen, scraping my hands and knees, but keeping silent. I heard Jo Jo's "shit" as she bumped into something. Then a flashlight popped on. The flashlight was in her left hand, the gun in her right. I could see her, but she couldn't see me. I grabbed a rock and winged it at her, but it missed, causing her to spin and shoot behind her. How many gunshots had there been? Four or five? I hadn't been counting. The .38 only holds five bullets. But was she carrying spare ammo?

"Josie, let's talk this over." Blinky now, somewhere in the darkness. "C'mon, I never would have flipped on you. Let's you and me work it out."

I heard her spin the cylinder on the .38 and looked up

in time to see her slipping bullets in. The flashlight beam struck Blinky squarely in the face.

A gunshot and a scream.

"You shot me! *Jesús Cristo,* Jake, she shot me in the fucking leg! I'm bleeding. She broke the bone. Jake!"

I kept quiet. I did not want to get shot in the leg or anywhere else.

I stayed huddled behind the right rear wheel of the Silver Queen's chariot. Another gunshot, and the sound of glass shattering. Above me, the lady's hair had fractured into a thousand shards and cascaded over me. I stayed put, struck a match to the rock floor and lit the fuse on a stick of dynamite. I crouched there, letting the fuse fizzle and crackle, keeping the flame between my cupped hands so it would not glow in the darkness, trying to figure what to do next.

I tried to calculate how long the fuse took to burn. I counted off the seconds, measured the inches, then realized it was about ten seconds from blast off. Extending my arm, I tossed a hook shot in the general direction of the entrance to the cavern. As I did, a flood of thoughts engulfed me. I didn't know the strength of one stick of dynamite. Probably more pow than a string of Chinese firecrackers, but not enough to bring down the roof. Right? Didn't Blinky talk about a circle of sticks just to knock a hole in rock wall? As my arm was following through on a pretty healthy toss, I thought of the old Road Runner cartoons. Wasn't Wile E. Coyote always tossing dynamite and having it tossed right back?

I intended it as a diversion. A little boom, and I would dash . . .

"Shit! Shit! Shit!"

All these years I've known Jo Jo Baroso and never had she been so scatological. Of course, then, I'd never thrown a stick of dynamite at her before.

The *floppity-flop* of her rubber boots across rock. A stomping sound.

"You're crazy, Jake!" Her voice, just this side of hysterical. "You'll kill us all. These timbers aren't stable."

At least she hadn't thrown it back at me.

From somewhere in the darkness, I heard the whimpering of my client who liked the privilege that kept me from testifying against him, but refused to adhere to any laws himself.

"Blinky, how about it?" I shouted out. "Is it safe?"

"Blow her up, Jake. Send her straight to hell."

I peered out from behind the chariot's wheel and saw the flashlight beam play across the floor until it found Blinky, curled up alongside an ore cart. "Jake, she's going to shoot me again. No, Josie, no!"

"I'll take care of you later," Jo Jo said, then turned the beam toward the Silver Queen. It flicked off, and I knew she was walking this way. I didn't hesitate. I struck a match, lit the fuse, stepped into the open, and tossed it underhanded along the rocky floor. It bounced two or three times, the fuse burning green in the darkness.

I heard Jo Jo mutter the same monosyllable. I heard the boots slapping the rock. I watched the lit fuse, tried to memorize the spot in the darkness as she approached it. The glowing fuse disappeared under a stomping boot and I charged the spot. I was going to hit her head on, legs churning, and wrap her up, a picture-perfect tackle. I was going to drive her to the floor and do something I've never done before: I was going to hit a woman.

She must have heard my leather soles smacking the floor. Or my labored breathing. Or her instincts were just too sharp.

I saw the flash from the muzzle before I felt the impact.

The bullet caught me in the right shoulder. It was a clean through-and-through that didn't strike a bone, a major blood vessel, or a steel pin that acts up when it rains. I felt a burning, the trickle of warm blood, and then a sharp pain as if an ice pick had been jammed into me and was still there.

I was still on my feet, but wondering why.

Shouldn't I be on the ground or something?

The flashlight flicked on, bursting through the darkness, illuminating a craggy formation of blue limestone and dolomite above me. I turned, tucked my head, went into a crouch and rolled onto my good shoulder, scrambling back behind the chariot.

Another gunshot, and again the Silver Lady took one for me. Or maybe it ricocheted off Plutus, one of the little diapered gods at her side. I felt around in the darkness for the last stick of dynamite. Where the hell was it? I found the big silver wheel of the chariot, ran my hand along the ground, and there it was. I drew a match from my pocket, struck it, and nothing happened. My pants, still soggy from my bodysurfing in the tunnel, had moistened the tip. I found another match. Soaking wet. Another one, same thing.

I breathed on the first match, trying to dry the phosphorous, wiped it in the dust, struck it again. Nothing, and now the tip started to crumble.

I heard Jo Jo's footsteps getting closer.

One last time, and it caught. I let the flame grow a second, then lit the fuse, waited a second and threw the dynamite as far as I could. I wanted to sail it over Jo Jo's head to get her turned around. When she headed to stomp out the fuse, I'd rush her again, but this time, I'd zigzag.

I waited to hear the dynamite hit the ground, but instead of the *smack* against hard rock, I heard a soft *thump*.

Then I heard Blinky's yell. "Jake, *ay, mierda!* Jake, *maldito sea,* it's on the timber over the ledge. I can see the fuse burning."

Then I heard Jo Jo. Her vocabulary hadn't improved. I watched the flashlight beam playing across the rocks above the ledge. Finally it stopped at the juncture of a vertical and horizontal timber. Wedged between them was a stick of dynamite with a glowing fuse.

The timber was at least twelve feet off the ground. In my younger days, I could dunk a basketball with a running start, but the basket's only ten feet. Twelve feet was out of the question.

"Jake, come here!" Jo Jo shouted at me. She was directly in front of the Silver Queen, maybe fifteen feet from the pedestal.

"Why, you want a clean shot at me?"

"No, you've got to put out the dynamite. Now!"

"Throw your gun over here, and I'll do it," I said, though I didn't have the slightest idea how.

"¡Chíngate!"

Well, at least she had expanded her stock of words. "The gun. Throw it out."

"First, the dynamite."

"No, first the gun."

"Would you two stop arguing and do something?" Blinky had picked up some rocks from where he was lying and was tossing them at the dynamite. I couldn't see where they landed, but I didn't think he was going to win a teddy bear at the county fair.

"Jake," she said. "Now!"

I quietly climbed up the rear pedestal of the silver lady's chariot. Jo Jo turned the other way, her flashlight aiming a beam at the sizzling fuse. I hopped into the back of Cleopatra's barge and shimmied up a silver pedestal until I could get my hands on top of the canopy. I hoisted myself up, swung a knee on top, and looked out at the darkness. I was twenty feet above the floor of the cavern. The fuse was still burning.

"Jake, where are you?"

The flashlight beam was there below me. I could creep to the front of the canopy and leap at her. It wouldn't be chivalrous, two hundred twenty-some pounds smacking into her, probably breaking some bones, but at the moment, she had the gun, and I was out of tricks.

I took a step to the front of the canopy.

"Jake, where are you? There isn't time!"

"Josie," Blinky called out. "We gotta get outta here. Help me into the tunnel."

I took another step.

"No," she called back. "If that timber goes, this whole

chamber will be sealed off. The statue will be crushed.''

I took a third step.

And the Silver Queen came to life. At first, I thought the two Greek gods at her side were moving backward. But they were standing still. Which meant we were moving forward.

The ship broke off the pedestal and sailed down a step, then a second, and a third, gathering momentum like a raft hitting the rapids of the Colorado River. When it smashed into the floor, the queen pitched forward, and so did I.

The flashlight beam turned, and I heard a gasp from Jo Jo.

The queen snapped in two at the waist. Her head separated and bounced across the floor. The top half of the queen's torso flew straight ahead. I leapt from the canopy just before it hit, and I rolled, this time on my bleeding shoulder, the pain shooting through my arm. I bounded to my feet and tried to stand, bracing myself with one hand against something soft and spongy. I looked down and found my hand inside the queen's head. I tossed it away, thinking how much lighter it felt than I thought it would.

I heard a cry from Jo Jo Baroso, an animalistic shriek of horror and pain, followed by a sickening gurgling sound. She was trying to say something but sounded as if she were underwater. I turned to look. The flashlight lay on the floor, pointing at her twitching feet. I picked up the light and shined it on her face.

The queen's scepter was lodged in her throat, the point of the star buried just below the chin. Blood poured from the wound, coating the oversized silver dollar that sat just below the star. The life draining from her, Jo Jo said my name, softly, and what sounded like, ''Why . . .''

I knelt beside her.

''. . . did you leave . . .''

Her lips were still moving when . . .

The explosion.

Echoing off the rock walls.

Sending a cloud of dust up and then down again.

Stillness. The roof didn't fall in.

A couple of rocks tumbled from somewhere above, and the timber groaned. Then a couple more rocks fell.

Then quiet.

Nothing happened.

Until a boulder the size of a Buick crashed from above, splintering the pedestal, from which the Silver Queen so recently sailed. The timbers groaned louder. Smaller rocks began peppering the floor like a stinging hailstorm. A storm of dust rose from the floor.

"Blinky," I yelled in the darkness.

But there was no reply.

Around the chamber, wood timbers shrieked and split. A roar from above grew louder, like an approaching jet.

I scurried toward the ledge with short, quick strides, then dived across headfirst, pulling myself into the tunnel just as the horizontal timber crashed to the floor, followed by what sounded like the entire mountain collapsing into the chamber. In seconds, the opening was sealed tight by a thousand tons of rocks. I lay in the wet tunnel and listened to the rumble of thunder just a few feet away. The floor shimmied, and the black water rippled as the mountain coughed and sputtered and rearranged its parts. When the noise stopped and the shaking subsided, it was over, and the mountain had reclaimed a piece of itself.

29

Chumming

"Have I ever told you about the time a Hialeah city commissioner walked out of his house to check his mail and found a human skull staring at him from inside the mailbox?"

Doc Riggs is a whiz at openers in conversation.

"Not recently, Charlie," I said.

"Hush, Jake," Granny cautioned me. "Listen to Doc, and you may learn something, and while you're at it, don't cut the squid so big. It would take a whale to swallow that bait."

"Orca or Moby Dick?" Kip asked.

We were anchored in about eighty feet of water near Spanish Harbor Key, a bit south of the seven-mile bridge. In the winter, just off the reef, it's a decent place to catch yellowtail snapper, which unlike their suspicious cousins, red and mangrove snapper, are more likely to bite lines with visible leaders and are less likely to hide in caves. We came down in Charlie's pickup, the one that nearly ran down a process server. In Islamorada, we hitched up Granny's trailer with the twenty-foot Boston Whaler and headed past Lower Matecumbe Key, Conch Key, and Burnt Point, stopped for cold beer in Marathon, then took the bridge to Bahia Honda Key where we put the boat in the water, and nearly did the same with the pickup.

I know the Keys are commercialized and overpopulated, and you can't go a mile on U.S. 1 without passing tacky strip shopping centers with your convenience stores, T-shirt shops, and souvenir stands, but they're still the Keys where the sun rises in the Atlantic and sets in the Gulf, and you can sometimes exchange whispers with a pelican or spot a deer hightailing it across the highway. God's stepping-stones, local sportswriter Edwin Pope describes these sandy spits of coral, and that's good enough for me.

"Anyway," Charlie said, "here's the commissioner and in his mailbox is this skull, and a coconut split in two, and a decapitated chicken, and fourteen pennies wrapped in a white cloth."

"An unusual campaign contribution," I said, "but maybe not in Hialeah. Probably violates postal rules, too."

"Some weird voodoo," Granny contributed.

"Sounds like *Black Sabbath* with Boris Karloff," Kip said.

Charlie let his bait drift to the bottom on a one-ounce sinker. He didn't like to fish nearly as much as he liked to talk. "In a way, you're all correct. It was a Santería ceremony, a fascinating combination of African rituals and Catholicism. They consider one of their gods, Babalu-Aye, to be the embodiment of Saint Lazarus, Oggun is Saint Peter, and so on. A santero was using black magic to cast a spell on the commissioner, who had voted against allowing animal sacrifices within city limits."

"Now I remember," I said. "Later the Supreme Court ruled the church had the same rights to kill chickens as Colonel Sanders. But what about the human skull?"

"Excellent question, in fact, the only question as far as the authorities were concerned, since it's not illegal to cast a spell on your antagonists."

"Remind me the next time I try a case against Abe Socolow."

Charlie harrumphed and kept going. "Anyway, a lot of skulls and human bones began showing up at the Santería ceremonies, and the police suspected the worst.''

"Human sacrifices," I said, trying a sidearm cast with my spinning rod, the only way I could do it with a mending hole in my shoulder. Earlier, from the foredeck, I tried to cast left-handed and nearly put a 1/0 hook in Granny's ear. The hook was tied to the end of a thirty-pound leader on twelve-pound spinning tackle. Yellowtail don't have great choppers, but I use the leader to keep from breaking the line on coral.

"That's what our local constabulary suspected because they had no experience with this sort of thing. As it turned out, there were plenty of dead chickens and goats, but no humans. The human bones were stolen from cemeteries.''

"Wow, *Night of the Living Dead,*" Kip chipped in.

"Metro kept delivering packages to the morgue marked 'unknown human remains.' We identified some from corpses whose coffins and tombs had been desecrated. Very upsetting to the families.''

"I suppose so, if Uncle Harry's femur turned up in a witches' brew.''

We all thought about that for a while, then I dropped a frozen chunk of chum over the side in an effort to entice reluctant snapper out of the reef.

Granny held her nose and called out, "Whooee! What'd you put in that, some of Doc's old chickens and goats?''

"It's my own recipe, Granny, and I'm not telling.''

"I don't blame you. Ye gads, it smells toxic, or maybe radioactive.''

"Radioactivity doesn't smell," Kip informed us.

Charlie reeled in an empty line and said, "I don't mind the smell of chum.''

"Of course not!" Granny yelled at him. "After ten thousand autopsies, fish guts would smell like roses.''

"What *did* you put in that?" Charlie asked, sniffing the breeze.

I gave in and disclosed my secret sauce. "Equal parts dolphin entrails, grunt heads, and ballyhoo so old the fish market threw them in the Dumpster a week ago. Chopped everything into a slurry that looks like Granny's blueberry pancake batter, then froze it all in milk cartons.''

"Chopped how?" Granny asked. "You didn't use my blender again?"

I didn't answer.

"Damn, boy, that's for making frozen margaritas. I got a meat grinder in the pantry, you know."

"I know, but it takes twice as long, and it hurts my shoulder to crank it."

"Pantywaist," she said. "You know, Doc, the boy could never handle pain . . ."

"Granny!"

"Or women . . ."

"C'mon."

"Or a real job."

We bantered for a while longer, then the talk turned to fishing. Granny claimed she pulled a seven-pound yellow-tail from this very spot a week before, so it must be my chum that was chasing the fish to Omaha or somewhere. Nobody had a bite, but we were all enjoying the warmth of the winter sun. The sky was a Caribbean blue. Not as deep as a Colorado blue sky, but with a hint of turquoise. The breeze was soft, and the temperature an even eighty degrees. I was wearing cutoffs and was barefoot. My shoulder was healing, and so was my reputation.

Granny squinted at me and said, "That persecutor fellow called when you were gassing up the boat this morning."

"Socolow, and he's a prosecutor."

"Same difference."

"What'd he say?"

"Said you'd want to know he squashed the indictment for the murder of that phony-baloney salesman."

"Quashed," I told her, but she paid me no mind.

"Then, not ten minutes later, like it was all planned, the persecutor fellow from Colorado called."

"McBain."

"That's him. Dismissed all charges up there, plus he

said to make sure to tell you he's impinging all records of your arrest.''

"Expunging," I said.

"Whatever.''

It had been a good week in the squashing and impinging departments. I also had received a letter from Tallahassee dropping disbarment proceedings, and Judge T. Bone Coleridge called to tell me he had tossed out the child neglect case and also asked my opinion of the recently concluded college bowl games. So, with the Colorado records expunged, it was still true. I've never been disbarred, committed, or convicted of moral turpitude, and the only time I was arrested, it was a case of mistaken identity—I didn't know the guy I hit was a cop. That made me think of Josefina Jovita Baroso, because she hated it when I said that.

"I always thought there was something strange about that gal," Granny said, sadly.

Strange the way that happens, you're thinking of something, and someone else puts words to it. Of course, Granny had raised me since I was a pup, to use her expression, and we're often on the same wavelength. I wonder if that's the way with a husband and wife, and if I'll ever get the chance to find out.

"I'm not saying I thought she was a killer," Granny continued, "but there was always something a little cold about her. Gives me the willies, just thinking about it now."

I tossed another icy block of chum into the water and cut more squid for bait. Kip had put down his gear and was napping on the aft cushions. Charlie's eyes were closed and his hat, made of green palm fronds, was pulled down over his face. The water will calm you, or as Granny says, peacify you.

"Who would have thought she'd be a whatchamacallit, a serial killer?" Granny asked.

"I think you probably have to kill at least three people to earn that title," I said.

''Number three would have been you.''

That gave me some pause.

''What *was* wrong with that gal?'' Granny asked, still gnawing at the thought.

''She had an inability to feel the emotions that most of us have,'' I said. ''Even her brother, a lifelong criminal, never could have killed a man. With Jo Jo, people were just objects, like a table or chair.''

''A sociopathic personality,'' said the voice from under the palm frond hat. And I thought he'd been snoozing. ''Used to use the term 'moral imbecility' referring to antisocial, morally irresponsible behavior. All the normal emotions of lust, anger, and greed are still there but without the tempering restraint of conscience.''

''Greed,'' Granny repeated, shaking her head.

''Indeed,'' Charlie said. ''As Virgil asked, '*Quid non mortalia pectora cogis, auri sacra fames?*' ''

''Good question,'' I admitted.

Charlie translated. ''What lengths is the heart of man driven to by this cursed craving for gold?''

''That reminds me,'' I said. ''When the shoulder heals, I'm going up to Colorado for a while.''

''Skiing?'' Granny asked.

''Not exactly.''

''Ice climbing in Box Canyon?'' Charlie guessed.

''No, getting too old for that.''

I let it hang there a moment, like a tern hovering in the breeze.

''So just why does the craving for gold remind you that you're going to Colorado?'' Granny asked suspiciously.

''In the mine, when the Silver Queen collapsed, I jumped off the top of the Silver Queen just before the explosion.''

''I know,'' Granny said. ''You blabbed about that more times than Doc tells about the land crabs that stole a ring from a corpse in the mangroves.''

''When I hit the ground, I put my arm down to brace myself, and my hand went inside the queen's head and touched something . . . I don't know, kind of mushy or spongy.''

"So?"

"Well, both Cimarron and Blinky both said the head and torso were carved from this massive chunk of pure silver. A year before the statue was made, miners dug a nugget—more like a boulder—out of the Mollie Gibson mine on Smuggler Mountain that weighed twenty-one hundred and fifty pounds. The purest silver ever mined, the largest nugget ever found. For a hundred years, the story has been that the statue was carved from the nugget, but if that were true, the head wouldn't have been hollow.''

Granny pushed her sunglasses up on her head and eyeballed me. "I'm still listening, but I don't know what that has to do with you going back to Colorado.''

"When they let me out of the hospital, I did some research. In the library, all the newspaper clippings of the time say just what I told you, the pure one-ton nugget, the statue, the whole shebang. But in the county historical society, there are handwritten notes from the artisans who made the Silver Queen, and they kept track of all the materials used, including three hundred eighty pounds of papier-mâché.''

"So what?" Granny asked.

"That's what I stuck my hand in. They filled that big mama with papier-mâché and coated her with a thin layer of silver!''

"So write a story for the *National Geographic*. What's it got to do with you?"

"The one-ton nugget has never been accounted for. I searched all the records. Every big event in the mines was duly recorded. It would have been major news if the nugget had been melted down or sold or put on display, but it simply dropped off the face of the earth.''

"Or back into someone's mine," Charlie offered.

"Exactly. Maybe the same someone who filched the Silver Queen from the museum put the nugget back in that mine, too. Or maybe it's in the Mollie Gibson, or who knows where.''

Granny had reeled in and found her hook missing its chunk of squid. "Don't tell me you're going to go look for it. Not after all you've been through.''

"I've got the maps, the charts, the old mining logs," I said.

"How'd you manage that?"

"Bought 'em. Bought Cimarron's stock actually."

"Of all the damn fool . . ."

"No, listen, Granny. The court divided the company's cash up among all the investors, about thirty cents on the dollar. Cimarron's stock passed to Jo Jo, who owned it at the time of her death.''

"You mean she killed her husband and gets his assets?'' Granny demanded, her sense of justice offended.

"She got them and never lost them because she wasn't prosecuted for killing Cimarron. The probate court in Colorado put the stock up for sale. Nobody wanted it, so I bought it—seventy percent of the company—for a hundred bucks. I already had ten percent.''

"You're not serious, Jacob. What do you want it for? It's cursed.'' Granny only called me by my given name when she was perturbed.

"Hey, it's not for the money. It's like a game, a scavenger hunt. You have these old maps and diaries from a hundred years ago, and you know somewhere under the ground is this treasure. Well, it just starts to take hold of you.''

"Uh-huh," she said, not sounding convinced.

"So I thought maybe Kip would come up there with me. He already feels comfortable in school there, and who knows, maybe we'll find the nugget just like Cimarron found the Silver Queen.''

Granny and Charlie seemed to chew it over for a while. Then Granny said, "No use trying to talk Jacob out of anything. Boy's got a stubborn streak inherited from Lord knows who.''

Charlie took off his hat, cleared his throat, and pulled a pipe out of a pocket on his fishing vest. He tamped cherry tobacco into the bowl and struggled to keep a match lit in the breeze. "What about the other twenty percent?"

"Blinky's share," I said. "It's being held in trust by the court until he's declared dead. There was no way to find his body in the rubble."

"Uh-huh."

When Charlie's brain cells are cranked up, he usually stays quiet a while. Off the bow, an osprey dive-bombed the water just off the reef and came up with a parrot fish.

After a moment, Charlie said, "Other than Kip here, you doing this treasure hunting by yourself?"

"I might find some help."

"From whom?"

"I thought I should get someone with a little experience."

"There's something you're not telling us."

I put on my innocent face. "Like what?"

"Where's Baroso?"

Granny growled at that one. "Dead, ain't he? If he was shot in the leg, he never could have gotten out of the cavern, and even if he did, he couldn't have climbed all the way up. Isn't that right, Jake?"

"That's the way I figure it," I said.

Granny nodded her approval.

"Unless he took the elevator," I added.

They both gave me a look.

"Blinky had this old elevator working off a couple of twelve-volt batteries. I missed it on the way in, but I found it on the way out, just before I got to the stone ladder. It's the way I got back to the top."

"You left that part out."

"Not when I told the cops. That's how I explained the blood."

Again, the look from both of them.

"There were fresh drops inside the cage. I added a few with my bleeding shoulder. The cops had no reason to test it because they figured it was all mine, and I mostly told the truth: The last time I saw Blinky he was in the cavern, and a couple of seconds later, it was a tomb.''

Charlie made a tsk-tsking sound. ''Misleading the police, I'm surprised at you.''

''I didn't mislead them. I just didn't go out of my way to help them.''

''Where'd he go?'' Granny asked. ''How'd he get away?''

''When I got out of the tunnel, Jo Jo's pickup was still there, but the Jeep was gone.''

''So he contacted you,'' Granny said, prompting me to continue.

''In a manner of speaking,'' I said.

''Jacob, don't be difficult.''

''When I got to my rental car, I almost missed it, but on the windshield, somebody had used a finger to write a note in the fresh snow.''

''Lordy, do go on!'' Granny shouted, excitedly.

''Please do,'' Charlie pleaded.

I didn't answer.

''Jacob!'' Granny demanded.

I still didn't answer.

Kip joined the chorus. ''C'mon, Uncle Jake. What'd he say? I'll bet it wasn't 'Rosebud.' ''

''You know, the three of you are the only people in the world I love with all my heart,'' I said.

''So?'' Granny demanded.

''So, I'm sorry.''

''What in hell's fire is that supposed to mean?''

''Attorney-client privilege,'' I said, and then I felt a tug on my line.